THE QUMRAN MYSTERY

THE QUMRAN MYSTERY

Eliette Abécassis

Translated by Emily Read

ORION

First published in France as *Qumran* by Eliette Abécassis
by Editions Ramsay, 1996

This edition first published in Great Britain
in 1998 by Orion
An imprint of Orion Books Ltd
Orion House, 5 Upper St Martin's Lane,
London WC2H 9EA

A CIP catalogue record for this book
is available from the British Library

Approximately 545 words (pp. 125, 299) 'The Seductress'
(pp. 273–274, 53 lines) and 30 lines from 'The Thanksgiving
Hymns 8' (pp. 203–204) from *The Dead Sea Scrolls in
English* by Geza Vermes (Penguin Books, 1962, Fourth
edition 1995) copyright © Geza Vermes, 1962, 1965, 1968,
1975, 1987, 1995. Reproduced by permission of Penguin
Books Ltd.

ISBN 0 75280 748 x (hardcover)
ISBN 0 75281 403 6 (trade paperback)

Typeset at The Spartan Press Ltd,
Lymington, Hants
Printed and bound in Great Britain by
Clays Ltd, St Ives plc

To Rose Lallier,
the book born of one of her visions

Whoever considers these four things:
What is above us?
What is below us?
What was there before the world?
What will there be after it?
Better for him that he had never been born.

Babylonian Talmud, Haguigah 11b.

PROLOGUE

I

On the day the Messiah gave up his soul, the sky was no darker than on other days: there was no bright light, no miraculous sign. The sun hid behind thick clouds, its rays just breaking through the opaque layers that seemed to promise fine rain or hail, but none fell to refresh the dusty earth. The landscape was not shrouded in darkness and the sky still shed a weak light.

In other words it was a day like any other, neither happy nor sad, dark nor light, not extraordinary, nor even totally ordinary. Maybe this very normality was an omen for a lack of omens, I don't know.

The death was slow and difficult. The Messiah's breathing had dragged out into a long groan of infinite despair. His colourless hair and beard no longer reflected the vigorous wisdom he had always dispensed, like a treatment or a cure. His eyes no longer blazed with the same flame that had fired his sage words, his prophecies announcing the advent of a new world. His body, ravaged and twisted like a cloth, was reduced to no more than a painful contusion, an open wound, with the bones jutting from the flesh in macabre ridges. His flayed skin was like a cloak shredded to pieces, a shroud ripped in two; it was a scroll unfolded and desecrated, a decayed parchment with letters of blood wandering on scratched lines, a scrawl dotted with erasures and second thoughts. His stretched limbs, stabbed by needles, purple-stained with bruises, seemed to have collapsed on themselves. Blood flowed from his pierced hands, clenched with pain; a warm gush rose from his heart into his parched mouth, void now of the gentle words he so loved to speak, frozen in its last expression before the attack, one of dumb fear and surprise. His breast, like a lamb trapped by a wolf, leapt up as if the heart itself would burst out, a naked, shining sacrifice.

Then he stiffened, drunk with his own blood as if with wine flowing from a press. Horror, and all other expression, drained from his pale, drawn features; his half-open mouth and eyes wide in ecstasy took on a look of innocence. Was he to rejoin the Holy Ghost? But the Holy Ghost had abandoned him at the very moment when, with a final glimmer of hope, he had seemed to invoke him, calling his name. There had been no response, no sign for him – him, the rabbi, the miracle-worker, redeemer, consoler of the poor, healer of the sick, the mad and the crippled. Nobody could save him now, not even himself.

They gave him water and sponged his wounds. Some said a bolt of lightning cast a blazing line across the horizon; others thought they heard him calling for his father in a loud voice which echoed for a long time, as if descending from the sky. Inevitably, he succumbed.

He was old, but not ill. Members of the community thought he might be immortal, and were divided about whether to expect an actual event – death, reappearance, resurrection – or the non-event implied by his very longevity – eternity. Thus whether he lived or died, it was a miracle.

It happened on an afternoon in April. According to the doctors amongst his disciples, a cardiac arrest had brought on the earlier coma. They stopped the transfusions between three and three-thirty, and his body was transferred by ambulance from the hospital to his home. There he was laid on the ground and covered with a cloth, according to tradition. Then they opened the office where the rabbi had prayed, studied and read. The faithful recited the sacred texts, and the many people who had loved him came to pay a final homage to their master. Millions of disciples throughout the world had had faith in him, had believed he was the Lord-Messiah, the apostle of a new era, the forerunner of a new kingdom, the one they had waited so long for, ever since the dawn of time.

The visits continued until evening. Then they placed the body in a coffin made of wood from the great oak desk where he had spent so many hours of study. Around the mortuary a police cordon could barely contain the crowd. Traffic in the town was at a standstill; no car could penetrate the serried masses of men in black, weeping women and young children, gathered in hundreds of thousands to mourn the rabbi. Some, stricken, held their heads in their hands. Others howled out their pain in the street; here and there people danced to old Hassidic tunes, some melancholy, some lively, and sang: 'He lives, our master, our rabbi, our King-Messiah.' This was no burial: they were waiting for a Resurrection, the end of the Exodus, the beginning of the final Deliverance. Then at last they would truly be in Israel and could call the land their own. Had he not said as much, with his parables and allusions? They had understood: after so much suffering, so many people scattering, so much persecution, so many killings. They had stopped saying 'later' – 'later' was too distant. It had to be him, here and now; he was the one who would come 'later', the one they had been awaiting so long.

The funeral was put off until the day after his death, to allow everybody to get there. Ben Gurion airport was crammed with Hassidim from all over the world, hurriedly flown in from New York, Paris or London.

When the disciples emerged from the house, they were surrounded by people wanting to approach the rabbi for the last time. The procession set off towards the cemetery, followed by a dark, silent crowd, like an immense veiled and sobbing widow, and began the climb up to the Jerusalem cemetery, high on the Mount of Olives.

Slowly and in silence they carried him to the stone marking the spot where his rabbinical predecessors had been buried for the last three hundred years. There they laid him in the ground, naked and wrapped in a shroud. The rabbi's three secretaries said the Kaddish, and the customary prayers were recited.

Then the rabbi's favourite disciple, the one he loved best of all, spoke.

'Brothers and sisters!' he said. 'Jerusalem, the gateway of all peoples, has today been torn asunder, her walls destroyed, her towers demolished; she is covered in dust; and now she is like dry stone. The rabbi, our master, is no longer with us. We are orphans on this earth, our homes are devastated, our souls crushed. We feed on our own tears. Our eyes burn and our throats are parched. But the people who walk in darkness will soon see a great light. Look around you! There are tens of thousands in God's army. People everywhere are preparing; each man in his own time and according to his own beliefs, but all are arming themselves and uniting in the great swarming movement of the new era.

'All around us, the world is collapsing in chaos. Like armour, our districts protect us against the wickedness of the encroaching Sodoms and Gomorrahs, with their steel and plastic disguises. We close our eyes to their depravity and lust, the cursed dynasties of madmen, emaciated beasts howling at the moon, wandering the empty streets with bulging eyes and long lank hair stuck to their necks, mindlessly killing their easy prey, defenceless children and lone women. Outside our houses sickness spreads through the world, isolating men from one another like a new leprosy. The sick are dumped in hospitals, temples of death, now, rather than of healing, far from Redemption and Resurrection, waiting for the end to be pronounced irrevocably by priests in white coats. Everywhere this cursed earth, this stinking bin, ravaged by technology and its refuse, has dried up, scorched by the sun. The desert has taken over, the water has drained away; the earth, shaken by sickly convulsions, throws up the stacked-up bones and blood still fresh from the last massacre or genocide. Can you not see the rising smoke, the dying flowers, the dry grass? This land will soon be home only to the owl, the hedgehog and the crow. Brothers, we have reached another time; we are at the end of time.

'The day speaks of another day, the night whispers to the coming dawn, dewdrops quiver in the wind and bring the news: our rabbi, the Messiah, is awakening from his secular sleep, standing up, resurrecting the dead to save the world. Already, like a refiner and purifier of precious metals, he is coming to judge us. The proud and the wicked will burn like chaff in the furnace of this new dawn; they will be consumed in its eternal flame. The light of his justice will shine down upon those who fear him, their eyes will see him, and they will say "Great is the eternal Lord." Those who cannot see will be destroyed by his immense vengeance, and his name will be glorified.'

Then the rabbi's disciples left the cemetery, making way for the waiting horde of faithful, who filed endlessly past through the darkness of this night, as dark as any other night. Perhaps he did leave the tomb and rise up to heaven, but nobody saw it – or if anyone did, they did not speak of it. Maybe, the night of the burial was simply like the day: the sky was neither lighter nor darker; there was no bright light, no miraculous sign. The moon, behind thick clouds, was neither full nor red. Grey clouds, hardly showing against the dark sky, had promised fine rain, but it never fell to refresh the heavy earth. The skies did not dissolve like smoke, nor roll back like a scroll. The earth did not shatter in pieces, nor stagger like a drunk, nor shake like a flimsy hut. The sea was calm. Mountains did not collapse or melt in flames. Saron was not laid waste like Arava; Bashan and Carmel were not denuded. There were no new skies, no new earth, no new kingdom: there was nothing. Who had buried himself, captive in the caves, for forty days, in order to read the sealed document? The potter's jar did not splinter into thousands of little pieces and no piece could have served to bring fire to the hearth or water from the pond. The potter's jar was full of a thousand holy treasures, and the excavations were rich in fragments.

The new wine was not in mourning, the vine had not withered, the lambs did not bleat any more than usual. The joyful rhythm of the tambourines had not ceased and the soft sound of the harp still echoed through the houses. The city had not been beaten and stripped, like vines after the harvest. Jerusalem, gateway of the people, had not become a city of peace, of sapphire stones and ruby crenellations and waving flags. The Temple in her bosom had not been rebuilt of cypress, elm and box. All was calm; there was no sound, no loud sound of the Eternal Lord, paying back his enemies; blowing on them the fire of his rage and punishing them with the terrible might of his fury.

And yet there could have been some sign, some tiny clue indicating that all was not completely normal. Someone could have pointed it out, had it been so. For the doctors had been wrong. He was so old, and yet so robust and vigorous in the sermons he gave all over the world, for the visitors he received endlessly, for the advice he gave, written and spoken, on the telephone or at home, in private or in public, face to face or through his disciples. It was as though he was clinging to life to keep it going. He was so old that they had not paid attention. They had foreseen this moment for a long time, with apprehension or fear; they had foretold it and had twisted the truth to fit their scientific prophecies. But who could have known, since he himself had announced his approaching end and future resurrection?

For he did not die of heart failure the previous day: he died of a brutal blow on the head. But hardly anybody knew that. Nobody except myself.

For the rabbi did not die a natural death. The hand of man had called him back to God. No, in truth the rabbi did not die a natural death; he was killed and it was I who murdered him.

For, behold, the day cometh, that shall burn as an oven; and all the proud, yea, and all that do wickedly, shall be stubble: and the day that cometh shall burn them up, saith the Lord of hosts, that it shall leave them neither root nor branch.

I was born in the year 1967 of the Christian era, but my memory stretches back five thousand years. I remember past centuries as though I'd lived through them; for my culture has clothed them with words, writings and exegeses spoken throughout the ages, accumulated and placed end to end, or lost for ever. What is left remains within me, a line traced by the work handed on from father to son down the generations. I don't mean History, that dry procession of figures caught in wax, on marble tombs, in museums, and in the frozen pages of history books, an eternity of death. No, I mean living memories, thoughts not subject to chronological order, for time ignores method; it obeys the rule of the senses, of life itself. Memory finds its true self in the present, by minute analysis and introspection, revealing the absence and unreality of the present, since it never really exists: the event passes, and, passing, is already passed and therefore *in* the past.

In my language there is no present tense for the verb 'to be'; to say 'I am' you have to use the future or the past. To tell my story in your language I'd like to be able to convey an absolute past tense, not the perfect tense, which treacherously mingles the present with the past. I prefer the past historic, with its beauty, simplicity and completeness – the proper language of history. The self-analysing present tense, like the historic present, pretends to reveal the past, which is a universal condition. In the Bible I read there is no present, and future and past are almost identical. In a sense, the past can be conveyed through the future tense: to form the past tense you add the letter *vav* to the future tense (called the conversive vav) – but *vav* also means 'and', so you have the choice of reading the verb as 'he did' or 'and he will do'. I have always adopted the second solution. I believe the Bible is written in the future tense, and only announced events that never happened, but which will happen – because there is no present, and the past I'm telling you about is the future. I'm unveiling the Apocalypse.

*

Two thousand years ago a story began which changed the face of the world then, and again for a second time fifty years ago, thanks to an amazing archaeological discovery. When I say 'amazing' I don't mean for my people, who knew about it from the earliest moments of the Christian era, but for everyone else; and it is for them that I use the word 'archaeology' – for myself, there is nothing more immediate and less historical than that particular science. I could say that in a sense I and my people both created it and are the object of it, but I will explain that later.

The story I speak of is a part of History, but not of mine: it is that of Christianity. I am not a Christian; I belong to a community of religious Jews who live on the margin, against the stream of contemporary society, and they are called 'the Hassidim'. They are dedicated by ancient Jewish tradition to the transcribing of important words and events, to keep their memory alive. So is my duty and aim here: to tell this story with truth and rigorous accuracy, to tell what happened.

But first I should say straight away that the Hassidim do not seek to persuade or convert. I write, not in order to be read, but to preserve the truth of events in perpetuity. I write for posterity: I learned from my fathers and their fathers' fathers that events and thoughts must be preserved and hidden in a small corner of the world, not for present-day readers, since we live a monastic life, away from society, but for future generations who will discover our secrets and understand our language. Writing is not a mere outlet for me, but a sacred ritual, which I embark upon almost unwillingly, as a duty. It is my way of praying, of seeking forgiveness, of making a sacrifice.

But I must confess that I am no meticulous scribe with a passion for detail: I tend to take huge steps as though running and leaping hedges. Beauty is not my strong point either – I'm not a visual person. According to the Talmud, one should not admire the landscapes, beautiful plants or charming trees that one might come across whilst studying: *Whoever studies while walking along a path and stops to say 'What a beautiful tree, what a pretty bush' deserves to be put to death.'* I have always kept that saying at the back of my mind. Besides, I'm short-sighted, and take off my glasses to write; when I look up I see a hazy world, where only a few shapes and movements can be discerned. Minor ones remain invisible, and what I can pick out is so vague that I guess more than I actually see. But I can at least set the words in motion, and by their movement express something, not of what I was, but what I am to become. He who can read my words will be able to decipher the future through the past, the synthesis through the analysis. I invent myself, understand myself through my text. *Each letter is a world, each word a universe.* Each person is accountable for what he reads as well as what he writes, since everyone is free with respect to his reading.

Like my forbears, I write on very thin animal skin; before starting I draw lines with a sharp instrument to stop my pen from wandering into space, abandoning its allotted path. The line is not superimposed in black ink, but cut into the skin: it must be deep enough to be seen, but must not pierce it. This a tricky operation, because some parchments are more fragile than others, and not all skins have been tanned in the same way: the paler ivory ones are more friable than the yellower ones.

My task progresses slowly. When I reach the end of a scroll I sew it up without damaging it, and then start on the next one. I write in a single flow, since I cannot rub out the text, nor keep starting again indefinitely. First, and most importantly, I gather my thoughts and memories – I can't afford any errors. However if it does happen that my pen or my hand slips, or my memory betrays me, I can correct the mistake, without erasing it, by writing a little letter above or below the wrong one. Or I can insert the missing correct letter in the blank space just above the line of writing. So to read the text properly, one must not forget to read between the lines.

Mine is not a beautiful story: it tells of cruelty as much as love. But if I relate it, it is because I cannot escape the law which commands me to record important events, and what I have to say is so extraordinary that people will try to forget or deny it if I do not put it down on paper. For me, as a scribe, it is like a prayer, my way of praising God; for a Hassid there is nothing more important than the liturgy, which keeps us faithful to divine law. I wish I could have been able to convey to mortals something of the life of the angels surrounding the throne of God and singing His praises, but I can only tell of misfortune. For thousands of years we have been waiting for our religion to reach a state of perfection in the New Jerusalem; throughout this tedious wait, without Temple nor Holy City, we have lived in obscurity, giving praise and dedicating our lives instead of making sacrifices.

And so the years have gone by as we have lived in monastic retreat in our hidden houses, following the strict rituals of our community, with its calendar of holy days and festivals. We knew about the changing times, we knew that out there our brothers the Jews were losing their identity among the nations, whilst we remained, guardians of the Scroll. And so we lived on until something happened that disrupted our whole existence: in 1948 the Jews got their own country, and a part of our community returned to the land of its ancestors, whilst the rest remained in the diaspora, awaiting the Messiah.

But I feel I'm getting ahead of myself here, and that's where the first scroll of my story begins, as does my work as a scribe.

For Zion's sake will I not hold my peace, and for Jerusalem's sake I will not rest, until the righteousness thereof go forth as brightness, and the salvation thereof as a lamp that burneth.

First Scroll

THE MANUSCRIPT SCROLL

Announcement of the birth of Isaac

After these things, God appeared to Abraham in a vision and said to him: 'Behold, ten years have passed since you departed from Haran. For two years you dwelt here and you spent seven years in Egypt, and one year has passed since you returned from Egypt. And now examine and count all you have, and see how it has grown to be double that which came out with you from Haran. And now do not fear, I am with you; I am your help and your strength. I am a shield above you and a mighty safeguard round about you. Your wealth and possessions shall multiply greatly.' But Abraham said, 'My Lord God, I have great wealth and possessions but what good shall they do to me? I shall die naked, childless shall I go hence. A child from my household shall inherit from me. Eliezer's son . . . shall inherit from me.' And He said to him, 'He shall not be your heir, but one who shall spring [from your body shall inherit from you]'.

Qumran scrolls, *the Genesis Apocrypha.*

I

You could say that it all began one April morning in 1947.

In fact it all began long before, more than two thousand years ago. In the second century before Jesus Christ, a Jewish sect was founded which gave its own interpretation of the the Five Books of Moses, his laws and commandments. They violently attacked the Jewish religious authorities in Jerusalem and accused the priests in the Temple of laxity and corruption. Wanting to live far from all this, they settled at Qumran, a deserted spot on the banks of the Dead Sea. All wealth was held in common, so that everyone could support himself. The little monastery had its own priests and sacraments; they believed that those in Jerusalem were not legitimate and that the Temple had not been built strictly according to the rules of purity and impurity. They lived at Qumran until the Romans came and destroyed it in the third year of the Jewish War. They were called the Essenes.

Or perhaps it all began five thousand years ago when God created the world, when He separated the sky from the earth so that the first man and woman, Adam and Eve, might live there. Then came the Flood, the age of the patriarchs, the flight into Egypt, and the time when Moses freed the Jews from slavery and Israel returned to the land of Canaan.

Unless, of course, it all began with the chaos that preceded everything, when the earth was deserted and empty, covered by the deep oceans, surrounded by the breath of God, plunged in darkness. That was when God decided to create the world – a crazy whim, no doubt, since we still have no idea why He did it.

One generation passeth away, and another generation cometh: but the earth abideth for ever. The sun also ariseth, and the sun goeth down, and hasteth to his place where he arose.

However, let us simply say that everything began on an April morning in 1947 AD – or began again, as nothing can be finished until the Messiah comes, there can be nothing new until His sun shines with its eternal light.

On that day the Essene manuscripts were discovered, where they had been for centuries, preserved, wrapped in linen and sealed in tall jars. They had been written at the time when the sect still occupied the Qumran site. Facing inevitable defeat by the Romans, they hid their sacred texts in inaccessible caves in the nearby cliffs, to save them from falling into the hands of the infidel conquerors. They wrapped and sealed them so well in the linen and jars that the manuscripts remained intact, until they were discovered on that fateful day in 1947. The men who found them also uncovered the ruins of the Essene settlement, their homes and buildings.

They broke into other caves and found other manuscripts, which they took to sell.

There was in Israel a man, a Jew called David Cohen. He was son of Noam, who was son of Havilio, who was son of Micha, who was son of Aaron, who was son of Eilon, who was son of Hagai, who was son of Tal, who was son of Rony, who was son of Yanai, who was son of Amram, who was son of Tsafi, who was son of Ham, who was son of Raphael, who was son of Shlomo, who was son of Gad, who was son of Yoram, who was son of Yohanan, who was son of Noam, who was son of Barak, who was son of Tohou, who was son of Saul, who was son of Adriel, who was son of Barzillai, who was son of Ouriel, who was son of Emmanuel, who was son of Asher, who was son of Reuben, who was son of Er, who was son of Issacar, who was son of Nemuel, who was son of Simeon, who was son of Eliav, who was son Eleazar, who was son of Yamin, who was son of Loth, who was son of Elihu, who was son of Jesse, who was son of Ythro, who was son of Zimri, who was son of Ephraim, who was son of Michael, who was son of Ouriel, who was son of Joseph, who was son of Amram, who was son of Manassi, who was son of Ozias, who was son of Jonathan, who was son of Reouven, who was son of Nathan, who was son of Osiah, who was son of Isaac, who was son of Zimri, who was son of Josias, who was son of Boaz, who was son of Yoram, who was son of Gamaliel, who was son of Nathaniel, who was son of Eliachim, who was son of David, who was son of Achaz, who was son of Aaron, who was son of Yehudi, who was son of Jacob, who was son of Yossi, who was son of Joseph, who was son of Mathan, who was son of Eleazar, who was son of Eliud, who was son of Akim, who was son of Zadok, who was son of Eliakim, who was son of Abiud, who was son of Zorobabel, who was son of Salathiel, who was son of Jekonias, who was son of Josias, who was son of Amon, who was son of Manasse, who was son of Ezehias, who was son of Achaz, who was son of Jonathan, who was son of Ozias, who was son of Yoram, who was son of Josaphat, who was son of Asa, who was son of Abia, who was son of Roboam, who was son of David, son of Jesse, who was son of Joped, son of Boaz, son of Solomon, son of Naasson, son of Aminabab, son of Aram, son of Esrom, son of Phares, son of Juda, son of Jacob, son of Isaac, son of Abraham.

And this man was my father, a scholar of great repute throughout the country for he knew the history of Israel from its beginning. The beginning above all: he was in charge of digs and excavations of ancient sites in Israel. Archaeology was both his passion and his everyday work. Extremely knowledgeable about ancient times, his aim was to rediscover every trace of them. He had written numerous books about his discoveries, which were very popular, as were his lectures, because they brought the past to life – when my father spoke about the past, it was as though he had personally lived through it, and his audience would live through it with him. He did not regard history as something finished, and felt no nostalgia for ancient times, but was always recalling memorable events, beginning his stories with 'Do you remember?', as if I could recall things that had happened thousands of years ago. He could do this – it was all in his mind, as if he had experienced and remembered it, without having to learn it.

He was fifty-five. His hair was as thick as Absalom's. He had the body of a muscular warrior: he was as strong and fierce as King David. His eyes were dark and bright, and his face glowed like the sun. But as far as I was concerned he was ageless; I was never afraid that he would grow old. When I looked at him I thought of what my rabbi used to say: 'It is forbidden to be old.' His almost divine spirit and ancient memory seemed to me to place him outside time, beyond all the usual signs of human decrepitude. He overcame all the obstacles presented by the times he lived in by sheer force of mind, driven by the vastness of his project.

I must explain that when I was still living with my father I had not yet joined the Hassidim, I lived amongst others, for I had not yet found my true vocation. I didn't know myself before this second birth when I met them. I lived in the modern world like any other Israeli. After the army, I went to university, and so it was at the yeshivah that I first learnt the Torah and the Talmud. I had also been there for three years, before military service, and without really knowing why, had already felt enormously attracted to this contemplative, reclusive life.

I had a friend, Yehudi, who I studied with most of the time. Son of a great Hassidic rabbi, he was very learned and knew the whole of the Talmud by heart. At first I couldn't keep up with him, as I had been brought up without religion and with no knowledge of the texts. My mother, a Russian Jew, was a militant atheist – the only vestige of communism that she brought with her from the USSR, along with her accent. The Sabbath was never observed in our household. For my father, archaeology was the Talmud, his own way of reliving Jewish history. Influenced by my mother, and by the scientific rationalism of his friends and colleagues, he never prayed, and only read texts if they were engraved on parchment or stone. Palaeography was his speciality; and it seems to me now that it was no coincidence that he devoted his life to the study of ancient texts.

Palaeography is not an exact science. It has none of the precision of, say, chemistry, nor any of the precise systems of classification of botany or zoology. I would even go so far as to say that it is not a science at all, even though dates can be estimated with a high degree of precision. It was no coincidence either that, just as Yehudi's father passed on the teachings of his own ancestors, so my first readings, and only prayers, were those that my father's hand guided me along, evanescent scratches on precious parchments.

He taught me to examine minutely the material on which the scribe had traced the letters, as well as the form of writing he had adopted; these were all clues which helped determine the historical and geographical origins of the manuscript. Thus, when inscriptions are engraved on stone or clay, where it would be difficult to draw curved letters, the writing will naturally be adapted to the medium and be 'square', like the ancient writings of Persia and Assyria, and, for a time, of Babylon. Conversely, in other parts of the world, when the scribe has used papyrus or parchment, the letters are 'round' and the writing cursive. My father taught me that the first fact to be taken into account by the palaeographer is the continuous change in the alphabetic forms used in the Scriptures. He taught me to recognise the transition from one alphabet to another, a difficult and tortuous process, strewn with false clues. An obsolete alphabet can continue to be used long after a new one has been adopted, either for a particular reason, or simply out of nostalgia. Periods thought to be distinct can thus be inextricably tangled together on a parchment, and a text thought to be definitively dated could belong to two different centuries, with no way of telling which.

Luckily the palaeographer has other clues at his disposal: the joins or dots between letters for example, or the position of the letters in relation to the lines. Sometimes the letters follow a uniform base line; sometimes they move between lines, the letters stretching towards the top line, with considerable variation at the base. My father used to say that man too is formed by his medium, carved out like vowels and consonants on stone. I believe he was like a parchment himself, a leather scroll covered in round, cursive writing. He never spoke of his past or his family, which I assumed had disappeared in the Shoah. Despite his distance from his origins, he had, also despite himself, passed on to me his handwriting, small and indecipherable. It was a part of myself, engraved on my heart, and it was only much later, after a series of dramatic events, that I was able to read it.

In my eyes my father himself was like ancient Hebrew, difficult and perilous to decipher: Hebrew has no vowels, just some consonants sometimes used as vowels, but they don't always have the same value, and their significance varies. With or without them, the word containing them is never quite clear, unless the reader knows it already. Holy texts were always read out loud, and sometimes were only transmitted by oral tradition. Thus the role of the written word was mainly to remind the reader of what he already knew. For centuries there was no difficulty about this, as long as the users of the original documents knew the meaning of the text. But this tradition gradually fell into oblivion, and when, some two thousand years later, archaeologists discovered ancient texts, the palaeographers had the greatest difficulty in understanding the consonantal words. The way was open to error and doubt, as well as interpretation and creativity. As one of the rabbis put it, a great deal of waiting and longing goes into attracting the vowels to the consonants, like a man wanting to perform his mitzvah. Just as the sexual act cannot take place without desire, the word cannot exist without the vowel. But I only really understood this later, when I was confronted with the power of carnal longing.

My father taught me the strict rules governing textual criticism; writing was first used in the Middle East around the beginning of the third millennium, for administrative purposes rather than prayers or holy texts. It was only around the year 2000 BC that it began to be used for artistic purposes, epic or lyric poems. I will always remember the shock I felt when he told me that Moses had not written the Torah himself. I was thirteen, preparing for my bar mitzvah and, for the first time, wanting a return to tradition, my teshuvah.

'But Moses wrote these texts under divine dictation,' I said. 'According to Deuteronomy, they were written by God's own hand.'

'Impossible. There are too many different styles in the Torah for there to be one single author. Three main authors have been identified: the priest, the Elohist and the Yahvist.'

'But if they're written by man, they can't be revealed.'

'They're the work of a human hand, but revealed insofar as they are built on a foundation of spoken words. Originally, writing was not intended for reading; it was no more than a support, an *aide-mémoire* to preserve the integrity of the oral tradition. It was only many centuries later, when the great libraries of the Hellenistic period were created, that writing was freed from the spoken word. Complete autonomy finally came with the invention of printing. The Torah scrolls as you know them weren't read out loud in the synagogue until the second century BC. It was only after the destruction of the Temple and the end of the sacrifices that it became the immutable book, of which not one iota of text, writing or language could ever be changed.'

When my father taught me to read, he did not let me use letters written in books. He wanted me to know everything by heart, without needing any support. He always said that it was much better to retain texts in one's head rather than carry exercise books around, and that in order to understand one must know. Surely these were the words of a Talmudist rather than a palaeographer? Like Yehudi and his father, my father knew the ancient scrolls by heart. His training enabled me to make stunning progress when I began to study the Talmud with Yehudi, the best pupil in the yeshivah.

II

Now it happened that in the year 1999 of currently recorded time (5759 as we record it) a crime took place in such strange and terrible circumstances that the army had to become involved. Nothing like it had been seen in Israel for more than two thousand years. The past seemed to surge forth like a demon from its confines, mocking men with a bloodless, sinister laugh: a man was found dead in the Orthodox church in Jerusalem's old town, hung on a great wooden cross, crucified.

And it happened that my father was rung up by the head of the Israeli army, Shimon Delam, asking for an urgent meeting. The two men had fought together, and although they had chosen different paths in life, one of political and military action, the other of reflection and study, they remained old comrades, always ready to help one another. Shimon was a true fighter as well as a cunning spy: this thickset little man did not hesitate, on a mission in Lebanon, to infiltrate a group of terrorists dressed as a woman. I had belonged to the same elite unit as his son, who was as brave and impetuous as his father, and we too had been linked in combat and shared adversity.

When they met at the army headquarters, my father told me Shimon seemed unusually worried and confused.

'I need your help,' he said. 'It's something my men aren't used to doing. A delicate matter – religion's involved. I need a wise man, a scholar and adviser – and a friend I can trust.'

My father was intrigued and asked him what it was about.

'A dangerous matter. Every bit as dangerous as the Palestinian problem and the war in Lebanon, every bit as important as our relations with Europe and the United States. In a way it involves all of that. I want you to do something. It's very delicate. It needs academic knowledge as much as military experience. Enormous sums of money are at stake and there are people out there with no scruples about human life, who are only after the money . . . Let me show you.'

They set off by car towards the Dead Sea. They took the road from Tel Aviv to Jericho, winding below sea-level through the powdery, baking desert for several kilometres, between the dunes of Jordan and the bare oppressive banks of the Dead Sea, which they finally reached at twilight. The wind had dropped and there was a smell of sulphur over the plain.

The wind goeth toward the south, and turneth about unto the north; it whirleth about continually, and the wind returneth again according to his circuits. All the rivers run into the sea; yet the sea is not full.

The silence was broken only by faint soundwaves from the depths of the desert. The merciless sun, scorching animals and plants, had not yet tempered its baking heat. Under a motionless sky they walked along the muddy shore and turned towards a terrace cut out of the bottom of a chain of rocky cliffs. In the distance the water glistened darkly in the sun. To its right there was a green patch, the oasis of Ain Feshka, land of Zebulun and Naphtali in Galilee.

Qumran stretches from the Dead Sea to the top of a high cliff, with three levels separated by steep, broken slopes, spreading out on a terrace of marly soil, with a small stream running through it. To the right the Wadi Qumran flows down to the salt sea. On the terrace are the ruins of Qumran and, recently established, a small kibbutz. Between them and the shore they overlook a steep slope of hard chalk which seems to eat slowly into the soft mud.

The old track and the new road from Sodom to Jericho pass along the bottom of the cliff. This is the most accessible part, with the most passable tracks and widest paths; the rocks here are easier to climb, softer because of the nearby mud. Some people, despite the best of intentions, get no further than this; they think they have reached the end of their journey, and refuse to make an effort. They stop there and gaze down at the bronze and gold earth, hardly sloping, tangible beneath their marble tread.

The second sloping terrace tells its own story; it lies on a former bank of the Dead Sea, which was much higher then. It slopes uniformly and is easy to move around on. This is where the ruin of Qumran lies, alongside the buildings of the kibbutz, which guards the site and cultivates the palms around the springs. The path is precipitous and difficult, but men in the past have marked out a few tracks and paved between the cracks of the crumbling rock, to guide the visitor higher and higher, towards the caves.

The more agile can therefore reach the third level, a chalk terrace high above the second one. Here history gives way to prehistory. Openings at different levels bear witness to the retreat of the waters. They can be reached only with great difficulty; you must scale hard rock, often under a beating sun, leap precariously over ravines, risk vertigo and plunge into every tiny crevice without fear of getting lost. Eventually, on the steep slope with its huge, sheer blocks of stone onto which occasional violent rainstorms bring down debris and rockfalls, you can distinguish some of the caves – while others are so well set back and inaccessible that they have yet to be discovered. The path appears to climb, higher and higher, right to the top of the great cliff, but it is impossible to get beyond the last level – anyone who tried would be leaping into the unknown, and would probably take their secret with them.

Qumran is certainly no Garden of Eden, lying as it does in the remotest desert. Its climate however does seem a little gentler, the air a little cooler, than down below on the shore of the Dead Sea. Intermittent but plentiful waters maintain a permanent pond on the second level, sufficient to support a human settlement. Brackish waters irrigate the palm groves, and deep ravines provide a natural rampart which almost completely sequesters the promontory: this was why, despite appearances to the contrary, life was possible there.

The Essenes chose to settle here, close to their origins, as if by nearing the beginning they had their eyes set on the end. This was why they built their sanctuary not far from there, at Khirbet Qumran, one of the most desolate regions on the planet, almost devoid of vegetation and inhospitable to man, on chalky, steep and labyrinthine cliffs cut through by ravines and pock-marked by caves. They chose to live amongst these white stones, beside the rugged and indelible scars left by the earth's convulsions and slow, painful erosion, in this lair of rebels, brigands and saints.

This was where Shimon took my father, to the ruined monastery. He picked up a small piece of wood and began chewing it. After a few moments, he decided to speak.

'You know this place. You know that more than fifty years ago they found manuscripts belonging to an Essene monastery, the Dead Sea Scrolls. It seemed that they dated from the time of Jesus and they told us things about religion that were new and hard to accept.

You know too that some of them were lost – or stolen, I should say. The ones we do have we've acquired through guile or force.'

My father indeed knew the area well, having carried out many excavations there. And he knew, of course, the saga of the scrolls, ever since that day in 1947, 23 November, when the telephone call had come for Eliachim Ferenkz, Professor of Archaeology at the Hebrew University in Jerusalem. It was from an Armenian friend of his, a dealer in antiquities who lived in the old town, asking to see him as soon as possible – on too grave and delicate a matter to deal with over the telephone.

At that time the country was at war. The United Nations General Assembly was about to pronounce on partition; Arabs were threatening to attack Jewish towns and villages. The region was like the desert just before a sandstorm; calm, but with the murmur of a distant and threatening hurricane. British barricades around a besieged Jerusalem watched the enemy and guarded the passage from one side to the other. Neither Ferenkz nor his Armenian friend were able to obtain passes, so they agreed to meet the next day at the border. Their conversation took place across a barbed-wire fence.

'So why the hurry?' asked the professor.

'An Arab colleague from Bethlehem came to see me,' the Armenian told him. 'Like me, he deals in antiquities. He brought some leather fragments covered in ancient script. I think they may be extremely valuable.'

'What Arab colleague?' Ferenkz sounded wary. Several times people had tried to sell him ancient objects which had turned out to be fakes.

'He got them from the Bedouin. They said they were pieces from leather scrolls found in a cave near the Dead Sea. Apparently there are hundreds of others like this one. They wanted to know what they are worth. That's why I came to find you – to get your opinion.'

'Show me. If they're worth anything, I'll make it my business to acquire them for the Hebrew University.'

The Armenian pulled a piece of parchment out of his pocket, and lifted it up to the fence so that the professor could examine it. Ferenkz peered closely at the text written on a fragile ochre parchment, which looked crumbly and was fraying at the edges. What he saw seemed familiar to him, like this land where parchment is almost part of the soil, like the other scrolls that had been found in various caves and archaeological sites; indeed, it was like the inscriptions he himself had found on first-century tombs around Jerusalem. Still, he was intrigued. He had never seen such an inscription on leather – a perishable material, unlike stone. Was it ancient? Was it a fake? Ferenkz was an archaeologist, used to analysing the remains of constructions, homes, fortifications, hydraulic installations, temples and altars, or the objects found on these sites – arms, tools and domestic implements, but never scripts or parchments. Archaeology on a parchment would be absurd.

And yet, without really knowing why, Ferenkz believed in it. On that day, at that moment, in front of the wire, he knew that this piece of leather was not a fake.

'Go to Bethlehem and bring back more samples. Meanwhile I'll get a pass so that I can visit your shop when I need to.'

The Armenian rang again the following week: he had some more leather fragments. Professor Ferenkz rushed to the shop and examined them carefully. For an hour he held them, inspected them with a magnifying glass, deciphered them, and concluded that they were genuine. He was prepared to travel to Bethlehem to buy the whole scroll. But there was the threat of war and tension was high throughout the country. For a Jew to travel from Jerusalem to Bethlehem by bus, through Arab territory, would have been extremely dangerous; his wife would not allow him to go.

The following evening he was still at home, miserable at the thought of losing the manuscripts, when he heard on the radio that the United Nations vote on partition would not be cast until the following evening. He then remembered what his son had told him. Eli was chief of operations for Hagganah, the Jewish secret army; he had adopted a codename, Matti, which he kept after the creation of the state of Israel. Matti had told his father that Arab attacks were expected after the United Nations decision, so Ferenkz decided that the postponement of the vote left him a whole day to try and save the manuscripts. He left home at dawn, crossed the barricades with his pass and woke his Armenian friend. Together they went to Bethlehem, where they met the Arab merchant, who told them what the Bedouin had said.

'They are Bedouin from the Taamireh tribe, which often herds its goats along the north-west bank of the Dead Sea. One day one of the animals got lost. They ran after it but it disappeared into a cave; when they threw stones into it there was an echo, as if they had hit pottery. They went in and found earthenware jars containing bundles of leather covered in tiny Hebrew writing. They brought them to me to sell.'

The merchant showed them the two jars, ancient pieces of pottery, as smooth and hard as the Qumran rock itself, coated over centuries or millennia by layers of orange-yellow dust streaked with grey. One, smaller and wider, had two handles; the other was taller and narrower. Both had lids sealing the contents. Ferenkz opened them and carefully withdrew the decayed and dusty cylinders.

In the light of day, after two thousand years of seclusion, they seemed almost to shake off the brown ashes of their tomb and to rise up, grave and fragile, resurrected. They were folded in on themselves like buds in spring, or eyelids stuck together after a long night's sleep, or cocoons just before they unfold. He recognised on these quivering corpses the actual script of the Bible, as if written by Hebrews millennia or centuries ago – or the day before. *They had not been looked at for two thousand years.*

Ferenkz returned, his secret clutched to his heart, and entered the Jewish quarter of the Golden City by the Jaffa Gate. These newly discovered parchments would soon be known throughout the world as the Dead Sea Scrolls.

As soon as he got home, he began to study the manuscript, until his family interrupted him to tell him what the whole world had just heard on the radio: the partition of Palestine had been agreed. Tears of joy poured down his cheeks. 'Just think of it!' said his wife, 'there's going to be a Jewish state!'

Despite the Arab attacks, the next day Ferenkz made the journey again to buy the scrolls. One of the manuscripts turned out to be the *Book of the Prophet Isaiah*: he didn't recognise the others, but he was sure that they too were about a thousand years older than anything he had ever seen before. He understood at once the enormous implications of this discovery for Biblical studies.

The other manuscripts were just as important: one was a prophetic account, in Biblical Hebrew, of an ultimate war in which good would triumph over evil, entitled *The War between sons of Light and sons of Darkness*. Another scroll, a collection of Hebrew poems resembling the *Book of Psalms*, was later known as the *Scroll of Hymns*.

Soon after buying the three manuscripts, Ferenkz learnt that there was a fourth. At the end of January 1948, he received a letter from a certain Kair Benyair, asking to see him about a parchment. This man, a converted Jew from the Syrian Orthodox community, was an emissary from Bishop Hosea, the Syrian master of the Monastery of St Mark in the old city of Jerusalem. After a complicated correspondence, Ferenkz and Kair Benyair finally met in the Arab section of the town. Bishop Hosea's emissary showed Ferenkz an old manuscript, explaining that he had purchased it from the Taamireh tribe, and offered to sell it to him. The professor saw at once that, like the others, it was more than two thousand years old. On 6 February 1948 Ferenkz and Kair Benyair met for the final transaction. But Hosea's emissary, after being offered a large sum of money, appeared to change his mind and prepared to leave with the scroll. Ferenkz tried to hold him back, bargained, pleaded in vain, but could only obtain a tentative arrangement to meet the following week. Of course he never came, and Ferenkz never saw the manuscript again.

The bishop's emissary had in fact been sent, not to sell, but to get an opinion on the authenticity and value of the thing. Hosea had bought the scroll from the same source as Ferenkz, and had shown it to several scholars. A monk, assistant librarian at the Archaeological Museum of Palestine had, after rapidly deciphering it, declared it a fake; the bishop then showed it to an erudite Greek priest studying in Jerusalem, who often came to St Mark's library; he said the scroll was a copy of the book of Isaiah, and of no great interest; a third researcher thought it was a collection of prophetic sayings, but was not sure that they were ancient; in August that year an expert from the Hebrew University dated the scroll as being from the Middle Ages: 'It's worth looking at,' he said, 'but it's nothing special.'

Hosea remained convinced that the manuscript was ancient. 'You don't think it could date from antiquity?' he asked.

The expert denied this and added that he thought it an absurd hypothesis. When Hosea persisted, he explained: 'Imagine it. Fill a box with manuscripts, forget it for two thousand years, hide it, bury it if you like – but I assure you, you'd never be in a position even to ask the question as to their value.'

As a last resort, Hosea took the manuscript to his superior, who advised him to give up and forget the whole story. But the bishop persevered. Convinced of the value of the manuscript, he decided to get confirmation from an expert who could unequivocally authenticate it.

He therefore sent an expedition to the caves in search of more scrolls. They brought back many manuscripts, some in good condition, others damaged or rotten. He also bought the two large pots in which the manuscripts had been hidden, hoping to get a good price for all these things. A friend thought he might be able to get a great deal more money for them in the United States, and suggested that Hosea get the manuscript evaluated by the American School of Oriental Studies in Jerusalem, and then leave the country, as Israel would go up in flames as soon as the British mandate expired.

At that time there were two seminarians at the School of Oriental Studies who were later to become famous in academic circles for their work at Qumran. The first was Paul Henderson, a graduate student from Yale doing research in the Holy Land, a fervent Catholic who shortly afterwards became a priest; and Father Pierre Michel, a French specialist in the archaeology of the Middle East.

Henderson was a slight man with a thin face, pale skin and red hair, like Esau and David. Although sometimes ill-tempered, he was not a wild animal like Esau; and although ambitious and swaggering, he was not warlike and passionate like David. He was reserved and methodical, like Jacob, which made him a good archaeologist; as pious as Abraham, Isaac and Jacob, sometimes as fervent as Isaiah and sometimes as pessimistic and disappointed in his faith as Jeremiah; above all, he was as absolute and intransigent as the prophet Elias.

Pierre Michel, on the other hand, was small and round, with the beginnings of a bald patch. Naturally spontaneous, he was much too responsive and plain-spoken to be able to hide his feelings or keep secrets. He sought for balance in all things, between justice and love, faith and reason, hope and despair. And he wanted answers, but was never satisfied with them; this made him weak and vulnerable, but he was still a long way from the susceptibility and stupidity of Samson. His soul was like a sea, calm on the surface, but rocked far below by powerful and destructive forces, currents which sometimes clashed with one another, like sharp waves against cutting reefs.

The professor of archaeology at the School was away and Paul Henderson was the only person there to meet Hosea, whose efforts were at last rewarded. The young theologian, after consulting several archaeological textbooks, realised that this was indeed an ancient scroll. Pierre Michel agreed with him. They studied the document together, and photographed it, with the bishop's permission. Then, for the first time, they identified the other fragments from the caves: the *Scroll of Isaiah*, the *Manual of Discipline* and the *Commentary of Habbakuk*. By now they realised that they had in their hands the greatest archaeological discovery of modern times.

The Arabs declared war on the State of Israel immediately after the proclamation of independence. Bullets rained down on Jerusalem, which was besieged on all sides and dying of hunger and thirst. In the Old Town the Jewish Quarter was burned to the ground. None of the three sanctuaries within the ramparts – the Church of the Holy Sepulchre, the Western Wall and the Dome of the Rock – was able to deter the deadly gunfire, and it seemed, in this final war, as if the Apocalypse had finally come to Judaea. In the circumstances it seemed wiser for Henderson and Michel to leave for the United States. Before they left, they persuaded Hosea to sign a paper giving them exclusive rights of publication; in exchange they promised to find a buyer very quickly. The bishop agreed, and on 11 April 1948 he too set off for America, and the Dead Sea Scrolls were revealed to the whole world.

When the news reached Ferenkz he was terribly angry, and suspected the Americans of having sabotaged his negotiations with Hosea. He wrote several letters claiming that the scrolls were the property of the new state of Israel, but to no avail. It was too late. Hosea had left Jerusalem with the scrolls in his luggage, determined to sell them to the highest bidder, and also to spread the Orthodox word throughout the world.

He rejoined Paul Henderson and Pierre Michel in New York, where they reached an agreement, and for two years they travelled together, exhibiting the scrolls at the Library of Congress, the University of Chicago and some of the major art galleries. In 1950 the first publications appeared, with photographs of the *Scroll of Isaiah*. The following year, the *Manual of Discipline* and the *Commentary of Habbakuk* were published in their entirety.

Ferenkz for his part began editing his three scrolls, and also worked on the hasty trancriptions he had made when he examined Hosea's scroll. He was convinced that it belonged to Israel, and he travelled to the States to meet Paul Henderson. The meeting was friendly to begin with, but when Henderson proudly claimed that he was the one who had discovered the scrolls, Ferenkz lost his temper.

'I think you know where the last scroll is, the one Hosea was going to sell me before he changed his mind,' he said finally.

'I don't know what you're talking about,' said Henderson. 'All the scrolls we possess have been published, or are about to be published.'

'You're lying,' said Ferenkz. 'You must return the scroll. It doesn't belong to you, and you have no right to interfere in this matter.'

'It's the Jews who have no right to interfere,' replied the Catholic.

War had been declared, but Ferenkz was not able to fight to the end. He died in 1953, with the bitter thought that 'his' scroll, the one he had glimpsed, was lost for ever. Little did he know that his son would get it back fourteen years later.

Matti resigned from the Israeli army in order to carry on his father's work. He oversaw the publication of Ferenkz's book on the three manuscripts, and wrote a detailed commentary on one of them, *The War between the Sons of Light and sons of Darkness*. In the mid-sixties, he received a letter from Bishop Hosea, offering to sell him a manuscript from the Dead Sea.

His immediate thought was that it must be the famous scroll that his father had failed to buy from Kair Benyair. He was right: Hosea had asked too much and had never found a buyer. After a series of convoluted transactions, a contract of sale was drawn up, but Hosea never delivered the scroll.

By now it was the summer of 1967, and with war looming again between Israel and her neighbours, Matti was recalled to the army as strategic adviser. The battle for Jerusalem took place on 7 June. Israeli paratroopers advanced through the Old Town, and climbed up the stone steps at the end of Tiferet Street. After a thousand years, they were once again at the Wailing Wall, which had protected the Temple before it was destroyed. They stood with their hands outstretched, their foreheads against the stone, sobbing and praying at the spot which had sheltered the place, beneath the hill, where Abraham, without God's intervention, would have sacrificed his son Isaac.

Then, after a fierce battle with the Jordanian troops, they captured the Archaeological Museum, in which lay thousands of fragments of Qumran Scrolls – the enemy was ultimately forced back as far as Jericho, north of the Dead Sea, so as well as the museum, the Khirbet

Qumran site, with its hundreds of manuscripts, passed into Israeli hands.

On the morning of 7 June 1967, in the midst of the battle, Matti and two other men entered the scrollery beneath the museum, hearts pounding. There was nothing at all on the long tables, normally strewn with fragments. They found the precious scrolls in the cellars; they had been gathered together in haste, packed in wooden boxes and taken down before the battle.

The next day, one of Matti's aides was finally able to confront Hosea's agent Kair Benyair at his Jerusalem home and take possession of the scroll, which Matti presented to the Archaeological Museum to complete their collection. The Israeli authorities, however, wanted no open quarrel with the previous owners of the second lot of scrolls, and an agreement was reached with Professor Henderson, who gathered together a team to study the manuscripts. This hand-picked group were given the task of deciphering each fragment and then publishing the results.

When the war ended, Matti came back to the museum to look at the famous manuscript and begin studying it. He searched everywhere, in the rooms and the cellars, but could not find it. After several days of fruitless searching and questioning, he was forced to accept the truth: the scroll had disappeared.

III

'Who knew this scroll existed?' my father asked, when Shimon had told him the story of its disappearance.

'Impossible to say,' said Shimon.

'You know better than I that the news of Hosea's acquisition spread rapidly among scholars studying the Qumran texts, and when the fourth cave at Qumran was discovered in September 1952, interest among researchers grew enormously. The Taamireh tribesmen who had made the original discovery at Khirbet Qumran had gone back in the hope of finding more manuscripts to sell. They dug into the rock and scratched through the accumulated soil and dust until they found the thousands of fragments still buried there.'

'Indeed. It was reported all over the world,' my father said. 'Every day some new treasure would appear, although since they were as yet undeciphered and untranscribed, nobody really knew their significance. Reading the scrolls was a slow and arduous task; only trained researchers and scholars could gauge their importance. They *did* realise that the scrolls would be the starting point for a new historical investigation: that quite soon they might learn the truth about the birth of rabbinical Judaism and the origins of Christianity, instead of relying on the sparse details of the life of Christ whose authenticity had become more and more questionable over the years. And what they had here were not just a few odd fragments – more were appearing every day. There were large pieces, and some smaller, folded and threadbare, some better preserved than others, some nameless fragments – and they were making history. But only the scholars knew that.'

'That's why I've called on you. It's possible that the manuscript could have been taken by one of the members of Henderson and Michel's international team – they were the only ones with access to the scrolls. Do you know the others?'

'I know who they were. There was Thomas Almond, a British agnostic, an Orientalist, nicknamed "the angel of darkness" because of his strange manner and the huge black cape he always wore; a Pole, Father Andrei Lirnov, a tormented, melancholy character; and a flamboyant French Dominican, Jacques Millet, easily recognised by his dishevelled white beard and big round glasses. They all had direct access to the scrolls, as well as control over access by anyone else. The team very rarely issued an official publication, and most of the fragments from Cave Four have only ever been commented on in closed seminars.'

'But a strange thing happened. In 1987, Michel, who was giving a lecture at Harvard, revealed some details about the contents of a fragment he was studying. What he said about it reminded Matti of the scroll he had quickly deciphered before it was stolen. There were two columns in Aramaic where the prophet Daniel interprets the dreams of a king. But the most remarkable part of the fragment, which Michel had dated as coming from the first century BC, was the interpretation of a dream predicting the coming of a "son of God" or "son of the Highest".'

'Exactly the words used by the angel Gabriel at the Annunciation in Luke's Gospel.'

'Michel refused to publish the document. Apart from a few words to fellow academics during his lecture, and the reading of a minute fragment that he had translated, the contents of the scrolls remain secret.' Shimon stopped for a moment, and pulled from his pocket a piece of paper, which he held out to my father.

They will be great on earth
All will venerate him and serve him
He will be called great and his name will be shown
He will be called son of God.
And they will call him son of the Highest
Like a shooting star.
His kingdom will be a vision
They will reign for several years
On the earth
And they will destroy everything.
Nation will destroy nation
And province will destroy province
Until the people of God rise up
And throw down their swords.

'Yes,' said my father. 'I know this text. But nobody has ever seen the end of the fragment, so we can't say with any certainty whether it mentions the coming of a Messiah sent by God.'

'Whatever, the fragment was never heard of again after the 1987 conference. Years went by and no new publications on the subject appeared. It was as if there had been an official decision to put a stop to all investigations – which is exactly what had happened. The international team went their separate ways. Henderson found a comfortable position at Yale University; Almond went back to England; Millet divided his time between Jerusalem, where he continued his excavations, and Paris, where he taught. Michel went home to Paris too. He left the priesthood and now works for the CNRS.'

'And Andrei Lirnov killed himself, no one knew why,' finished my father.

'Yes, indeed . . . As you know, archaeology isn't really my thing,' said Shimon, after a slight hesitation. 'But it appears that the Israeli government is searching for the lost manuscript, not for theological reasons, although they're complicated enough, but because it belongs to us by right. Also it contains crucial evidence about the history of the Jewish people.'

'And you think that was the fragment read out during Michel's lecture?'

'Yes, it's highly likely.'

'Any idea about the contents of the rest of the scroll?'

'We don't know, though we think Jesus is explicitly mentioned.'

'A threat to Christianity?' asked my father.

'It certainly might be best kept in the vaults of the Vatican, along with other forbidden fragments,' said Shimon drily. 'We do know that it didn't disappear by accident, and we have our theories. The other manuscripts belong to the Qumran sect, which the evidence suggests was Essene. They date more or less from Jesus's lifetime, but none of them mentions Christ. However, it could well be that the missing scroll contains important revelations about Christianity.'

'I see what you're getting at, but I can't accept this task, Shimon, it's not for me. I'm not a fighter any more, and I've never been a spy. These days I'm a researcher, a scholar, an archaeologist. I can't go rushing all over the world looking for this manuscript. It may be lost, anyway, or burnt.'

Shimon stood quietly for a moment, thinking. My father knew him well, he would not easily be put off. He recognised that particular ironic expression. He was clearly a spy, no matter how much he tried to conceal the fact. With his slow and solid demeanour, Shimon always seemed to be absorbing and accumulating information, always watching and measuring, reacting cautiously to what people said. At this moment, thought my father, he was thinking fast, searching – his speciality – for a weak spot which he could use to persuade him.

'Exactly – a scholar is what I need, a specialist, a palaeographer, not a soldier . . . And I know about your interest in the manuscripts. Do you remember how you felt when they were discovered? We were fighting together, and you could think of nothing else; you said it would change everything.'

'That was in 1947, fifty years ago, and things were very different. Qumran was in Palestine, in the British Mandate, with the kingdom of Transjordan to the east. There was no road along the Dead Sea, only an old Roman road through the scrub, and even that had virtually disappeared. The only human presence in that landscape was the Bedouin. I was amazed by the discovery because I couldn't understand how the manuscripts could have got out of such a place. Now the roads are all marked, there are endless excavations, and you talk to me about international strategic stakes. We've given the Jericho palm groves to the Palestinians and are even thinking of handing over, for the sake of peace, a part of the Judaean desert, including the Qumran area. All this is too complicated for me; it's not my business any more, can't you see that? I know these manuscripts; I already know that the Essenes, who lived at the same time as Jesus and were careful scribes whose only purpose in life was to record everything they saw, *never mention Jesus in their writings*. I presume that's why you want to find the last scroll. Will it mention him? What will it say? Was Jesus an Essene? If he was, is Christianity a branch of Essenism? Or perhaps it won't mention him. Would that mean that he came after the Essenes, or not at all? Did he ever exist?

'You see why this is a dangerous line of research. We must avoid a revolution. We know nothing about this manuscript and perhaps it's just as well. Surely it's better to leave things as they are than risk making them worse. Israel doesn't need this. It's a lethal weapon that could go off in your face.'

'Listen,' said Shimon, 'I'm not asking you to analyse the contents. Others can do that, if you don't want the responsibility. If it turns out that it would be better kept secret, we'll do that. Trust me. All I want you to do is to find it, get it back from whoever's got it, whether they be Christians, Jews, Bedouin or Arabs, and bring it to me.'

'Supposing the Christians have already got it – the Vatican, I mean?'

'Impossible.'

'Why?'

There was a silence. Shimon chewed his twig for several minutes as if, once again, he was weighing up pros and cons, evaluating the importance of the information he was about to give, calculating the risks.

'Because the Vatican is searching for it too,' he said. 'Desperately.'

'How do you know?'

'Have you heard of the Papal Biblical Commission?'

'A little.'

'It's an institution created at the beginning of the century by Pope Leo XIII, to fight the tide of modernism. Its job is to watch over Catholic scriptural studies. You might think things would have changed in the last fifty years, particularly since Vatican Two. Not so. Today the Jerusalem Biblical School, to which most of the international team belong, is as much involved with the Commission as it ever was. Most pupils from the school are placed as teachers in seminaries and other Catholic institutions. So in practice, it's the Commission that decides what the general public can or cannot know about the contents of the Dead Sea Scrolls. In 1955, when the Copper Scroll was deciphered in Manchester under the supervision of Thomas Almond, the Vatican called the Commission to a special session to counter any revelations it might contain. More recently, it issued a decree on Biblical studies in general, and specifically on the historical truth of the Gospels, stating that anybody interpreting them should do so in a spirit of obedience to the authority of the Catholic Church.'

'How far would they go to get hold of the scroll?'

'A very long way. There's another organisation which depends on the Commission, called the Congregation for the Doctrine of the Faith, principally a tribunal, with its own judges. Their specific task is to pinpoint delicate points on which the Commission will be pronouncing. Such investigations are generally aimed at anything which might threaten the unity of the Church. They're carried out in conditions of total secrecy, as they were in the Middle Ages. Until 1971, the Commission and the Congregation were held to be two separate organisations; that pretence has now been abandoned, and although they're still separate groups, they're housed in the same office in Rome. Their guiding principle is very simple: whatever conclusions are reached, whatever the scrolls reveal, nobody, either in writing or teaching, can contradict the doctrinal authority of the Commission. And, I may add, the history of the Congregation goes right back to the thirteenth century. Only the suppression of dissidence can ensure the revival of a unified Faith and Dogma. These men believe that those who do not share their ideas are blind or, worse, evil. It appears that Paul Henderson, one of the first to work with Pierre Michel on the scrolls, himself a member of the international team, is the actual director of the Congregation for the Doctrine of the Faith. We know he had the scroll in his hands and that he probably read it when he was still at the Biblical School in Jerusalem. But he hasn't got it any more and he's looking for it. We know he'd do anything to get it back. We've been following his tracks and those of his emissaries, for several months and in several countries.'

'Who are they?'

'Members of the international team, in particular his right-hand man Pierre Michel. And Father Millet too, another member of the team.'

'Which means . . .'

'That these men are the Grand Inquisitors of the present-day Catholic Church.'

My father thought for a moment.

'Who had the scroll first?' he finally asked.

'The Orthodox Bishop Hosea, who sold it to Matti. But we think Henderson may have taken it and given it to Michel to study.'

'What became of Hosea? Did he know what the manuscript contained?'

Shimon hesitated again, and then said: 'He's dead, David. Murdered last week, as he was passing through Jerusalem. The money he had with him disappeared, along with the scrolls. The thieves must have been well-informed about his movements. They may try and re-sell them, in which case we must find them, wherever they are in the world, as Matti did.'

'But he was a general, and had plenty of help,' my father said angrily. 'I can't do it alone. I'd have to talk to scholars, and others, perhaps even crooks and murderers.' He shook his head. 'No, it's not

38

for me. Apart from anything else, I'm too old. There's no point talking about it anymore.'

'Okay. No hope of changing your mind?'

'None.' But my father knew him too well to think that he would give up so easily. His last question meant that he was about to bring out a trump card.

Shimon gazed down at the stony earth. Then he said: 'In that case, I can tell you everything. I was going to keep quiet until you accepted, so as not to put you off. But since you're refusing, you might be able to enlighten me. It's not just the Vatican. It's true the Christians are looking for the scroll, but there appears to be a political element as well, and the police are involved. This must be strictly between you and me.'

'Of course.'

'I told you Hosea was murdered; that's not quite accurate. It was more complicated. The police have decided to hush it up for the moment. They want to investigate without spreading panic.'

Shimon was not normally a man who minced his words, and my father was surprised to see him so reticent. 'What happened?'

'You won't believe it . . . He was crucified.'

My father started. 'What do you mean, crucified?'

'Like Jesus. Nailed to a cross. Well, not exactly like Jesus. It was a different sort of cross, with two horizontal bars, one big and one small.'

'A cross of Lorraine?'

'A sort of decapitated cross of Lorraine. The poor man's wrists had been nailed to the crossbar, and his feet to the upright. He died quite quickly, asphyxiated. At first they thought it was the work of some maniac. And – this is what I'm getting at – we don't know why, but we think it's something to do with the scroll.'

'Really?'

'Yes. We know that Hosea rushed back from the States because of it. He appeared to be trying to escape . . . It seemed almost like an execution, the ceremonial, the cross . . . David, I don't know what's going on, but if it is a madman, he could strike again.'

'Yes, I . . .'

Shimon saw his confusion, and pulled out his trump. 'You'll need someone with you, someone young and strong, a fighter. He would have to be a soldier and a scholar.'

'I suppose so,' said my father, resigned.

'I know just the man, and so do you.'

'Who?'

'Your son Ary. I've read his army dossier. I know he saved my son Yacov's life. Your son's a brave young man who would have made an excellent soldier if he hadn't chosen a more contemplative life.'

'You've thought of everything, haven't you?'

Second Scroll

THE SCROLL OF THE SAINTS

When I was young, before I wandered
I longed for wisdom and I searched for it
It came to me in all its beauty
And I studied it deeply.
The flower of the vine too produces grapes
When the bunches ripen which gladden the heart.
My foot has trodden on a single land,
Because I have known it since I was young.
I have listened
And heard a lot.
And the earth was my nurse
And I pay the homage that is due to she who taught me.
I meditated as I played
I longed for good without reward.
I was myself inflamed for her,
And I did not turn away,
I hurried towards her,
And on her heights I did not rest.
My hand opened her gate,
And I discovered her secrets.
I purified my hands to go to her,
And I found her in purity.
My heart was intelligent from the beginning
Which was why I did not abandon her [. . .]
Listen, o multitudes, to my teaching
And you will acquire gold and silver thanks to me,
May your soul rejoice at my penitence
And do not be ashamed of my songs!
Accomplish your works with justice
And you will receive your reward in time.

Qumran scrolls, *Pseudo-Davidic psalms.*

I

After the creation God looked upon what he had done, the light, the firmament, the stars, the sun and the moon, the earth and the sea, the plants and the animals, and he saw that it was good.

His satisfaction sometimes surprised me. Were the beauties of this world really comparable to those of the next? Why then had I devoted my life to asceticism in order to attain the latter, when I was allowed to enjoy the former? *I said in mine heart, Go to now, I will prove thee with mirth, therefore enjoy pleasure: And, behold, this also is vanity.*

I was no prodigal son. On the contrary I was a fitting son for David Cohen, even if, at that time, I did not quite realise what the proposition entailed. But Shimon, who had known me in the green uniform of the land army, would have been surprised to see me then. I was tall and bearded, with my Russian mother's blue eyes circled by small round spectacles. My beard was sparse, not abundant like that of the old sages. My body was like my father's, slender but muscular. It was useful in the army, but I had let it go since joining the Hassidim.

Like all my brothers, I had long twisted meshes of hair on either side of my face, traditional side-locks, which I sometimes tied up on top of my head, beneath my hat. Day and night, even when I had my hat on, I wore a black velvet skullcap, which covered most of my head. My shoes were flat and black, without laces; welcoming my feet in their black stockings. Black, too, were trousers, in accordance with tradition. I wore a white shirt beneath a long dark coat, and beneath the shirt a small prayer shawl made of two cream woollen squares with an opening for the head, one flap hanging down on the chest, the other on the back, and showing below, attached to each corner, a ritual fringe in memory of the Covenant. I did not wear a tie: a too-distinctive attire of the non-Jewish world. Around my waist was tied a cord, the *guertl*, a long ribbon of plaited black silk, which separated

44

the controlling half of the body from its prosaic parts. On the Sabbath and feast days I would wear a black frock coat of gleaming silk.

I had studied archaeology with my father, and had helped him with his work and his research, but that was before I started at the yeshivah, a place as exclusive and jealous as the God of Israel. From a very early age I had accompanied my father on his digs: I was his only son and only child. But I was very pious; that is to say very practising. An 'orthodox Jew', as the Jews call us.

Unlike my father, who observed neither the Sabbath nor a kosher diet, I would attach phylacteries around my arms each morning, and on the Sabbath, when he and my mother would set off on expeditions into the countryside, I would put on my big white prayer shawl and bless all my comrades at the yeshivah, for son of Cohen, I was a Cohen, and a descendant of the priests whose function was to bless the people of Israel. My life, down to the smallest detail, was lived according to the rules. I prayed each morning on rising, I said the blessing before eating, I prayed each night before sleeping; I studied every single day. According to the law, time inhabits space; hence the *mezuzot* on the lintels, the candlesticks on the Sabbath table, and at the windows at Hannukah. And according to the law, the word becomes flesh: I could only eat animals permitted by the Torah, ruminants with cloven hooves, and fish with scales and fins. And according to the law, the flesh is joy. On Friday nights and Saturdays at the yeshivah, we rested without light, without pencil or paper – we were forbidden to touch any work tools – but we sang and danced all night, according to Hassidic custom. As one of our rabbis said, 'You don't sing because you are happy, you are happy because you sing'. We did not live a life of mortification; we lived together, in a community, young and old, women and children, and all were happy to be together in the peace of the Sabbath, sharing the prepared dishes and the golden *chollah*, listening to the words of our masters and laughing at their puns. As soon as the first star appeared over Jerusalem, announcing the day of rest, Mea Shearim sank into lethargy. Young men ran to the borders of the neighbourhood and placed barrels on the roads to stop the traffic, while others put stones in their pockets to throw vengefully at passing cars. Sirens mingled with the sound of the *shofar* announcing the arrival of the bride – the Sabbath – and a carefree crowd dressed in its finest clothes swarmed through the main streets to the many synagogues, some of which were no bigger than a small house. Some rabbis would stand at their doors, already in their black and white prayer cloths, calling to passers-by, trying to complete the minian, the quorum of ten worshippers necessary for the service to take place. Piercing chants floated down from open windows, psalmodies and prayers interspersed with vibrant shouts, as the young students intoned songs of joy.

If there is any pure area left in the world, it is Mea Shearim, stuck between the old city of Jerusalem and the new Jewish town. The place seems to have been built by Jews to cut themselves off from other Jews, as if their desire for difference could never be satisfied. The area is certainly an anachronism, lying as it does at the margin of the State, of society and of everything representing the reality of Israel. And certainly we were relics, and in time we may well disappear. But it could also be that the future is on our side, and that we would endure, despite everything, thanks to our faith and our high birth rate: for our families were as numerous as the stars in the sky, as grains of sand by the sea, and they had grown and multiplied as God, our God, had commanded them to.

Mea Shearim consists of one main thoroughfare lined with low houses built in a style reminiscent of Central Europe, with the steep roofs of rainy countries – this in a land where every drop of rain is a blessing from God – wrought-iron gates, tiny balconies, and court-yards turned to chasms by a maze of alleys. At the entrance to the neighbourhood sat the eternal beggar, a wandering Jew with a heavy black coat and large hat, holding out his wooden bowl at the foot of a placard, saying in English, Yiddish and Hebrew:

Jewish woman, the Torah commands you to dress with modesty. Skirts should be below the knee and married women should cover their heads. We ask visitors not to shock our religious feelings by walking our streets in immodest garb.

For the few thousand Jews of Mea Shearim, the clock of time is still set on the ghettos of Central Europe, which for the most part, the Sephardic and indigenous inhabitants never knew but which they re-invented, with the help of the strudel and the Yiddish language, since the holy language is not for profane use, nor for the trivialities of daily life. Mea Shearim, spread over a few square kilometres, means in Hebrew 'the hundred gates'. Some say that when it was built by Hungarian Jews during the second half of the nineteenth century, the windows and terraces were purposely built facing inwards onto the courtyards, with only a few doors giving access to the outside, in order to exclude bandits and unbelievers from the stronghold.

I was seventeen when I first entered Mea Shearim. My parents never went there; it was not their sort of place. I was surprised at first by the density of the population, the nervous hurried crowds in the narrow streets, the steady tempo of the Hassidim, despite the crowd; a picturesque, talkative, bearded world, always on the move, always gazing, it seemed to me, towards eternity. Old rabbis stopped in the middle of the road to dispute for hours about a single word of the Talmud, stopping the traffic, without regard for anyone around them, rejoined little by little by pale, serious young men who would argue ardently. They were the *bahurim*, students of the *kolelim* and the yeshivahs. I eventually joined one of these curious schools which provided no diplomas and whose only goal was to explore more deeply the world of divine communion.

At that time I thought that the entire population of the area was dedicated to the study and celebration of Jewish life. I had not thought of the economic side; that question seemed shrouded in a magical, impenetrable aura. Later I discovered that actually half the inhabitants were devoting their time and money to spiritual matters, the other half were supporting them. The jobs they did were of the kind that allowed them to observe their laws: they were scribes, slaughterhousemen, circumcisers, ritual bathkeepers, makers of wigs and *mezuzots*, hatters and cappers, goldsmiths and artisans making candlesticks for the Sabbath and Hannukah, working in wood or stone, silk or velvet. They were also supported by communities abroad, particularly Williamsburg, the Hassidic quarter in New York. Thus the rest, the students, could live, precariously but without starving. Studying was all they knew how to do in this world; they started learning the Torah at five; by twelve they already knew the Talmud. Only when they reached forty were they considered worthy to study the mystical texts of Zohar, the *Book of Splendour*.

I did not realise, either, what enormous variety of thought lay behind the apparent unity of their lifestyle. Every detail – a trouser-leg turned up, or hooked up to the knee, black shoes or boots, short coats or long with a vent, Borsalinos, streimels or Russian caps – reflected some dynasty, some school of thought with its own particular customs.

I envied the ones lucky enough to have been brought up in the tradition from their earliest youth. I had everything to learn, and little time. I felt I had lacked education and would have to be, in a sense, re-made, starting from the beginning. But here again I naively ignored the extent to which I was predisposed to find an ultimate refuge inside this citadel, the world of dreaming old men with their hats and beards and coats, with strings of children born at nine-monthly intervals; a hieratic people, with their hasty step and same pale faces framed with curled locks of hair. An unusual palace, where silk and velvet glowed, some outdated place with girls in shawls and women in wigs and hats, with long skirts and wool stockings. They dressed for a Polish winter – here where it was forty degrees in the shade – harking back to austere beginnings in Podolia. There, during the sermons and pogroms, hatred had been instilled in the womb, slowly but surely preparing the ground for the catastrophes of the centuries that followed. So the only safety was to be found in the home, within the hundred gates, within the community; here the hated Jew and his poor and rejected family could find a precarious barrier against attack, bound together by their studies and teaching. Within the gates, the texts before him, each could at last feel master of his historic destiny, and enriched by his own ancient culture. It was a fortress within which each man was both king and subject, and there was no slave and no martyr.

When they brought the ghetto with them into the heart of Israel, they also brought escape from it, a new openness towards other aspirations, the mystical breath of the Caballa. They brought within the hundred gates real life and true actions, and the possibility of creative movement. To protect themselves from this world, they invented a future one and called it 'rapture'.

I knew about rapture before I knew about Hassidism. I had always been prone to exultation, and sometimes I was possessed by huge strength and immoderate appetites. I had gone into trances, and had felt divine forces within me so that I could have faced any obstacle, and, driven by this faith, I pursued my religious studies in spite of my parents' protests. This zeal drove me towards the Hassidim, for I knew that they alone understood such a possession. I can hardly admit it; could I describe it? At times I reached a state close to *devekut*, the supreme bliss, the fullness which is for them a rule of conduct.

At the yeshivah, they taught me the preliminaries necessary to achieve this state of ecstasy: the praying techniques that aided concentration, the intense staring at the texts, which would unite

48

the soul with the inner light of the Hebrew letters, giving life to word and thing. I knew fruitful thoughts; I fasted; I learned exactly what doses of magic powders were needed. Sometimes wine alone was sufficient, for wine releases secrets – but with powder, the whole soul is lifted.

Then it was as if I had emptied myself, as if I had managed to lose myself, and possessed, I did not possess my soul anymore. Freed from selfish bonds, my spirit would blossom into opaque and magnificent splendour. I felt my body levitating. I walked out of my dead and abstract self towards a heavenly world. I had abandoned time and space and reached essential truth; in that instant, close to eternal peace, I felt the sudden inspiration of the Eternal One, and I relived the wonderful truths and dreams of creation. I contemplated glorious ideas. I wrote books, I read the Torah, I was Moses and Elijah, I was both king and prophet. My thoughts flew beyond our earth to a future world brought about by me, for I was the Messiah.

We would hold banquets where we danced all night, close together around a brazier, until dawn, breathless. Our hats, edge to edge, formed a dark and ceaselessly undulating sea. Sometimes one of us would detach himself from the group and dance alone in the middle of the circle, close to the fire. When he danced in front of the flames, like a disjointed shadow, his face lit up with fire and ecstasy.

We would gather in one of the courtyards with an orchestra, and perform incantatory dances. Some virtuosos could juggle sticks and bottles, twist their heads and bend their bodies backwards into a horizontal position. One of the dances, the *volatch*, involved one dancer bringing back to life with cunning movements the one pretending to be dead, until both were dancing together to an infernal rhythm.

When God created man, it was by contraction. His infinite will turned into a finite being. By contracting Himself into Himself he made way for the creature. *Tsimtsum*. I return myself to nothingness, lose my subjectivity, in order to find original wisdom, the wisdom of the beginning with all its possibilities, the unceasing changes and evolution of pure will. In this way I discover things I could never have suspected in my conscious state. I find another self that I never knew was there. I become the creator about to make his first brushstroke. I find the divine universe, with its total otherness, its complete transcendency, at work within me.

To achieve this state one must practise asceticism: give up worldly preoccupations, self-interest and pride. Sorrow, too, as tears make one forget God. One must empty oneself of everything; to understand what was there unknown, words, desires and memories. The captive will must be surrendered totally, to give it back all its strength.

Rapture was the centre of our life, the core of our redemption. For the Messiah will come through it, like God, not revealing himself in his entirety, but by retraction. And when he saves us, he will gather together in each thought, each word and each act, the divine sparks that are dispersed among us.

II

In the morning sow thy seed, and in the evening withhold not thine hand: goes the saying, *for thou knowest not whether shall prosper, either this or that, or whether they both shall be alike good.* When I was a Hassid, I would rise early and cross the Arab quarter to reach, after Mea Shearim, the heart of the old town, the white quarter, gleaming in the dawn, which encircled little Jerusalem in a phosphorescent aura. I knew where I was going then, and went happily. My heart was under the city light; Jerusalem was looking at me like a bride. From time to time I would be overcome by a strange feeling of peace and accomplishment. Sometimes my feet would lead me on mysterious detours through forbidden areas, but I would always find my way back to the Wall.

It always came as a surprise, at the end of the dark and winding streets, standing huge and still, guarding the town like the noblest of Tsahal's guards. It was no longer the Wailing Wall; but rather the Western Wall built by Herod to protect the Temple, and now, by a sad irony, protecting only itself. I would kiss the wall, and say my morning prayer, touching it with one hand. When I had finished, I would leave, walking backwards as all religious Jews do, not to turn their backs to it out of respect for the destroyed Temple.

I would then go to one of the many yeshivoth in the quarter, to pursue my Talmudic studies. I would spend the whole day there, poring over the pages from thick volumes of the Talmud, seeking the clinching argument, knowing all the time that there was no such thing – and so we would resort to the traditional formula of the tekou: *when the Messiah comes, all questions and all problems will find their solution.*

This was where I met him for the first time. He was standing in a corner of the room, swaying and chanting, stroking his beard, a book in front of him, without looking at the young and brilliant Talmudists.

'Israel is a rose amongst thorns. What does the rose represent? The community is red or white, like a rose, and lives sometimes in harsh times, sometimes lenient.'

I asked one of my comrades who was this man.

'Don't you know?' He was surprised. 'That's the rabbi.'

'What rabbi?'

'*The* rabbi,' he said, as though there were only one.

Later, when I had studied with him, and learnt much from him, I came to know what a great man he was. He would say: 'It is not your duty to perform this task, but you are not free not to do so.' He said too that thousands of years ago, when the Jews were a small semi-nomadic people moving from place to place in the land of Canaan, the tradition of Jewish study was already in place. He taught me that it was essential to develop one's intelligence. If we were not totally concentrated on our work, he would get into a towering rage, saying that the whole point was missed once you lost track of the argument. The result was meaningless. You had to follow the reasoning step by step, almost like a police investigation. We were trying to find the hidden meaning of the law, and it required an enormous effort. He did not, like some of the masters I have come across, simply want his pupils to ingest information; he thought they should learn to think for themselves. There was no jealousy between master and pupil – our independence was no threat to him.

It would usually begin with the rabbi asking one of us to read a page from the Talmud. The subject hardly mattered; it could be something odd, some specific case which was unlikely to occur, where you didn't know what was at stake: a tower floating in the air, a mouse bringing crumbs into a house on a day of Passover, a foetus transplanted from one womb to another. Six or seven lines of text could involve two hours of argument. If you missed a single day or a single hour, it became impossible to follow the reasoning.

Sometimes I wondered: what goes through the mind of a young man of eighteen who decides to spend ten years of his life in a yeshivah, studying the Talmud, when he could be doing a thousand other things? What was the attraction of such a lonely path? Most of my comrades weren't *baal teshuvah* like myself, turning back towards tradition. They were there because their fathers had placed them there, to become scholars. I had seen the light and was searching for fulfilment.

Study therefore was less satisfying for me than the contemplation of the aura around it. For us, knowledge was not supreme value. Like most Hassidim, I felt that the minute examination of textual detail and the tortuous discussions of minutiae were, although necessary, both inferior and subordinate to the true aim of the exercise, which was to attach oneself more and more closely to God.

It wasn't easy. We were not allowed to leave the yeshivah, except in cases of absolute necessity. Magazines, newspapers and radios were forbidden. The rabbi said that the yeshivah was not like any other school; it demanded depth, purity and sanctity from its pupils, and those who deviated from this ideal had no place there. So as long as one was in the school one was forbidden to take any interest in what was happening outside. It was a shelter from the outside world, preventing any intruder from coming in – or its members from leaving.

We were not allowed to see girls. The rabbi said that boys should not meet any girls until a year before their marriage.

'But how do you know when it's a year before your marriage?' I would say. 'You've got to meet the girl first.'

'Well, if you're eighteen and starting university, you probably won't get married for four years. But supposing you meet the right person when you're eighteen? It's very difficult to go out with a girl you love and only talk. Much better avoid the whole situation before you're seriously involved.'

'But the students say they want to meet girls sooner than that, otherwise they won't know how to behave with them.'

'You either know how to behave or you don't – you won't learn by mixing with lots of girls. People who start late make just as successful marriages as those who start early.'

We were not allowed ovens; our concentration would be affected if we were always wondering what we were going to eat that night. The cinema was forbidden, too, because it might be a source of temptation. Although cassettes were not allowed, some students borrowed the teachers' tape recorders, pretending it was for work.

I used to like the movies, but after I joined the yeshivah I wouldn't go, even if I had been allowed to. What would people think, seeing me there with my streimel and locks? And I tried not to look at women in the street either. When I had to speak to them I would lower my eyes. The rabbi said one had to be especially vigilant in summer, when they wore scantier clothes.

I believe that when you live in such a different and isolated world, you have no alternative but to read and study. The school hardened us, preparing us to fight against the evils of the modern world; we kept preparing and arming ourselves for the struggle; we were ready to resist and fight. We were the battalions of the new age.

I didn't hate the rabbi. I didn't worship him, the way the others did, but I firmly believed in him as a prophet and a fine man. So I couldn't hold it against him when my best friend Yehudi was forced into a marriage with his daughter, even though I knew it saddened him. He was younger than me, only twenty-four, and had no thought of marriage, but I was not shocked that it was being imposed on him, or that he didn't even know his fiancée; that was how most marriages were arranged.

It all began with his sister, who had reached marriageable age; their father had gone to the marriage-broker in order to find her a husband. The broker knew a brother and sister who were both available, and, knowing that Yehudi was single, he suggested a double arrangement. Yehudi's father refused at first, thinking Yehudi could wait a little longer. However the broker persisted, this time approaching the mother, whose influence in these matters was crucial; when she heard that the brother and sister in question were the rabbi's children, she couldn't refuse. Financial matters were settled, and Yehudi was received by the rabbi. A certain distance had to be maintained until the engagement was final, and so they met at the yeshivah. The object of the interview was to ascertain the young man's scholarly talents; Yehudi had prepared a lesson, and he performed brilliantly. The rabbi asked a question from time to time, and after ten minutes nodded. The girl's name was Rachel and she was eighteen; she could cook and do housework, and wanted to be a seamstress.

'You see,' said Yehudi, 'it's such an honour to marry the rabbi's daughter. Can you imagine! My parents are wild with joy.'

'But what about her, your wife? What's she like?'

'I've only seen her once, I don't know. But through her I'll be closer to him.'

Yehudi and the rabbi met one more time before the marriage. They walked together through the streets of Mea Shearim, talking of the yeshivah and other things. When they parted, the rabbi smiled faintly and said 'Gute Nacht'.

A few weeks later they shattered a glass in memory of the destroyed Temple. Thousands of Hassidim from all over the world came to the sumptuous wedding, at which the bride walked seven times around the groom, according to the custom.

As the rabbi's son-in-law, Yehudi had unique access to him, and was privy to his every word and gesture, a unique piece of fortune for a Hassid.

Although I knew perfectly well about arranged marriages, I couldn't help feeling sad; I felt that a new life was beginning for him and therefore for me: soon I would have to start preparing for my own marriage. There had, of course, already been a few propositions. I was not an ideal match, as my parents were not religious, but I had completed my teshuvah; I was a fast learner and one of the best pupils at the yeshivah, and I had a good reputation: *a good name is better than precious ointment; and the day of death than the day of one's birth.* Several fathers and mothers had boasted to me of the merits of their daughters, but I had never spoken to them because to do so would have been to seal the union. And what could I do if the time was not right for me?

For my parents, my departure to the yeshivah had been like a death. I could no longer eat with them. At first I would accept a glass of tea, or a cake, but I gradually stopped visiting. How could I enter a house where the mezuzots on the lintels were not kosher, where everything in the kitchen was *taref*, and where they mixed milk and meat, ate shellfish and forbidden animals, and even, God forgive me, pork? How could I eat with people who did not wash their hands and pray before eating, or say grace after the meal? How could I live with people who cooked, had lights on and went out in the car on the Sabbath, and whose married women did not cover their heads? My own parents were blasphemers, my mother a renegade who could not understand how her son could have become a Hassid. For her it was a step back to the Middle Ages, to the prison of the ghetto. She had come to Israel to escape from all that. She said I was too young to live an ascetic life according to antiquated laws, and too free-spirited to believe in the superstitions and merciless rules which prevented people from enjoying life.

But for me the rules were not restrictions but the path to meaning. It was forbidden, above all, to be old: beneath my austere streimel and black coat, I knew that I must remain young, with all the naivety of youth. The clothes were merely an armour against the senility of the world protecting me against the superficiality, hypocrisy, depravity, pettiness, the pursuit of money for its own sake, in short everything that disfigures the world and makes the young so old, sad and cynical. As the rabbi said, youth, like happiness, is unaware of itself, and disappears when you search for it. *Rejoice, O young man, in thy youth; and let thy heart cheer thee in the days of thy youth, and walk in the ways of thine heart, and in the sight of thine eyes: but know thou, that for all these things God will bring thee to judgement.*

I had been in the army, unlike most of my yeshivah companions, who were not Zionists and had rejected it for religious and ideological reasons. My parents had wanted me to, and so had I. The country had given us a great deal, and the least I could do was to spend three years defending it, and therefore ourselves, and indeed the Hassidim. I had been in Lebanon, and had lived through sleepless days and weeks in tanks, watching the enemy. Fear had been a constant companion; there was never a week without a military funeral, the tearing, hopeless roar of gunfire over the grave of a young man of my own age, killed in action. War, for me, was no game, no imaginary exercise; it was real, proof of how tough our times were, how precarious and threatened our lives, our very existence on earth. It was David versus Goliath, Jericho reconquered and lost again, the Golan invaded by the four Mesopotamians, cast out in turn by Abraham. It was Masada all over again: a fortress, a little patch of land attacked from all sides, awaiting the final countdown; the same cities, the same struggle, the same hopes. Soldier that I was, with my green uniform and sub-machine gun, I still prayed whenever I could at the Western Wall, with my head against the stone; I prayed that this war would be the last, that the exile and return should not have been in vain, that we should continue to revive the language, and make the desert bloom; that we should be able to gaze on summer evenings at our city bathed in bronze and gold light. *For Gaza shall be abandoned, Askelon shall be devastated, Ashdod shall be abandoned at high noon, and Eqron uprooted.*

During my three years in the army I discovered drugs, alcohol and parties, but I was never drawn into this world, or seduced by it. I had known a few girls and had occasionally had a taste of an artificially-induced paradise, but I had felt like a visitor or an anthropologist, and had never wanted to repeat any experience. The others called me 'the other one'; they could see that, although I didn't dislike or even despise them, I was different. They would say that I was from another century, another world, and they were right – I was a living antique, something to study, like a well-preserved parchment, young somehow despite its great age, able to reveal new and fresh truths as well as events from centuries past.

My father was not like them. Unlike my mother, he never said that what I was doing was backward-looking folly. He never said anything. It was only later that I understood his silence on the subject. I hadn't realised that he had been extremely pious as a young man, and I couldn't understand how a Cohen could have become so 'assimilated'; I thought he had no idea why I dressed in the clothes of the Polish ghetto, even in the stifling Israeli summer.

But he knew, and better than I did. For him the past was his religion, and research into the past his job. Archaeology was our common passion: when we worked on digs together, or studied old documents, we were truly father and son, and son was no prodigal.

III

So, if Shimon had not intervened, if my father had not called upon me, I might have married, and put down roots for the rest of my life – for the texts say you need to keep studying to be able to study. But without realising it, I had been waiting for this. It was as if everything I had learned was for some other purpose. Even though, by my understanding of it, study was its own reward, I did vaguely feel, unlike my comrades, that it was not the ultimate purpose of my existence. I felt that it was preparing me for something that was still to come. *I communed with mine own heart, saying, Lo, I am come to great estate, and have gotten more wisdom than all they that have been before me in Jerusalem: yea, my heart had great experience of wisdom and knowledge.*

In fact, a painting would describe me better than a long essay. I was like a faintly drawn and pale watercolour. At that time I was righteous and innocent; I had seen evil but had had no contact with it. I was like a newborn child, not because I had never sinned – I was like any other man – but because nothing so far had shaken my integrity. I was whole, still with my own choices, dreams and wishes. Nothing could stop me, I was afraid of nothing. The fact was, I had not lived. Now that I have, I miss that time, because everything was still possible then. Afterwards, when it was too late for hope, I simply had to try to carry on living with my haunting memories.

When my father told me about the manuscripts, I was not surprised. I knew the strange history of their discovery and had always felt curiously drawn towards Qumran, where I somehow knew, as if it had been written, that a part of my life would be played out. *The thing that hath been, it is that which shall be; and that which is done is that which shall be done: and there is no new thing under the sun.*

'I remember your excavations there,' I said to my father. 'The ruins of Khirbet Qumran were near Wadi Qumran, and not far away was a cemetery containing a hundred and ten tombs. They lay facing north to south so they couldn't have been Muslim ones, and there were no familiar symbols on them.'

'Yes. They were Essene tombs.'

'I didn't know a manuscript had been stolen . . . I can understand them wanting to get it back, but why is Shimon involved? What's it got to do with the army?'

'The manuscripts are politically important.'

'Why?'

'The government wants to find the scroll before the Vatican gets to it.'

'Is there some threat to Christianity?'

'We don't know what it contains, and we don't know who's got it.'

'But why come to you? And why do they want me to go with you?'

'I think it's because we know the subject without actually being involved.'

'And what am I supposed to do?'

'Follow me, escort me, maybe protect me.'

'It must be dangerous, then, if you need a bodyguard?'

'Yes, perhaps,' he admitted.

'When do we go?'

'Now. Tomorrow. As soon as possible.'

'But I can't. I'm studying at the yeshivah, and you can't just leave your studies like that.'

'Who said anything about abandoning your studies?' he said mischievously. He thought for a moment, and then added: 'If we find the manuscript, we'll study it together. We may find something important . . . We may have to keep it, and only show it to Shimon, perhaps not even to him. In any case, you musn't say anything to your rabbi.'

He leaned towards me, and breathed: 'Nobody, without my permission, understood?'

I nodded. It was the first time he had ever asked such a thing: to choose between the respect and obedience I owed him, and my blind trust in the rabbi. He knew that I had already made that choice when I had abandoned his traditions, or rather his non-traditions, as I saw them, but the confrontation had never before been direct; it had remained implicit, but always there, a question hanging in the air. So I felt that this was sufficiently important to make me observe the fifth commandment and keep it from the rabbi, even if, by doing so, I was betraying in the name of the Torah the actual giver of the commandment.

He didn't mention the hideous murder connected with the manuscripts – I only heard about it later. Perhaps it was better like that. I don't think the terrible shock I felt would have been any the less had I been prepared for the idea. But as yet I knew nothing; I wanted to find out about the manuscript out of curiosity, and because I was drawn to it by something indefinable, some nagging memory.

We went into the Jordan valley, because my father wanted to show me Qumran, as Shimon had shown him. The site he took me to, near the caves, overlooked the landscape. To our left, to the north, the silvery river wound between the thickets; behind us, to the west, lay the dark escarpments and yellow dunes of the Judaean desert and, in the distance, the green oasis of the Jericho palm-grove. The grey water of the Dead Sea lay like a lake before us, reflecting the steep blue mountains around it. My father stared fixedly at the western shore, where the promontory of Ras Feshka, behind a huge cliff, overhung the bright green spring at Ain Feshka, he knew that, right by the spring, and a little to the north lay the marl terrace by the cliff overlooking the coastal plain and the ruins of Khirbet Qumran. We could not see them from where we stood, but I understood later that he could easily have visualised them.

I had been there before, on many outings with my parents or friends. For myself as for many others, it was still a lonely spot in the middle of the desert, inhabited only by the Bedouin in their tents. Only later did I understand that Khirbet Qumran, described very briefly by early explorers of Palestine, was one of the most renowned and holy sites on earth. From this wild, featureless, Dead Sea landscape, which bore no trace of man or beast, had emerged the only thing such a landscape could produce: a single God, without name, face or body; a pure being, with no physical trace or manifestation. These dunes and this sea were no place for nymphs or sirens.

We walked to the old Essene monastery at Khirbet Qumran, built of grey blocks of stone at some distance from the sea. In the hills behind were black patches: the caves where the scrolls had been found. Between the Dead Sea and the monastery lay the necropolis, a large rectangle of earth paved with large pebbles and harsh rubble. A two-storey tower to the north-west protected the site.

The monastery contained a kitchen, with an oven and refectory. There was another room where the Essenes gathered, with an adjoining scriptorium built of plaster and brick. Three bronze and two clay inkpots had been found there, still containing dried ink. Rain from the hills filled six cisterns which supplied the community; a large pool had been unearthed, the *mikveh*, which served for the purification of the brothers.

'Before the excavation,' said my father, 'there was only a heap of stone and one choked cistern.'

'Do we know how the inhabitants lived?' I asked.

'The men spent their days writing, reading, and studying. The community had an enormous library, with several hundred volumes. Some were Biblical, others were the sect's own literature. They were fervently read for the edification of the community. The non-Biblical literature had to reflect the opinions of the sect. In those days books had no author: if a scribe thought the text he was copying could be improved upon or embellished with additions, omissions or modifications, he would do so. Not so long ago it was the custom for copyists to display their talents by changing the texts they worked on.'

'Even sacred texts?'

'If they were sure that it was sacred, they tried to copy it exactly. Remember the legend of the Seventy. Ptolomey II of Egypt gathered seventy-two scribes from Jerusalem, six for each tribe. He asked them to work for seventy-two days translating the Laws of Moses from Hebrew into Greek. Each one was isolated in a cell on a Mediterranean island, working, according to the legend, under divine inspiration. At the end of seventy-two days, the completed translations proved identical.'

'What was this room used for?' I asked, pointing at the remains of a vast enclosure that appeared to be one of the main rooms.

'It's the refectory and assembly room. One the Essene rituals was to sit down together to partake of a banquet presided over by the Messiah. Nobody could touch the bread or wine until each one had been blessed in hierarchical order. The ceremony was a foretaste of Heaven; the priest replaced the Messiah if he was not present, and acted in his name.'

'Like Jesus at the Last Supper?'

'Yes, and Jesus there identified himself with the Messiah.'

'Do you think there's a connection between Jesus and the "Master of Justice" mentioned in the Qumran scrolls?'

'The scroll known as *Habbakuk's Commentary* – not in good condition, unfortunately – alternates quotations from the *Book of Habbakuk* with descriptions of subsequent events which fulfil the prophecies. The book mentions a 'Master of Justice', a dissident priest of the Temple, who was pursued and killed by the 'Wicked Priest'. It appears that the Master of Justice was venerated as a martyr: according to the Essenes, he received revelations directly from God, and was persecuted by the priests. They also believed that their Master of Justice would reappear at the end of time, after the war between Sons of Light and Sons of Darkness. According to their predictions, the Master of Justice would kill the Wicked Priest, take power and lead the world into a Messianic era.

'So,' continued my father, 'there are curious similarities between this Essene and the Christian Jesus. Like the Master of Justice, Jesus preached penitence, poverty, humility, love of one's fellow man, and chastity. Like him, he commanded respect for the laws of Moses. He too was the Chosen One, the Messiah of God, the saviour of the world. He too faced the hostility of the priests, the Sadducees in particular, was condemned and put in prison; and at the end of time he too will be the supreme judge. He too founded a church whose faithful fervently await his return. And finally the Christian church and the Essene community share as their most important rite a sacred meal, presided over by a priest. A great many common features but, for the moment, no proof.'

My father spoke with the passion he always felt when visiting archaeological sites and reliving the past. I loved the deep sound of his voice on these occasions: vibrant, but almost choking with the effort of getting the words out clearly. He sounded then almost like one of the most vehement of the ancient prophets.

A bit further on, some men were busy excavating the base of a wall. The one who appeared to be in charge of the operation was a plump man of medium height, with a white beard and curly hair and large horn-rimmed spectacles. His ruddy complexion indicated consumption of more than just communion wine, and his shape, beneath the Dominican robe, betrayed a weakness for good living.

This was Father Millet, one of the French members of the international team. My father recognised him at once – they had often met at digs and conferences; he was friendly and talkative, and we found ourselves easily engaged in conversation.

'Where have you got to?' asked my father.

'We've cleared a group of buildings which stretches eighty metres from east to west and a hundred metres from north to south,' he said, showing him a map covered in scribbled notes. 'And we've been able to distinguish and date several periods of occupation by examining the walls and floors, and the coins and pottery fragments that we found. The earliest human habitation of Khirbet Qumran goes back to the Israelite period: the walls with the deepest foundations are built on an ashy layer containing shards from the Second Iron Age. These have been found particularly at the angle of sections 73 and 80, and to the north of the site, against the foundations of the eastern wall. One team found a jug handle beneath section 68 bearing the stamp 'Lammelech', meaning 'to the king', part of a well-known series, and an ostracon engraved with Palaeo-Hebraic characters. The position of the shards and the level of the foundations enabled me to reconstruct the plan of a rectangular building comprising a large courtyard and rooms along the eastern wall, with a projection at the north-east corner. There's another wall along the east side of cistern 117, but I don't know what it's for.'

'Probably the western wall of the building,' said my father, glancing at the map.

'But there's a sort of enclosure in front of it.'

'With an opening on the north side?'

'Exactly.'

'That's where the water drained out into the large round cistern, the deepest one at Khirbet Qumran. Have you been able to date the building?'

'Yes,' replied Millet, surprised by the speed with which my father had automatically drawn his conclusions. 'The shards give the date – the end of the seventh century BC. This is confirmed by the Lammelech stamp, which dates from the end of the monarchy, and by the ostracon, whose characters are from not long before the exile. It also seems clear that this building did not survive the fall of the kingdom of Judaea; the ashes around the Israelite shards suggest that it was destroyed by fire. It had been in ruins for a very long time before the next group came to live at Khirbet Qumran.'

'These were the priests in revolt against the Temple?'

'There are several hypotheses about that. Whoever they were, they were the founders of Essenism. Here, look what we've just found, which certainly belonged to them.'

He showed us a tiny phial which, according to him, dated from the time of Herod or his immediate successors. It looked as though it had been deliberately hidden in the ruins, because it had been carefully wrapped in palm-fibre paper.

'You see,' he said, tipping the bottle, 'it contains a very thick red oil, unlike any you would find nowadays. I think its the balsam oil used to anoint the kings of Israel. But we can't be sure, because the tree that produced it has been extinct for fifteen hundred years.'

'May I see?' I said, and he handed it to me.

'Have you read the Copper Scroll?' my father asked, still pursuing his idea.

'Yes, I read Thomas Almond's transcription, which has just been published. It describes a priceless treasure, of gold, silver, precious ointments, holy robes and vessels, and the sixty-four places around Jerusalem where it was hidden in ancient times. It also contains a detailed map of these places, ponds, tombs, tunnels, with precise instructions about their names and positions. The researchers estimate the treasure to be so great, according to the scroll, that one wonders how it could have been accumulated.'

'Don't you think it probable,' said my father, 'that, bearing in mind the frequent mention of ritual vessels in the Bronze Scroll, there might have been some link between the Qumran community and the priests of the Jerusalem Temple?'

'The Qumran community seemed to have been founded by dissident priests from the Temple . . . You really think so? And what would that mean?' said Millet, unconvinced.

'Supposing the community had been founded by former priests who were rivals of the Sadducees: that would bring the Christ-figure closer still to Essenism, remembering Jesus's quarrels with the Temple. It would also explain their final vengeance against him, the crucifixion – if Jesus was the Essene Master of Justice, he represented a political threat.'

'True, if one admitted that Jesus was an Essene, but that hypothesis has never been proved,' said Father Millet.

'Pierre Michel's famous lecture was a step in that direction,' replied my father.

'But it was never published, and nobody has seen the text it referred to.'

'The text has disappeared.'

'Like a lot of the Qumran scrolls, which were published afterwards . . . But why are you so interested in Qumran studies?' The priest was suddenly worried.

'I'm researching the Dead Sea Scrolls as Professor of Palaeography at Jerusalem University. What about you, when did you start working on the scrolls?'

'Oh, well, you know,' said Millet, relaxing slightly, 'it was really chance. I came from the South of France, and I studied Latin and theology. One day I decided to learn Hebrew after finding some old books in the library, and got permission from my bishop to go to Paris. Later I became a friend and colleague of Paul Henderson, who became director of the international team. He entrusted me with some of the most important Aramaic texts from the Dead Sea Scrolls. Then I joined the Archaeological and Biblical School in Jerusalem. I've worked on the scrolls for twenty years, ever since I began to study archaeology.'

Father Millet then expounded on his passion for the subject, and he and my father talked for almost an hour about digs, parchments and ancient history.

I studied his features during this animated conversation. It seemed simple enough: like Joseph, he had a regular and sympathetic face. Looking more closely, I noticed two horizontal veins on either side of his forehead, which throbbed as he spoke. At the tip of one of them, two capillaries crossed a vertical one. The whole thing seemed to form the Hebrew letters *vav* and *tav*. These two letters could form a word: *tav*, which means 'note'. I thought this man must certainly possess a pleasing inner harmony, which was reflected in his appearance.

At one point my father asked him: 'Don't you find it strange that there isn't a single Jew in your international team? A specialist in Jewish history might have been useful . . .'

'I know. It's a form of academic apartheid that's hard to justify.'

'What would have happened if one of the researchers Henderson used had insisted on contacting a Jewish academic, as an expert on some particular question?'

'There would have been an international incident, I should think . . . In any case, the Qumran caves were on Jordanian soil until 1967, and the Jordanian army would never have allowed a Jew across the border.'

'But don't you think the Jewish academics might have shed some interesting light on the interpretation of the texts, with their know-ledge of Jewish law and rabbinical literature?'

'I don't recall any member of the team mentioning rabbinical literature as being of any interest in the translation of the Qumran texts. The position as regards Jewish academics was simple: we couldn't work with them, therefore it was a waste of time even discussing it . . . I know that must appear unacceptable, but that's the way it is. Archaeologists, too, are victims of their own prejudices. You know,' he went on, after a short pause, 'I used to think that archaeology was a precise science, which could reveal the truth about history, and that a well-run dig could provide an objective picture of a site. I realise now that every archaeologist approaches a site with preconceptions about what he does or doesn't want to find there. It's impossible to work through a mass of rocks, debris, dust and broken pottery without having some idea of what kind of buildings or utensils you expect to find.'

'What are you implying? That the members of the international team might not have "seen" certain things?' said my father, beginning to understand what Millet was hinting.

'No . . . Nobody would have suppressed any evidence. The team did its best to measure very precisely the soil levels, and the position of all vessels, pottery and coins, and to draw up a detailed map of the site. Today, of course, nobody doubts that a community lived here, but what sort was it? You need a lot of faith, looking at ruins like these, to imagine furniture, assembly rooms and refectories.'

'What exactly was Henderson looking for when he began excavating the site?'

'As far as he was concerned, the Qumran story is that of a group of religious dissidents who, in about 125 BC, left their homes and families to settle in the ruins of a Bronze Age fort. How were they able to establish and support themselves there? Henderson couldn't answer that. He suggests that they built a monastery with a large tower, assembly rooms and workshops, an elaborate water system, with cisterns and ritual baths. The sect, according to him, expanded during the reign of Alexander Janneus. He thinks the Qumran site was reduced to rubble, not by the thirty-five-year civil war that ravaged the country, nor the Roman invasion, nor even by King Herod, but by the earthquake that destroyed the area in 31 BC.'

'But what about the evidence that contradicts that interpretation?'

'Such as?'

'Utensils, coins, manuscripts even, that show that the site didn't disappear in 31 BC, but well after that date, meaning the Essenes could have had contact with the early Christians.'

'It's very likely that such "evidence" as you call it, never "existed".'

As though he felt he had said too much, Father Millet said goodbye. He was already hurrying away when I realised that I was still holding the little phial of red oil. I ran after him to give it back. He took it and then, on a sudden inspiration, gave it back. 'No, you have it,' he said.

'But why?' I asked, amazed.

'I don't know. Look after it.'

He seemed quite certain, but I sensed a sort of sadness, almost an entreaty. I accepted the strange gift. 'Here's one piece of evidence at least which won't disappear,' I thought.

A few days later we met Shimon, and he gave us our tickets for the United States and England, where we would try and see two other members of the international team, Paul Henderson and Thomas Almond. We would also meet Matti, who was attending a conference in New York.

Before leaving, Shimon wished us luck. 'Above all, be careful . . . Here, Ary, this is your farewell present.'

He held out a little leather pouch which contained a small pistol. Seeing my surprise, he said: 'Watch out, it's loaded. I believe you know how to use it . . . I hope you won't need it, but you never know.'

Before I could react, he took it back. 'I'll have it sent by post to your hotel; obviously you can't take it on the plane. Do the same when you move from place to place, so that you always have it with you.'

With those words, he turned and left. We felt strangely uncomfortable seeing him go.

The day before we left, we went to meet Kair Benyair at the Orthodox monastery in Jerusalem; he had been Bishop Hosea's intermediary during the negotiations with Matti over the last of the four Qumran scrolls. It was crucial to talk to this man: he had seen the manuscripts, and might know who had killed Hosea.

The Orthodox monastery was at the end of a narrow street in the Armenian quarter. We found ourselves in front of a heavy medieval door, with a modern mosaic above it. When we rang it opened slowly, and a suspicious-looking deacon appeared. Few tourists visited the church, its rich library, nor even the room at the bottom of the building where, according to Syrian tradition, the Last Supper had taken place some two thousand years earlier, and this apparently made the monks all the more suspicious of visitors.

The deacon directed us to the priests' quarters, and Hosea's rooms, at the top of one of the buildings. On the way we passed the sanctuary, where gold icons hung, lit by candles, above the altar covered in Syriac inscriptions. Solemn prayers echoed off the rocky walls of the crypt – for several days they had been mourning their bishop.

Outside Hosea's apartments a woman greeted us coolly. She looked up and down at my streimel and my black coat, wondering why a religious Jew had strayed so far from his quarter. My father told her the reason for our visit, and she replied that Kair Benyair was away in France, where he had gone in a hurry after Hosea's death. He was wanted, if not as a suspect, at least as a witness in the affair. But he had left no address, and no one knew where to find him.

While my father was talking to her, I went quietly on up to Hosea's rooms. The door was open, and I went in. There were three large and splendid rooms, with stone vaulted ceilings, antique furniture, jewel-encrusted trinkets, ancient musical instruments and gold plate.

All this treasure, I thought, and it ended like this. *I gathered me also silver and gold, and the peculiar treasure of kings and of the provinces.* I automatically moved towards the desk, which was covered with boxes and papers, books in Syriac and various files. I noticed a folded piece of parchment in the midst of all this. It was a fragment of scroll. I pushed it into my bag and went back down.

Downstairs the woman, who had not noticed my absence, was refusing my father permission to visit the apartments. The mystery of Hosea's death was unsolved, and in an atmosphere of undirected suspicion strangers were particularly unwelcome: the ancient foundation had turned in on itself, fearing scandal, as though hiding a guilty family secret.

Outside, when we were far enough away, we looked at the manuscript I had stolen. My father immediately identified it as a fragment from Qumran. It was in good condition, and we soon deciphered it. Together, with our hearts thumping, we translated the tiny, carefully drawn characters:

1. In the fortress which is in
The vale of Achor, take forty paces
To the east beneath the steps.
2. In the burial place
In the third row of stones
Bars of gold.
3. In the great cistern
In the courtyard of the peristyle
In the plaster of the floor
Hidden in a hole opposite the higher opening
Nine hundred coins.
4. In the place of the pool
Below the water channel
Six paces from the north towards the pool
Gold plate.
5. At the top of the staircase to the sanctuary
On the left
Forty bars of silver.
6. In the house of two pools is the basin, the plate and the silver.

'It's part of the Copper Scroll,' said my father. 'The one that Thomas
Almond partly deciphered. It describes the position of some buried
treasure.'

'What treasure?'

'Who knows? It may be the fabulous riches of King Solomon. His
temple, you remember, had double gates of gold, gold ceilings and
candlesticks, sacred furniture, an altar covered in gold leaf; the floors
were inlaid with palms, and within the Holy of Holies guarded by
cherubs in olive wood, was the most sacred object, the Ark of the
Covenant.'

'But Solomon's temple was destroyed by Nebuchadnezzar's armies
in the sixth century BC!'

'Yes, and the riches it contained disappeared. There have been
many legends about them, passed down from generation to generation. One of them, in the second book of the Maccabees, says that
Jeremiah was one of the guardians of the treasure; after the fall of
Jerusalem, he went to Mount Nebo and placed the tabernacle, the
altar and the incense in a cave. Another says the treasure was taken by
the Jews during their exile in Mesopotamia and buried on the site of a
temple; they hid the seven-branched candelabras and seventy gold

69

tables in a tower in Baghdad. Some also said that a scribe had found the jewels and gold and silver, and had shown them to an angel who had hidden them. Others say that the holy plates and the treasure are under a stone in Daniel's tomb, and that anyone who touches it will die instantly – it's supposed to have actually happened to one archaeologist. This text suggests that the treasure is hidden near Jerusalem, in a region behind rocky valleys, lower than the mountains, but cut off from them on three sides by deep ravines. All these sites can be found around Qumran. Do you remember what we saw at Khirbet Qumran?'

'Of course! The text must refer to the big double cistern on the lower level. *In the house of two pools is the basin, the plate and the silver.*'

'Perhaps. In any case, it does look as though Hosea was after the treasure. It may be why he was killed.'

'But why did he want it? Hadn't he made enough money from the scrolls?'

'Remember what it says in Ecclesiastes . . . 'He that loveth silver shall not be satisfied with silver; nor he that loveth abundance with increase: this is also vanity.'

We decided to stop in France on our way back, to try and find Kair Benyair – although we had, as yet, no idea how we would go about it.

That evening I went to see the rabbi, to tell him I was going away, without being able to explain why.

'Is it something you are ashamed of, that you can't tell me?' he said suspiciously.

'No. I have an honourable purpose. I'm going with my father.'

'Your father?' He was surprised. He knew that my father was not a religious man – I could tell by his tone that he probably thought of him as an *apicoros*, an Epicurean, a renegade, a man without law.

'Don't go away and forget the law. There are many temptations in the outside world, and you take the risk of not being saved when the Messiah comes, which will be soon. At least try and save yourself – never forget the coming of the Messiah. At every moment his footsteps can be heard approaching Israel, his people.'

I shivered. We had waited so long, and now the rabbi was telling me that the time had come: God was about to repay the eternal trust that had been put in him. We would be the last generation in exile, the first of the Deliverance. Everything in the world was ready for this revelation, and now he was coming. 'Mashiah is coming,' he prophesied. He had told us not to be afraid during the Six Day War; when Communism had collapsed, and during the Gulf War, he had announced that Israel was the safest place to be, and that the time of destruction had not yet come. He had been right. Many thought that he was inspired by God, others that he himself was the Messiah. Others said that the coming of a Messiah was a spiritual matter, and could not be placed in a historical or contemporary context. *For man also knoweth not his time: as the fishes that are taken in an evil net, and as the birds that are caught in the snare.*

'Don't forget,' he said before I left – a final piece of advice, or perhaps a first commandment – 'don't forget that you must ceaselessly prepare for his coming, and hasten it with prayer and the study of the Torah. Pray that the spiritual birth will take place, and soon. You will be like the people of Israel in their Egyptian exile, crying to God for deliverance. God was only waiting for us to show the strength of our longing. For that, you must always consider yourself half deserving and half guilty. One single mitzvah can tilt the whole world towards good and bring with it freedom and ultimate deliverance.'

Some thought the rabbi had all the attributes of the Messiah, and that they should immediately, as the people of Israel did in ancient times, express their commitment towards the future King David and say: *we are your bones and your body.* They too wanted to make it known that the rabbi was the King-Messiah of their generation.

I, although so devoted to him that I would do anything he said – the sound of his voice alone was a profound inspiration – still had doubts. The wait for the Messiah was not for me, as it was for them, the only element of their observance. My respect for our rabbis – and this one in particular, whom I considered to be the greatest amongst them – was constant, but quite separate from the wait for the Messiah, which I thought would still be a long one. I used to have long arguments with my fellow-students on this subject, which often left me perplexed.

'If he is the Messiah, why doesn't he prove it?' I would ask.

'But he has already proved it by his prophecies.'

'Then let him save us, if he is the Saviour.'

'That's what we're waiting for, and praying for night and day,' they replied.

They would end up thinking me an atheist, an infidel, I thought – I who lived only for my religion. They didn't like my questioning spirit, even though it was not rebellious.

When I left, my fellow students of the yeshivah simply said: 'Goodbye. Let's hope that you will be back amongst us before the Deliverance.'

I left with the curious sensation that I too was searching for the Messiah, every bit as much as if I had remained, studying texts, with them. Was it so certain that he was amongst them? I needed to find out for myself whether he wasn't elsewhere, far away, somewhere in the wide world. *I the Preacher was King over Israel in Jerusalem. And I gave my heart to seek and search out by wisdom concerning all things that are done under heaven.*

The night before my departure I had a strange dream, which woke me up with a start, and made me deeply uneasy for several days afterwards. Later I forgot it almost completely, until events intervened which made sense of it . . .

I was in a car driven by my friend Yehudi. We were not in Jerusalem, but in a town which, without knowing why, I associated with Europe. We wanted to cross a river, but there was no bridge; Yehudi decided to try and ford it and drove towards the bank. At the last moment, the path seemed too dangerous and the river too deep, and I shouted to him to turn left. He reacted too late, and instead of plunging into the water, we were lifted to the sky, flying towards the clouds. I waited for help, for someone to bring us down to earth. But the car went on rising and nothing came. Then Yehudi gave me a desolate look, as if to say that he had not done it on purpose. I cried: 'Not now!' and woke up.

Third Scroll

THE SCROLL OF WAR

The First War of the sons of Light

The Rule of War on the unleashing of the attack of the sons of light against the company of the sons of darkness, the army of Satan: against the band of Edom, Moab, and the sons of Ammon, and against the sons of the East and the Philistines, and against the bands of the Kittim of Assyria and their allies the ungodly of the Covenant.

The sons of Levi, Judah, and Benjamin, the exiles in the desert, shall battle against them in . . . all their bands when the exiled sons of light return from the Desert of the Peoples to camp in the Desert of Jerusalem; and after the battle they shall go up from there (to Jerusalem?).

[The king] of the Kittim [shall enter] into Egypt, and in his time he shall set out in great wrath to wage war against the kings of the north, that his fury may destroy and cut off the horn of [Israel].

This shall be a time of salvation for the people of God, an age of dominion for all the members of His company, and of everlasting destruction for all the company of Satan. The confusion of the sons of Japheth shall be [great] and Assyria shall fall unsuccoured. The dominion of the Kittim shall come to an end and iniquity shall be vanquished, leaving no remnant; [for the sons] of darkness there shall be no escape.

Truly the battle is Thine and the power from Thee! It is not ours. Our strength and the power of our hands accomplish no mighty deeds except by Thy power and by the might of Thy great valour. This Thou hast taught us from ancient times, saying, A star shall come out of Jacob and a sceptre shall rise out of Israel. He shall smite the temples of Moab and destroy all the children of Sheth. He shall rule out of Jacob and shall cause the survivors of the city to perish. The enemy shall be his possession and Israel shall accomplish mighty deeds.

By the hand of thine anointed, who discerned Thy testimonies.
Thou hast revealed to us the [times] of the battles of Thy hands that
Thou mayest glorify Thyself in our enemies by levelling the hordes
of Satan, the seven nations of vanity, by the hand of Thy poor
whom Thou hast redeemed [by Thy might] and by the fulness of
Thy marvellous power. (Thou hast opened) the door of hope to the
melting heart: Thou wilt do to them as Thou didst to Pharaoh, and
the captains of his chariots in the Red Sea. Thou wilt kindle the
downcast of spirit and they will be a flaming torch in the straw to
consume ungodliness and never to cease until iniquity is destroyed.

Qumran scrolls, *The War Rule.*

I

We then began our long journey, across thousands of kilometres and through thousands of years.

We were in fact following a path which would lead to war, but we did not know that: at first, we were not afraid. We did not yet understand the atrocities that man can commit when his faith has been shaken. I am not talking about the banal, thoughtless sins which have no consequences, but of absolute evil, long planned and ripened, premeditated, whose victims are simple and good souls, the just and the wise. Nobody knows what it is seeking revenge for, with its refinements of perversity; nobody knows why it flourishes only by destroying innocence; nor why it recurs infinitely. The Evil's evil must be something terrible, to cause such pain and inspire such cruelty.

Absolute evil can only be satisfied by ravaging with all its power the weakened forces of good, but can never succeed, because the forces of good are as infinite as the forces of evil. Absolute evil is by its essence incomplete, never satisfied.

After God created the world, he made man in his image and likeness, so that the fish in the sea, the birds in the sky, all the earth and animals that move upon it would be his subjects. When he saw what he had done, he was satisfied and thought it good. But perhaps he did not realise the sinister plot hatching behind his creation. He had not created a mirror-image of himself in man. He had created evil.

Our Bible tells us that the Messiah will come after a terrible war between good and evil. The scrolls call this *The War between the Sons of Light and the Sons of Darkness*.

We set off. It was the first time I had been in an aeroplane, and I felt as if I were leaving my native land for ever. Speed seemed to make distance eat up time, and I felt I had grown older by the time we reached New York.

Our hotel was in Williamsburg, in the Hassidic district of Brooklyn, and I certainly felt at home there: it was very similar to

Mea Shearim. The people in the street were just like myself, with beards, side-locks and streimels. Their clothes, however, were more diverse, with many more subtle differences. Some wore a *holot*, instead of a coat, a kind of dark dressing-gown with short round lapels, and a belt attached to the coat by buttons and bows. The richer ones had sable tails attached to their streimels. The less fortunate wore a *kapel*, a large, wide-brimmed felt hat with a matt silk ribbon. One could tell which group each one belonged to by their clothing: there were Hungarians, Galicians, members of the Satmar, an American anti-Zionist group, the messianic missionary group Habad, spread throughout the world, the Gour, dedicated to study, the Vishnitz and the Belz. All walked with the typical hurried step of the Hassidim. Everywhere there were groups of students deep in animated discussion, and everywhere large families, older children trailing younger ones who in turn carried babies. *Go forth and multiply.*

We arrived on the Sabbath evening. Hundreds of Hassidim crowded the streets, going to the synagogues. I decided to go and pray, and, by some miracle, managed to persuade my father to come with me. He managed not to appear ill at ease, lost in this dressed-up crowd, without streimel or black coat. The others asked what I was doing with him, was he my father or a friend, or perhaps a new recruit, a *baal teshuvah*, of whom there were many.

We were invited to spend the evening with the Hassidim, since it is the custom to receive guests on the Sabbath. That night there was a banquet, and the faithful drank and danced as if possessed. The rabbi, as head of the community, presided over the table, which had been sumptuously decorated in honour of the Sabbath. My father was surprised to see several young men around their leader, staring at him, not eating.

'To watch the rabbi eat and drink is a great honour for a Hassid,' I explained. 'His smallest gestures must be observed, as they might contain some important sign or some new direction for life. When the rabbi lifts his finger, the whole world trembles.'

'Supposing the rabbi is just an old man, incapable of eating properly? Look, he's drunk too much – he's falling asleep.'

'For them, that old man is the link between heaven and earth; he has taken upon himself the suffering of the world. He may be the last of the Just, and his virtues will save the community. The wine he has blessed, the herring he has left on his plate, but has touched, are holy objects: they teach us that eating is a religious act, not for the satisfaction of basic needs, but for the purification of the human body, thanks to the divine life contained in the food. It's a mystical act of communion, like the devekut.'

The rabbi got up. Immediately, one of the Hassidim at his side rushed forward to eat up the remains of his meal. My father looked at me.

'Eating the remains of the rabbi's food, drinking the last few drops of wine in his glass, ensures eternal blessing,' I explained.

'You don't really believe that, do you?' He was almost pleading with me. 'Tell me you don't believe it.'

'I believe in the power of rabbis. I believe we owe infinite respect to this man. I believe,' I added weakly, 'that we should talk to him about the manuscripts. I am sure he could help us.'

'Help us? He doesn't know anything about it!'

'You never know . . .'

The following evening we had an appointment with Matti, son of Professor Ferenkz, the original discoverer of the scrolls, who was in New York for a conference. We wanted to talk to him about how the scroll had disappeared, and also about its contents, which he might have been able to guess at in the brief time when he had it in his hands.

This brave researcher, this warrior, was one of Israel's legendary heroes, one of those who had fought from the beginning for the liberation of his country, and had been instrumental in the creation of the State of Israel. He had been Chief of Staff in the army during the war of independence, and had afterwards followed in his father's footsteps. He had become as famous for his many excavations as for his wartime exploits. He was a militant Zionist, like my father, who, although passionate about archaeology and biblical research, had remained a convinced atheist.

We met in the bar of his hotel. He was still handsome, with short thick hair and black eyes. He looked rather as I had always imagined Moses when I was a child: there were none of the distressing symptoms of old age, no shaking or trembling, only the maturity achieved through strength and wisdom. Most striking was the texture of his skin: it was not thin and wrinkled, nor grainy and dull like an over-ripe fruit, but thick, firm and dark, like clay encasing his head, with his cheekbones rocky promontories, his fleshy mouth a chasm, illuminated by his bright black eyes. His face, suntanned and weather-beaten by wind and sand, had become the mirror-image of the eroded landscape of Judaea, where he had spent so much of his life. It had adhered to him like sand to the fossil, the fossil to the stone, the stone to the rock.

'Yes, I know, David,' he said, cutting short my father's explanation. 'I searched for that scroll, some years ago, and when I found it it slipped through my fingers . . .'

'What happened?' asked my father.

'It was stolen from the Museum of Antiquities in Jerusalem.'

'Did you have time to decipher it?'

'Alas, no.'

'Do you know who stole it?'

'It's hard to say . . . I might as well tell you everything I know. I received an anonymous letter from someone wanting to sell me a manuscript. It quoted a statement to the press by Thomas Almond, the English member of the international team they called the "angel of darkness", to the effect that a scroll had disappeared, and claiming to be able to obtain it. The writer enclosed as proof a photograph of a fragment, which convinced me that this was the scroll that my father had seen but been unable to acquire. He wanted a hundred thousand dollars for it – an enormous sum, but what is the price of a priceless object? Assuming the Israeli government would back me, I agreed to pay. A few weeks later the reply came: 'I must tell you that the Jordanian prime minister offered three hundred thousand dollars before he was assassinated. Negotiations are therefore still open.' It was signed by Hosea, the Syrian Orthodox archbishop.

'I had already met him in America, and we had begun negotiations which had come to nothing; now he was re-opening them and raising the stakes. I controlled my rage, because I badly wanted the scroll, and we continued our correspondence: Hosea, who travelled a lot in Arab countries in the Middle East where any relationship with Israel was forbidden, would contact me through an intermediary, a certain Kair Benyair. I tried to guess from the letters what was really going on between him and his contacts in Jordan: he appeared to be involved in dealings with government and court officials, who led him to believe that several manuscripts, including those in the Jordanian Museum of Antiquities, were for sale. The number of scrolls on offer changed all the time, but the one I was most interested in was the one in the photograph.

'I wrote and told him that I was ready to discuss his demands with my friends, and if they seemed reasonable, we might reach an understanding. A few days later Hosea sent me a small fragment of the manuscript so that I could date it. It had no incrustation and was legible without infra-red: I recognised at once that the Hebraic characters were the work of a scribe of the same school as those of the Dead Sea Scrolls. I could also say with certainty that the language was not the same as that in the Bible. After this brief examination, I photographed the fragment and returned it to Hosea, as I had promised, with replies to his questions: the fragment did appear to be from the Dead Sea, it was written in Hebrew, by a good scribe, but the piece was too small to show whether it was an apocrypha or a document composed by the Dead Sea sect.

'Then I wrote to Paul Henderson, the director of the international team, whom I had worked with before. I knew that he had had dealings with Hosea in the past. I asked him to try to convince Hosea to sell me the famous schroll. I was careful, but could not hide my excitement about the fragment. I suggested that it might be one of the most important yet discovered, and that it was the duty of the academic world to buy it from Hosea, and the duty of the Jewish people to restore it to its historic home in Israel. I begged him to do all in his power to save this scroll from disappearance. He replied that Hosea, claiming expenses and rival offers, was now asking seven hundred and fifty thousand dollars, a hundred and fifty immediately and the rest on delivery. I was furious and refused by return of post.

'Some time later, I went back to New York to give some lectures. There I received another letter from Hosea, using a very different tone this time. He asked for a final offer for the scroll; I said I would pay a hundred thousand dollars, and he accepted. To protect myself, I conducted the negotiations through lawyers. A detailed contract, which included Henderson's name, was drawn up and signed by Hosea and his representative, Kair Benyair. Several clauses certified the authenticity of the document, which was to be delivered into my hands ten days after signature. The fragment would be handed over by Kair Benyair, and once it had been joined to the scroll, it could no longer be contested.

'Ten days went by. Then Kair Benyair, back from Jordan, told me, to my great surprise, that the manuscript was still in Hosea's hands, and that Hosea doubted the validity of our arrangement and wanted more money, because the Bedouin were asking him for more.

'Hosea wrote to Henderson, saying that he was sorry not to be able to send the scroll, but that the troubles between Jordan and Lebanon were making it difficult to move between countries. He explained that he would have to bribe several people and take a lot of risks, and that the price would have to be revised.

'All that time I kept a careful eye on all articles on Qumran in the academic journals, in case the scroll had been sold to someone else. I found no mention of it – apparently its existence was known only to Hosea, Kair Benyair, Henderson and myself.

'It was now May 1967, and the Six Day War was about to break out. I was called back to Israel to co-ordinate between the prime minister, the minister of defence and the chief of staff: military matters took precedence over the scrolls.

'Early in the morning of 5 June, the war began – Jordan, Egypt and Syria against Israel. After two days' fighting, the Israeli army had beaten the Arab armies, occupied the Jordanian sector of Jerusalem – including the Old Town and the Museum of Antiquities – and beaten the Jordanian army back to the eastern shore of the Jordan.

'That night, I was woken by a call from the army chief of staff: Lieutenant Colonel Yanai, of the information services, would be at my disposal to help find the scroll. The next day Yanai went to Kair Benyair's house. Kair was not a brave man, and a few threats persuaded him to dig out from under the floorboards a shoebox containing the scroll and a cigar case with the detached fragments.

'That afternoon I had to attend an important meeting of the Defence Committee, at Headquarters, about the Syrian situation. In the middle of the discussion, I was handed a note saying that Yanai was waiting for me outside. In my position as the prime minister's adviser, I not only had to listen to each person's opinion, but analyse it and give my own; I tried hard to concentrate and restrain my impatience. Finally, I went outside and found Yanai waiting calmly in the corridor. He handed me something and said: "I hope this is what you were looking for."'

Matti stopped for a moment. He took out a pack of cigarettes, offered them to us, lit one and took a long drag. His face was impassive, but his eyes shone.

'I went into the nearest empty office and carefully unwrapped the shoebox. Inside I found the scroll, wrapped in a napkin covered in cellophane, with the fragments in a smaller wrapping. Matters of life and death, involving thousands of men, were being discussed in the room next door, but I couldn't resist examining this treasure. What I found left me both satisfied and disappointed. The upper edge of the scroll was uneven and wavy; some parts seemed to have dissolved; others were in poor condition, disintegrated and stuck together by damp dust. The most damaged side of the parchment was the one exposed to damp – not from the cave where it had lain for centuries, but from its more recent hiding place. What was extremely strange was that the characters were written backwards like mirror writing, from left to right like Hebrew.

'The next day I placed the scroll in a hermetically sealed laboratory, in an atmosphere of controlled temperature and humidity. The most important thing was to separate the fragments that had got stuck together in Kair Benyair's hiding place. The ones in a reasonable state of preservation were detached, and then placed in normal conditions of humidity at seventy-five to eighty degrees. The more damaged pieces had to be softened first at a hundred degrees of humidity, and then refrigerated for a few more minutes. Each stage required the greatest care, as the operation could irreparably damage the writing.

'The Archaeological Museum was now under our control, and I decided to keep the parchment there. The international team was pursuing its researches there, as the Israeli authorities had wished them to do, in a desire for toleration and respect.

'Then one morning I found the table on which the scroll was usually laid empty. I was astounded. Only the researchers had access to this room, and I didn't think them capable of such a theft. We searched the museum for days, and I gradually had to resign myself to the fact that the manuscript had disappeared for good; it was as if some unknown curse was preventing us from seeing it . . .

'Twenty years later, in 1987, I attended an international conference, along with most of the Qumran specialists. Imagine my surprise when Pierre Michel mentioned in his speech an unpublished scroll whose style and text strangely resembled the missing one . . .'

'Do you think he stole it?' asked my father.

'It's possible. It would explain why he won't publish it – he knows I could identify it. Unless someone else stole it and then sold or gave it to him . . .'

'Were all five members of the team at the museum at the time of the theft?'

'Yes. Pierre Michel and Paul Henderson, whom I completely trusted, were there more or less permanently. The three others – Father Millet, the Pole Andrei Lirnov and the peculiar Thomas Almond – were there less regularly.'

'Could Michel have deciphered the manuscript in 1967?' I asked.

'Certainly. The preparatory work had been done; all he had to do was reflect the text in a mirror to read it the right way around.'

'If Pierre Michel is the thief,' my father said, 'why would he risk detection by revealing the contents of the scroll, if he'd kept them secret for twenty years?'

'It is odd. But having worked in the army, I can tell you that it often happens with the most important secrets. The more important it is, the harder it is to keep; the longing to share it becomes too strong, and one day one does so. Then, of course, one regrets it, but it's too late.'

'Have you got the photo of the fragment you deciphered?'

'No, it's in Israel, but I'll send you a copy in a week, when I get back. It's very short, I can recite it almost by heart:

In the beginning was the word,
And the word was with God,
And the word was God.
Everything was in Him,
Nothing that was
Was without Him.
In Him was life,
And life was the light of men,
And the light shines in the darkness
And the darkness did not understand it.
There was a man, sent by God;
His name was John.
He came as a witness,
To bear witness to the light
So that all men would believe.
But his words were cut short
His words were changed,
And the word became a lie
To hide the truth,

The true story of the Messiah.
And to him,
By the sacrament of the priests of Qumran,
Will be given the treasure.

We remained silent for a moment, puzzled.

'Do you have any idea of what's in the rest of the scroll?' my father asked again.

'Alas, no. I didn't have time to read it all. But I'm sure that, from what I did see, it's not an apocrypha, but an original document from Qumran. And from what I gathered from Pierre Michel's words at the conference, it must contain new revelations about the Essenes, and their demand to be considered as the true heirs to the Zadokist priests. For the Qumran sect, the key to the inner meaning of the Scriptures could only be found through divine revelation. You know that in all apocalyptic speculation, the one who holds the key to all mysteries and hidden laws is the messenger of God. The Essenes regarded themselves as the "Sons of Light"; I believe they were simply a sect intent on persuading their co-religionists that their vision of the world was the right one. They saw in everyday events the realisation of a divine scheme. I think the "Kittim" or "Sons of Darkness" so often referred to in the scrolls are the Romans, who worshipped goddesses of victory and fortune, and whom the Essenes hated most of all.'

'So Qumran was one of the main centres of resistance to both Roman imperialism and the Jewish aristocracy, who collaborated in order to amass huge fortunes?'

'We don't know whether the Essenes' motives were political or theological. At the height of the sect's influence in Judaea, its envoys travelled all over the Mediterranean, far from the political upheavals in Jerusalem, with only a roll of parchment, a sort of gospel, preaching modesty, purity and poverty.'

'But in Judaea, for those struggling to preserve the old codes and laws, and battling against the economic domination of the Romans and the Jewish aristocracy, preaching a new gospel calling for the abandonment of the laws of Moses must have had some political significance. That was the problem with Jesus.'

'I see what you mean. You're wondering whether this scroll is at last speaking of Jesus, and if so, in what terms. All I can tell you is that he's not mentioned in the little I've seen of it. But you could look

85

for someone with the same characteristics, instead of a specific individual called Jesus. The historic Jesus could equally well have been Arthronges, the self-styled Messiah referred to by Flavius Josephus, who became Greek and then Roman during the *Pax Romana*, and was recognised as the Messiah by a good many Gentiles in the Roman Empire. It is by no means certain that the Jesus described in the Gospels actually existed. From what we know at present, only two of the people mentioned in the life of Jesus are proved to have existed: Pontius Pilate, the prefect of Judaea, whose name was found on a Latin inscription in Caesarea in 1961 by some Italian archaeologists; and the high priest Caiaphus, whose family tomb was discovered in South Jerusalem in 1990. Everything we know about the life of Jesus derives from Christian literature written about a hundred years after the events described.'

'You remember the three Central characters in the Qumran texts: the Master of Justice, the Wicked Priest, and the "sofer" or Man of Lies,' said my father. 'Some think that the latter was Paul, mentioned with deep disdain in the *Commentary of Habbakuk*, which contains the account of an argument between the Man of Lies and the Master of Justice about the strict observance of the purity laws and of the Temple rites.'

'Let me guess what you're getting at . . . Paul laid the foundations for a whole new religion, based not on Mosaic law, but on faith in Jesus. According to him, the spirit of the law had defeated the law itself. He spread the word throughout the Mediterranean, to Ephesus, Corinth and Philippi. Because of him Christians saw the Jews as a people with a harsh and terrifying God. The idea of Christianity as a universal religion began with him, which would mean the conversion of all Gentiles . . . Because of him, Christians regarded themselves as the new Israel, and rallied the Romans to their faith, so that in less than three hundred years the Roman Empire had become Christian . . . Perhaps the scrolls were stolen to cover up the fact that it was Paul and not Jesus who achieved this . . .

'I think you're on the right track,' said Matti, with a small, mischievous smile. 'But first you must go and see Paul Henderson.'

'Have you stayed in touch with him?' I asked.

'No. I worked long enough with him to appreciate his intellectual capacities, but after a certain incident, I decided to break off contact.'

'What happened?'

'It was shortly before the scrolls were stolen, during a party at the museum. Henderson was a little drunk. He raised his glass to propose a toast. "I want to drink to the greatest living man of the second half of the twentieth century – Kurt Waldheim." I almost fell off my chair. There had been rumours about him in the Israeli press, but until then I hadn't believed them. I don't think Henderson is very sound, if you know what I mean . . .'

'Have you seen him since?'

'Yes, of course, but only in the distance. I particularly remember one conference in 1988, a gathering of academics in charge of the process of publishing the scrolls. Amongst them was the editor of the *Biblical Archaeological Review*, Bartholomew Donnars. He's a familiar figure at archaeological conferences, from San Francisco to Jerusalem. He always sits in the front row, taking notes in a little yellow book. He's an irreverent and uncompromising idealist, a real toughie behind the beaming smile and non-stop chat. In 1988 there were still dozens of unpublished documents in the hands of Millet, Michel, Almond and Henderson, material that Donnars wanted to see communicated to the Israeli teams. He pressed Henderson for a timetable for future publications, and forced out of him the announcement of the pending appearance of a work called *Discoveries in the Land of Judaea*, to be followed by ten volumes regrouping different Qumran texts in the three following years, and ten more volumes between then and 1996. Of course this was impossible, and Donnars wrote an editorial headlined 'They'll never do it', a declaration of war on the international team. The article stated that the time had passed for excuses and equivocation; that this team, which had published nothing for thirty years, would never publish anything; that the Israeli Department of Antiquities was accomplice to a conspiracy of silence; that the only way to end this obstruction was to permit free access to the Qumran scrollsto any competent academic. Donnars was finally heard, but it was too late for the crucial scroll, which had disappeared in 1967.'

We talked to Matti for a little longer, and then left, pleased with all he had told us, convinced we were on the right track.

After leaving the hotel, which was in the middle of Manhattan, we walked for over an hour. We hadn't the heart to visit anyone else, and we needed to think about what Matti had told us. We became caught up in the life of the city by night: it was almost two in the morning, and we caught passing glimpses in the lights of streets as drab in the dark as they were by day.

We were in another world, but the geometric layout of the streets prevented one from getting lost. By day you could see the sea in the distance, but at night the twin towers of the World Trade Centre were the only horizon. We wandered, side by side, intimidated by the smooth glass towers of Babel on either side. We gazed up, wondering what it would be like to be master of an empire, or just a yuppie at the top of one of these skyscrapers, looking out at the graduated steel elevations, the ziggurats with steps of concrete, glass or asphalt, mirroring one another ad infinitum; to watch, from on high, the worship of speed in this city, men moving like animals driven by a carnivorous survival instinct, and a desire for money: a world where financial earthquakes could be set off by a small electronic gadget. How intoxicating it must be, up there, to have this raging, despairing horde scrabbling at your feet.

These towers had not been built for man to reach up to the Almighty, to gaze upwards; but rather, to look *down* from above. They were for man to imagine himself *as* God, to see men as small and absurd scurrying insects, like the ones to be found in every dwelling in the city, rich or poor, clean or dirty, overcrowded or empty; scuttling cockroaches with gleaming shells, and apathetic worms cowering in slimy bodies. Were we really as miserable and pathetically repulsive as that? Were we so monstrous?

We left the prosperous, well-lit main streets and plunged deeper into the night. It was March and still cool. Gusts of steam blew up from the pavement. There was noise everywhere, sirens – ambulances, fire engines, police cars – signalling a disaster at every step we took. We took a taxi, and ended up near the East Village, in Alphabet City.

Here were the gates of Hell. Beggars in rags, half-drunk and half-asleep, lay slumped in doorways, stinking, their grey and purple skin layered in dirt, as if they had recently been exhumed. Strange creatures spilled out of crowded, smoky bars, dressed in plastic and vinyl, with spiky multicoloured hair. We passed young people with faces or bodies covered in tattoos and pierced with rings. Some were on the ground, injecting needle-marked arms; others vomited on the pavement, close to the tramps and the dustbins; one man stood in the middle of the road yelling obscenities, and nobody took any notice. At the end of an alley, figures in leather and chains grappled with one another beside their motorbikes.

It was a land of demons, a refuge for every bird of ill omen the world had ever known. The whore of Babylon was lifting her skirt and revealing her nudity to all. At the entrance to a nightclub, a man dressed half as a lion, half as a horse, swallowed fire for the amusement of passers-by. He stamped those wanting to go in with the name of the club: 666, either on the hand or the forehead.

My father shuddered, and dragged me to the other side of the road.

'Let's get out of this place, before we become caught up in its sins and suffer the inevitable punishment.'

II

The next morning, we took the train to Yale, about an hour and a half from New York, where we met several archaeologists with whom my father could catch up on old controversies started long ago.

His colleagues seemed surprised to see me with him, all in black, with my locks hanging down beneath my large-brimmed hat. They couldn't understand how a son could be so different from his father. What they didn't realise was that deep down we were the same – but I was all that he was not. With my hat and prayer book, I filled in what was missing in my father; I was his complement, the garments he had shed. Or perhaps he had only taken the outer casing, and I was his real self, for as his son I represented his past as well as his future. Although he had no beard or hat and wore ordinary trousers and checked shirts, he was not in the least embarrassed by this strange Hassidic son, but the professors certainly seemed to find us a curious couple.

Eventually we were able to meet Paul Henderson in person, a small and well-preserved seventy-year-old famous for his enormous knowledge of the Church Fathers and mediaeval theology. He had fading red hair streaked with tarnished gold, and youthful green eyes that lit up his face, contrasting with his extremely pale and wrinkled skin, with broken veins on the cheeks and small spots on either side of his nostrils, which were crisscrossed with more tiny veins. I narrowed my eyes to work out their pattern, and I could distinguish three Hebrew letters, ק, ר and ת, forming the word *qarat*, to cut.

His desk was littered with reviews, history books and an impressive number of Bibles. There was a small microfiche reader for examining photos of ancient scrolls. My father asked him to tell us about the international team.

'I founded it, with Pierre Michel,' he replied. 'I began work on it a little before he did, in the summer of 1952. At first all I did was clean, prepare and identify all the scrolls found in the caves. There wasn't that much material, about fifteen pieces. I would open a box, take out a fragment, put it in a bowl to dampen it, and then place it between two panes of glass to flatten it. Often they were darkened by urine crystals, probably from goats lost in the caves, and had to be washed; I used castor oil for the most soiled ones. But we made one terrible error, despite all our care: we used Sellotape to join the pieces together.'

'Nowadays researchers spend hours removing hardened sticky tape from the fragments,' said my father.

'At the time we had no idea what a mistake it was; we knew a lot less about restoration techniques. The most important thing for us, during those first three years, was deciphering and identification. I soon began to work with Pierre Michel. He had the most extraordinary talent for deciphering what appeared to be totally unreadable. He knew the rarest words in Hebrew or Aramaic, and had complete confidence in the accuracy of palaeographic analysis when it came to the study of ancient manuscripts. He was convinced that the scriptures had evolved smoothly over the centuries, and aimed to establish a chronological sequence. Thus he distinguished three successive types of Hebrew script in the Qumran fragments: the archaic, dating from between 200 and 150 BC, the Hasmonean, 150 and 30 BC, and the Herodian, 30 BC to 70 AD. They covered crucial phases in Judaean history, from the Selucid conquest until the destruction of Jerusalem by the Romans, allowing us to state that the scrolls belong to the Essene sect, as described by Philon, Josephus and Pliny the Elder . . . But you know all this. Tell me how I can help you.'

'We would like to know how you obtained the manuscript you gave to Pierre Michel, and which he mentioned in his lecture in 1987,' said my father baldly.

Henderson was taken aback. 'From Bishop Hosea. He was our regular supplier, except when we went into the caves ourselves. But why do you want to know?'

'Because that manuscript belongs to the Jerusalem museum, and we're trying to get it back. Didn't you realise that it was the scroll that Matti bought, and deposited at the museum, and which was then stolen?'

'Not at the time, no. I hadn't had time to look at Matti's scroll, which I had helped him negotiate for. How could I have known it was the same as the one Hosea offered me later? I only learned that after

Pierre Michel's lecture, when Matti asked for it back. But by then it had disappeared . . . with Pierre Michel.'

'Did you read it after you bought it?'

'Alas, no. The letters were reversed, as if in a mirror, and a cursory reading was impossible. I gave it to the Polish member of the team, Andrei Lirnov, and he gave it to Pierre Michel before he killed himself.'

'Do you think his suicide was connected with what he had read?'

'It's possible. I don't know. I'd like to have read it as much as you, out of scientific as well as theological interest. Although I'm inclined to think it's better this way,' he added hesitantly.

'Why?'

'I was very surprised by Pierre Michel's lecture. It had been some time since he'd shared the results of any of his researches with me, as he had always done in the past. I wondered about his mental health . . . It wouldn't be surprising, after all that happened . . .'

'What happened?' said my father doggedly.

He gave us a black look, and said abruptly: 'The scrolls are cursed. Ever since the Shapira affair, anyone who touches them is damned. They kill themselves. They're murdered. Like Lirnov. Like Hosea. They say he was stabbed, but it's not true.'

'How do you think he died?' I asked.

'He was crucified.'

'How do you know?' said my father.

'I have my sources.'

I glanced at my father, but he froze me with a look.

'Not only do I know nothing about the missing manuscript,' said Henderson, 'but I don't really think it's that important. Ten years after the first discovery, a new science came into being, Qumranology, with a bibliography of two thousand works. There are now innumerable research centres, reviews and books on the subject. Your manuscript is a drop in this ocean, and I can't get excited about it. I very much doubt that it contains anything different from the other manuscripts, none of which said anything new about Christianity or Judaism.'

'On the contrary, it seems to me that if so many people are interested in the texts, a missing document is crucial!' I said.

'Crucial for whom? The relationship between Essenism and early Christianity was noted by the eighteenth-century philosophers, who held that Christianity was a phase of Essenism. King Frederick II wrote to Alembert: "Jesus was really an Essene." It was the Age of Enlightenment, they wanted to demystify everything, undermine the foundations of religion. Is that what you want to do? Surely that's an old battle.'

'We want to find the way to the truth,' said my father.

'Do you think it will lead you to a revolution? Religion has been through many of those, and has always recovered.' Henderson got up suddenly, his face contorted with fury. 'What do you want to do? Put the whole Christian message in doubt? Overturn the foundations of our beliefs?'

'Surely the church cannot deny the importance of the revelations in the scrolls,' said my father calmly. 'For example, the story of the Master of Justice, in clear dispute with official Judaism and the cult of the Temple, persecuted by the "Wicked Priest". Who was he? Was he put to death, crucified even, as the scrolls suggest in the phrase "suspended alive on the wood"? Is there a connection with Jesus? Is it blasphemous to suggest that the Master of Justice and Jesus are one and the same person? And what is one to say about John the Baptist? There's no doubt that the prophet who baptised Jesus was, at the very least, in contact with the Essenes, who, like him, lived in the desert and practised baptism.'

'But John could equally well have been an anchorite, a hermit rather than a member of any community. And don't forget that Jesus preached the word of God, while the Essenes followed an esoteric doctrine. Personally I find that the Qumran documents shed light not so much on Christianity itself, as on the environment it emerged from, that's to say first-century Judaism. Nobody knows what the Essenes believed; that was all lost with the last worshippers, after the Jewish revolt, when Qumran was destroyed by an earthquake.'

'The Essenes decided to live on the fringe of society because they had declared war on the Temple. And they were waiting for the end of the world, constantly studying apocalyptic writings . . . Christianity certainly grew out of a messianic atmosphere.

'We need to know more, and that's why we want the missing scroll,' my father continued. 'It's a scandal that documents discovered in 1947 should have been confiscated, and still remain unpublished.'

'What more do you want?' Henderson was getting angrier. 'You have the manuscripts from caves 1 to 11; by 1951, the Americans had already published three out of the four manuscripts from St Mark's Convent. Then there are the posthumous edition of the texts that

Ferenkz worked on, the second Scroll of Isaiah, the War between the Sons of Light and the Sons of Darkness, and the Hymns. Four manuscripts from St Mark's Convent, transferred to the United States in 1948, have since been acquired by Israel, and placed in a sort of shrine in the National Museum.'

'It's this manuscript we want, not the ones we've got already,' replied my father drily. He thought for a moment, and then added gently: 'You're probably worried about your faith. Is it the Biblical Commission that has ordered you to act like this? I mean the Congregation for the Doctrine of the Faith, which I know you work for.'

'Certainly,' he replied at once. 'I'm not fooled by your manoeuvres – you want to shake centuries of faith in the Lord. You're the ones causing scandal.'

He pointed to the door; the interview was over.

My father seemed defeated. Having dedicated his life to antiquities, he suddenly saw the scrolls scattered throughout the world, amongst the four scholars, bringing nothing but fear and trouble in their wake. Men had died, savagely murdered, others had gone mad or killed themselves. Although he was a rational atheist who believed in rigorous scientific tests, my father believed in portents. It always seemed strange to me that a man so detached from religion should be so reluctant to disturb what he called the natural order of things, which I called divine order.

His discouragement surprised me. Knowing his passion for search and discovery, I couldn't understand why he felt, without yet having really tried, that we would probably never find the manuscript or, even if we did, that it would bring nothing but disaster in its wake. I understood later that fear of the Devil, inculcated in him in childhood, had remained anchored within him, like a different geological layer in his cynical scientific outlook. He was afraid the scrolls were possessed by the Devil.

'It's the opposite of what Father Henderson says – the content of this manuscript must be very important, and he must know it. So we have to carry on,' I said.

'I don't know. I don't know where to begin.'

'What's the Shapira affair Henderson mentioned?' I asked.

'The Shapira affair . . . In the summer of 1883, London was buzzing with the news of the discovery of two ancient Hebrew manuscripts from Deuteronomy, written in cursive Hebraic-Phoenicean script, known from the famous Moabite stele at Mesa, which dates from around the ninth century BC. Shapira had brought back from Palestine fifteen or sixteen crudely folded leather strips, which he offered to the British Museum for a million pounds, and for several weeks there were articles almost daily in the British press, and even translations of the texts. Finally, Shapira committed suicide in a squalid hotel in Rotterdam.'

'Another death ascribed to the scrolls,' I said.

'Yes. Probably the first, and perhaps not the last. The most worrying part of the story is that the manuscripts were never found. They appear to have vanished in Holland. It may sound stupid, but it all frightens me.'

'Why? Have Henderson and his Congregation managed to persuade you that the scrolls are cursed? Do you think they're the basis for some new heresy?'

'Perhaps. That crucifixion scares me. Who could have done that? It wouldn't make sense for Christians. Jews? Crucifixion was forbidden under Jewish law, but we know that Alexander Janneus used it a great deal. It may be that the Jews, crucified in great numbers under Antiochus IV Epiphanius, might copied their persecutors during and after the Maccabean wars, but that hypothesis has never been proved. The Romans are the most likely candidates . . .'

'There aren't any Romans now,' I cried. 'All that was thousands of years ago. Things have changed. It could have just been some madman . . . I think we should ask the advice of the Williamsburg rabbi. He'll tell us whether to carry on or not.'

I don't really know why I said that . . . Perhaps it was just seeing him so distraught, or perhaps it was a straightforward Hassidic reaction.

He looked surprised but interested. 'The old rabbi we saw at the Sabbath?' In his present state, it didn't take long to convince him.

Two are better than one. Because they have a good reward for their labour. Far if they fall the one will lift up his fellow: but woe to him that is alone when he falleth; for he has not another to help him up.

As I had mentioned my own rabbi in Israel, we had no trouble getting an audience. We went into the little Williamsburg house where the court was held. Disciples were seated on the floor of the room in which the rabbi gave his judgements, with their hats pushed back, hanging on the master's every word. The *gabbai*, the rabbi's assistant, went to and fro, sometimes handing him a *kvitl*, a written petition. The rabbi could give judgements on anything from commercial matters or medical treatments to potential marriages, which would most likely be cancelled, if he was not in favour. He had never previously met any of the parties, who might have come from anywhere in the world; requests sometimes came by telephone from Europe or Israel. And the rabbi always had a reply.

The *gabbai* introduced us, and I briefly explained the purpose of our visit without giving precise details (my father had requested this), and asked whether we should continue our search or abandon it. He withdrew briefly to consider, said something in his assistant's ear and then, shaking his head, said: 'You must continue your search. It is dangerous, but you must continue.'

He blessed us before sending us away, putting his hands on both our heads. 'God will help you,' he said to me.

I looked up and caught a piercing stare from beneath the thick eyebrows which joined up with the imposing white beard. I lowered my eyes, embarrassed. He leaned down and whispered words that froze my blood: 'Take care of your father; he is in great danger.'

Wild singing began behind us: Hassidic judgements always ended with hymns and dances by the disciples, more cheerful than prayers and more conducive to bringing on the devekut. I looked back. The 'ah, oy, hey, bam, ya' were repeated with increasing intensity, their joy kindled by a kind of invincible solidarity; I knew that by now the disciples would have their arms round each other's shoulders and waists and would carry on dancing until they reached a state of trance. Magic circles of dancers linked up with one another endlessly, carried along by the increasingly pounding rhythm. It would become hotter and hotter; coats would be removed and more and more elaborate contortions would be attempted. The most accomplished would form a smaller circle in the middle, and the others would watch them, hallucinating, clapping. Everybody would be enslaved by the dark magic of the rhythm.

We continued towards the hotel; the rabbi's advice seemed to have calmed my father. But whereas his enthusiasm for our mission was renewed, it was now I who felt only despair, and without being able to confide in him. If the rabbi had wanted him to hear, he would have spoken out loud. And he had told us to continue. Now I, for the first time, felt panic at my throat, turning my stomach. Once again I was being forced to betray one loyalty in order not to betray the other.

Eventually my father noticed my anxiety, and asked: 'What did the rabbi whisper to you?'

'It was a secret, otherwise why would he have whispered?'

We were deep in our thoughts, and didn't notice a strange figure, dressed in black, discreetly following us.

We stayed a few more days in New York, talking to scientists and archaeologists in libraries and universities, all of whom told us that our researches were both fruitless and dangerous.

My anxiety gradually faded, despite the sinister atmosphere surrounding the manuscripts, I was proud of both my father and myself. I believed that this alliance between the generations was the secret of power and success. And, unlike my father, even though I was more religious than he, I did not believe in the devil, or in evil, for I had never seen it. To me death was a myth invented by man to frighten man.

For dust thou art, and unto dust shalt thou return.

On the morning we left New York, the receptionist at the hotel handed us a package that had just been delivered. Inside was a small piece of dark-brown parchment. We had no idea who might have sent it: it was too soon for the one Matti had promised us, and in any case he was only going to send a photo, not the original, which of course he didn't have. We still had to put the gun in the post, so we decided to examine it later.

When the plane had taken off, we got it out again, and my father unfolded it carefully.

'This is strange,' he said. 'I don't know what sort of skin this is – it's too dark to be lamb or sheep. I've never seen parchment like this.'

It was thick and smooth, unlined and soft, as though it had never dried out, unlike the Qumran scrolls, which always seemed about to crumble to pieces. This leather, although tanned, was malleable and rolled up easily. It appeared surprisingly fresh, as though from an animal that had recently been killed. We deciphered some words in Aramaic script, written in black ink, that had run in places, and strayed into tiny wrinkles in the skin, underlined by tiny red scratches, like blood. The words were familiar:

97

This is my body
This is my blood
The blood of the covenant spilled for the many.

'It's the Eucharist,' my father explained. 'When Jesus identifies himself with the bread and wine at Easter, announcing the Calvary.'

'But why was it sent to us? And by whom?'

'I don't know. If it were a piece from a Qumran scroll, it would be proof of a link between the Gospels and the scrolls. But this is less than six-months' old . . .'

'Is someone playing a trick on us?'

'Or trying to frighten us . . . To show us we're being watched.'

We examined the parchment again, intrigued: it was certainly unlike any we had ever seen. The words had been written by a good scribe, and the letters were well-formed, but it had been done in a hurry, without any lines. And the soft texture of the skin was somehow worrying. The more I stared at it, the more I had the sense of having seen it somewhere before. Could it have been in a museum, on some reproduction, with my father in Israel? But I thought it was more recent than that . . .

Suddenly my father gave a cry of horror, interrupting my thoughts. Beads of sweat appeared on his forehead, and for a moment he couldn't speak.

'Ary, it's not parchment. Ary . . . It's skin.'

'I know it's skin,' I said, not understanding.

'I mean *human* skin.'

I looked again at the fragment in my father's shaking hands, and then I understood, and a shiver ran up my spine. I did recognise that brown skin: it was Matti's.

III

When we reached London we rang Matti's hotel. They said he had disappeared two days before, and the police were searching for him.

We checked into a hotel near the Centre for Archaeological Studies, where Thomas Almond was supposed to be working. We were weak with fear, and our legs were giving way beneath us, as though we'd had a sleepless night. Once in the hotel room, for want of anything else to do, my father rang the police to find out more; they said Matti had probably been kidnapped, but no trace had been found.

We had no doubt what had happened, but why? Had he been watched? Was somebody trying to prevent him from giving us the copy of the fragment? Did he know something else that he hadn't told us? And why the barbaric warning? There were thousands of unanswered questions.

That afternoon we went to the Centre, more as a distraction than in pursuit of our mission. My father had often worked there and knew it well, but now found it hard to recognise. Archaeology had been computerised; all the files, maps and fossils were now on microfiches, easier to handle and less fragile. The secretary told us that Almond hadn't been to the Centre for several years, and lived near Manchester, translating manuscripts and writing a book.

Our tedious journey continued: Almond lived miles from anywhere. After the train, we took a bus which dropped us in the middle of nowhere, and then we still had a long walk through woods. Dark rainclouds were gathering, and we heard strange noises behind us: crows flying up suddenly, cracking twigs.

We finally reached it, a little grey brick cottage, overgrown with brambles. We knocked, and a man of about fifty, with long hair and a black beard, dressed in dark clothes, appeared in a crack of the door. My father introduced himself as Professor of Archaeology at Jerusalem University. He explained why we were visiting him, mentioning Father Henderson, and only then did he let us in.

Inside, the house was a repository of dusty relics, as old as Methuselah, scattered all over the floor, pinned to the walls, piled on tables. He showed my father some rare pieces, wearing gloves, like a horticulturalist with fragile plants. Passionate about archaeology, he was the sort of slightly mad academic who is lost in his researches, and would be lost without them. He showed us an old table at the end of the room, with the fragments he had been given to translate. Both my father and I stared greedily at them.

This was the real thing, and I was seeing it for the first time. Very old parchments covered in tiny Hebraic script, with no margins, paragraphs or punctuation, an unending and undeviating line. Sometimes it jutted to a long *lamed* or the hook of a *yod*, but it would always return to its rightful furrow and follow its invisible path. As delicate as paper, as soluble and crumbly as compost, it had somehow survived for two thousand years. As fragile and tenacious as the Jewish spirit, as exposed and proud as the face of a consumptive, it reminded me of the little phial of oil that the Maccabees lit in their temple after it had been sacked by Greek soldiers, whose flame, instead of flickering out after a few hours, had lasted eight days; that was the miracle of Hannukah, which enabled the rites to be carried on despite the war. And before me was the miracle of the scrolls.

We leaned forward and read in silence:

And I am part of ungodly humanity
Of the mass of the flesh of perversity.
My iniquities, my faults, my sins, my straying heart
Condemn me to the gathering of the rotten,
Of those who walk in darkness.

For it is not for man to decide his path
And nobody can steady his pace.
The judgement is for God to make,
His hand procures the right conduct
And through his knowledge came everything that happened.
All that happens is guided by his plan,
And without him nothing can be.

'Look at this one,' he said, showing us a manuscript in rather better condition than the one we had been reading. 'It's the Copper Scroll. When we found it, it was so shrivelled up that it was impossible to unroll, so I devised an ingenious system of slicing it into small fragments.' He pointed to a curious contraption made of a saw and some rails. 'The parchment is cut lengthwise by a needle, and then carried along on a little contraption on wheels directly under a circular saw, so that it's the manuscript that moves, not the saw. There's a fan to blow away the dust and a magnifying glass enables you to control the depth of the cut. To prevent the scroll from breaking up when the blade touches it, the outside is wrapped with adhesive tape and warmed so that the skin remains supple. The line cut by the blade is neat, as you can see, and diametrically opposite the edges of the parchment. So there's a margin between the two columns of writing, and you can slice off exactly the amount of letters you want. This is the result.' He proudly handed us a narrow fragment.

'Do you know the contents of the scrolls that were entrusted to your colleagues in the international team?' asked my father.

'No, I never read them. I don't go to lectures on Qumran – nor do they, for that matter. But I do know that they say that nothing in the contents could cause any concern, or force them to revise their ideas about early Christianity. And yet, if you only knew . . . I've found extraordinary things. One describes arms, shields, swords, bows and arrows, all richly decorated with gold, silver and precious stones, for the use of resurrected men at the coming of the Messiah. This text very precisely describes an army divided into battalions, each under a different flag with a religious slogan. The deployment of troops and military tactics are spelt out down to the last detail: everything has been prepared in advance for the coming of the Messiah. When he does come, all he will need to do to win the final war is follow the texts.'

'Which war?' I asked.

He put on a mysterious expression, and then declaimed, in a booming voice: 'The War between the Sons of Light and the Sons of Darkness! There's a whole scroll devoted to it, beginning with the declaration of war by the Sons of Light. The Sons of Darkness are the armies of Belial, the Philistines, the men of Kittim of Assyria and the traitors who helped them, the sons of Levi, Judah and Benjamin. The Sons of Light are the exiles of the desert. Then comes the battle between Egypt and Syria, which puts an end to the Syrian regime and places the Sons of Light in control of Jerusalem and the Temple. For forty years, they struggle against the descendants of Shem, Ham and Japheth, in other words the whole world. The battle against each nation takes six years, and ends in the seventh, in accordance with the law of Moses. After forty years all the Sons of Darkness are wiped out.'

'Some people say the scrolls endanger the true faith and bring bad luck,' said my father.

'Who says that? The Sons of Darkness?' roared Almond.

'Yes . . . well, no. I mean some scholars.'

'Dogma is everything to them, they're stuck in the Middle Ages. I want facts, not dogma!' He struck the table, making us jump. 'The theologians can't even say where Jesus was born, or when, or even who he was, nor explain the discrepancy between his image in the Synoptic Gospels and St John's Gospel. Yet they *know* what Christianity owes to pagan religions, and about the striking resemblances between the Essenes and the early Christians, and the likelihood of some contact between the two, and claim that it doesn't worry them. But I say to them: surely truth is a religious obligation? Didn't the four Gospels say "Truth will set you free"? They reply that the New Testament gives a coherent account of the life of Jesus and the early Church. That's a lie! All we know of the story of Jesus comes from a few contradictory episodes, which don't make up a coherent whole. As for the so-called account of the beginnings of the Church . . . It's by no means certain that Jesus founded, or had any intention of founding, the Christian Church.'

'Exactly,' said my father, emboldened by Almond's speech. 'We want to find out exactly who Jesus was and what his real story was.'

'I very much doubt whether the life of Jesus could ever be pieced together; there's too little evidence. But I'll tell you why the scrolls have been dispersed and why misfortune strikes those who become involved with them . . . including you, if you persevere,' he said, pointing a long bony finger at us.

'Theologians have always insisted that, despite the many contradictions in the Gospels, the story they tell is true. Now, for the first time in centuries, with the discovery of the scrolls, we have the opportunity of finding out whether Jesus was an Essene or a Pharisee, whether he existed, whether there were several Jesuses, or perhaps none at all. For a long time the Gospels were the only historical source of information, and when you think that three out of the four overlap so much that they were certainly copied from one another, it's a very fragile and unreliable one – the scrolls could easily cast doubt upon them.'

'But there's a short passage in Josephus which mentions Jesus,' I said cautiously, wanting to push him to the limit of his argument. 'And he was a serious and scrupulous historian.'

'All the most respected schlolars have dismissed that passage as a fake, probably added by a copyist in the Middle Ages. It happened quite often. We must submit to the evidence: all we have comes from the Gospels, and the Dead Sea Scrolls give us an opportunity to distinguish between legend and truth. But there are people, whom I won't name, who are determined to prevent this from happening.'

He was in full flood, and nothing could stop him. Outside, night was falling, and the fading light threw strange shapes on the walls of the room. Almond continued in a low voice, as his imprecatory gestures cast giant shadows on the walls.

'Presumably you're familiar with the story of the three kings at the nativity. But do you know the story of the Tiridates of Parthia, three Magi bringing gifts to Nero, whom they venerated as "God-King Mithras"? Or the one of the Magi in search of Fravashi, whose birth was announced by a star? Do they remind you of anything?'

'Who was Fravashi?' I asked.

'A pagan God – you should study pagan culture, young man,' he said patronisingly. 'And what about the announcement to the shepherds? And the Magnificat: was it really spoken by Mary and reported by witnesses, as Luke says, or was it a liturgical chant, adapted for the occasion? Scholars certainly know that it's later than the story itself. I ask you,' he said, lifting his arms and raising his voice as if addressing a huge audience, 'which passages of the Gospels were *not* rewritten or adapted by their authors or the copyists? The earliest manuscripts we have date from the fourth century, which gave the Fathers of the Church plenty of time to modify the scriptures to suit their theological tenets. Do you realise that it's not even possible to prove that Jesus was born in Bethlehem? And if it were, would it be Bethlehem in Judaea or in Galilee? And if there really was a child-killer seeking to murder the new-born Jesus, as the Gospels say, who was he? There is no written evidence of him.'

'Herod, they say,' said my father.

'But surely someone as well-informed as Josephus would have recorded such a barbaric act; he mentions plenty of Herod's other crimes. It may be an invention of Matthew's, to confirm the prophecy about Rachel crying over her children. Just as he could have sent Joseph and Mary and the baby to Egypt to confirm the prophet's words: "I will call my son from Egypt".'

Almond carried on, unstoppable: even with such a small audience as my father and myself, he seemed to be speaking to thousands of others, alive and dead.

'What does a believer think? He thinks Jesus preached the Gospel, died as Messiah, was resurrected, and through his apostles founded the Christian church, which spread throughout the world. Or if he doesn't believe in the Resurrection, he believes the apostles, moved by the spirit of Jesus, founded the Church according to the Gospels. He recognises – at least I hope he does –' (he gave an ironic smile) 'that Jesus was a Jew, inheriting the Jewish tradition. He will also believe that the apostles interpreted the words of Jesus, deducing his doctrine from them, which emerges not as it really was, but as coming from what they saw him to be: the Saviour, King and Son of God. In any case he always believes in the complete originality of Christian teaching. He has no idea of what came before – apart from the prophecies of Moses and the rest about the coming of Christ – or of anything not in the Bible.

'But the scholar knows, if the believer doesn't, that there were a number of pagan divinities at the time of Jesus, in whose names similar doctrines were preached. Mithras was the Saviour of humanity, and so were Tammuz, Adonis and Osiris. The idea of Jesus as Redeemer isn't a Jewish one, nor is it a common theme amongst the early Christians in Palestine. The Messiah whom the Jews, and the Christian Jews as well, awaited, was not the son of God, but the messenger of God, who would save the world not by the gift of his blood and his body, but by the arrival of a Messianic kingdom on earth. The Christian Jews did not expect a deliverance which would take them to heaven, but one which would establish a new order on earth. It was only when Christianity spread into the pagan world that the idea of Jesus as Saviour took hold.

'I'll tell you why the scrolls are going to bring trouble and scandal. Because not only do they supply a picture of Judaism at the time, but it is an exhaustive picture. If Jesus existed he must have been in contact with, or even part of, an Essene sect; but not a single one of the scrolls, to my knowledge, mentions him. At the most they speak of a Master of Justice, but there's nothing to say that the Master of Justice is Jesus.'

'Could there have been several prophet figures, and the conflation of these into one single figure came after Jesus?' I asked.

'The figure of Jesus is inspired by others who came before, such as

Mithras,' he continued, pleased that we were following his argument. 'The twenty-fifth of December, the date chosen by the early Christians for Jesus's birth, was the same as Mithras's, around the winter solstice. And the Sabbath, God's day of rest after the Creation, was abandoned in favour of Mithras's day, the day of the conquering sun.'

He turned to the wall and unhooked a painting of Christ on the cross, which looked like a true Caravaggio. Holding it in both hands, he continued with his lecture.

'As for the figure of the Virgin with her dying son, she was everywhere in the Mediterranean world at the time of the expansion of Christianity. In the beginning, she symbolised earth as virgin and mother each spring. The son was the fruit of the earth, born only to die and, returning to the earth, to begin a new cycle. The drama of the Saviour and the Mater Dolorosa is the drama of nature: the rhythm of the seasons parallels the cycle of Heaven. And there's the Virgo constellation which rises in the East, when Sirius heralds the rebirth of the sun: in pagan myth, the passage of Virgo over the horizon corresponds to the Virgin giving birth to the sun. Does that remind you of anything? Similarly the place long associated with the birth of Jesus, was previously connected with that of Horus, the son of Isis and Osiris, who gave his life to save his people. Isis was the Mater Dolorosa. These ancient myths are rife amongst the priesthood; Christian sacraments originate from these cults, and nowhere else.'

He put down the painting and reached down a couple of old books, which he leafed through frantically, as though searching for irrefutable proof.

'The idea of the Eucharist, too, was borrowed from Mithraism, and the blood of the lamb is another part of its tradition. Christianity owes so much to pagan religion that there's little left that can properly be described as Christian. So what the scholar knows and the believer does not, is that Christianity would have spread *with or without Jesus.*'

He paused for effect, and then continued: 'The only important element not found in pagan cults is Jesus as master or rabbi. But between the third century and the Renaissance, when the invention of printing ensured the spread of the Bible, the rabbi-figure completely disappeared from sight, and was forgotten, overtaken by the Christ of the sacraments, the Saviour, whom the Christian church had promoted for more than a thousand years. Jesus of Galilee was almost unknown.

'The only person who tried to restore the Jewish Christ was Paul of Tarsus, a Pharisee but a Hellenist, and an inspired Jew with a profound knowledge of paganism. It was his inspiration to make a synthesis between Israel and Athens, to mingle the dying Temple of Jerusalem with the Mithraic sacrifice, the Essene Jew with the unknown God of Areopagiticus. He was a "christianos", not a Christian, a gnostic who thought that Apollo, Mithras and Osiris should bow down before his Hebraic Yahweh. This could only be achieved by assimilating the "Saviours" and the "Redeemers" – and so the Messiah of Israel became the Christ of the whole world.'

At that moment there was the sudden and deafening sound of a gong, repeating itself: the clock thunderously struck seven. Almond continued throughout, shouting above the noise.

'It could all have happened differently, and still have been called Christianity,' he enunciated, as if addressing us from the top of a lighthouse. 'The scholar is not worried by what the manuscripts contain, because he already knows that Christianity is not a religion founded by Jesus and spread by his disciples. The believer doesn't want to know this, and dreads what he may find in the manuscripts.'

'What have you found in your texts?' said my father, when the noise had died down.

'They don't trust me, and they haven't given me the most interesting ones. I'm not even really a part of the international team any more. Even so, I suspect that I know more or less what they contain. But I'm afraid I can't tell you any more for the moment, because it's the subject of the book I'm writing.'

His tone suddenly changed, and he said, with a strange look: 'Did you know that certain mushrooms can produce extraordinary hallucinations? Come and see.'

He led us to a dark corner of the room, where he lit a small lamp. There was a sort of altar, and, beside it, some little red mushrooms with white spots, the sort one avoids picking in the woods. They were covered in dried mud, and looked soft and slimy and unappetising.

'I burn some every day and inhale the fumes. That's how I discovered what you are still searching for.'

He took a handful of the mushrooms, placed them on the coals that covered the altar, and set a match to them. Black, suffocating smoke began to rise, and Almond stood imperturbably in the midst of the nauseating cloud enunciating like a high priest, his forbidden rosary.

'Christianity comes from the magic mushroom; that's the theme of my next book. I will demonstrate that Jesus never existed, any more than Christianity – we are all victims of hallucinations caused by one type of mushroom, which I have found here, near Manchester. I'm studying its effects on myself. When I inhale this smoke, I have Christian visions of crucified men and virgins with child. Surprising, isn't it? Don't you want to try some?

'Man's dream is to become God, to be omnipotent. But God is possessive of His power and wisdom, and will not suffer rivals. He does, out of the goodness of His heart, allow a few mortals at His side, but only for a very short moment, during which they can only glimpse the beauty of omniscience and omnipotence. It's a unique experience for the lucky few: colours are brighter, sounds clearer, each sensation is magnified, every natural force multiplied. Men have died in order to glimpse eternity, to attain this mystical vision, and their sacrifice has given birth to the great religions like Judaism and Christianity.

'How can one attain the mystical vision? It's an esoteric skill acquired through centuries of observation and risky experiment. Those who knew the secrets of plants weren't priests, and rarely wrote down what they knew, transmitting it only to the initiated. Only during abnormal times, such as persecutions, would they record the names of plants, how to use them and with what incantations, and then in coded language so that only the dispersed communities could understand them.

'This is what happened when the Temple was sacked and Jerusalem destroyed after the Jewish revolt of 70 AD. Christians then discovered a way of entering the spiritual world so successfully that they forgot the secret on which their experience hinged, the key to eternity: the sacred mushroom, *amanita muscaria*.' He held up a mushroom. 'You see the red skin and little white spots – it contains a powerful hallucinogenic. The Ancients thought the phallic shape represented the god of fertility. Yes, I tell you, this is the Son of God, the divine seed, God manifested on earth.'

I interrupted. 'What's the connection between the mushroom and the scrolls?'

'Can't you see?' He frowned. 'It's obvious! Look at the Sumerians' cuneiform writing. The alluvial soil in Mesopotamia produces a particularly fine clay with which they made diamond-shaped tablets. But the oldest tablets are circular, and striated like the underside of a mushroom!'

He's half-mad, I thought, but not entirely; what he says isn't complete nonsense. But my father clearly thought the man was possessed by the devil, and was eager to go: we left him to his demonic inhalations.

We dined gloomily back at the hotel in Manchester. My father once again bitterly regretted having let himself be persuaded by Shimon to take on this mission. In the past, when he had spent hours scratching the soil to find an old stone, or months studying old maps, searching for lost cities, he had been fighting with time and space. Here he was up against a different, abstract, enemy, which became more shadowy the closer he got to it.

And the Lord said unto Satan, whence comest thou? Then Satan answered the Lord, and said, From going to and fro in the earth, and from walking up and down in it.

I had a strange feeling that I would have to start taking the lead, and that he, instead of being a guide, an ally and a master, had become almost an enemy despite himself, almost as afraid of the truth as those who were hiding it. I saw his fear and, remembering the rabbi's words, felt a growing anxiety. But I had to remain calm, and try to reassure him.

'This is the second country we've visited, and we haven't made any progress,' he said. 'We seem to run up against either brick walls or madmen.'

'We've only just begun! Think of your excavations – they take three, ten years, more. Think of this as an archaeological dig.'

'No – the find was made years ago, we're just sticking together the pieces. This is a job for a spy, not an archaeologist. We're not cut out for this, I should never have agreed to do it.'

'If we want results, we should go back and see Almond again tonight.'

'Tonight? You must be mad! You saw how we left him. God only knows what he's doing now . . .'

Late that night, I slipped out of the hotel and took a taxi back to Almond's house. I felt that he must know important things that he would only reveal under the influence of his drug, and I knew my father would not want me to go. I knew, from my experiences, that some things only emerge from a trance-like condition, of the sort Almond must reach with his mushroom. I could not have explained this to my father – the devekut is a Hassidic secret that few people know about, although Almond may have been one of them.

I rang his doorbell about midnight, and he opened the door at once. I said I had come to try his magic mushrooms, and he let me in. The room was filled with a thick and sickly smoke from the burning fungi, and the smell made me feel faint, as though I had lost control of my limbs. But this was very different from the rapture, because I was not conscious of what I was doing.

Terrifying images came into my mind: I found myself in a watery mire, a sinister area of bogs full of slime, with rivers of blood and fire, barren valleys, impassible lakes patched with green ice, empty plains and primitive, infernal caves full of dark plots. And there was the Devil himself.

His face changed all the time. Sometimes he looked like Almond, sometimes Henderson, sometimes like Beelzebub and his demons. Seraphim and cherubim with angels' wings and children's faces stirred up conflict and wreaked havoc. Belberith implanted thoughts of murder in the minds of good men. Astaroth, prince of Thrines, the demon of sloth, spread antagonism and hatred. Azazel, the prince of demons, taught men how to make weapons of war. And I was like the scapegoat, innocent and yet stained by the sins of the Jewish people, cast out from the city into the wilderness to expiate sins he had not committed – blasphemy, perjury, theft, murder and massacre – seeking my dark master.

A terrible shriek tore the night. It was the cry of the seven whistlers, mysterious birds which haunt the night sky and which, according to legend, represent the souls of Jews unable to find peace after the crucifixion of Christ. Then the face of Azazel gave way to the face of Satan.

He was horrible to look at: his mouth dribbled the blood he had sucked, the blood of the poor, the slaves, the innocents. His eyes were flames, giving off sparks. There were several crowns on his head and two horns, sharpened like blades. His deformed, boneless body was draped in bloodstained garments. Sharp, filthy claws grew out of his hands and feet, and a long tail hung between his legs.

He approached the altar where the mushrooms were burning, and covered it with a black cloth. All around, dark candles gave off acrid, bitumenous fumes. The Caravaggio Christ lay on a table beside the altar; I leaned forward to look and saw that it had been totally transformed. The crucifix was reversed and the Christ was naked, his neck contorted, his face had an obscene thick-lipped smile and a lolling, dribbling tongue.

The Devil then intoned hymns and prayers, which he sang backwards. He lifted a chalice full of water to his lips; when he poured it over my head it turned into wine. With false oaths he announced that the day of judgement was approaching.

'Master of all murder, disciple of all crime, master of sin and vice, God of true reason, here is your manuscript,' he said with a cruel smile, handing me a roll of black parchment. 'Sell it, you will get a million dollars.'

At these words I rolled on the carpet, kicking and crawling obscenely on my stomach. My tongue clicked against the roof of my mouth; the noise was so loud that it echoed against the walls. The pupils of my eyes were dilated and my head flopped on my shoulders. I heard Satan's blasphemies, as he loudly sang 'This is my body', impaling a black goat on his horns. *Acquerra Beyty, Acquerra Goity.*

'Give me the money,' I cried. 'I'll take the scrolls and sell them!'

A familiar voice replied: 'Is that what we've come for? What has happened to your *galut*? Have you come all this way to worship the golden calf and forget your mission?'

'No,' I replied remorsefully. 'The writings are worth more than all the money in the world.'

I was lifted by a powerful wind onto the roof of the cottage. He held the scroll up to me, saying: 'Here's the scroll, come and get it. It will be yours.'

I could see the manuscript from the roof. One small step and it would be mine. I was not afraid of the void; on the contrary, I was irresistibly drawn towards it. I felt the breath of the Devil as he whispered: 'Come! Just one step, it's so easy . . . All you desire is here, one step away.' I was magnetically drawn downwards, like an object in free fall. The more I contemplated the emptiness, the more fascinated I was. I closed my eyes, and stepped forward . . .

But suddenly I had a vision of my father sleeping peacefully, waiting for me; I could not betray his loyalty and trust.

'No,' I said, stepping back. 'Life is worth more than manuscripts.'

Then Satan brought me back to earth. He held out the scroll.

'Take them and read them. You can rule the world, if you promise to worship me.'

'No,' I cried. I realised that the only way to avoid temptation was to refuse without thinking. 'You will worship the Lord your God, and serve him alone,' I recited.

'You will read them!'

He came close to me, his eyes brands of fire, his mouth foaming, his torn hands dripping blood. He pushed the scrolls towards me, shaking with rage. Then I ran away, as far as I could, panting, through the deserted countryside. I struggled on for over an hour, terrified by the thought of the pursuing Satan, until I collapsed, exhausted, and lost conciousness.

I awoke very early the next morning, beside the road a mile or so away from Almond's house. A lorry took me back to the hotel, where I slept until midday. When I woke up, memories of the night before jostled in my brain, like a bad dream. I decided to try to forget it, despite a persistent hangover.

We left London for Paris in the late afternoon. In the taxi on the way to the airport, we at last glimpsed the city we had not had time to explore. The old buildings, relics of centuries I had never before seen the remains of, seemed to me both splendid and flamboyant. Beside our precious relics, London was a young city, but it was still a marked improvement on the modernity of New York, which I had found so discomfiting. Here I saw monuments for the first time in my life: in Israel there were walls, sarcophagi, abandoned sites, ruins, but no real monuments. My country was a series of historical layers, cities razed to the ground, eroded by war and neglect. In London, the old houses stood proudly, as though defying vain and ephemeral human passions, usurping the power of time, becoming its true incarnation.

I saw a bored-looking type wandering in Piccadilly, his hair in multicoloured quiffs, with chains on his jeans and holes in his jacket, with nose, lips and even his eyelids pierced. His eyes were blank and hopeless. It occurred to me that this man was, in a way, like us in Mea Shearim – awaiting the end of the world. He too was a soldier of the new dawn, a visionary of decadence, a doomed apostle of the future.

Still haunted by terrible images, I tried to study the Talmud on the plane to calm my mind. Study for me was an intoxicating experience which transported me far beyond the scriptures. So, like all Hassidim, I was cautious about it: the Talmud is forever reinterpreted, contradicted, refuted again, with no result nor dogma. It is like a thriller in which the reader is sent urgently forward from one page to the next; but it is also a book of philosophy in which each page, each line, each word is important and requires intense concentration to be understood. Unlike a thriller, however, it has no ending: even if one read all the treatises and every volume, there would still be a thousand possible interpretations of every passage.

So study, like novels, distances the mind from the contemplation of the divine; after every hour spent reading, the Hassidim must stop to think about God. However, at this moment, escape was what I needed.

My father leaned over to ask which treatise I was studying. I looked up, and saw a headline in the newspaper his neighbour was reading:

CRUCIFIXION NEAR MANCHESTER

We asked the air hostess for a paper, and read:
A palaeographer was killed last night, apparently by a maniac. Professor Thomas Almond, who was preparing a work on the Qumran scrolls, was discovered, crucified, on a large wooden cross. His murderer has not yet been found. There seems to be no clear motive, and Manchester CID are appealing for any information.

We read it twice, trying not to believe what we were reading. It was as if we had suddenly gone back two thousand years in time. Reality had overtaken scholarship and research. For my father, the horror was all the worse for the fact that it had happened straight after our visit, as though the murderer was laying a trail of death behind us.

I was terrified. The murder had happened the night before, and I knew that I had probably been with Almond until dawn; but I could remember nothing, except that he was still alive around midnight. Had I, unwittingly, helped with his execution? What could possibly have happened to make me forget?

My father was calm now, motionless as a block of stone. It was as though he knew that the curse of the scrolls was inescapable, and would run its course whatever the cost.

So I returned, and considered all the oppressions that are done under the sun: and behold the tears of such as were oppressed, and they had no comforter; and on the side of their oppressors there was power; but they had no comforter.

Fourth Scroll

THE SCROLL OF THE WOMAN

[The woman]
  . . . speaks vanity
and . . . errors.
She is ever prompt to oil her words,
and she flatters with irony,
deriding with iniquitous l(ips).
Her heart is set up as a snare,
and her kidneys as fowler's nets.
Her eyes are defiled with iniquity,
her hands have seized hold of the Pit.
Her legs go down to work wickedness,
and to walk in wrong-doings.
Her . . . are foundations of darkness,
and a multitude of sins is in her skirts.
Her . . . are darkness of night,
and her garments . . .
Her clothes are shades of twilight,
and her ornaments plagues of corruption.
Her couches are beds of corruption,
and . . . depths of the pit.
Her inns are couches of darkness,
and her dominions in the midst of the night.
She pitches her dwelling on the foundations of darkness,
she abides in the tents of silence.
Amid everlasting fire is her inheritance,
not among those who shine brightly.
She is the beginning of all ways of iniquity.
Woe (and) disaster to all who possess her!
And desolation to all who hold her!
For her ways are ways of death,
and her paths are roads of sin,
and her tracks are pathways to iniquity,

and her by-ways are rebellious wrong-doings.
                                    Her gates are gates of death,
and from the entrance of her house
she sets out towards the underworld.
None of those who enter there will ever return,
and all who possess her will descend to the Pit.
She lies in wait in secret places (. . .)
On the city's squares she veils herself,
and she stands at the gates of the towns.
She will never re(st) from wh(orin)g,
her eyes glance hither and thither.
She lifts her eyes naughtily
to stare at a virtuous one and join him,
and an important one to trip him up,
at upright men to pervert their way,
and the righteous elect to keep them from the commandment,
at the firmly established to bring them down wantonly,
and those who walk in uprightness to alter the statute.
To cause the humble to rebel against God,
and turn their steps away from the ways of justice,
to bring insolence to their heart,
so that they march no more in the paths of uprightness;
to lead men astray to the ways of the Pit,
and seduce with flatteries every son of man.
                              Qumran scrolls, *The Seductress.*

I

When God put man in the Garden of Eden after the Creation, he saw that it was not good that he should be alone. So he took one of his ribs and made woman. Man, seeing that she was bone of his bones and flesh of his flesh, attached himself to her, and they loved one another, and once again became one flesh. Then the serpent appeared and tempted woman, and she persuaded man to sin.

Was it necessary for evil to be mixed up with love? The original sin was not the union between man and woman; it entered into it, like a spreading disease, from the serpent to the woman, from the woman to the man, after love.

Jesus said: 'Love one another.' He also said that greater love has no man than he who lays down his life for those he loves. So why so much hatred, always?

I thought the answer to these questions might lie in a book I had often heard of – from my father, mostly – without ever having read it, a book that the whole world knows, reads, and often quotes, sometimes without realising it.

I mean the Gospels. At the yeshivah we were not allowed to read any text not issuing from Jewish orthodox culture; so very few essays, and certainly no novels.

I had a confused feeling that there might be something to be found in these books, and by the time we arrived in France I had one thought only: to understand what was going on. I had to know.

The rabbi, although he said you should never be ashamed to ask questions and look for solutions, would never have allowed it. It was strictly forbidden to read the Gospels, or even pronounce Christ's name. But as soon as we arrived, I bought a Hebrew translation of the New Testament.

My heart pounded as I opened it, and my hands trembled as I turned the pages. I knew I shouldn't be doing this, but I had to. I could almost say that I tasted the sharp and delicious taste of forbidden fruit. At last I would understand.

I was more surprised than I can say by what I discovered. Not by its strangeness, but by its curious familiarity. I will try to convey what I read, as far as I can remember it, because I never repeated my sin.

He was born in Bethlehem in Judaea, at the time of King Herod. He was the son of Joseph and Mary, conceived by the Holy Ghost, as the prophet had predicted: *the Virgin will conceive and give birth to a son Emmanuel, which means 'God is with us'*. At his birth, wise men who had seen magic signs came from the East. When they reached Jerusalem they asked where lay the King of the Jews, to whom they had come to pay homage. They met Herod, who gathered the rabbis; they said the King of the Jews would be born in Bethlehem, according to the texts. So they set off for Bethlehem. They were guided by a star, and found Mary, the young mother of Jesus, and paid homage to Him. Then they went, leaving behind them clouds of incense and leaves of myrrh.

Then Joseph had a dream telling him to flee into Egypt, because Herod was searching for the child in order to kill him. *A voice has been heard in Rama, tears and a long threnody; it is Rachel crying for her children and she cannot be consoled, for they are no more.* They remained in Egypt until the death of Herod, then returned to Galilee and lived in a town called Nazareth.

There was also a man called John the Baptist, who cried in the wilderness for Judaea to convert, because the Kingdom of Heaven approached. *A voice cried: 'Prepare the way of the Lord, make his paths straight!'* John wore a garment of camel-hair, with a belt around his loins; he lived on grasshoppers and wild honey. Many flocked to him to be baptised in the Jordan, and to confess their sins. Many Pharisees and Saducees came and he exhorted them to repent.

Then Jesus came from Galilee to the Jordan to be baptised by John. At his baptism, Jesus saw the Holy Spirit in the shape of a dove; he remembered Noah's bird of peace, and further back, the breath of creation. Then he went into the desert and was tempted three times by the Devil. But, remembering the word of the Bible and the prophets, he emerged triumphant from the test. *You will worship the Lord thy God and none other.*

When he heard that John had been arrested, Jesus went back to Galilee, then to Capharnaum, by the sea. *Land of Zabulon, land of Nephtali, road to the sea, country beyond the Jordan, Galilee of nations! The people that walked in darkness have seen a great light: on those who live in a land of deep shadow, a light has shone.*

Travelling throughout Galilee, surrounded by his disciples, he taught in the synagogues, proclaimed the good news and cured all types of illness and infirmity with his miracles. Great crowds came to hear him. Then he went into the mountains to proclaim the 'Beatitudes'. *Blessed are they that mourn, for they shall be comforted, and the meek shall inherit the earth.* He cured a leper, a centurion, Peter's mother-in-law, the daughter of a rich man, two blind men and a possessed man who was dumb.

He spoke in allegories, like the psalms and like the Midrash; he was proclaiming things hidden since the beginning of the world.

He then went to Jerusalem. Approaching the Mount of Olives, Jesus sent two of his disciples to the village, where he said they would find a tethered donkey, with her foal beside her. The disciples found them, just as he had said. He set off. The crowd went before him, crying: 'Hosanna to the son of David! Blessed be the name of the Lord who comes!' When he got to the Temple, he threw out all those who were trading on the steps.

Then he said to his disciples: 'In two days it will be Passover. The son of man will be betrayed and crucified.' The high priests and elders gathered in the palace of the high priest Caiaphas. They agreed to arrest Jesus. It was Judas Iscariot, one of his disciples, who would betray him.

On the eve of Passover Jesus knew he would be arrested. He sang psalms, and with his disciples, set off to the Mount of Olives. *The shepherd will be struck down and the sheep scattered.* They spent the night at Gethsemane. Then came the traitor Judas, one of the twelve, accompanied by armed men sent by the high priests. He kissed Jesus: that was the sign. Then Jesus said: 'That thou doest, do quickly.'

He was arrested. Peter tried to protect him, but Jesus said, 'Don't you think I could call on my Father, who would send more than twelve legions of angels? How would the prophecies in the Scriptures be carried out?' Then he addressed the crowd: 'All this is happening so that the words of the prophets can be fulfilled.' Then the disciples abandoned him and ran away.

Jesus was taken before Pilate. Seeing him captive, Judas was filled with remorse and gave back the thirty pieces of silver to the priests and the elders, saying: 'I have sinned by betraying innocent blood.'

But it was too late. He hanged himself. Judas had given the reward for his treachery back to the priests; but they could not keep the money from their crime, and they gave it to the potter's field.

Pilate gathered the crowd and offered to release either Jesus or Barabbas, a thief. The crowd chose Barabbas. Pilate washed his hands: the responsibility was now upon the crowd. So Jesus was crucified, in the place called Golgotha. They gave him wine mixed with vinegar. They drew lots over his clothes. Passers-by nodded their heads at him, saying: 'You who destroyed the sanctuary, save yourself now.' He trusted in God, let God save him now, if he loves him.

At midday, darkness suddenly fell over the town, remaining until three. Before he died, Jesus cried: *Eli, Eli, lama sabachthani?* 'My God, my God, why hast thou forsaken me?'

I felt troubled. I understood the importance of the discovery of the manuscripts: if John the Baptist was an Essene, if Jesus was an Essene, could his teaching be interpreted in the same way as before? If Christianity turned out to have emerged from a Jewish sect, its image would surely be radically changed.

But above all I was struck by the betrayal, the passion and the suffering of Christ. I could not understand the reasons for his death; they seemed obscure of me. Were the Jews responsible, the Romans guilty, or was it the opposite? And which Jews? Which Romans? The priests, the crowd, the disciples who abandoned him? Why did Judas, one of his disciples, betray him? Was it for the money, or was there a deeper, doctrinal, motive? And why did Jesus allow it to happen, when he knew he was about to be arrested, had never ceased announcing it and warning his disciples, right up to the Last Supper? Why did he even encourage Judas, telling him to do his work quickly: it was as though each one had his role that night, as though it were a plot, planned by the two of them, Jesus and Judas, a secret agreement between victim and traitor.

It appeared to have been necessary that he should be put to the test at that fateful hour. But why, then, had the other disciples not realised and understood this? Why had they abandoned him at the very moment when he needed them most?

I felt suddenly dizzy. The problem was at last clear to me. It was both as simple and difficult as this: who killed Jesus? I felt in a confused way that the answer to that question would bring with it the solution to the mystery of the deaths of Almond, Matti and Hosea, as well as that of the disappearance of the manuscripts.

Finding the answer, however, would be a complex matter. Judas the traitor was clearly guilty. But had he acted on his own, or was he an instrument? What was the understanding between him and Jesus? The Romans had carried out the deed; they were the state and the law. But they had left the final decision to the Jews, which made the whole thing singularly complicated. They – the Jews – had voted for his death. But which Jews? Not the entire population, not the Pharisees, who were not there, only representatives of the Sadducees and of some of the Temple priests.

Were they guilty, then? Jewish law did not encompass death by crucifixion, and the tribunal did not have him stoned. So the guilt is once again shared between Jews and Romans, who could not simply 'wash their hands' of the matter. Finally, what were the motives of both parties? Why did Pilate have him arrested? Was he really such a threat to Roman authority, when all he did was speak for the poor and the infirm, with no political or revolutionary message? Who were the people in this fanatic, manipulated crowd who called for his death? Did they really prefer the thief Barabbas, when previously they had acclaimed him as John the Baptist's Messiah?

And why such animosity from the priests? Were they really afraid that this simple rustic from the faraway province of Galilee could be a threat to their power in Jerusalem? Why wish for his death, when they had no real charge against him?

Why did Judas betray him? Could it really have been simply for the money? Could the son of a Zealot, a Zealot himself, have been so venal? And, finally, why did Jesus allow himself to be betrayed?

It was as though Jesus had been murdered three times: by Judas, by the Romans and by the priests, with the crowd as their instrument. And perhaps a fourth time – 'My God, why hast thou forsaken me?', he said before dying. The question remains, and it did not escape the Romans, the passers-by, even the thieves crucified beside him: if Jesus really was the Son of God, his father could have saved him – indeed, he could have saved himself, he who had performed so many miracles. Maybe he chose not to perform a miracle this one time, in which case his death was his own choice, a sort of suicide. Judas had been his accomplice, Judas whom he had embraced, urging him to perform his task. He foresaw betrayal and death, and yet did nothing to avoid his fate – so Jesus himself was one of the guilty parties.

Unless . . .

I shuddered. An extraordinary and blasphemous idea struck me: Jesus knew he was going to be betrayed, but perhaps he thought he would not die. Right up until the end he thought God was going to save him: at the very last moment, the great cataclysmic miracle would happen, the triumphal, radiant coming of the Father. He was expecting the Kingdom of Heaven. Why else would he have said: 'My God, why hast thou forsaken me?'

They were his last words, summing up a life, and a death. But they were not the words of a martyr on the cross, expressing the final victory of a man offering himself as a sacrifice to save humanity, nor even the longing to rejoin his Father in the glory of another, better, world. 'Why hast thou forsaken me?' The words have a different resonance – regret, surprise, recrimination, even anger.

So the dying Jesus on the cross accuses God of having killed him. *Why did God abandon him?*

I found it hard to wake up the next day, after a restless night of long nightmares in which I saw Jesus struggling with his enemies and Satan as I had seen him in my evil visions. We set off for the theology department of the university, to find Father Jacques Millet, who had returned from Qumran, and whom we thought might tell us where to find Pierre Michel.

It was a difficult journey; St-Germain-des-Prés was completely blocked by a huge crowd shuffling slowly along, waving banners and chanting slogans. Cars waited at a standstill for the demonstration to go by. We had read that morning of massive jams all round Paris, bumper to bumper, a long procession of monsters belching poisonous fumes. The drivers sat, sheep-like, resigned, with nothing to lose, nothing to do but wait; after six hours they were still able to wave to one another, the time for anger had passed.

Each group of demonstrators had its banner: the sweeps, the postmen, the teachers, the unemployed. A man with a loudspeaker harangued the crowd: 'The government refuses to listen. They want us to believe that the survival of the nation depends on some being poorer than others. They say sacrifices must be made to end unemployment, but it's always the same people making the sacrifices.'

It was not an angry mob. They were simply at a loss, and calmly demanding their right to jobs and pensions; they demanded that the government should resign. The slow procession conveyed gloom and fear of the future, rather than any real political fury. There were some, however, who tried to push through the police barriers, and were repelled with coshes and tear gas; some were roughly thrown into black police vans. The Kittim, I thought. The people were crying their desolation, their dread of poverty, and the police, afraid of the anger of a hungry man, struck them down and arrested them.

We managed to push our way through the compact mass of humanity, and reached the university. We found Millet in his shabby office, scattered with books and files. He was no longer the jovial and welcoming figure we had met before, and was not inclined to lively conversation, as he had been at Qumran. The letters etched in the veins of his temples were still there, but more blurred than before.

'I didn't expect to see you again so soon, and here in Paris,' he said, shaking hands. 'But I knew there would be some contact with Israelis, after what's happened.'

He said, since the savage killings, he was ready to answer our questions, and to co-operate fully with the Israeli authorities. Like Andrei Lirnov, he had left all his manuscripts with Pierre Michel who, soon afterwards, had left the priesthood and come to France to work as a researcher. The greater part of the non-Biblical manuscripts, apocrypha, and writings of the sect were now in his possession. According to Millet, he had a total of a hundred and twenty fragments, but he refused to disclose an exact list of what they were. He gave us Pierre Michel's private address, warning us that he would probably not receive us, as he nowadays saw nobody.

He appeared embarrassed and his Hebrew was more hesitant than when we had last seen him, as though he were afraid of saying too much. My father clearly had the same impression, and asked him outright:

'Do you know what the scroll Pierre Michel mentioned at the 1987 lecture contained? Did you decipher it when you worked at the Archaeological Museum in Jerusalem?'

'No, I didn't have time.'

He had answered my father's question. Pierre Michel's scroll had been the one stolen from the museum. There was an awkward silence, and we prepared to leave. Then the priest suddenly asked me: 'Do you live at Mea Shearim?'

'Yes.'

'It's a pretty district, isn't it?' His face lit up with a nostalgic smile.

'Yes, indeed.'

'I always miss Israel when I'm in France. It's different there – I feel well and safe. It's such a wonderful country . . . Do you remember the little phial of oil I gave you?'

'Of course. I carry it everywhere with me. Do you want it back?'

'No, it's yours. Keep it . . . Keep it carefully. You know what our Lord Jesus Christ said: "Give, and much shall be given to you . . ."'

He stopped, and then added quietly: 'The fact is . . . When I was working in the scrollery, I was under quite strong pressure from certain authorities not to examine that manuscript. I don't know what's in it, but if you really want to know, I don't think they trusted me.'

'And they didn't get it back from Pierre Michel, after he left the priesthood?'

'They tried,' he said, giving no indication as to who this 'they' was. 'That's why he left Jerusalem. But now he doesn't have to answer to any ecclesiastical authority, unlike me.'

'Surely you must have glanced, even superficially, at the manuscript?' my father insisted.

'Yes, I did, just before it disappeared. When I mentioned what I had glimpsed, so to speak, to Father Henderson, he told me not to mention it to anyone under any pretext. In other words, to forget all about it. He said the same thing to Lirnov. But the poor man could not bear what he knew . . .'

'What?' said my father.

'I can't answer. I promised I would be silent, and I can't break my silence. But try to see Pierre Michel. Here's my home address.' He handed us a card. 'Don't hesitate to call me, I'll do all I can to help you, without breaking my oath, you understand.'

'Are you afraid of something or someone?' asked my father. 'Perhaps *we* could help *you*.'

There was another silence, and no reply.

'Do you think the Congregation for the Doctrine of the Faith might be involved in these crimes?'

'I've belonged to the Congregation for years, and I know what they're capable of. But not this, believe me. No, I'm not afraid of them. The only reason for my silence is the promise I made, nothing more.'

He indicated that the interview was over. As I shook his hand, I was struck to the heart by the sadness in his eyes.

We had not learned much from him, but for the first time I felt that an obstacle had been removed. We knew nothing yet, but at least we knew *that*.

Then I saw that wisdom excelleth folly, as far as light excelleth darkness. The wise man's eyes are in his head; but the fool walketh in darkness: and I myself perceived also that one event happened to them all. For there is no remembrance of the wise more than of the fool for ever; seeing that which now is in the days to come shall all be forgotten. And how dieth the wise man? As a fool.

That same evening we went to Pierre Michel's flat in the XIIIth arrondissement. It was in the Chinese quarter, on the twelfth floor of a gloomy, tall grey tower block. We rang. There was no answer.

We then rang Father Millet from a telephone box opposite: no answer either. We set off again, walking northwards. It was twilight, and the sun was fading gently in the spring mists. The soft light was reflected in pastel shades on the stone buildings.

We reached the VIth arrondissement, driven no doubt by some unconscious logic – *Satan, the temptation of the abyss* – and walked in silence towards Father Millet's parish. At his house, we deliberated.

'Since we're here, why don't we go and see him?' I said.

'Now? Isn't it too late?'

'No. He urged us to come, and perhaps he'll speak more freely away from the university. I think he trusts us.'

'He trusts you, you mean, and I wonder why. Still . . . I don't know what more he can tell us, but I'm worried about him. I'm sure he was frightened of something.'

'Perhaps the only way of protecting him is to get him to tell us everything . . .'

My father hesitated, and then said: 'All right, let's go in.'

We rang the entryphone, but there was no answer, and we went up to the apartment. The door was open and my father went in first.

What we saw froze us with a terror that would remain with us for the rest of our lives. No day or night passes when I do not wake up horrified by the memory of what I saw. For a long time I prayed to be released from the hideous images which kept me awake at night, and haunted my days; but I could never forget the horror of human wickedness, which no demon can equal.

Therefore I hated life; because the work that is wrought under the sun is grievous unto me: for all is vanity and vexation of spirit.

Father Millet hung upright, his arms up, and his head leaning to the left. He was practically naked, and his white body had become soft and fleshy, boneless. His face was frozen in an expression of intense suffering, his eyes like stone: their cry of pain, fear and incomprehension, their longing for death as deliverance, had finally been answered, but the expression remained. The white hair was stuck to his skull by the sweat of suffering, like the sweat of an old man lost beneath an eternal beating sun, devouring himself in the process of malignant disintegration. A yellow bilious liquid dribbled from his open mouth. There were still thin dried-up trails of blood on his temples, and on his hands and feet, which were fettered with heavy black ropes: the last traces of life. His hands were curled up around their wounds, as though trying to protect them, and his skeletal feet hung down on top of one another.

Precariously perched with one buttock on the cross bar, he had been hung on a large wooden cross, a headless cross of Lorraine. His wrists were nailed to the crossbar, his feet to the upright. His body was dislocated, twisted sideways; large nails had been driven into his flesh, leaving pustulating wounds.

He had been crucified.

We stood bewildered, unable to take our eyes off this macabre scene. We were Cohens, and Jewish law forbade us to touch a body; we had to remain pure of all contact with death.

But we were morbidly drawn towards this dead man. Death is a sinister power, attracting the great forces of life towards it, sucking them into the fatal void; the man who gazes upon death is like somebody leaning over an abyss, knowing that he too can end it all with one step. Death is a terrifying seducer, a bitter-sweet intoxicating wine. You have to be solidly anchored in life, or forcibly attached to it, to withstand its power; will-power alone is not enough – it can do nothing against the longing that death inspires, the end of existence, the gate to eternity.

We left the apartment and plunged into the dark night, nothing compared to the darkness within us.

It is better to go to the house of mourning than to the house of feasting: for that is the end of all men; and the living will lay it to his heart.

My father felt himself somehow responsible for what had happened to Father Millet; he believed our search had become a calvary, a *via dolorosa*. He kept on saying that this mission was not for us, that it was our fault that he had died, that Almond's crucifixion and Matti's death were linked. It was clear now that somebody was following us, trying to prevent us from continuing our search by destroying any evidence we might discover. If we, as Cohens, were not allowed to touch blood, surely we were equally forbidden to draw it. Shimon had been wrong to think that we might succeed, or perhaps he just never imagined the tragic consequences of such an investigation. And the next message would be no warning any more; we were up against Romans, barbarians prepared for anything.

'I think we should go home to Israel,' he said.

'We can't just give up. We must solve the mystery, whatever it costs.'

'But Ary, you can't explain everything; some things have to remain secret. Sometimes simple appearances can be the most deceptive, and what lies beneath them is so terrible that it's best to turn away. You know it's impossible to look God in the face, and a mortal sin to try to. He must remain hidden. Whoever tries to unveil his mystery will be cursed and destroyed.'

'What are you talking about? Is there something else you know about these murders?' I cried, terrified. 'You don't believe in God anyway, you don't keep the Sabbath, or even obey the Ten Commandments. What are you saying?'

'I don't know whether God exists or not, but I don't want to contradict his will, or ignore his signs.'

I couldn't help smiling, despite our terrible situation. Our roles had been reversed. I thought I was the believer, and now I was suddenly the one putting the atheist, rationalist point of view. He, the atheist, now appeared more religious than me.

'You're wrong to think these are signs; or God has been mistaken in sending them,' I said calmly. 'We can't abandon everything. We must find the manuscript. Somebody's hiding it, I don't know who. It may not be one man, it may be a group, some institution that's been suppressing it for centuries. Whatever it is, we must carry on. We can't be like Jonah, refusing God's command to preach repentance to Nineveh, or we'll be swallowed by a whale.'

I really did feel that we should persevere; and if the barbarians wanted war, then we should accept their challenge. I wasn't frightened. I thought I was immortal, and so were the people I loved. We were life, we were the sons of light, they were the sons of darkness; and was it not written that the Messiah would come after this battle?

The next day we returned to Pierre Michel's apartment. Again nobody answered the bell. Shimon had sent me a skeleton key along with the pistol, that other ominous farewell present: I opened the door quietly.

The apartment was tiny and dark; the shutters were closed. We crept down the narrow corridor and went into the main room.

A woman was crouching in front of a drawer, digging out papers and looking through them. She turned round with a cry of alarm. 'Who are you?'

'It's all right,' said my father. 'We're archaeological researchers, looking for Pierre Michel.'

She looked calmer. 'Pierre Michel has gone away, and if you're looking for the manuscript, it's not here either. I'm looking for it too.'

'Why? Who are you?' I asked.

'I work for the *Biblical Archeological Review*, for Bartholomew Donnars. We want to publish the entire collection, including the one that was fraudulently removed.'

'Yes,' I said warily. 'Everybody knows your magazine earns its living from the manuscripts.'

'These documents are just as important for historians as for priests. Their concealment is the real scandal, not our attempts to find them and publish them,' she said calmly.

'How did you get in?' asked my father.

'The same way as you, I should think. I suspected Pierre Michel wouldn't be here. Ever since he left the priesthood, he's been getting death threats from people trying to get the manuscript back. I think he's run away. I had a lot of trouble finding him, and even when I did it was very hard to get him to agree to talk. I explained that it was his only hope.'

'His only hope of what?'

'Of staying alive.'

'You've heard about the murders?' I said.

'Who hasn't? They've been in all the papers.'

'But *who* wants to kill him?' asked my father.

'He said he didn't know, but he supposed it was Henderson. He had given the manuscripts to Michel right at the beginning, when they were close colleagues; but he didn't know about Michel's doubts and apostasy, and when Michel began leaking the contents at the 1987 lecture, he was furious. Then Michel disappeared, with the scroll. And now' – she looked gloomily around the room – 'no way of finding him.'

She was young, with long blonde hair and a pale freckled face. She said her name was Jane Rogers, she was the daughter of a clergyman, and her work at the *BAR* was inspired by the love of truth, which for her was the same thing as the love of God.

'You see,' she told me, with the serious expression I was to come to know so well, 'I want to publish the manuscript for the sake of Christianity.'

I had hurt her feelings, and I bitterly regretted it.

'I'm sorry,' I said. 'I was wrong to criticise.'

Her face lit up with a childlike smile. 'It's all right, I'm used to . . .'

She stopped, looking terrified: I turned, and saw two menacing figures.

My father stepped towards them, as though to protect us. They grabbed him and hit him on the head with a cosh; he collapsed.

For a moment I stood frozen, unable to move. Then the sight of my father prostrate on the floor filled me with murderous rage, and I threw myself on his attackers.

I punched one of them in the stomach, but the other one got in a blow to my head, which stunned me for long enough for them to carry away my father's unconscious body.

I tried to chase them, but the pain in my head made me stagger. I could hear Jane Rogers' voice, as if from a great distance, calling: 'No! Don't go after them, or they'll kill him, like the others.'

I lost consciousness.

When I came to, I saw, through a thick haze, a golden angel bending over me, wiping a soft, cool cloth across my forehead. I shut my eyes, and opened them again: this was no heavenly vision, but a worried Jane Rogers. I could feel the gentle pressure of her hands on the compress.

'Are you feeling better?' she said. 'Shall I call an ambulance?'

'It's all right. Why did they kidnap my father? How do they know who he is?' The terrible events of the last hour came flooding back.

'They must have known you were looking for the manuscripts . . . Unless they thought he was Pierre Michel – obviously neither of us could be . . . Are you a Hassid, or are you in disguise?' She watched curiously as I desperately tried to replace my black velvet yarmulka.

'I live in Mea Shearim.'

'Oh, I see . . . Perhaps they were just looking for the treasure.'

'What treasure?'

'The Bedouin knew about it through their oral tradition, I believe. One of the texts mentions a treasure of gold and precious stones.'

'Yes, the Bronze Scroll. It's the treasure of the Temple. How do you know about that?'

'I work on that file at the *BAR*, and we get all the latest archaeological news. But we can talk about that later; we can't stay here. Anything might happen.'

The fresh air did me good. We walked together for a while, then went to our separate hotels, after exchanging telephone numbers.

I couldn't get to sleep. I still had a piercing headache, and I was frantic about my father. I could see no way of finding him. If they realised their mistake, or that he knew no more than they did, they might kill him. Tormented by the image of the crucified body of Father Millet, I tossed and turned feverishly all night. Who could have killed him? Fanatic Christians, or fanatic anti-Christians? Jews, Muslims or Christians? Bloodthirsty maniacs, anyway. But what did they mean by this ritual re-enactment of the death of Christ?

They might be simple criminals looking for the Essene treasure, who thought my father held the key to it. Or fanatics who, dreading the revelations in the manuscripts, had also killed Almond and Millet, Matti and Hosea.

One thing struck me when I thought about this: the common factor was that the kidnappings were always linked to the manuscripts, one way or another. So the way to save my father, if there was still time to, would be to attract the kidnappers by drawing attention to the manuscripts.

At five that morning I rang Jane Rogers.

'It's Ary Cohen. I'm sorry I woke you.'

'It doesn't matter, I wasn't asleep. How's your head?'

'A bit better. Listen. I must find my father. I don't know where he is, who took him, or why. But I do believe it was because of the manuscripts.'

'Did he know anything about them?'

'No more than I did.'

'What exactly were you looking for?'

'Pierre Michel's scroll.'

'The one he quoted in the lecture?'

'Yes.'

'That's why I was sent here too. Are you sure your father hadn't found out something he was keeping secret from you?'

'I don't think so.'

'If he doesn't know anything, they might not kill him, and there's still time to find him.'

'I'm afraid they may just disappear. We must do something to draw them to us; pretend we know something, or that we've got what they want.'

'Anything in particular?'

'Do you think your journal could organise a symposium on the manuscripts; something people will hear about, and read about in the papers?'

'It's happening already,' she said. 'In three weeks there's a big *BAR* Qumran symposium, and all the scholars are invited. What's your plan?'

'To make them believe we've tracked down the last scroll.'

'You'd need at least that to make the great Qumranologists come. Last time, very few turned up.'

'I hope it's not too late . . .'

'Don't think about it now,' she said. 'Try and sleep, and tomorrow we'll draw up a battle-plan.'

'I'll force them to come, if necessary,' I replied.

She seemed surprised.

'With moral force, I mean.'

The next day I rushed frantically around Paris. I went back to Pierre Michel's apartment, looking for clues. I rang Shimon, not to tell him what had happened – that might endanger my father's life – but to see if he knew anything. He appeared not to.

Then I went to the Israeli embassy, without any particular plan; I just wanted to tell them everything. But at the last minute I changed my mind.

The day after that, a small package arrived at my hotel from New York. I opened it with trembling hands, my heart pounding: inside was a worm-eaten wooden cross, with a Hebrew inscription, just four letters which made my flesh creep. INRI: Jesus of Nazareth, the King of the Jews, the inscription on the Cross. There was no doubt it was a message from the kidnappers that they knew what we were looking for and that my father was threatened with crucifixion.

What exactly did they want? Were these fanatics prepared to crucify everybody involved with the Qumran manuscripts? What on earth could be in them, to provoke such hideous murders?

The symposium was now my only hope of finding an answer, and I decided to go to New York with Jane Rogers.

II

We left the following day. Jane had persuaded me that it would be pointless to stay in Paris, since my father was probably not there any longer, and I wouldn't have known what to do in Israel; to tell my mother or the authorities would certainly put his life in danger. Since the package had come from New York, it seemed likely that he had been drugged and taken there; anyway, I would be able to make myself useful with the preparations for the symposium.

When we arrived, I moved into a small hotel near the offices of the *Biblical Archaeological Review*. For three weeks I lived there in torment, not knowing whether my father was alive or dead, feeling half-dead myself. I rang my mother several times, with cheerful messages, saying my father was too busy to talk to her. I would then put down the receiver and burst into tears. *I am weary of my crying: my throat is dried: mine eyes fail while I wait for my God.*

During that time I began to understand that I was not invulnerable. For the first time, my universe was shaken. As one of our masters used to say, 'the world is a narrow bridge and the important thing is not to be afraid.' The narrowness of the bridge had never frightened me when I walked firmly, guided by the Talmud and the Cabal, certain of their value and that of my people, the chosen people, of whom I was one. I was chosen amongst the chosen. Suddenly, now, I could see the abyss; I was only kept from falling by a thread. For the first time I doubted and wavered. *I sink in deep mire, where there is no standing: I am come into deep waters, where the floods overflow me.*

It was the first crack in my armour, and it would never be mended. From the day I first became aware of my fragility, that consciousness never left me. My carefree state turned into one of metaphysical inquiry; I became like the wise men of old who questioned the meaning of life, forever unsatisfied, haunted by death, seeing the world as a house of sorrow.

Sometimes these people can be caught up by life: they fall upon it with voracious and insatiable appetite, trying to escape from their terrible fear by filling the world with distractions created by their anxious minds. But they are never at peace; they always search for new horizons – their souls thirst after God, the God of life. It is not a nostalgic search for the past, for the country where they were born, it is the desire to fill an empty shell, to find something missing but undefined. The others, the carefree people live amongst their fellow human beings as though it is perfectly normal that they should be there, on the planet known as Earth, where the sun rises, dew falls on the earth, dawn, cradle of the day, stretches out langorously each morning and leaves with a hasty yawn, until the unimagined end of time; as though it is quite natural that the world should have no beginning and no end, that the earth, a tiny speck in the vast universe, should continue its ceaseless diurnal course, a never-ending and minute movement contemplating ironically the finite being, the dust of time, the germ within the microcosm. For the carefree human being, nothing could be more natural; he hears everything, but sees nothing. Nothing could surprise him, not the baby born, covered in blood and fluids, the child growing up, learning to talk, the man growing old and dying, amidst blood and fluids. He sees the world as a sphere on which to travel, another artefact; he does not suffer from vertigo, nor does he lean over the bridge to observe the precipice. He continues arrogantly on his way, oblivious to the vanity and futility of human endeavour since all will come to dust. He is one of the Blessed, untouched by the impurity of death, able to grasp and use the concrete reality of life.

Childhood had been a period of unconsciousness, in which events succeeded one another, with no sense of past or future; the army had provided a rigid frame, based on outside events which, like electric stimuli, caused semi-automatic reactions. It had provided a regulated, secure existence – everything becomes so simple when no decisions need to be made, and one can just follow orders. Now, for the first time, I faced the chaos of real life. And it terrified me. No more rules, no law; everything was permitted: kidnapping, theft, crucifixion. My horizons, with their infinite possibilities, narrowed strangely when I thought of death. Who were they? Where were they? Why did they do it? *O my God, I cry in the daytime, but thou hearest not; and in the night season, and am not silent.*

My father had foreseen danger, and had told me his fears; I bitterly regretted having persuaded him to carry on. I feared his suffering almost more than his death. I no longer had the strength to study the Bible. I had no friends and I missed Yehudi: he always had the solution to the most intractable problem I put to him. Perhaps he would have devised a *pilpul* to show where my father was hidden. He would have begun by summing up the known facts:

'First: you and your father are looking for a manuscript which was in the Qumran cave and has been stolen by X. Second: in the course of your search you meet three people, all of whom die violently. Third: your father disappears, kidnapped by unknown people. Therefore,' he would conclude, 'it is obvious that he is in . . . St Catherine's monastery in Ankara.'

'Why?' I would have asked, amazed.

'It's quite simple,' he would have replied, pleased with my reaction, and launched into a Talmudic argument, linking the Bible, the kidnappers, the rabbis, and others with no connection to the affair. This was the way Yehudi's mind worked. But I knew, of course, that there was no question of a *pilpul* here, and that pure reason would not bring us any closer to my father.

I used to go for walks with Yehudi in the white Negev desert, at times when we needed to think. We would set off for several days of total solitude, climbing steep escarpments which looked like papier-maché cut-outs, and gazing at the cinematic scenery for hours before setting off again. I missed my country, now that I was vulnerable and alone in the diaspora. One's country is like a father, solid ground when one is about to collapse and lose one's footing.

Oh that I knew where I might find him! that I might come even to his seat! I would order my cause before him, and fill my mouth with arguments. I would know the words which he would answer me, and understand what he would say unto me.

Can I admit it? Dare I say it? I thought a great deal about Christ at that time, a forbidden thought I could share with no one, not even Yehudi. I dreamt about Him, as one does in the midst of suffering and injustice, and found comfort. One day, in Manhattan, passing a baroque church among the skyscrapers, I decided, on a sudden impulse, to go in. It is, of course, strictly forbidden to us to enter a church, and even more so to do what I then did.

I sat on a bench, facing a statue of Jesus. For the first time I looked at the figure, not as a pagan image, the forbidden representation of an non-existent God, but as a crucified man, a good man. I thought of him not as one thinks of God, but as a character in the Bible, and this consoled me. He at least was there, in flesh and in spirit, and if one could believe in his existence everything else followed miraculously: the world to come, the meaning of life, creation, happiness and the resurrection of the dead.

Yes, my father would return: if not in this world, then in the next. The more painful and undeserved his suffering, the closer he would be to Christ. In that case, why do anything? Perhaps there was no need to search for him or find him, since God would save him. But supposing Christ did not exist, supposing there was no God, or only the hidden God of the Jews, the withdrawn, abstract God who never intervenes, even faced with the greatest atrocities nor even, perhaps, after death? Then everything was permissible. Virtue would never be rewarded, crimes would remain unpunished; man could do anything he wanted, all would be absurd. But in that case, why do anything?

And yet something had to be done. Just because to do nothing would have been a greater absurdity.

To keep my ailing mind busy I helped Jane to prepare for the symposium. She threw herself into it, telephoning all over the world, lunching journalists, writing articles. Her aim was to attract as many people as possible, and she persuaded the *Review* to adopt as its theme 'Did Jesus exist? The extraordinary revelations of the Qumran scrolls.'

The *BAR* intimated, through Jane, that for the first time all the Qumran scrolls would be assembled; and the press took the bait.

And not just the press. Shortly after an article by Jane had appeared in the *Times*, Pierre Michel rang her. He was in New York, and explained that he had had to leave Paris in a hurry to escape his pursuers. He was at last prepared to reveal his scroll to the public, his only chance, he thought, of staying alive. He would, therefore, be at the symposium.

'Let's hope he can help us find out where my father is,' I said to Jane.

'He might, if we can get our hands on the last manuscript. Your idea was brilliant, we're groaning with requests for invitations. We've sold almost as many copies this week as *Vanity Fair*; that must be a record for an archaeological magazine.'

'I don't care about the manuscript if it means I'll never see him again – it's not worth a man's life.'

'Don't give up, Ary. I'm sure we'll find him.'

'If we do, it'll be thanks to you . . . Why are you doing all this for me?'

'I'm doing it for myself as well. I've learned a lot of useful things. I've changed a lot, you know.'

There was a short silence, as she lowered her eyes and hesitated before adding: 'To answer your question . . . Perhaps it's also because I care for you, more than I should.'

She blushed as she said it, and my heart leapt.

I had known girls in the army, but none had really interested me. My friends used to joke about the attraction women felt for me – they used to say that with me around they stood no chance. They would beg me to accompany them on outings, so that they could use my magnetic attraction to their advantage. Men, too, would listen to me, and seek out my company.

With women it was different: they would look at me in a particular sort of way which I found atrociously embarrassing. I could feel them watch me go by, and hear them whisper my name. My friends thought it was something to do with my bewitching stare; they would laugh and say that my eyes were pools of love one could drown in. They were blue, like my mother's, with my father's burning look.

Others thought it was my indifference that attracted women, and it is true that I had other things on my mind and felt quite detached. With Jane it was different. We were comrades in arms, with a common cause and a true fellow-feeling. But I had never thought of her as a woman, or anyway as my woman. At first, when she spoke, I was careful not to look her in the eye, as I had been with women ever since entering the yeshivah. Little by little she had become a *haver*, a fellow-student, with whom I would discuss problems and make plans, look for the best ideas, create scenarios. Her presence inspired creativity; with her by my side I could solve the thorniest of problems. She was a good listener as well as a good speaker, both imaginative and realistic, able to follow unusual lines of thought, but rigorous enough not to take unnecessary risks.

And when my glance met her fierce, dark-brown eyes, I would lower mine, ashamed to be caught looking at a woman. For it was not allowed. Not that love was a bad thing, nor forbidden by my religion – but she was not a Jew. And she was a Christian, the Protestant daughter of a pastor.

Had she been Jewish, or had I not been a Cohen and a Hassid; had I been a goy, Protestant or Catholic; had we both been atheists; had I been agnostic and she Protestant; had I remained like my parents – then, yes, I believe I could have loved her. She was so different from the girls we married: timid and reserved, humble and self-effacing. She was none of those things. Her destiny was not to be a pious housekeeper and mother of children; indeed she was not predestined to be anything. She was independent and active, afraid of nothing, especially not of the truth, which she pursued fiercely, like a knight of old, guiding me when I hesitated, urging me on when I flagged.

We would have long theological discussions, about Jesus, her religion and mine. We respected one another even when our points of view diverged and, as often happened, we failed to understand one another. The more we expounded our ideas, the greater the chasm between Judaism and Christianity seemed to be. Our conversations were based on what we had learned from teachers and books, the accumulated wisdom of centuries of ignorance, error and misunderstandings. We explored these contradictions at length, either to comfort ourselves, or perhaps to get closer to one another. Sometimes, after hours and hours of argument, we would separate, too tired for anger – dialogue, even argument, always unites people.

Once, when I expressed astonishment at her interest in and knowledge of Judaism, she said: 'It's the Shoah. I couldn't understand why this people had been so persecuted; I wanted to know what had so frightened people over the centuries. Then I saw that there was nothing to understand about this hatred, but that, on the contrary, knowledge of Judaism and Jews was a sacred duty for a Christian.'

Sometimes there were long silences, never uncomfortable, which reflected our spiritual communion as it became ever deeper, and which I soon identified as being the consciousness of mystery. It was like the silence of the desert, in which all extraneous elements, all futile thoughts, fall away, leaving the central core of truth. I felt for the first time that silence might be preferable to words; if by 'silence' one meant intuition. But why, then, have language and objects at all? Why all these writings and words, laws and commandments? What was their power based on? Were the words creators, or had they themselves been made and adapted?

'Made by God,' she said. 'He made language, and the mind, and the link between words and things. And vision, and all that is. You and me.'

Certainly if He did exist – and I knew He did – He was amongst us.

I felt infinitely close to Him, through her, even though her God had a name and mine was abstract. If concepts are unworkable without intuition, I needed her help, her faith, to bring me closer to the God of truth.

She wasn't vain; she wore no make-up on her pale face, and her long blonde hair fell straight to her shoulders. She dressed modestly, in simple loose clothes, sometimes trousers or jeans. Or perhaps I just saw her like that, as a sort of angel, with no feminine graces, in order to persuade myself that she was not one of the Jewish Janes promised me by the rabbi.

After Jane made her feelings known to me, I suffered a crisis. As though to protect myself, to erect barriers between us, I started visiting the Hassidic ghetto; her declaration of love drove me back there with some kind of automatic survival instinct. I began frequenting the small synagogue in Williamsburg that we went to, and soon got to know all the regular worshippers.

And so I came to meet the rabbi of this congregation again. I told him of my father's kidnapping and my despair. I did not tell him about Almond and Millet, or the crucifixions.

'I warned you of the danger,' he said. 'But you musn't lose hope: you must wait, and practise the devekut.'

'The devekut? Why?'

'To find out who was following you.'

I didn't understand. Had he foreseen the danger after seeing someone following us? Who was it? And why the devekut? However, I was a Hassid and accustomed to blind obedience to the words of the rabbi, and so I tried to achieve the devekut, as he had ordered.

I wish I could describe this state of ecstasy in words, but I fear it may be impossible. At first we simply drank wine to make ourselves happy; then we began to sing. We were accompanied by a musician with a powerful synthesiser, which produced the sounds of drum, clarinet and guitar to accompany our hypnotic chant.

Before my teshuvah I had experienced rock music, with its exciting, limb-twitching rhythms; I had gone to raves in Tel Aviv discos, where huge crowds of young people invoked the end of time with their night-long rhythmic movement. In a common trance, but with no communion between them, these young automatons jogged their heads and shoulders, without conviction, to a brutish rhythm occasionally improved by the faint faraway hint of a musical phrase.

Hassidic songs were different: they brought joy to the heart. And I know no other music which brings so much happiness and cures so many sad hearts. It begins cautiously, *Oy va voy*, building up speed, *Machiah, Machiah*, to the final collective climax, *I believe, yes I believe with all my faith in the coming of the Messiah*. The happy band galvanises and inspires the faithful to the final battle, to receive at last in their soul its mighty victor.

They gave us a sweet and unfamiliar drink. Because of the wine and the dancing, we drank too much of it, and soon I was overcome by a strange torpor, and felt myself gently losing control, rocked by the steady rhythm of the music. Part of me tried to resist, while another, deeper, impulse allowed and then urged me to let myself go. I closed my eyes, concentrated, and breathed deeply from the pit of my stomach. I lay on the ground, with heavy limbs and a thick head, and gradually found myself flying towards other horizons.

Here and nowhere, now and forever. For twenty minutes my consciousness expanded; burning lava seemed to flow from my soul, bringing me to the state of pure memory that one sometimes experiences, in minute doses, through a smell, sound or colour, a perfect, intact memory. The devekut brought on this miracle a hundredfold: piercing souvenirs flew through my mind. I was drunk with their speed, dazzled by light, caught in a whirl of extraordinary colours, celestial sounds and sublime flavours. I seemed to be dancing ever faster and higher, spinning towards the cosmos, while an invisible force held me on earth. Caught between the two I would reach upwards and then collapse back.

At one moment, reaching upwards, I experienced some extraordinary intuitions. Obscure passages in the Talmud, over which I had struggled for hours, suddenly became crystal clear. Then another image appeared in my mind: I saw the Hassidic court I had attended with my father. I relived the whole scene; every word and gesture, right up to the moment when we left the rabbi's house and heard the music behind us.

Then I saw. I had turned round to watch, almost regretfully, as the house the frenetic music came from disappeared. I remembered the moment clearly: one second a figure appeared from the house, the next, its slender silhouette came closer to us. I tried to concentrate, to see the face, but my state of ecstasy seemed to throw me in other directions.

I made a desperate effort. Suddenly I shuddered violently; for several minutes, which seemed like hours, I entered a trance-like state, at the height of which I saw the face.

I sobbed with relief, and then blind anger. It was Jane.

How long wilt thou forget me, O Lord? for ever? how long wilt thou hide thy face from me? How long shall I take counsel in my soul, having sorrow in my heart daily? how long shall mine enemy be exalted over me?

Terrible days followed. I suspected the worst of Jane, too much to tell her of my discovery and ask for an explanation. Suppose she was involved with the kidnapping? Or had something to do with the crucifixions? Was she really Protestant, or Catholic, a member of the Congregation for the Doctrine of the Faith? There was no doubt that she had been following us since New York, and perhaps even earlier, and she had held me back when I wanted to pursue my father's kidnappers. Perhaps she knew where he was and was simply keeping me busy to prevent me from looking for him. If so, she was dangerous: I might suffer the same fate as my father, or worse.

All the same, I found it hard to believe in her treachery. I could not find any trace of duplicity or evil in her face, try as I might. All I saw was an honest and loyal woman who appeared to love me – I couldn't imagine cruelty or evil behind those calm features.

Or was it all a game? Examining her further, I saw her in a different light. Sometimes her eyes would wander, or light up with strange ferocity. Once I met her by chance in the street: she was brightly made up, and her hair was curled around cheeks that were pinker than usual; she wore a short skirt and high-heeled shoes. I should never have stared at her, but I had to be sure it really was her. Where was she going, dressed like that? Who was she? Was she a virgin or a whore?

Why had she followed us? What was this trap we had fallen into? When we had surprised her in Pierre Michel's flat, apparently there on her own account, was that premeditated? If so, what was her motive?

At times I thought I hated her. She was betraying me; perhaps she only pretended to love me. Then, having rejected her love, I began to value it as one can only value something unattainable, or lost for ever. For the first time I began to examine my own feelings for her. Ever since her declaration, I had maintained the silence imposed by our laws on the subject, refusing to examine the nature of our relationship, partly because of the serious matters in hand, partly for fear of discovering that I had been caught in the feminine trap. And of all women . . . A goya, my rabbi would say, a shiksa.

Had I been caught? Was I trapped? Was this love? I asked myself furiously, at the same time suspecting her of having kidnapped my father. But then, love is like war. I was fighting on two fronts, one against an invisible enemy, and for a cause which was beyond me, the other against my undefined feeling for Jane, which threatened to overwhelm me; it was a war against myself, trench warfare, which had me, at times, huddled in bed, the telephone within reach, forcing myself not to ring her and confess defeat at the hands of the beast – a beast which would not relinquish its prey, surviving on the hopes it maintained.

I would try, often with little success, to avoid the longing which could overwhelm me at any moment: the sight of an object would remind me of her, or the memory of something she had said would flood back with the odd phrase or thought. It was worse, of course, when she was actually there. Then I would be tortured by the thought of leaving her, or by the knowledge that she was not there just for me, that her attention might stray, perhaps in the direction of Machiavellian plans for my destruction. Missing her when she wasn't there was an almost unbearable torment, but at least I could imagine her, dream of her as I wished her to be, and be alone with her in my thoughts. I would relive moments we had spent together, words and gestures that had delighted me; the same images would recur time and again, throwing me into the same confusion. I would try to drive out these images, and discover others from the depths of my memory; then disagreeable ones would surface, moments which revealed that she was not all she seemed, but another, malign Jane, pursuing me with evil intent. I took pleasure in weighing up the pain and disgust this induced in me, and I would rehearse over and over again, like an actor on an empty stage, particular moments that had caused me fear or pain.

But longing for her when she was actually there was worst of all, because there was no comfort in the imagination, and the pain could not trigger any subtle pleasures of the memory; on the contrary, it simply withered the spirit. With her before me, everything seemed incongruous, empty and absurd: our meeting, my presence, my longing. I felt myself turning into a ridiculous inquisitor, a shameful figure doomed to failure. I would ask myself what was the use of continuing – I had lost this war, and in the most humiliating fashion. She had taken my father; let her have me now.

But I still had my pride, and it was my strongest weapon. When I felt myself weaken it would restrain me, making any possible gesture or word seem ridiculous. But she had surrendered her pride, I would argue, when she declared her love. Yes, implacable pride would reply to love, but that was part of her plot; if I had declared myself, I would have been lost. And so pride saved me, always calculating and manipulating, a true rebel, inspiring the finest rebellion of all, against beauty, with only revenge to follow. Pride was my friend, my only ally. Was I disobeying my laws by embracing pride? But the law itself forbade the union. I no longer wanted Jane; I wanted to slay her with my pride, to love myself more than I loved her.

And I find more bitter than this the woman, whose heart is snares and nets, and her hands as bands: whoso pleaseth God shall escape from her; but the sinner shall be taken by her.

'Well, do you love me?' she eventually asked outright.

It was dark and wet, and we had been walking for quite a while side by side in Central Park. I didn't quite know what to do: I wanted, without betraying myself, to get her to reveal the dangerous game she was playing.

'I don't know; I'm too worried about my father to think about anything else. And I'm afraid.'

'Of it being forbidden by your laws?'

'It's not just that.'

'But it's a law you've chosen of your own free will, you and no one else. And you've picked the most demanding law of all, haven't you?'

'Yes, indeed.'

'But your mother, for instance, doesn't think like you, does she?'

She looked me straight in the eye. I tried hard to hold her gaze – at that moment, without knowing why, I thought she was sincere.

'No,' I admitted. 'She came from the USSR, and broke away from her idea of what orthodox Judaism was. She's an atheist, both scarred and influenced by communism.'

'It doesn't matter. There are millions of people like her, who haven't got the same history. Most Jews are like her, certainly all the ones I've known until now.'

'Of course, there's no reason why you should ever have met somebody like me. People like me don't normally mix with people like you.'

'They're normal people, Ary. You bury yourself away because you're afraid of the outside world – you want to remain anchored in your certainties.'

'I agree, I'm different. I was not before, according to your criteria.'

'Does your law forbid us to love one another, then? Mine is prepared to welcome you. Why is the God of Israel such a jealous God? Your religion has always welcomed strangers, has never been involved with inquisitions, witch-hunts, deportations or extermination camps; why is it so intolerant towards us? Why don't you want me?'

'Mixed marriages are forbidden.'

'Are you one of those people who think mixed marriages will achieve what Hitler failed to do?'

'I think they're a mortal threat to our people, yes.'

'But what is a mixed marriage? All marriages are alliances, unions of two different people, always some sort of mixture.'

'I want you to remain as you are. I wouldn't love you if you changed . . .' I stopped, biting my tongue. I had said too much. Had I been trapped once again?

Her face lit up. 'So you *do* love me? If I became like you . . . Why can't you be like your mother? It would all be so simple. I believe that if you loved me enough – that is, if you were able to get out of yourself – there's nothing I couldn't do for you. But that's not really the problem, is it? The truth is that you have a vocation. You're a monk Ary, a Jewish monk.'

III

It was true; I had become a sort of monk. It was like being in love: I had become close to God in a completely new way. I imagined Him clothed in myrrh, aloe and cinnamon, more desirable than spun gold, sweeter than new honey. He would help me at the break of day, and anoint me with soothing balm when I woke afraid in the night, my heart pounding in my breast. Then I would call His name, and I knew that He would save me from danger, and punish those who spied on me.

During such nights I would beg for the wings of a dove, to fly to the desert for a night of peace, in a safe haven far from this tempest. Far, far away from this city of violence and discord, of night prowlers, of streets riddled with brutality and crime.

A man is persecuting me;
All day he fights and oppresses me.
Spies harass me every day,
But up there a great army fights for me.
When I am afraid I count upon You,
On God, in whom I trust, for what could a mortal do for me?
All day they have made me suffer,
They think only of harming me.
Secretly they spy
And watch my movements
To threaten my life.

My soul thirsted after him in my agony: I was parched in the desert, and He was a perennial spring, a sanctuary of strength and glory; the oil and fat I needed in my starvation. *When on my bed I think of You, I spend hours in prayer.* I clung to him with all my strength, to resist the fetters of the woman. I could not allow myself to be joined to this fleshly creature, who might belong to the Devil, who had followed me, who had perhaps killed, cut up, crucified . . . I thought of my father and shuddered.

*

147

One morning I waited until she left her house and followed her. She went to the *BAR*, spent two hours there, then came out and caught a taxi. I took another and we followed for about ten minutes before she got out and went into a café, where she appeared to be waiting for someone. I watched through the window and saw man come and sit opposite her, with his back to me. He seemed old, with white hair, and his solid shape was vaguely familiar.

They seemed to know each other well, and talked animatedly for over an hour. Finally he handed her an envelope, which she opened: I saw that it contained bank notes. Then the man got up, took his coat and left, saluting her briefly. He turned, and I could at last see his face. It was Paul Henderson.

I went back to the hotel, shattered. I knew now that she was a spy. She was strong and beautiful, bad and cruel, wicked and cunning, like Delilah. I had been fooled, made ridiculous, poisoned. Who was she? What did she want? Who had sent her? Was it Henderson and the Vatican, or was she manipulating them too?

She was an informer in the enemy's camp, and had brought the enemy into her own camp, the better to watch him. My father was probably on the other side of the world, and I was here, doing nothing, being made a fool of. If anything had happened to him . . . Like Samson, I would push the grindstone in prison. The Devil was present in this woman, and, through her, infiltrating himself amongst men. Unless it was the other way around – that she was manipulating the Devil. Yael, Judith, Delilah, Jane, with her soft blonde hair on her round shoulders; my head was spinning. White hands with sharp fingers, rapiers; the delicious horror of feeling them around my neck, dug into my bleeding heart. Please, one last effort.

I could not sleep that night. Looking for something to read I found one of the Qumran writings, the Rule of the Community. I leafed through it distractedly, and found a passage entitled 'On Reprimand'.

They shall rebuke one another in truth, and humility, and charity. Let no man address his companion with anger, or ill-temper or obduracy, or with envy prompted by the spirit of wickedness. Let him not hate him [because of his uncircumcised] heart, but let him rebuke him on the very same day lest we incur guilt because of him.

Then I decided to make a clean breast of it, whatever the result. I was suffering torments. And if she had played any part in the murders or the kidnapping, at least I might be able to find my father's tracks again; I was prepared to risk my life for that. I made an appointment with Jane in a café, to demand an explanation.

'I know everything,' I said. 'Enough play-acting – you've lied from the start. I don't know what it is you do for the *BAR*, but I know it's only a front. I don't know who you're acting for, but I do know that we didn't meet in Paris by chance. You'd been following us since New York.'

Her eyes widened; she certainly wondered how I knew. She hesitated, and then said:

'It's true I followed you from New York. I took the same plane. But, Ary, you're wrong about one thing. We did only meet by chance – I was following Pierre Michel too, and I never thought you would be on his track so quickly.'

'How long have you been following us? Who are you working for? Where's my father?'

'Ever since you went to see Paul Henderson. I'm his student. He supervised my thesis. He asked me to follow you.'

'Why?'

'I was to find out where you were going, and tell him everything you discovered. He said you were dangerous; that you were planning to undermine the foundations of Christianity, and must be stopped.'

'By any means?' I said.

'No, of course not. I swear I don't know who kidnapped your father. I was as surprised as you when those men broke in.'

'But if Henderson had us followed, he could as easily have arranged the kidnapping.'

'I wondered about that too, and I asked him. He denies it. You must believe me, it's not him. He's not a wicked man, he's just afraid for the sake of his faith.'

'How can I believe you, after all these lies? Why didn't you tell me, after . . .'

'I didn't want to lose your trust.' Her voice had changed. 'Given your intransigence, I was frightened of losing you. I'm doing all I can to make amends. The symposium will take place, and I'll do everything in my power to help find the killer, and your father. You must believe me, Ary . . .'

She seemed sincere. She had admitted everything at once, as though it were a relief to tell the truth at last . . . But she had lied. She was a dangerous woman, prepared to do anything, follow men in the street and on planes, break into flats.

'You took money,' I said. 'You sold me. You sold *yourself.*' But even as my anger grew, I realised that it was more disappointment than real rage.

Her eyes were filled with tears, and her face tense with shame and misery. 'How could I ever hurt you?'

Do we not have the same father?

Jane then told me at length about her past as a theological researcher, and her relationship with Paul Henderson. At first she had been impressed by his scholarship and his openness towards other religions, Judaism in particular. But she had come to realise that, behind this apparent broadmindedness, lurked an intransigence that came close to fanaticism. She owed him a lot for helping her career, and he had promised her that she would succeed him when he retired. He appreciated her discretion, and her knowledge of ancient languages had been useful to him in his research. When he offered her this task, it would have been difficult for her to refuse. However, she now bitterly regretted what she had done, and begged my forgiveness.

We were never closer than during those days before the symposium opened. Our discussions began again, keeping us up for long hours after our day's work. I would tell her about Hassidism and the Caballa, unveiling the mysteries of those letters of the alphabet known only to the wise men who plumbed the ultimate depths of knowledge. I taught her the א *aleph*, symbol of the universe, whose central bar represents the link between the upper hook, the higher universe, and the lower, the world beneath. And the ב *beth*, representing creation, with its image of the home, welcoming, sheltering and protecting; ג *guimel*, around which throngs of angels hover, protecting it with their opalescent wings; ו *vav*, proud and straight, like the just man; י *yod*, the sacred point; ז *zain*, representing freedom, whose object is to open what is closed, be it the breast of the sterile woman, the tomb of the buried man, the gate of Hell. ה *Heh*, the holy letter, twice present in His name, the word of words, the four consonants incarnating the unpronounceable, our God, YHWH.

I taught her to read the signs on the face, which change according to the person's condition. For the twenty-two letters of the alphabet are imprinted on each soul, and this is reflected through the body. If the man is good, the letters are arranged regularly; if not they become inverted. I showed her the man who walked in the paths of righteousness, easily recognisable to a cabalist by the horizontal vein on his temple, with two stripes crossed by a vertical one, forming the mystical letters ו and ת. A man, on the other hand, who has lost his way, in whom impurity has replaced virtue, looks different. He has three red spots on both cheeks with small red veins below, inverting the ר and ת, as it is written, *the shame of their face bears witness against them.*

I spoke of the prodigal son, who after following the wrong path, returns to his master, and feels shame at being looked at, because he thinks the whole world knows of his past. His face is alternately yellow and pale, with three veins: one comes from the right temple down to the cheek; another above the nose mingles with two marks on the left-hand side, and a third joins them. All this disappears when the man is completely free of vice and used to a virtuous life; the letter ז then appears on his forehead. And the man who returns to earth to atone for faults committed in a previous life has a vertical wrinkle on the right cheek, by his mouth, and two identically placed deeper ones on the left. This man's eyes never shine, even when he is happy.

'And what type am I?' she asked.

There were a few very fine lines on her face. I knew them by heart. They formed several delightful letters: *aleph, heh, beth and heh* הבהא

I saw her every day, and every night I prayed fervently, for prayer is the strongest weapon against evil. I tried to convert the transports of joy that uplifted me when I thought of Jane into divine passion, to replace earthly love with holy ardour. I prayed to God to give me the strength to resist temptation, but I knew that He had given us free will to fight evil alone.

It was a terrible struggle. I longed to be a pure soul alongside God, but my heart was tainted with earthly desires. I wanted to fight the good fight, but my tremulous spirit burned with anxiety. I wanted to be as dry as a block of wood, but I was damp with desire. I prayed and even sometimes banged my head against the wall.

But despite all my efforts, and against my will, I was tempted. The Hassidim say that this too must be used to serve God, and sin is a necessary condition in which to totally serve Him: the Holy Spirit hovers over sin, and dwells within it. I thought I might achieve salvation by going beyond forgiveness, which seemed unachievable, and reconciling higher and lower forms of truth. In my dreams I opened the Holy of Holies, the sacred centre of the Temple, where I found cherubim tenderly embracing. Was it possible that bodily powers could have some godly force? No. I longed to be pure, and believed myself to be strong.

Never before had I longed so impatiently for the tikkun, the messianic end of the world. It could be my only salvation; only some cosmic event could counteract the power of my desire. But I also knew that, in order to achieve the final salvation, each person had to become his own Messiah and enter into a personal relationship with God, through the devekut. At times – dare I admit it? Can I say it? – its effects did not counteract the strength of the temptation. Was this a sign of the presence of God? Even when I was about to betray him and disobey his commandments, I could feel his presence all around me. *There is no place without him.* I was closer to God than I had ever been, and yet I was tempted. Like Job, I had lost everything: my rabbi, my land, my father; like Job, my human frailty had been ensnared by the female form. So deliciously female, with her plum-coloured lips, her tight trousers, her skirts slit at the back, her high heels!

As I prayed so fervently, I would see her name in the words I read. The consonants would be swelled by vowels, inflaming my heart: my books would start a sort of diabolical dance, enticing me, drawing me towards them with sultry looks, voluptuously awaiting the movement of my lips. They slid on my tongue: it was no longer Kaddish, it was Kaddisha, the prostitute, not the saint. Sacred and profane came closer to one another. God can only be defied from the very heart of evil, forced to show himself.

It would be convenient to say simply that the thoughts flooding my mind had been put there by the Devil, but I could not help feeling that they were very much my own, unthinkable as they were. Do I dare admit to them? Must I write them, set them free, or hush them up for ever, bury them deep in my heart, alongside all the other crimes that will be weighed in the balance at the final judgement? I want to bear witness, so that future generations will know what it was I wanted, what I lived through, so that my actions, like evil itself, will resound throughout the universe. *We have sinned before you. We beg your forgiveness.*

To commit the sin. Let her mouth kiss mine, her breath mingle with mine; that is what the words said to me. Kiddushin, sanctity, but also marriage, one of the peaks of human existence, closest to the presence of God. Among the Hassidim, married couples slept in separate beds and had intercourse in darkened rooms, face to face, the man on top of the woman. My rabbi used to say that it was best to remain as much clothed as possible, or use a sheet with a hole in it. Polish Hassidic women had short hair, Hungarians and Galicians shaved heads.

But why had God given us flesh? Why did my skin burn when I was near her? Why did my flesh cry out when my eyes, reddened by the shame of lust, glimpsed her immaculate skin? Why have bones and nerves, if they were not also in the image of God, if only the soul was essential to man? Why this cursed terrestrial garment, if it was only to be shed once night had fallen? Even if the body is a mere accessory, surely its form conceals some other concept? My forehead, hands, feet, all bore the stigmata of desire.

My furtive glances were drawn irresistibly to her rosy cheeks, her almond eyes, the curve of her breast and stomach beneath her dress – I would almost faint with pleasure. A pearl or flower earring, a dewy wrist, a sunkissed ankle would thrill my soul. It was as though I was seeing for the first time, as though until now I had been blind. I had never looked at women before; now my gaze would linger, despite myself, on forbidden areas no Hassid had ever ventured into. I did not possess them, but I knew them.

Surely the whole body cannot be sinful, if the senses are an integral part of it? Why did I feel so ashamed, no longer worthy of our masters' teachings, or of the Torah itself? In fury I buried my books in a book cemetery, as is the custom; it is forbidden to throw them away. The next day I dug them up, and begged forgiveness.

Tortured by my father's disappearance, I desired her. A Hassid with streimel and locks, I desired her. Before praying, after studying, I desired her. I desired her when eating or sleeping, when going in or out. Our hearts were scarred by the deaths all around us, and yet I desired her. If it had been the end of the world, I would still have desired her. *Turn away thine eyes from me, for they have overcome me.*

She was my soulmate, and drew me to her at will. The love she gave me, her soft words and gestures, were as sweet as honey. Her beauty filled me with eternal joy; how I pined for her grace and charm. I wanted her to open to me her pavilion of peace, for the world to be illuminated by her glory; for my happiness to be within her.

I devoured every glimpse of her. Her glowing face was scattered with very pale freckles; her lips seemed like strawberries and raspberries in the midst of the desert; her ivory neck was as pale as the Negev. Her skin was like a white stone in the salt sea, close-grained, milky and smooth; it was a silky casing, as supple and white as paper, the result of centuries of progress, of generations of beauties. Ink would flow over such skin, never sinking in, drying on the surface after sliding like a dancer over it.

One could not make holes in such a surface; only lightly-drawn figures. All the letters of the alphabet appeared there, forming incantatory words; twenty-two subtly-drawn, curved lines, from which I, the meticulous scribe, would form words, guided by divine inspiration, following the silent thread of my imagination. I prepared, smoothed, scored the satin-smooth skin with a thousand words from the most ancient of traditions, each one divinely inspired, consonants swelled by vowels, stretching on towards infinity. Sifted memories, epiphanies, respectful profanity, an everlasting interpretation of this most precious of parchments, my heart would beat, dead, then brought to life by this careful exegesis. I was writing a whole new history, built of subtle pilpuls, delayed desire, melodious sounds, and faith, hope and endless waiting. How I longed for the end! It would be the end of time, Parousia, the coming of the new world, the liberating tikkun, so long awaited down the millennia.

Sometimes I would dream when wide awake: her mouth would be the most delicious of nectars, her whole being a refined perfume. She was my dove in the hollow of a rock. I could see her face, hear her voice; and the voice was melodious, and the face beautiful, her eyes like birds, her lips a scarlet ribbon.

Here and nowhere, now and forever. I was seized and lacerated by flashing bursts of energy, both intoxicating and dazzling. I felt bright colours, saw celestial music and tasted supreme flavours. I whirled ever faster, ever higher, never stopping. An invincible force was propelling me towards the cosmos, whilst another held me in the depths of the earth.

The thought of my father kept me sane. Some days I would rush around the places where I might meet Israelis and archaeologists; sometimes I thought I saw him, and my heart would leap. Sleepless, nightmare-filled nights left me haggard and bleary-eyed during the day. Often I wondered if I had done the right thing, or if I should have pursued those men who had taken him before my very eyes, and I would be seized by remorse. What was I doing here, if he was still in France? But what could I do in France, if they had brought him here?

One night, we were talking in the hall of my hotel, and I broke down. She accompanied me to my room, where I lay in despair for an hour on my crossed arms. Jane sat patiently beside me. When she leaned over to see if I had recovered, her long hair brushed my face. Her scent of camphor acted on my inert body like a healing balm, and I sat up. She gazed at me with her dark eyes and then left, leaving a faint trace of her perfume.

Fifth Scroll

THE SCROLL OF THE DISPUTE

Progress and eternal triumph of light

[The sons of righteousness] shall shine over all the ends of the earth; they shall go on shining until all the seasons of darkness are consumed and, at the season appointed by God, His exalted greatness shall shine eternally to the peace, blessing, glory, joy, and long life of all the sons of light.

On the day when the Kittim fall, there shall be battle and terrible carnage before the God of Israel, for that shall be the day appointed from ancient times for the battle of destruction of the sons of darkness. At that time, the assembly of gods and the hosts of men shall battle, causing great carnage. On the day of calamity, the sons of light shall battle with the company of darkness amid the shouts of a mighty multitude and the clamour of gods and men to (make manifest) the might of God. And it shall be a time of [great] tribulation for the people which God shall redeem; of all its afflictions none shall be as this, from its sudden beginning until its end in eternal redemption. On the day of their battle against the Kittim [they shall set out for] carnage. In three lots shall the sons of light brace themselves in battle to strike down iniquity, and in three lots shall Satan's host gird itself to thrust back the company [of God. And when the hearts of the detach]ments of foot-soldiers faint, then shall the might of God fortify [the hearts of the sons of light]. And with the seventh lot, the mighty hand of God shall bring down [the army of Satan, and all] the angels of his kingdom, and all the members [of his company in everlasting destruction] . . .

Qumran scrolls, *The War Rule*.

I

After they had sinned, the man and the woman heard the voice of God resounding in the garden at the break of day. Then they hid; and God called the man, who replied that he was hiding because he was naked. And God asked him how he knew he was naked: had he learnt it from the tree from which he was forbidden to eat? The man confessed that he had eaten the forbidden fruit, but that it had been the fault of the woman whom God had placed near him. And the woman said that it was the serpent who had tempted her. And so they had to explain themselves before God, just as one day everybody has to pay his dues, confess his sins and pay for his crimes. But why is it that everyone, out of cowardice or wickedness, casts the blame onto others and, incapable of repentance, tries to unload the sins he has committed?

The long-awaited day of confrontation arrived at last. The *BAR* had hired a big lecture hall panelled like a courtroom for the symposium. We were amongst the first there: while Jane busied herself, I watched people arriving, singly or in small groups. There were journalists, teachers, researchers, churchmen and rabbis from many countries; all pressed forward, looking anxious and curious. Some wore set smiles – atheists, or those who thought that the truth was at last going to emerge, that a final verdict would be announced. Others looked tormented.

Several television companies were broadcasting the event live. I had no idea how many people would see and hear what was about to happen, but I prayed that amongst them, either in the hall or watching a screen, there would be someone who could help me find traces of my father.

After the kidnapping in Pierre Michel's apartment, my father was taken about two hours' drive from Paris, his eyes bandaged and his hands tied. Nobody said a word in the car.

Eventually they reached a house in the country, and he was locked in a room where he was able to move about, but which he could not escape. The kidnappers left him there for several days, which seemed like an eternity. When they brought his food he questioned them in Hebrew, Arabic, all the languages he knew, but they never said a word. He had no idea why they were holding him, nor what they could possibly want; he wondered if they had really intended to take Pierre Michel and got the wrong man. He remembered the crucifixions, and was desperately worried about me. Locked up, with nobody to talk to and nothing to do, he became profoundly depressed. His limbs were numb for lack of exercise, and his head hurt from constantly lying down.

Then one day they began questioning him, in English. They wanted to know about the manuscripts; who had them and who was looking for them. He told them all he knew, which was not very much.

Then the men took him from the house to a small plane, in which they travelled for about six hours. They arrived in the middle of the desert, the monotonous rocky landscape my father knew so well. The sun was setting, and he could see, against the purple hills, a road crowded with people and animals returning home at the end of the day. He was in the Mesopotamian plain.

The crowd was enormous; everybody had come. The many scholars were sitting, with paper and pencil, waiting to take notes. Journalists talked animatedly amongst themselves: some were already taking photos, others reading the papers. One headline read: *Did Jesus exist? Revelations about the greatest archaeological discovery of all time*. The article explained the importance of the Qumran discoveries, and described the mysteries surrounding them.

Little by little, small discussion groups were formed. Rabbis and priests gradually drew together, as though feeling that the time of confrontation was approaching, perhaps the ultimate confrontation. They knew that after this meeting any final doubts would be gone, and there would be no further chance of cheating: bad faith would have to give way to either pure faith or apostasy. The truth would emerge, and with it would collapse centuries of ideology and obscurantism, ignorance and make-believe.

Occasionally the most courteous exchanges and the most ecumenical intentions would give way to sharp altercations. Here and there one could hear snatches of conversation: 'Jesus was not an Essene,' or 'We're sure of the existence of John the Baptist, but Jesus as a historical figure, no.' Words like 'blasphemy', 'lies', and 'Hell' flew like arrows around the room. Finally the hall was full, and the talk merged into a great murmur of sound.

Jane came back, accompanied by a small, round, agitated man – Pierre Michel, the man we had tried so hard to find! The three of us sat down in the front row, and he began to re-read feverishly the paper he had prepared for his talk, looking nervously around. This man belongs to the fourth category, I thought; he has come back to earth to atone for a sin committed in a previous life. He had a vertical scar on his right cheek, and his face was deeply wrinkled and tired. His eyes were the most striking thing about him: they were completely blank, devoid of expression, like the glass eyes of a doll or a stuffed animal.

'Who are you frightened of?' I whispered to him.

He looked up, surprised. 'The Inquisitors,' he replied. 'The people from the Congregation. I left them and they haven't forgiven me. If you want my opinion, they're responsible for all these deaths. They're taking revenge for what was done to Jesus, with this lunatic ritual. Now I'm on their list because I know too much, and because I betrayed them, by letting out a bit of what I knew at the 1987 conference. It was after that the threats began, and I was forced to disappear with the scrolls. I feared for my life then, and I haven't had a good night's sleep since. I live in terror – I tell you, I'm their next victim.'

The first speakers appeared on the platform; historians, philosophers and philologists. Jane pointed out several well-known scholars in the Qumran field: Michelle Bronfield, from Sydney University, a supporter of the thesis that John the Baptist was the Master of Justice, and Jesus the Wicked Priest; Peter Frost, one of the first to recognise the importance of Hosea's scrolls in 1948; and Emery Scott, a Baptist academic, who was spending his retirement drawing up the definitive bibliography of every book, article or other publication concerning the scrolls.

A medium-height, well-built man came to sit down beside us; his face was framed by large black whiskers, rather like side-locks. Jane introduced me to her employer, Bartholomew Donnars, editor-in-chief of the *BAR*. He was in a state of high excitement.

'Delighted to meet you. I've heard a lot about you from Jane. I'm so pleased that you're here on this great day! I've been waiting so long for it to happen. All this time I've been mocked for demanding a target date for these publications. As for the Department of Antiquities in Jerusalem, who are still doing nothing about the missing scroll . . . I can't understand it. Surely it's time the manuscripts were seen by the whole world. I even confronted Henderson directly at the Princeton forum last November, asked for some access, even just photos of the scroll. Naturally he refused, and what's more he tried to turn his colleagues against me. He announced that henceforth he would avoid mentioning the unpublished manuscripts, since it would be like reading a menu without being able to eat the food. And he attacked me in the media, too. On *Good Morning America* he said: "It seems we have a horde of flies, whose only occupation is to buzz around our heads." Do you want to see what my revenge is going to be?'

He pulled a dummy magazine-cover out of his briefcase. 'Here's the next cover of the *BAR*,' he said.

It was a close-up, highly unflattering, photo of an unshaven, glowering Paul Henderson with greasy hair and mouth twisted in a rictus grin. Above, framed by a television screen, his words about flies were printed in heavy type; a whole constellation of well-known academics were drawn buzzing around Henderson and his international team. I couldn't help smiling, and observing that he certainly had a lot of enemies.

The conference chairman, Professor Daniel Smith, opened the session with a short speech about plagiarism between scholars since the discovery of the scrolls; he gave several examples – one where a passage from one book reproduced a page from another almost word for word, including translation errors – and finished with a severe condemnation of such practices. Then a professor from the New York Centre for Ancient Manuscripts spoke, protesting against what he described as the 'possessiveness' of academics, who worked for years without revealing the smallest result of their toils.

'But it's long-term work, and we have so many other day-to-day tasks that it's impossible to hurry,' objected one of the scholars on the stage.

'No one's fooled by that excuse,' he retorted. 'It's intellectual censorship, really. Everybody's either afraid of censorship, or practising it themselves. I think these scrolls are of revolutionary importance, and I'd like to have access to them in order to verify my hypothesis.'

The professor explained that the Dead Sea Scrolls offered unhoped-for proof of fraudulent alterations to holy texts over the centuries since, unlike the latter, they were not affected by any. His hypothesis was that Christianity and Judaism were merely two degraded ideologies, late distorted echoes of an earlier messianic religion. He believed that Judaism had become Messianism via Essenism, which had engendered the Christian religion. Most of the academics present disagreed, and a debate began about the extent of the church's censorship and alteration of sacred texts over the centuries.

At last it was Paul Henderson's turn to speak. Pierre Michel was more and more nervous, shifting around on his seat. He leaned towards us.

'That's the man who wants to kill me. He's been looking for me ever since I left the monastery. Henderson is a name he took when he emigrated to the United States; his real name is Misickzy. When we first worked on together in Jerusalem, he used to let us all see the manuscript, and Lirnov began to decipher it. But he couldn't bear what he found, and killed himself, after giving the scroll to Millet. Then *he* began to study it, and when he realised what it contained he told Henderson, who decided to make it disappear. I remember the day Matti came in to decipher his manuscript, and couldn't find it – we were all laughing up our sleeves, we knew perfectly well who had it. That was when Henderson gave it to me to study secretly. When I began to reveal its contents, he asked for it back, and when I refused, he threatened me and sent men after me to take it. I tell you, this man is capable of anything, he might even . . .'

At that moment Henderson saw Michel. He looked surprised, stared at him for a second, and then began his speech.

'The Dead Sea scrolls contain no new revelations about Jesus,' he said.

A great murmur rippled through the hall.

The roar of an engine sent a wave of sound through the silence of the desert. A car picked them up and took them to a fortified village, inhabited by Samaritans, where they went into a house overlooking the Arab town of Nablus, the Biblical Sichem.

My father knew all about the Samaritans, who recognised only the Pentateuch and the book of Josiah as holy texts, and rejected all other

Biblical writing; believed that the true Temple, the house of God, was at the top of their mountain, and that the idolatrous Solomon had built a false one in Jerusalem. Like the Essenes, they were scribes, and copied out the Pentateuch, working for five or six hours a day on the calligraphy of a twenty-five-metre scroll, finishing one every seven months. They were also soothsayers and astrologists, a tradition inherited from a sect that Moses had brought back with his people from the Pharaoh's court, whose formulae were contained in a book dating from the time of Aaron.

After a few days of respite in this place, the Samaritans began packing their things and gathering provisions. They moved to another dwelling, this time at the top of Mount Gerizim, close to a spring and an olive grove. In the distance, leafy Nablus clung to the side of its hill. My father understood that this was a pilgrimage: it was the beginning of the Passover, commemorating the return from Egypt.

Then he was locked into another house, which belonged to priests and contained the oldest book in the world, the *Abishua Torah*, three thousand six hundred years old. Three different keys were needed to open the tabernacle containing the precious manuscript, each one kept by a different priest.

My father was present at one of their ceremonies. The three officiating priests disappeared behind a little velvet tent which concealed the tabernacle, and emerged, wearing prayer shawls, one carrying the ancient Torah wrapped in gold-embroidered silk, which he placed on a wooden bench. Then they solemnly removed the precious wrapping and, carefully placing their hands on the two silver pommels, turned the lid. The cylinder opened into three sections, and the ancient goatskin appeared, naked and white, spotted with antique letters. They brought the ritual objects from the cupboard; kiddush glasses encrusted with gold and precious stones, cherubs, and the twelve-stoned plaque carried by the high priest of the Temple at Yom Kippur. They gave all these objects to the mysterious kidnappers.

Then my father remembered the legend of the Samaritans: their sanctuary on Mount Gerizim had been destroyed by the priest-king John Hyrcan, between 135 and 104 BC, and it was said that they possessed his treasure, part of the riches of the Temple, which they would not bring out until the coming of the Messiah. He remembered a phrase from the Copper Scroll:

> On Mount Gerizim
> Beneath the upper entrance,
> A cupboard, and its contents,
> And sixty silver talents.

So his kidnappers were there to recover the Samaritans' treasure. But why were they surrendering it so easily? For money, or something else? And why was he being made to watch the transaction?

The ceremony continued. The *shohet*, the sacrificer appeared, carrying long, sharpened knives. Everybody left the synagogue. Women, children, old and young men, dressed in tarbooshes and long striped robes, all busied themselves preparing for the Paschal sacrifice. The young readied the enclosure, dug barbecue pits, brought wood, prepared straw and clay, fetched pans of water and made wooden skewers. Others picked hyssop and the bitter herbs which prevent coagulation that the Samaritans use to preserve the lambs' blood they traditionally smear on the lintels of doors.

My father wondered why he had been brought to watch this ceremony, when he was usually confined to his room. Two Samaritans stood close to him, making flight impossible.

Everything was finally ready for the sacrifice: the altar, the sacrificer, the knife and the lambs. But there were two altars: one large, and a smaller one beside it. The big one, no doubt, was for the lambs, but the smaller . . . What animal was that for? Everything was there, except the sacrificial victim.

Unless that victim were himself . . .

Pierre Michel wriggled about on his chair, visibly unhappy, as Henderson continued his oration.

'All the Dead Sea Scrolls can tell us is something about the way Jesus might have lived, and the sort of world from which Christianity emerged. My aim will be to shed some historical light on the context in which the scrolls were written. It was, of course, Judaism, and that is why I will now explain, from a strictly historical point of view, what was happening before and during the period in which the Essene sect was writing these scrolls.'

He then rambled at length about this and that, carefully avoiding any mention of the scrolls. Occasionally he glanced at Pierre Michel, who watched him with mingled hatred and fear and, becoming more and more exasperated, several times raised his eyes to the ceiling, as though scandalised and calling on God to witness his horror.

Suddenly he lost patience, rose, and climbed onto the platform. He spread some papers on the table in front of him and looked around the auditorium, as though weighing up an adversary.

Henderson stared at him with a mixture of threat and anxiety, but neither he nor the others on the stage dared say anything. The audience, knowing Pierre Michel was in possession of the most important papers, seemed to hold its breath, and there was total silence by the time he finally spoke, vibrantly, like a prophet without hope or pity.

'I cannot allow this hypocrisy to be piled on top of centuries of lies,' he said, hammering out each word with his fist on the table, as though beating the drum for the last battle. 'Why can't we, Jews and Christians, admit the truth? Why lie to ourselves, why be so afraid?' He looked at Henderson. 'We are lost sheep, trying to find our way, and all we do is take the same wrong turning again and again.

'Do you want to know the dates of the scrolls? Do you want to know if they mention Jesus, or if he's just a myth? And if he existed, whether he was an Essene or a Pharisee, whatever sect he belonged to, who killed him and why? Or would you rather go on being treated like children?

'You believers, with your complacent obscurantism, you worship idols as though they were proofs of faith, and you do not despise those who cannot look the truth in the face. You prefer ignorance. You atheists want to know nothing about Christianity, even though it has shaped the world you live in. You mock believers and their foolish faith, but you don't understand that the reason for your scorn is your own longing for belief: you lack the courage to pursue your dissatisfaction to its conclusion.

'So now I am going to tell you what really happened at Qumran. For some of you it will be good news, a rebirth, a purification from all the deposits left by centuries of ignorance. For others there will be only shock and scandal.'

'The Qumran texts are mediaeval!' shouted a man in the audience.

'In that case, they would have no bearing on the origins of Christianity. Is that what you're getting at?' replied Pierre Michel.

'No!' said another. 'They date from the second or third century AD.'

'Then the connection with Jesus, if there was a connection, would be unimportant . . . But if,' he raised his voice until the microphone vibrated, 'if they were written in the centuries immediately preceding the Christian era, then they would be vital to our knowledge of both Judaism and Christianity. The community described in the scrolls revered a certain "Master of Justice", who was martyred. This is why the date is the vital question. As you have all realised, we're talking about the origins of Christianity. And the essential question is, were the early Christians a part of the Essene cult?

'Even for believers, a historical question must have a historical reply. For the last two thousand years, the Church's line on the origins and significance of Christianity has been clear: Jesus was the Messiah come to carry out the prophecies of the Scriptures, not just for the Jews, but for all mankind. He was sent by God, who had made him a Jew, but his teaching is radically different from that of Judaism. Now, if the scrolls change this view, force us to recognise that Jesus and the early Christians were part of a Jewish sect, with an almost identical organisation and the same sacraments, then centuries of belief will be brought into question. It will then be necessary to draw the obvious conclusion from these historical facts, and admit that Christianity did not spring from a supernatural intervention, but was the result of a natural social and religious evolution.

'So, what do the scrolls tell us? I'll tell you. They tell us that Christianity, far from being a faith spread by the saints in Judaea, is in fact Essenism, which grafted itself onto the other religions of the gentile world until it became an autonomous system of beliefs, i.e. Christianity.'

'The scrolls are fakes,' came another voice from the audience, rapidly called to order by the chairman. This did not stop another from adding: 'They are Karaites, and date from the tenth century.'

Pierre Michel replied calmly: 'The Jewish Karaites sect was dispersed in the eighth century throughout Babylonia, Persia, Syria and Egypt, as well as Palestine. In the eleventh century, it declined in those countries, whilst increasing in Europe. Its distinctive feature was a literal interpretation of the Bible, in terms of rule of worship. Archaeological and palaeographic finds have invalidated any connection between this sect and Qumran.

'But of course I can see why the dating of the scrolls should cause such anxiety . . . Certainly there are worrying connections. One finds the apocrypha of the Old and New Testaments amongst the writings rejected by the Fathers of the Church, as well as the Pseudepigrapha.

That is clearly no coincidence. You all know that apocrypha means "hidden". I think these texts were set aside because they wanted their meaning concealed from the mass of the faithful, and only accessible to a few of the initiated. We must not forget that there were many esoteric writings at the beginning of the Christian era, and that they are very important to the understanding of the origins of the faith. I suggest that the curious connections between the two sets of writings can help us to shed light on both . . .'

He stopped for a moment and drank some water. Then he slowly drew from his briefcase a package wrapped in pale-coloured cloth, which he slowly unwrapped, revealing a scroll: one of the Dead Sea scrolls, I saw at once. He raised it above his head to show it to the audience, who stared, open-mouthed.

It was a very thin and ancient piece of parchment, light brown, spotted with dark patches, ravaged by time, insects and humidity. The two ends remained rolled, like hesitant arms, fearful of revealing their naked truth. It seemed so fragile, so delicate, as if it might at any moment disintegrate before our eyes and disappear, for ever unseen. It was so old, had seen so many centuries go by, it was almost as if it wanted to end its long calvary, tell its story and then collapse into dust, no longer solid proof for forgetful men, but just a wisp of memory, an idea, a word for parents to pass down the generations. Soon it would surrender itself to other words for which it was only a support; already it hovered between the spiritual and the material world, the tangible and the intangible, the real and the imaginary, the pure memory of these engraved words, forever lost, now rediscovered. It had reached the end of its strength and was worn out by its struggle and its travels. But here it was, before everybody, its mission not quite accomplished – there was still something that needed, finally, to be said.

Pierre Michel started again, in a loud voice. 'You want to know whether Jesus really existed? The answer is here in this document. Yes, he existed, and is mentioned here. No, he is not what you thought he was.'

There was uproar in the auditorium. All eyes were fixed on the scroll, which Michel still held up above his head. He lowered his arms and, carefully placing it on the table, said:

'Everybody knows the similarities between the Essenes and the early Christians can't be pure coincidence. Both communities held their goods in common, kept in a central treasury and redistributed as necessary for community purchases. When Jesus told the rich man to give all he possessed to the "poor", he meant his brother Essenes, who used the word "poor" to describe themselves: everyone who joined them had to give up their riches to the central funds. So, when Jesus invites the rich man, saying: "Come, join us," he is asking him to join the Essene community, of which he was himself a member.'

There was another clamour from the audience. He continued impassively.

'Above all, the Essenes and the early Christians lived in the same way. The Essenes avoided cities and preferred to establish themselves in villages. They refused to sacrifice amimals. Their teaching was based on principles of piety, justice, holiness, love of God, love of virtue and love of mankind. This was why they were much admired by many Jews, who saw the contrast between them and the corrupt priests of the Temple who collaborated with the pagan occupying forces.

'The two communities had a similar vision of the world, too: both believed in a cataclysm at the end of time, and a kingdom of God announced by a Messiah. Both saw themselves as the elect – sons of light battling against the sons of darkness. Essenes, like Christians, placed themselves at the centre of a cosmic conflict.

'In order to achieve this great destiny, they evolved a similar messianic set of beliefs and a similar communal organisation into a religious movement, with a similar concept of the universe. One has only to compare the *Handbook of Discipline* with the *New Testament*. All the elements tally, *because they are referring to the same community*. I tell you, Essenes and Christians were one and the same. Which means that, until the Church was founded, Christianity was an intrinsic part of Judaism.'

There were more confused murmurings from the audience. Pierre Michel continued, raising his voice to drown the noise.

'We must put an end to centuries of corruption of texts. Consider, for example, the *Testament of the Twelve Patriarchs*, which was long thought to be by a Christian, since it mentioned the Messiah. It is now known that it was written by a Jew. And that's only one example among many!

'One can now understand the mystery of John's Gospel, and its almost irreconcilable differences from the other gospels. For John, Jesus was a kind of rabbi. His public life went on for longer, three years instead of a few months or a year. He lived entirely in Judaea, never in Galilee. He was the Messiah from the beginning.

'Now I have discovered that the Gospel according to John quotes almost literally certain phrases of the Qumran manuscript I have been studying; it must therefore have been written very early on, in Palestine, the meeting-place between Christian and Hellenistic thought – in other words, at Qumran. I have every reason to believe that the Gospel according to John was written by a member of the Essene sect.

'Can't you see how close the character of Jesus, as described by John, is to the Essene Master of Justice, the exalted priest, the prophet who is martyred and reappears as the Messiah? The author of John's Gospel tells the story of the life of Jesus in accordance with the teachings of the Master of Justice: *I am the way, the truth and the life; nobody cometh unto the Father, but by me,* John quotes. Reading this manuscript has enabled me to resolve the mystery of John's Gospel: it is a theological treatise in the form of a biography of Jesus, containing doctrines preached by the Master of Justice.

'I will go further. Everybody knows, even if nobody will admit it, that John the Baptist was an Essene. He preached baptism, the Essenes' most important ritual; came from the desert, like the Essenes and, like them, announced the coming of the kingdom of Heaven. In which case, what is the significance of Jesus being baptised by John? It is no longer certain that Jesus's own teaching differed in any great degree from John's. His disciples were probably Essenes too – or how could they abandon their occupations so quickly when he told them to follow him? He told them to go forth and preach, two by two, and to accept neither bread nor money. How could they have survived? Where did they sleep? Either there were hospitable people in Galilee, or the disciples were amazingly well-off in friends and relations. Or perhaps they expected to be received by the Essene sects described by Philon and Josephus, based in towns and villages. Since they were Essenes themselves, the sacred rules of the sect would guarantee them shelter.

'Finally, when he was twelve, Jesus quarrelled with the priests of the Temple. That must have been the moment when he was initiated – while still a child, according to Essene custom. That was when he learned the canonical scriptures, as well as the Essenes' own writings. It would explain why he knew the Scriptures so well; he must have learned them somewhere. At that time everybody had masters. It is quite impossible that Jesus was not initiated by someone, and that he did not belong to a sect.'

He stopped for a moment to drink again and gather his thoughts. Beads of sweat had appeared on his brow. Henderson looked blackly at him: he would clearly have stopped Michel from speaking had he been able to. The audience, reticent at first, and then surprised, seemed gradually to have been won over by this little man's words. Some were smiling, radiantly happy to hear what they had been longing for. Others looked worried and shocked.

He was unleashing trouble and scandal. Once embarked, he continued, unstoppable: nothing was sacred any more. He was like a man possessed, undermining dogmas elaborately constructed over centuries, errors carefully implanted deep in the consciousness by the Church, leaving men with no voice of their own. But still they listened, because they knew that what they were hearing was beyond the Church: they were hearing Jesus, standing alone with his words and his faith. They knew this, and so they listened.

'How else could Jesus have spent forty days in the desert?' he continued. 'He couldn't have survived without shelter. But the monastery of Qumran was in the Judaean desert; it's possible that he lived in the caves there, as other Essenes did.

'How else could he attend a synagogue? The synagogues were the meeting places, and he certainly didn't frequent the Pharisees, of whom he was violently critical. No, he attended Essene gatherings, what they called the meetings of the "many".

'How did he come to be called the "Nazarene", when there was no such town as Nazareth at the time?' There were exclamations of surprise from the audience. 'Nazareth is never mentioned in either the Old Testament, the Talmud or Josephus – even though the latter, who was commander-in-chief of the Jews during the war against the Romans in Galilee, noted down everything he saw. If Nazareth had been an important town in Galilee, how could he have failed to mention it? The fact is that Nazareth was the name of a sect, not a town. It was Matthew, obsessed by a literal interpretation of the prophecies, who wrote that Jesus had gone to Nazareth, in order to confirm the words of the prophets who said the Messiah would be a Nazarene. He's referring to Isaiah's prophecy about a sprig – *netzer* – from the line of Jesse. But actually, it turns out that the Essenes were called Nazarenes, meaning "believers in the Messiah" . . . just like "christianos".'

Henderson was boiling with fury, his face taut and his hands clenched on his knees. At times he looked around him, seeming to count how many people were hearing these words. Then he would plunge his head into his hands, as though he couldn't bear to see or hear any of what was happening.

My father watched the preparations, completely stunned, crushed by what he suspected was about to happen, hardly able to believe it, paralysed with fear. Some people were boiling the bitter herbs and wrapping them in unleavened dough. Others had lit fires in large cylindrical furnaces: flames leapt from them, fed by branches and logs. Young Samaritans wandered impatiently about in their finery, pretending to busy themselves around the fires. Children played with the lambs.

Eventually, they all went home to perform the ritual ablutions and put on traditional sacrificial robes; the elders wore finely striped tunics, with a white prayer shawl over the shoulder. They then reconvened in procession, with the high priest at the head of it, followed by the elders, then the older members of the community, then the young.

The high priest stood before a block of stone, his face turned towards the top of Mount Gerizim, away from the setting sun. Twelve other priests stood around the sacrificial altar, chanting piercing prayers and lamentations, and the congregation joined in the refrains. The high priest climbed onto the stone block and began to intone. At the precise moment when the last ray of sun disappeared behind the mountains, in an instant of silence and emotion, the hundred-and-forty-sixth descendant of Aaron recited three times, in a resounding voice, the Biblical injunction: 'And all the tribe of Israel will cut his throat in the evening.'

The sacrificers tested the blades of their knives on their tongues and then, holding the wildly struggling, terrified animals, cut their throats in one movement. A great cry tore through the sky, and blood flowed from the slashed necks.

In one minute, twenty-eight lambs were slaughtered: the holocaust was greeted with an explosion of joy. The twelve priests then approached the altar, still reciting from Exodus. When the injunction came to put a red mark on the lintels of the doors, fathers plunged their fingers into the bleeding throats and marked their childrens' foreheads and noses.

Then everyone came forward to pay homage to the high priest. They brought steaming plates of food and kissed his hands, and hugged and embraced one another. The younger ones threw the sacrificed animals into boiling water in order to remove the skin more easily; once flayed, they were hung from posts, cleaned, cut up and salted, to get rid of all the blood. The priests checked the animals for defects, to decide which ones could be eaten. Those which were not perfect were thrown into the fire along with the wool, entrails and feet of the others.

By this stage my father thought that perhaps he had been wrong, and that the small altar, still immaculate, was not destined for him. The crowd, young and old, was infected with youthful enthusiasm and religious exaltation, as the priests tirelessly continued to intone the Exodus, moving around amongst the faithful. He wondered if they had forgotten about him, and would simply finish their sacrifice and go home. The spitted animals waited to be roasted on the great altar, and the young people stood around them, waiting for the words which would authorise them to throw them, all at once, into the flames.

'Remember the passage in Exodus,' said Pierre Michel, 'where Moses takes the blood from the sacrifices and sprinkles the people with it, saying: "This is the blood of the covenant that God has made with you, based upon his words." Does that not remind you of anything? Is it not the basis of the Eucharist, in which Jesus identifies the wine with his blood, renewing the Mosaic promise? But it is also reminiscent of the Essene rite which used bread and wine as a symbol of the flesh and blood of the Messiah at communal meals.'

He paused, appearing to weigh his words, and then said: 'The Essenes believed that the man called Jesus the Nazarene, Jesus the Essene, was their Messiah, the Master of Justice.'

'What do you mean?' cried Henderson, unable to contain his fury. 'The Christian Messiah is the same as the Essene Master of Justice? Don't you know that Christians awaited a single Messiah, whereas the Essenes spoke of two?'

'It's possible that the two became one, and equally possible that the Christians made a later synthesis of the two,' Michel replied calmly. 'Both communities believed they were part of a "new contract", which means the same as "New Testament". For both the early Christians and the Essenes, this was based on the Law of Moses. It was Paul who broke away from that law, to ease conversions and the development of the gentile Church.'

Henderson interrupted abruptly. 'You can't base the New Testament on an historical foundation. It's a theological problem.'

'You say that, but you know perfectly well that you're not completely satisfied with a Christ whose existence depends on blind faith alone. You want to know more about this enigmatic figure, you want the historical Jesus. It's circular reasoning: you want to establish a theology that can sit in judgement on history, and you want historical problems to be based on the Bible. If the story of the New Testament isn't based on facts, how can one believe in the chief protagonist? How can faith remain linked to fact?'

'Most of human history is subject to doubt, and some kind of faith is almost always necessary to give history its meaning.'

'That's not a tenable position for a theology founded on what's in the Bible. You can't base the beginnings of Christianity on something that cannot have happened, simply because you wish it to be so. Certainly you can build an imaginary world like that, in which you can think of God and worship him with symbols, but then you're outside the real world. I am religious, but I still retain a certain sense of history, and I want to remain in contact with reality. And I don't think that a belief in present-day theology is sufficient to determine what happened in the past.

'What makes the Qumran scrolls so fascinating is that they are real, tangible evidence. There they are, they exist. Theology can't make them go away. They have something substantial to tell us, and no amount of theology can suppress the implications of what they say. It's not just the scrolls, either: there are the caves, the monastery ruins, baptismal fonts, scriptoriums. And so, thanks to Qumran, history comes to life.'

He descended from the stage, and began talking to various people in the audience, waving his arms as though preaching, or perhaps giving blessings. He stopped from time to time, gazing at the smiling faces. He seemed transported, carried away by his speech, surrounded by an aura of heavenly grace. His voice was both gentle and warm, fired with passionate energy. His long-awaited day of glory had come at last.

'The scrolls exist,' he continued, 'and with them something of even greater significance. They are signposts, markers on the map of history. The long-dead Essenes speak to us through these scrolls, and what they say provides new answers to ancient questions; from these answers many other answers may follow, to give us a final account of the history of Christianity.

'So, for example, the figure of John the Baptist in the desert becomes not just a man suddenly inhabited by the holy spirit, but an Essene living an austere life, seeking purification, like his brothers, through ritual baths.'

'You're forgetting the big difference between John and the Essenes,' Henderson interrupted. 'What is there in common between the contemplative Essene way of life and John's fiery prophetic teaching, his proclamation, like Elias or Amos, that judgement was nigh, his denunciation of the scandals and corruption at the court?'

'What about the eschatological outbursts in the *Rule of the Community*?' replied Pierre Michel. 'Under the leadership of the Master of Justice, the new community was already convinced that the end of time was approaching. The *Scroll of War* proves it: Belial unleashed his rage against the penitents of Israel, and the hour of justice approached. The commentator of the *Scroll of Habbakuk* also observes that time has continued longer than predicted, and deduces that the final judgement against the sinners of the Covenant will be all the more terrible. The *Scroll of War* is the work of the extreme wing, which would join the Zealots in the struggle against Rome: it describes, in terms both realistic and apocalyptic, the holy war between the sons of light and the sons of darkness. The Essene community was obsessed by the end of the world, and provides a totally understandable setting for the figure of John the Baptist.'

'You say John was an Essene,' said Henderson. 'It's not true, but let's accept it for a moment. I defy you to prove that he had any contact with Qumran. As you know, there were several forms of Essenism, and the few inhabitants of Qumran represent a mere handful compared to the many families constituting the Essene order. According to Philon and Josephus, the majority of Essenes lived near towns and villages.'

'John most certainly had contacts with the Qumran sect. The monastery is close to the place where he held his meetings – that's no coincidence. What's more, Luke was Essene too; he describes the desert where he grew up, and we know that only Essenes brought children into the desert to instruct them in their doctrine.'

'John the Baptist was no Essene,' Henderson cut in. 'His father,

Zachariah, was a priest at the Temple, one of those attacked by the Essenes.'

'He led the life of an ascetic,' replied Pierre Michel, 'similar to that of the inhabitants of Qumran, scrupulously respecting the *Rules of the Community*. But more significant is John's behaviour in the desert: he wanted to renew the tradition of prophetic teaching. You know the spiritual and religious importance of the desert. The prophet Hosea had announced that God would lead his unfaithful people there to break off the alliance. Ezekiel describes the desert in which God would pass judgement on his people. The second book of Isaiah describes the new Exodus into the desert as a paradise, inviting his compatriots to carve a way for the Lord. This text is twice quoted in the *Rule of the Community* to justify the Essene abandonment of the Temple for the desert. The desert always appears as the last phase of the preparation for the great day.

'Moreover, John shared some of his contemporaries' ideas, particularly those in the Apocalypse, but differed from them in his radicalism. This is what brought him close to the Qumran Essenes, who had set up their little community in opposition to the corruption of Israel, to be, as the prophecy says, the precious keystone which will not shake. He's close to the Qumran Essenes when he threatens the people with the fury of God, and predicts that the children of Israel cannot escape it without a radical conversion.'

'John was an itinerant preacher who wasn't afraid of mingling with crowds,' said Henderson. 'Your Essenes were very snooty when it came to matters of purity, and kept their distance from sinners.'

'His aim was to purify all men through baptism, which was an Essene rite. They placed the greatest importance on "the purification of the many" by ritual baths.'

'But John presided over the baptism of others, whereas each member of the Qumran community took his own purifying bath, without the help of any mediator. And John's great evangelical welcome to all sinners was very different from the enclosed and integral nature of the Dead Sea communities. His humility before the "one greater than himself" marks him as a true Christian, and it's for good reason that he is traditionally regarded as the precursor and harbinger of Christ our Lord . . .'

'I was just coming to Christ.'

They hadn't forgotten him. When they had completed their tasks they approached my father. Slowly, they gagged him and tied him to the altar with a rough rope.

He was weeping, and his body trembled convulsively, but his executioners remained impervious to his dumb pleas. Nor had his calvary ended: the Samaritans returned to their houses to meditate and read, with their families, the history of the Hebrew people in Sinai.

Bound and gagged, he gave up all hope of rescue. Every terrifying minute seemed like the last, but brought with it, unbearably, a tiny glimmer of hope, that made him cling to life, suggesting to him that God might yet not abandon him. He began to hate this hope, that made him expect he knew not what – a rescue, natural or super- natural; anything that would get him out of this desperate situation. On the brink of a violent death, he was still expecting something to happen; he was, after all, a man.

The ropes dug into his bruised wrists. He lay on his back on the stone altar, arms bound to the two top corners, his legs bent to the left, and his ankles tied to the third corner. This twisted position restricted his circulation: he could hardly breathe, and his legs became more and more painful.

He began to pray. As if to accompany him the sound of the shofar rang out, as it does at Yom Kippur to announce the end of the fast, the great deliverance, the divine judgement which will bring reward and punishment to all. But this was not Yom Kippur, this was no renewal or purification: it was a human sacrifice. Where was God, for the love of God? Had he been abandoned? Tears came to his eyes again as he begged forgiveness in a burst of fervour, begged God with all his strength to save him, not to abandon him.

The patriarchs emerged one by one from their houses, each holding a stick and a prayer mat, with a blanket over the shoulder. The high priest, followed by the whole community, returned. They formed a circle around the altar and chanted psalms. Then the high priest slowly approached him, knife in hand. My father closed his eyes, and felt the sharp blade on his knotted throat.

'No!'

The cry echoed through the hall. Pierre Michel determinedly marched back up to the stage.

'You won't stop me speaking out, Henderson, saying what you and I know perfectly well: that Jesus and the Master of Justice are one and the same person. The "Kittim", the sons of darkness, the cruel executioners described in the scroll, who are going to lance and crucify him, are none other than the Romans.'

'Rubbish! The word was used to describe the Latin and Greek peoples of the Mediterranean islands. "Kittim" can just as well be applied to the Seleucids, who were Greek. And if it's the Greeks who are being attacked in the scroll of the Master of Justice, that would make it second century BC.

'Who the Master of Justice was, and the Wicked Priest mentioned in the scroll, remains a mystery. Plenty of historical figures can be connected with both. The Wicked Priest could well have been Onias III, the high priest banished by Antiochus, or Menalaus, the merchant priest who persecuted him. Or Judas the Essene, a holy figure who confronted the terrible Aristobolus I. Besides, the Master of Justice *was* a priest, perhaps even a high priest of the Temple. He belonged to a religious order, whose members he taught the meaning of the Scriptures, plus his own teachings and prophecies. He was persecuted and put to death, and then worshipped and venerated by the Essenes as their great martyr-prophet, who would return in the Messianic era. But this Master of Justice lived in the first or second century before Christ!'

'That's what you'd have us believe. But you and I know a great deal better, since we've both deciphered the last scroll; here it is, the key to the secret, in my possession, despite all your attempts to steal it from me,' said Michel, pointing an accusing finger at Henderson.

The audience was aghast. Something was going on between the two men, some old rivalry, perhaps older than themselves, but certainly a quarrel between two former friends – they no longer concealed the fact that they knew each other well.

'Jesus existed,' Pierre Michel continued, 'but he was not who we think he was. The time has come to reveal the contents of this scroll. It tells us not only who he was, but also who really killed him, and why. And that frightens you, Misickzy, hiding behind your pseudonym, Henderson; that's what you can't face. Today you're going to hear it, and the world is going to know everything. I'm going to tell the world what happened that Passover when Jesus died.'

Henderson, now wild with rage, began to shout. 'Traitor! You stole our manuscripts to injure us. I'm going to tell everyone what you did, and what motivates you. This man has not simply apostatized,' he told the audience. 'He's – he's converted to Judaism!'

179

Henderson finally gave free rein to the hatred that contorted his face, twisted his mouth and swelled the veins in his temples. 'You have converted to the people who killed Jesus. Because Israel is guilty, none other, and you have adopted its folkloric, obsolete, deicide religion!'

'I might have known you would seize on that anti-semitic calumny, directly responsible for all the suffering and unspeakable persecutions inflicted on Jews throughout the centuries. The Catholic Church may have changed its stance on the accusation of deicide, but only recently and half-heartedly: I'm ashamed of it, and of you.

'I know your motives, you and the Congregation for the Doctrine of the Faith: self-preservation and the survival of your opulent aristocracies. The truth, which you refuse to accept, is that the Saducee priests who condemned Jesus didn't have the support of the Jewish masses; they were in the employ of the pagan occupier, and trying to preserve their precarious position vis-à-vis the Romans.

'The Qumran community was founded after the Maccabean war, as a protest against the distortion of the Jewish religion by the Saducee-led authorities at the Temple. The Essene priests were strict followers of the precepts of the Torah, and called for God's justice to fulfil the prophecies. They thought that no political or military force could free Israel from the yoke of the oppressor; only a supernatural intervention from the Messiah, the Lord's Anointed, could establish a new order. So they turned to the past, re-reading the sacred scriptures in order to understand the significance of the destiny of the people of Israel. The texts shed a new light on contemporary events, and the history given by God had to be transcribed onto parchment to enable it to be read and re-read. And so the scribes of the sect began to produce not just copies of the sacred texts, but their own writings, about the sect itself.

'But what's all that to do with Jesus?'

The audience was anxious and impatient, and hung on his every word. His voice softened.

'He was no humble carpenter, nor a gentle shepherd preaching love and forgiveness through his parables, nor a divine incarnation come to sacrifice himself to redeem the sins of mankind. No. The Messiah of Israel was a triumphant warrior, a judge, a priest and a sage. There was nothing symbolic about his messianic fervour. The Qumran Essenes firmly believed that the Romans and their Judaean agents were the incarnation of the forces of darkness. They believed that only a bloody religious war would defeat the Devil and his evil power. Only then could there be a period of renewal, peace and harmony. The people of Israel had to play a part in their own redemption, and, guided by the Messiah, the Essenes would rebuild the world. But things turned out unexpectedly. Those who premeditated the killing of Jesus, the murderers, were . . .'

'Shut up!' yelled Henderson, now beside himself with rage. 'You have no right to speak. Christianity supplanted Judaism. A Jew's only proper response to Christianity is to convert. You're just a throwback embracing a decayed and anachronistic religion. The occupation of Jerusalem is founded on an enormous lie. Well, we can't deport the entire Jewish population of Israel, but we can get rid of one . . .'

When he felt the knife on his throat, his body shook and his eyes bulged with fear. He struggled and screamed, terrified. The fire was ready, the murderous flames awaited the murdered flesh, to send its breath up to God, who would then answer their prayers.

There was the deafening sound of a gunshot, then a second, and a third. Then a roar of panic from the crowd.

It was a weak, innocent lamb, rearing away from the fire, terrified. Its panting, sweating fear did not deter the man: the sacrifice was for God. The priest pressed the sharp blade against its throat and cut it with one sharp movement. The lamb gave one last cry, like a sob, and died. The blood was still flowing as they put it on the fire.

Pierre Michel crumpled to the ground.

It was a tiny creature, still suckling its mother when they took it from the herd. At the last moment, instead of sacrificing my father, they released him and killed it in his place on the small altar. Then he understood what had happened: they had relived the sacrifice of Isaac, when Abraham, after tying up his son, lets him go at the order of God and kills a lamb instead.

As this dawned on him, his nerve finally broke and he lost consciousness.

The crowd pushed in every direction. Some tried to get out, others to get closer to the scene of the crime. All wanted to know what had happened.

What had happened was simple: Paul Henderson had shot Pierre Michel and then dropped the gun. He stood now, flanked by security guards, bewildered and dazed by what he had done.

Jane and I tried to get to the stage, but the security cordon pushed everyone back. After a few minutes, ambulancemen arrived to take away the body; the barrier opened for a minute and Jane pushed through, but soon came back to my side, not having got very far.

We saw Pierre Michel's body go past, and then a handcuffed Henderson, escorted by the police. There was wild panic all around us.

We left, miserable at Pierre Michel's death and at the thought that we had been, unwittingly, the cause of it. I was filled with gloom. It seemed that not only had I failed in my quest, but I had also been responsible for the death of a good man.

I had set a trap, with Pierre Michel as the bait. It seemed as though I travelled the world to spread the bad news, like the Wicked Priest. Torment and horror dogged my footsteps. People I met who showed me the way, or just spoke to me briefly, suffered horrible deaths. I began to wonder whether it was something to do with me. Or perhaps Henderson was right: the scrolls were cursed.

I had to see him, to find out more about the reasons for his deed, whether rational or not.

II

Henderson had committed a murder in front of thousands of witnesses. It was the only crime he was charged with, but he was also a suspect of the crucifixions of Bishop Hosea, Almond and Millet, and the murder of Matti – whose body had finally been found, horribly mutilated. He denied all these, admitting only the death of Michel. Jane thought he was telling the truth.

'He couldn't commit a crime in cold blood,' she said.

'But this one was certainly premeditated. He'd been threatening Pierre Michel for a long time. He came to the symposium with a gun.'

'We must talk to him.'

We went to the prison where he was being held.

No longer the arrogant, self-confident man I had met with my father, he was deflated and enfeebled, and the deep wrinkles on his forehead throbbed nervously. We sat around a table in a glassed-in room, where we had been left alone. Jane explained, gently and calmly, why we had come, and then asked him why he had done it.

'I killed Pierre Michel because he betrayed us and abandoned the Christian faith,' he replied.

'Was it you who was threatening him?' she asked.

'He stole the scroll. I searched for it and, yes, I did threaten him several times. That scroll belonged to me, you see. He had no right to take it.'

'You're the one who took it,' I said. 'It belonged to Matti.'

'But who helped him to get hold of it? I negotiated with Hosea – I was in constant communication with him.'

'You used Matti to buy the scroll – though I'm sure the Vatican would have paid gladly, but then they would have wanted possession, wouldn't they? And then you stole it from him.'

'Yes, because it should have come to me in the first place. Hosea wouldn't give it to me, even after all I'd done for him. He wanted too much money, he'd become greedy. So I used Matti. But then, after I got it from the museum, I made a great mistake: I gave it to Pierre Michel to decipher and translate, because he was the best and I trusted him. But he was a viper in my bosom – he betrayed me.'

'What's in the scroll that makes it worth killing a man?'

He didn't reply. I repeated my question. Still no reply. Then I said: 'Do you know anything about the disappearance of my father?'

'No. I didn't know he'd disappeared.'

'He was kidnapped, Henderson,' I said, my voice trembling with rage. 'So if you know anything at all about the scrolls, you'd better tell me.'

He said nothing, but gazed at me with an ironic stare, the same arrogant look as when we had first met. I could no longer restrain myself and, leaning across the table, grabbed him by the collar.

'Ary!' said Jane. 'What are you doing?'

'I warn you,' I said, looking him straight in the eye, 'if you're implicated in this affair in any way, I'll make you pay for it, with my own hands.'

'Ary, please . . .' she said again.

'You call yourself a Christian, but you're a crook and a murderer. You stole our scroll, and not content with that, you tormented and killed Pierre Michel – all because you're an anti-semite.'

'Stop, Ary!'

'What about Hosea, Almond and Millet? And Matti? Answer!' I yelled, out of control.

'Let go of him, Ary!'

'I had nothing to do with any of that,' he said in one breath, when I finally let go of him. 'I hardly knew Matti. I have no idea who did that, or who took your father. I killed Pierre Michel, but not the others. Almond wasn't a Christian, and I didn't mind what he said. Anyway, he didn't have the important manuscript. I killed Pierre Michel because he'd been my friend and had betrayed me, and because he was about to reveal the contents of the scroll. I'd do it again tomorrow.'

'Come on, let's go.' Jane took my arm and dragged me towards the door. 'We won't get any more out of him.'

'What came over you?' said Jane, as we came out of the prison.

'I thought he knew something he wasn't telling us.' To tell the truth, I no longer believed he had committed the other murders. But it

184

seemed more and more clear that my father's kidnapping was connected with them.

'But why the violence?' She seemed shocked.

'Do you know what my name, Ary, means?' I said.

'No.'

'It means "the lion" . . . Look, I can't stay here. I must go back to Israel. The answer has to be there.'

'Let me come with you.'

'No. Where I'm going you can't come. Stay here. You're safer in New York, and away from me.'

The next day, the eve of my departure, we ate in a kosher pizzeria in the diamond district, surrounded by Hassidim, the men in frock coats and hats, and the women, some of them very elegant, in wigs of all kinds, long and short, curly and straight.

'Are you sure you don't want me to come with you?'

'Yes.'

'I've been terribly upset by Pierre Michel's revelations, and by his death. I'd like to know more, and I'd like to help you. It's important to me, and important for my faith.'

'You've done plenty already . . .'

'But I know you must go,' she went on. 'I'll only have you for a short time more . . .'

After supper, I walked her home. We stood in silence for a while outside her door. 'Since we've got to part,' she said finally, 'let me give you something.'

She pulled out of her bag an oblong object neatly wrapped in white cloth and, unfolding it carefully, handed it to me. I couldn't muzzle a cry of surprise. It was an ancient scroll, of crumpled parchment, covered in cramped black writing.

'I managed to get past the ambulancemen and onto the stage. I took it off the lectern. There was such chaos nobody noticed.'

I hadn't even thought about the scroll in the rush of events, assuming the police had it. But there was no time to voice my surprise further.

A man burst past me from behind and grabbed Jane's arm, forcing her to drop the cylinder. He hit her and she fell, her head crashing against the pavement.

I caught his elbow as he bent to pick up the scroll; he whirled round, pulling a knife.

We fought, rolling on the pavement. I felt his breath on me as his weight crushed me. I wasn't as strong as he was, and my bulky Hassidic garments hampered me, but I managed a few punches to his stomach and ribs that dislodged him.

Using all the techniques that I had never used since the army, I gouged skin, pulled organs, broke teeth, smashed my elbow into his jaw.

Then I felt the blade pierce my hip, and I lost my grip, startled by the pain. He punched me, ready to run. I felt my bones crack and my stomach retract under his blows, and realised that my only hope now was Shimon's revolver.

I plunged my hand into my pocket, but found only the little phial of oil. He grabbed it from me and smashed it on my head; thick, foul-smelling red liquid spread over my hair and down my face.

With a final effort, I found the gun and thrust it into his ribs. The fight stopped at once.

Jane, meanwhile, had come to; I helped her up, and, still staggering, she picked up the parchment and put it back in her bag. Then she pushed open the door of her apartment with one hand, holding her head with the other, and I pushed the man in ahead of me.

I asked Jane to hold the gun while I tied the prisoner to a radiator with the curtain cords. Keeping it within reach, we dealt quickly with our injuries. Jane cleaned her grazed knees, and held ice to the cut on her forehead. I bandaged my bleeding hip, and tried to wash off the stinking, viscous liquid that coated my skin and stuck to my hair. I looked at myself in the mirror: my face was swollen and bruised, with red and blue patches.

My adversary was in a similar condition, but he seemed more alert. He must have been around fifty, dark-skinned, with curly grey hair that must once have been black, and nervous brown eyes. I asked him in English who he was.

He replied in Hebrew: Kair. Kair Benyair.

At last we've found someone, even if it is our worst enemy, I thought. The symposium ruse hadn't been a waste of time after all.

'Why do you want the scroll?' I asked.

'The same reason you do.'

'What's that?'

'Because it says where the Essene treasure is.'

'How do you know? Have you deciphered it?'

'No, Hosea told me. He had already found some of the Temple treasure, thanks to the scrolls, a real fortune in precious objects. It's all still there, in his apartment.'

I remembered seeing some fine objects there. Now I knew where they came from.

'But he still hadn't found the final hiding place, where he said the most important treasure was.'

'Do you know where my father is? Who kidnapped him?'

'No. I don't know who your father is.'

'And do you know who killed Hosea?'

'Yes, I saw them. I was in the next room when they came. Hosea seemed to know them. They had a violent argument about the treasure. They said to Hosea that he would never find it. He said nothing would stop him. Then it was horrible. I ran away. But I'm afraid. They know I worked with Hosea, and I'm sure they're looking for me. That's why I left Israel.'

I realised that if I wanted to find my father I would have to track down the treasure, and therefore decipher the scroll.

I opened it carefully and began unrolling it with trembling hands. I felt the cracked skin open up as if by magic, and the fine, tightly packed writing appeared. It was certainly the missing manuscript: as Matti had said, the writing went from left to right, the opposite to normal Hebrew writing. This made a cursory reading impossible, or at any rate very difficult.

However, what had seemed to us all to be part of a sinister plan now had a perfectly natural explanation. I saw that, because the document had been rolled up very tight, the humidity had caused the writing to offset onto the back of the piece it was rolled against, leaving the original piece blank. So the transference and inversion of the writing had not been intentional, merely an accident. To read it, all you had to do was hold it up to a mirror, which I did. The Aramaic letters reappeared in their original order, just as the scribe had written them down.

Alas, if only I had paid more attention when my father taught me the ancient letters. Why had I wasted time in vain pursuits?' And how I was being punished! To be so close to my goal, but unable to reach it. Two hours later, I was as ignorant as I had been several months earlier.

Only a very few specialists could decipher the tiny writing of the

Qumran scribes. It was impossible for me, without my father's help – half the letters were missing, and reading it in such conditions was an arduous task of interpretation and guesswork. I read and re-read until the letters seemed to dance before my eyes, but I could not understand what I was reading. All I could do was stare like a fool at the old parchment that I had so longed for. *Wisdom is better than weapons of war: but one sinner destroyeth much good.*

I didn't know what to do. It was out of the question, of course, to consult another scholar: even if I had known who to ask, I would not have known whom to trust. But it was clear that I must return to Israel, where the treasure and, perhaps, my father was. I didn't want to release Kair, in case he alerted his accomplices. But he didn't seem to want to go. He suggested a deal: since we all wanted to know what the scroll meant, why didn't we work together?

And indeed, it was in our interests to stay close to him.

'You need me now,' said Jane. 'Otherwise who's going to keep an eye on him?'

'I can do that on my own. I don't think he'll escape. He's too frightened and it's not in his interests, since the police are looking for him. He needs us to get him over the frontiers, and to hide him.'

'But you can't risk losing him. And you can't be with him and look for your father.'

'I'll manage.'

'Okay, if you're going to be like that, I'll have to resort to other means. If you won't take me to Israel, I'll tell the whole story to the magazine. I'll go to Bart Donnars – who, I may say, is frantically searching for the scroll himself. Believe me, one well-crafted article by him would wipe you out.'

'You wouldn't do that!'

'No, I wouldn't. But I'm quite capable of coming, whether you want me or not. I don't need your permission to travel to Israel. And the manuscript does belong a little to me too . . .'

Such is woman – a help against oneself. I knew that I shouldn't give in: by prolonging our association I would only become even more attached to her than I already was. But she was determined, and I did give in. And so our curious group set off for Israel, where I felt lay the solution to all our problems.

A thousand memories assailed me as the plane approached Jerusalem in the setting sun at the end of summer, with a cool, sometimes icy, breeze on evenings when one could feel winter coming on. The golden light at such moments, tinting the white walls of the old town with ochre, and bathing the Mount of Olives in a saffron glow that seemed to reflect everything – sun, moon, stars, lightning, roses and candelabra.

I remembered one of the oldest quarters outside the walls of the Old Town, Nahalat Shiva, which the modern world keeps trying to annexe. There is a small synagogue in one of its gates that I used to attend, one of the oldest in the city, its walls covered in plaques commemorating lives long since crumbled to dust. In the narrow streets, people jump from pavement to pavement every time a car passes, or sometimes the cars mount the kerb to avoid crushing the pedestrians. Some streets are so narrow that one has to walk in single file. The modern world now besieges such places, and the holy walls, hardly touched by the light of sun or moon, seem about to go up in flames.

Awake, awake; put on thy strength, O Zion; put on thy beautiful garments, O Jerusalem, the holy city: for henceforth there shall be no more come unto thee the uncircumcised and the unclean.

III

I was immensely happy to see my homeland again. I had hardly
been able to restrain my impatience in the plane: it was as if
something wonderful would happen as soon as we landed, some
decisive new event, some major change. And effectively, that is what
happened.

As we began to fly over Israel, I gazed down at the long beach at Tel
Aviv, and the buildings along the coast. It was like a return, an *alyah*;
I felt like the immigrants returning to a place lost for centuries, a far
country, never before seen which is nonetheless home. I rediscovered
my identity. In the diaspora I had been nobody, and had had to seek
out Jews like myself. Here I no longer needed to justify my existence,
find a community. Here was a place of rest, where everything came
naturally. I felt as though I had been in the diaspora for centuries, and
now, at last, had come home. The wandering Jew puts down his
luggage.

My heart was warmed by the soft air that enveloped us as we made
our descent, and in the taxi to Jerusalem I felt completely at peace.
Nowhere had I ever felt this sensation of well-being: I was part of
something unique and extraordinary, and no longer had to fight for
my life.

The first bend in the road: we were beginning the climb towards
Jerusalem. I had driven this road a thousand times, and yet I was
desperately impatient. It wasn't just a return home, or the longing for
rest after a long journey. As we climbed, I realised that I looked
forward to arrival as one looks forward to a better world. I could
already see in my mind the walls of the city, and eventually they
became real, and my heart leapt and my soul rose up. I felt divinity
touch me, and was drunk on it. Eschatological impatience inhabited
me, made my soul leap. I was troubled.

I remembered a psalm, which said that if I stumbled, God in his
goodness would always save me, and if I tripped the justice of God
would defend me, and if I was oppressed, He would save me from the

pit, make my steps firm on the road. It said that in His justice He had judged me and by the abundance of His goodness all my sins had been expiated, and by His justice, He had purified me from the sins of mankind, so that the justice of God and the majesty of the Highest should be forever praised.

I thank Thee, O Lord,
for Thou hast not abandoned me
whilst I sojourned amongst a people.

[Thou hast not] judged me
according to my guilt,
nor hast Thou abandoned me
because of the designs of my inclination;
but Thou hast saved me from the Pit.
Thou hast brought [Thy servant deliverance]
in the midst of lions destined to the guilty,
and of lionesses which crush the bones of the mighty
and drink the blood of the brave.

Thou hast caused me to dwell with the many fishers
who spread a net upon the face of the waters,
and with the hunters of the children of iniquity;
Thou hast established me there for justice.
Thou hast confirmed the counsel of truth in my heart
and the waters of the Covenant for those who seek it.
Thou hast closed up the mouth of the young lions
whose teeth are like a sword and whose great teeth are like a
pointed spear,
like the venom of dragons.
All their design is for robbery
and they have lain in wait;
but they have not opened their mouth against me.

For Thou, O God, hast sheltered me
from the children of men,
and hast hidden Thy Law [within me]
against the time when Thou shouldst reveal
Thy salvation to me.

My heart and spirit were uplifted by a divine intuition, which carried me regardless towards union with the Creator. I invoked my father through him, as though he were there, in me, a part of me, as though God himself were telling me that he was alive, living through me and Him and that soon we would be reunited. It was a great consolation. Reason had told me not to give up, and told me, in familiar words, that supernatural intuition and spontaneous action were merely lazy thinking, the opposite of rationalism. But reason was vain, and I was inexplicably transported.

The town was not very big, nor even important in the modern sense of the word. It shouldn't really have been there at all. Like Ur of the Chaldees and ancient Babylon, it should long since have collapsed into rubble, and become a pasture for cattle. Why was its name changed, not to be obliterated? The empire that did that collapsed itself, and a rebuilt Jerusalem emerged from the ashes of destruction, and continued to survive. Throughout the centuries, no invading force held it: not the Byzantines, the Persians, the Abbasids, the Baghdadis, the Fatimids, the Mamelukes, the Egyptians, the Ottomans, and nor the English.

Jerusalem is eternity. The stone steps which circle the walls of the city like the bride the groom, seven times like the seven gates, like the seven candles on the candelabra, like the seven days of the week, and the seventh before the first; the golden light on the walls, the men in hats, the prayers and muttered requests; beyond the walls the Temple Mount, where the first father confronted God, who cursed the dwellings of men. The steep hills beyond the gate, where the city of the conquering king, huddled on the slope above the valley of Kidron, drank from the perennial spring, and above, the mountain of small trees, the ancient soil of great souls, and, at the foot of the valley, the tomb of the rebellious son and the pyramid of the angry prophet, with pillars to represent the heavens and bas-reliefs for the earth. The tomb of the warrior king, transformed into a mosque with a vaulted ceiling lit by flickering candles; the room next to it, containing desecrated scrolls, burnt pages, rejected words. The Via Dolorosa, the bloody calvary of the oppressed, the Messianic cross, the stations of the agony, everlasting life for man, abandonment by God. Omar's mosque, supported by the columns on which the scales will be hung to weigh each soul at the last judgement. Roman numerals, strange inscriptions on walls, on the ground and beneath the ground; the undulating cornices, the white houses, the new stone; the call from the Holy Mountain to Ezra and Nehemi returned from exile, from the ghettos of Sanz, Mattersdorf, Ger or Bez, from mellahs and casbahs; when they returned they understood, they read on the unfathomable walls, coated with dust and flies: this is my land; I will never forget it.

When the sun rises over the hills of Judaea, the Old Town is in shadow. But through the Kidron valley to the east, one hill captures every ray of sun. On its slopes is the oldest Jewish cemetery in the world, and, at its feet, there are olives and cypresses: this is Gethsemane, where things happened long ago, things that have remained hidden since the beginning of time; where, in his passionate longing to preserve the past, man repudiated graven images. It is easy, when the light grows pale on the hillside, to feel disillusion and disenchantment. This is the place that Jesus loved, where he sought peace, prayer and solitude; where he sheltered for the night – where, they say, he was betrayed.

Beyond the hills the desert is being driven back. Below, behind the ramparts, the town wears its antiquity with disconcerting insouciance. At the centre, the Wall, and, at the invisible centre, the Temple, twice destroyed, the Holy of Holies; at the heart of the ancient palace of gold and cedarwood, the House of God, where He would always find shelter. Nobody was allowed to enter, except the high priest at Yom Kippur. It is said that when the Temple was sacked, a Roman general went in, to see at last this place the Jews kept for God; when he lifted the curtain, he saw nothing. The centre of everything, the Holy place, the burning heart of Jerusalem, the burned heart of the Temple, was just an empty space, a place of emptiness. *Vanity of vanities, all is vanity.*

We went to a small hotel outside the walls, not far from the Old Town. I avoided my parents' house, in the new town, at Rehavia, so as not to have to tell my mother that my father had disappeared. But I wanted to see Mea Shearim again, and to show it to Jane. We left Kair at the hotel: he did not want to go out and run any unnecessary risks. He knew the police were looking for him, as well as the mysterious crucifier.

We took a bus to the new town and found ourselves in the prophets' street in Mea Shearim. Jane had dressed modestly, in a long skirt and a long-sleeved shirt, but it was unusual for a Hassid like myself to be seen walking alongside a young unmarried woman. So we made a rapid tour, and I showed her my old haunts: the synagogue, some of the yeshivoth, my friends' houses. Then I saw Yehudi, my old comrade, on the corner of a street. I shouted, and he ran up to me.

'Where have you been all this time?' he asked. 'You might have kept in touch.'

'My journey took longer than I expected,' I replied. 'This is Jane.'

She didn't offer her hand – she knew that a Hassid never touched a woman, unless she was his wife.

'Well come on, let's talk,' he said. 'I've got something important to tell you, Ary.'

We sat down in a café, one of the few in the area, run by a Hassid. Yehudi told me he spent his days in the yeshivah, and his wife worked in a kindergarten.

'So, have you heard the great news?' He looked both proud and mysterious.

'No?'

'It didn't reach the States?'

'No, what's going on?'

'The rabbi has spoken about the Messiah. He has revealed himself at last.'

'What did he say?'

'He announced himself.'

'Who?' I was dumbfounded.

'The rabbi, for goodness sake! He said that he is the Messiah and that the end of the world is approaching.'

I was speechless. What had made this man of eighty-two say such a thing? Why now?

'Do you believe it?' I asked him.

'Well at first, I confess I was as doubtful as you, Ary. But now I'm his son-in-law and his disciple, I know him better. I think he is a truly holy man, and more. I believe the rabbi will save us.'

I understood. When I had last seen Yehudi, he was a young man, fresh from the yeshivah, newly married; now he was one of the rabbi's close entourage, probably with some official position. He was one of the elect, envied by all the others, living close to the rabbi, and part of his daily life.

'Can't you see how bad everything is in the world,' he said. 'War, misery, injustice, it's all getting worse. They thought the horrors of the Second World War could never happen again, but we've had the

Gulf War, ethnic cleansing in former Yugoslavia, genocide in Rwanda: evil everywhere. And here, on our own soil, permanent conflict since the creation of the State of Israel, the clash between Gog and Magog! Look at Jerusalem! At least we can hope for a better world in the very near future. Revelation is at hand – we expect it at any moment. Can't you feel it? God has heard our prayers at last. He has chosen the rabbi and sent him to earth to save us.' His voice became hoarse, and he leaned towards me, gripping my shoulders. 'Ary, next year is the year 2000.'

'We passed the year 2000 long ago; three thousand, seven hundred and fifty-nine years ago, to be precise. We're not Christians – it doesn't mean a thing to us.'

He lowered his arms and shook his head.

'You don't realise what we're about to witness . . . If you don't repent, you won't be saved, you won't be part . . .'

' . . . Of the kingdom of Heaven,' I said, almost automatically. I suddenly remembered the dream I had had before setting off for the States, when I was in a car with Yehudi, following a bus, and climbing up to the sky. The bus represented the outside world, the Christian world, already saved by Jesus, and our little car represented our own world.

But I had woken up crying: 'Not yet!' I was not sure I wanted the Messiah to come so soon. What did this other world really hold for us?

'You know that tomorrow is the festival of Lag Baomer,' said Yehudi. 'The Hassidim are going to have a stand there, as usual, and this year I'm in charge of it. We're going to announce the news there. Why don't you come along?'

I agreed to meet him again the following day. It was not that I was carried away by the news, but a plan was forming in my mind, which was moving along the same lines as Yehudi's – not entirely a coincidence, as I was to discover later.

After we left Yehudi, Jane asked a lot of questions about us both. I told her he was married, and how that marriage had come about.

'Would you do the same?'

'I'd have to go to a special marriage broker, because my parents aren't religious.'

'Are there brokers for people like you?'

'There are ones who deal with slightly delicate matters: people who haven't quite adapted to society, who pray too much, or too intensely, or study too hard, or fast, or have nervous breakdowns, or emotional problems. Nobody is forgotten, you see.'

Night was falling, and her face reflected the golden light. Her eyes shone with sadness.

'They deal with mixed marriages too – I mean between Sephardis and Ashkenazis, and Sephardis who have studied in the yeshuva and become "black" – they wear only black, and they want to marry an Ashkenazi girl. The brokers try and find them one with some physical handicap, or some inheritance problem.'

'Supposing a Sephardi girl is looking for someone?'

'It's unlikely she'll find anyone, because neither Ashkenais nor Sephardis want to marry Sephardis.'

'What about women with emotional problems; do they ever find anyone?'

'In general, women don't have emotional problems before marriage. At least,' I added, seeing her surprise, 'not that the community knows about. The family would never mention it in case they didn't find a husband. For boys it's different – it would be harder to hide. They're out all the time, at the synagogue or in the street, whereas you only see the girls once a year at the synagogue.'

'What happens once the matter's settled?'

'The couple meets for the first time in the presence of the parents. After the introductions, there's some general conversation, then the parents go into another room in order to leave the young people alone together. The door is left open, as it's forbidden for an unmarried couple to be totally alone together.'

'And what do they talk about?'

'Their studies, general matters. Sometimes they don't say anything. The girl is usually very shy. Then they separate and don't meet again until the wedding day.'

'Can either of them refuse the match?'

'No. They believe their parents know what is best and trust their choice.'

'How many marriages have been arranged like that at Mea Shearim?'

'All of them, I think. Even if parents know each other and think their children would suit one another, they prefer to call in a broker, so that things can be arranged by a third party.'

'And afterwards?'

'After the marriage, the girls work until the first child is born; they teach or find a job in the community.'

'She supports the couple?'

'Yes, because the boy is studying. But they are provided with an apartment by the marrriage contract. They scrape by with the help of their friends and family, and loans from the bank.'

'And supposing it's a goya who wants to marry?'

I started. She knew the answer to that question – it was just bravado. I hadn't realised that by telling her about these marriages, I was reminding her of the impossibility of ours, and hurting her feelings.

On our way back to the hotel, we passed the Western Wall. It was five in the afternoon: night was falling. Climbing the little stone steps above the esplanade, one could see both the people praying by the wall and those returning from the Mosque of Omar after the last prayers. The afternoon sun lit the stone with a bronze glow, and one could imagine the missing Temple in an ideal Jerusalem, with great blocks of white stone surrounded by the rectangular wall. This holy and empty place, the site of horrors, revolts, usurpations of the line of Zadok, and the exhibition of idols by Antiochus, destroyed, reconstructed and destroyed again, had still not reached the end of its story; lost and found again, dreamt of before being experienced, experienced and then dreamt of again, ever since the riverside at Babylon, amongst the exiles, when the skies opened before the enraptured prophets, and a tempest came from the north, and the faithful were dazzled by a blazing fire. In their prophecies, they saw again the great square platform which contained the sanctuary of God, and, in very precise visions, the doors and chambers and the Holy of Holies; in their trances, they saw, as though before their own eyes, the precise dimensions of each wall, door and window; for them, to imagine the symmetry, the mirrors and the holy spaces was the secret code of their religion; in their trances they saw all the measurements, the mirrors, the holy spaces. But it was a utopian vision, and when the exiles returned from Babylon, and erected their Temple on the top of Moriah, the priests, penitents and pilgrims quarrelled within the sanctuary instead of uniting around plans for a perfect Jerusalem. And Herod completed the abomination when he, a despot imposed by Rome, began the great reconstruction of the Temple on Mount Moriah, and placed the seal of the golden eagle, symbol of pagan

Rome, on the finest construction in the Roman Empire. When the Dead Sea Scrolls were written, the Temple was a den of impurity: sacrifices were made each morning for the health of the emperor, and each day the holy dwelling lost a little more of the presence of its iconoclastic God.

And now, two thousand years later, they were searching for his traces, not beneath Omar's Mosque, which had hitherto been thought the site of Herod's Temple, but a bit further on, where digs had revealed parts of it. And so I began to imagine a Temple reconstructed again, if it were really possible that these excavations could show the exact site.

In my imagination I saw it as an open structure, with no wall around it, only lintels and doors, like an enormous circular bridge, with easy access to the central enclosure through the inner courtyards. Awnings and wide alleyways formed large enclosures, all giving onto an interior courtyard, all looking onto and communicating with one another. Each had different measurements: a rectangle twelve metres by eight; a triangle with fifteen-metre sides and a ten-metre base; an isosceles triangle with twelve-metre sides; then a perfect twenty-three-metre square, and a circular room sixteen-metres in diameter, another huge one with a sixty-four-metre diameter; there was a hexagon with eight- and twelve-metre sides, and a fifty-two-metre oval, an ellipse, another of indeterminate shape, square then circular, an unusual oblong shape; one with a very high ceilings, another very low, one paved, another with a shiny parquet floor, another with an oriental carpet. Some had chandeliers, others plain lamps, some had blinds, others curtains, some were brightly painted, others were in plain wood. All gave on to one another and formed an entity beneath the giant bridge.

In the courtyard there were four tables, on which were unrolled the Torah scrolls, and at the side of one of the outside doors, at the entrance to the north-facing one, two more. And two others still, opposite, so that there were a total of eight stone tables for the daily offices, one-and-a-half metres in length, and one metre in height and width. Each was reserved for a particular priest: a Sadducee priest, an Essene monk, or a Pharisee rabbi. Others would be for orthodox, liberal and reformed rabbis, the latter being a woman. And one for he who wanted, and another for he who did not want. Of the rooms with windows, some were reserved for the cantors, and gave onto inner courtyards; others, looking outwards, were for the rabbis who were in charge of the House of God, the ones closest to the Lord, the descendants of Levi.

In the centre was a hall, reached by several staircases. It gave onto the secret part of the Temple, which was seventy metres long and forty metres wide. The outside was made up of wood-panelled pillars and windows and rooms; even the floor was wood. The panelling was carved with palms and cherubs, each with two faces, each face different. All around were wooden sculptures, and the cherubim and the palms reached from the floor to the windows.

It was the Holy of Holies, the dwelling of God, where only the high priest could enter. He called himself the Son of Man, and appeared to me with the features of the rabbi. Was he the Messiah king, the saviour of all Israel? The high priest, the Wicked Priest, the Son of Man, the son of darkness or the son of light . . . Who was he really?

I suddenly emerged from my reverie.

There was no one left on the esplanade. We stayed there a little longer, and only returned to the hotel late that night. I was like a sleepwalker, moving slowly and hesitantly. To my great surprise – was this a dream, a vision, a prophecy, imagined or real? – the Golden Gate on Mount Moriah, opposite the Mount of Olives, walled up since 1530, was open that night. We went through it and back to the hotel, cooled by Jerusalem's fresh breezes.

Then said the Lord unto me; this gate shall be shut, it shall not be opened, and no man shall enter in by it; because the Lord, the God of Israel, hath entered in by it, therefore it shall be shut.

The next morning I explained to Jane why I had decided to go to the festival of Lag Baomer, which commemorated Bar Kochba's final short-lived attempt at Jewish independence in 135 AD. Bar Kochba had been supported by rabbi Akiba, who believed he was the Messiah on whom all mystical and nationalist hopes rested. The festival therefore attracted mostly very pious Jews, amongst them the Hassidim. It was an occasion for everyone, Sephardim and Ashkenazis alike, to honour the rabbis who had upheld these traditions, such as Rabbi Shimon Bar Yochai. But it was also an opportunity for the Bedouin, who came to sell their products, and I knew that the Taamireh, the tribe who had discovered the scrolls, would be there.

I asked Jane to stay at the hotel to keep an eye on Kair Benyair, and took the bus to Meron. Fourteen hundred buses and as many lorries and cars had spilled out of a clogged-up Jerusalem, and a human tidal wave had arrived at the foot of a hill in Galilee. A hundred thousand people would climb it before the end of Lag Baomer. Some pitched their tents on the rocky slopes, close to the tombs of the rabbis. Sick people were carried precariously along narrow paths on stretchers. Beggars in djellabahs and others in Hassidic clothes stationed themselves at the entrance to the sanctuary. They bickered, protecting their bags, and tried to attract attention by jingling coins in their tins. Sellers of pious objects, drinks, falafel and articles of every kind had put up rickety stalls all over the site.

I plunged into the crowd, looking for the Hassidic tent, and eventually found it close to the tomb of Rabbi Shimon. I leaned in and looked inside: there were a few planks on trestles, and pious books and tefilin scattered about. I could see Yehudi at the other opening, with a loud-hailer, shouting to passers-by: 'The Messiah is here! He is coming! We are entering the messianic era!' He caught a young soldier by the arm, and tried to make him wear a phylactery.

The soldier argued, and finally gave in.

Then Yehudi turned to me. 'Ary, I'm glad you've come. You can help me.'

'I'll look around for a bit, then I'll join you.'

Close to the Hassidic tent were old ladies telling fortunes, putting cards out three by three on a wooden plank. 'Come and see,' they cried, 'come and see if Bar Yochai is with us.'

Further away, young men fought for the privilege of carrying, for a few metres at a time, the scrolls of the Torah, which they held above their heads, followed by a procession of others doing improvised dances. A group of Hassidim followed them with a placard saying: 'We want Mashiah now.'

The Torah reached the tomb of Rabbi Shimon, amid general enthusiasm. Each celebrated the anniversary of his death in his own way: frenetic dances, warm greetings, animated discussions and lavish meals in the huge tents. Every now and then they would interrupt their celebration and run over to throw an offering of candles or incense on one of the rabbis' tombs, and beg for their prayers to be answered.

At last I found the Bedouin tent, and approached it. They were selling all kinds of trinkets and hand-made objects. I bought a small plate, without bargaining, and began talking to them.

'Where is the Taamireh tribe?' I asked.

'We are the Taamireh.'

I briefly explained that I wanted to talk to them about the caves and the manuscripts they had found there long ago in jars. They appeared to understand what I was saying, and went to get an old sage. I repeated my request.

'You must go and see Yohi,' he said, and disappeared into the tent.

'Who is Yohi?' I asked the others.

'Yohi is the one who went away.'

'Went away where?'

'He is the guardian of the tomb.'

I went back to the tomb of Rabbi Shimon Bar Yochai. It was a small stone house, and one had to go through dark corridors and small interior courtyards before reaching the central room where the vault was, at ground level. Inside were beggars, cripples and other poor creatures who could not afford a tent, praying for an improvement in their lot.

I recognised him at once, although I had never seen him before. His skin was brown and dessicated, and he had piercing black eyes, and grey hair, almost hidden by his turban. He sat at the entrance to the room and appeared to be meditating. I approached him, and said: 'Are you Yohi?'

'Yes.'

He seemed to expect me to give him a coin, as people did when they entered the mortuary. I put a note in his cup. He looked up, surprised.

'Have you left the tribe?'

He nodded.

'When?'

'Some time ago.'

'Why did you go?'

No answer.

'I made him go, Ary,' said a voice behind me.

I jumped – that slightly hoarse voice was familiar. I turned around slowly: it was Yehudi.

'I found him this job, and took him away from the tribe. What do you want with him?' I had never heard him speak in this tone.

'What do *you* want with him?' I said, amazed.

'This man is useful to us, because he knows the place where the Qumran manuscripts were found.'

'The Qumran manuscripts! What have they got to do with you? Did the rabbi send you?'

'Yes. He says he is mentioned in the scrolls. He wants them because they speak of the Messiah, and announce his coming for the year 5760.'

'Is that true?' I asked the Bedouin. 'You know about the manuscripts?'

He was silent for a moment, then said: 'The Qumran scrolls?'

'Yes.'

'It was my father who found them.'

Night was drawing to a close and the first rays of dawn were appearing when Yehudi and I finally left Yohi. Outside, the Hassidim were covering themselves with talith, and attaching their tefilins in order to begin their morning prayers. The songs and dances of the night before had given way to silent piety. In the early-morning light, in the scent of half-dead braziers, all the Hassidim stood, facing the Western Wall, swaying vigorously to and fro.

A small group meditated in a circle, sitting on the ground, to the sound of a melancholy tune played on clarinets; each phrase, improvised as it seemed, was punctuated by loud sighs that seemed to come from the depths of the soul. To be a Hassid, one's heart must encompass all happiness and all sadness, rejoicing with the fervour of messianic expectation, and bleeding from the indelible wounds left by the destruction of the Temple.

If suffering is necessary to the Hassid, then certainly I was one that morning. My suffering was too great, and my joy was tarnished. There was too much evil, too much evil for Him.

And I have been silent, when my arm was torn from its ligaments and my feet walked in the mire. My eyes were closed so as not to see the evil, and my ears blocked so as not to hear the killings. My heart was dulled by the evil scheme, because it is Belial that you see when their true leanings are shown, and all the foundations of my structure cracked, and my bones were disjointed, and parts of my body became like a boat in a tempest. And my heart beat almost to extinction, and a vertiginous wind made me stagger because of the evil of their crimes.

Sixth Scroll

THE SCROLL OF THE CAVES

I have told in my Scriptures of all the blessings and rewards which will come to them, because they preferred Heaven to their own life in this world, even though they were crushed by the wicked, and covered by them in shame and opprobrium and persecuted all the time that they blessed Me. And now I will call the spirits of the virtuous born into the light [. . .] as well as those who have not received in their flesh honour worthy of their faithfulness. I will bring out into a bright light those who have loved My holy name and I will place each one on a seat of glory. They will shine forth for all time, for the judgement of God is just: He gives His trust to the faithful in the place where they followed the paths of righteousness. They will see those born in darkness thrown into darkness, whilst the righteous will shine forth. The sinners will groan to see them in their splendour, and they themselves will go to the place ordained for them by the writings of the days and the times [. . .]

And now I tell you this mystery: sinners change and rewrite the words of truth, they alter most of them, they lie and forge great fictions, they write the Scriptures in their name. Would that they wrote all My words in their name, without deleting or altering them, but faithfully recording My testimony. I know another mystery: the righteous, the saints and the wise will receive My books and rejoice in the truth [. . .] They will believe in them and rejoice in them, and all *the righteous will* rejoice *when they learn all the paths of truth.*

Qumran scrolls, *Book of Enoch.*

I

After the beginning, after God had created man and woman and after they had sinned, He began to curse these creatures who had escaped Him. He told the woman that she would give birth in pain and that she would long for man, who would always dominate her. To the man He said that he would toil in sorrow, and that he would return to the earth whence he came, and that, being dust, he would return to dust. Then He placed cherubim on the eastern side of the Garden of Eden, so that with the flame of their sword they would guard the way to the tree of life. But why had God created man with free will, if he then had to pay the price of this freedom with his life? Why give, only to take back?

'Your father found the scrolls?' I asked Yohi.

'Yes.'

'Where is he now?'

'Dead. They killed him.'

'Tell me,' I said. 'Tell me what happened. I won't harm you. They've kidnapped my father and I want to find him.'

So he told me. There was no lost goat, or stone thrown into the cave: that was not how the manuscripts were found. One day a man had come to the Taamireh encampment: he looked like a Bedouin, but spoke an unknown language. Like all strangers he was received with the customary hospitality; they unrolled a blanket, and served sweet tea on the finest tray the tribe possessed, then served coffee in beautifully decorated cups.

That day, as usual, the tents were arranged in a long line, facing south-west. All was perfectly calm, everyone coming and going at his own pace. The summer heat was such that no one wanted to do anything but lie in the sun, and then, at its height, in the middle of the day, sit in the shade of the tent, whiling away the suffocating hours.

When the stranger had been fed and rested, they asked him what he was doing and where he was going. Because he did not speak their language, they called Yohi's father, who used to go and sell things in Israeli towns, and spoke Hebrew and a little English. He was able to speak to him quite easily: the stranger's language was like Hebrew, although not quite the form of it he normally heard.

In the tent were the sheikh and several important men of the tribe, and Yohi's father as interpreter. The stranger said that he had brought objects of great value, which he hoped to sell in the town. He thought that if the Taamireh would help him, they could share the profits. In his bag were some ancient jars out of which he drew, with infinite care, some very old pieces of parchment. The Bedouin watched curiously.

'Are you sure those old skins are so valuable?' asked the sheikh doubtfully.

In reply, the man passed a parchment to the men, so that they could look at it more closely. They studied it carefully: the scroll was covered with little black marks in regular patterns. They could not read, but they felt, seeing the man so proud of his discovery, that this must be something important. So they held a short council, at the end of which it was decided that Yohi's father, whose name was Falipa, should try to sell the scrolls when he next went to the town.

It was getting dark, so they invited the man to share their traditional supper of rice with raisins and onions. He slept in the sheikh's tent and left the next morning, at dawn, having agreed that he would meet the Taamireh again at their next encampment, in a month's time.

A week later, Falipa went to Jerusalem, where he laid out, amongst his other wares, the jars and the scrolls. Several days passed and nobody stopped. Then one morning a man passing through the souk gave a start when he glanced at them, then studied them carefully.

'Where did you get these?' he asked finally.

'I was given them,' said the Bedouin.

'How much do you want for them?'

Falipa had no idea what they were worth, but he thought it might be a lot, by what the man had said; and the proceeds would have to be shared, too. He gave a price at random, the equivalent of seven hundred shekels, thinking that the customer would bargain and reduce it by half.

But he paid up without a word, and Falipa returned to the camp, delighted to have obtained such a sum. When the man came to the rendezvous, he took his share of the money, and offered more jars

207

and manuscripts. These were eagerly accepted, and so began the traffic in scrolls.

After a few months, rumours began to spread around neighbouring Bedouin encampments that the Taamireh had become rich, and had had a good year: their camels were fat, their humps so round that it was hard to tell if they were camels or some other type of animal, and thirty-six young had been born recently. It was true. Thanks to the scrolls, which Yohi's father continued to sell, always to the same person, the tribe had become rich. The other tribes became jealous, and jealousy turned to covetousness.

The desert at that time was not at peace, and there were constant raids and counter-raids. Enemy tribes attacked one another, pillaging and sometimes killing. Bedouin wars followed strict rules, to ignore which would bring shame and dishonour on a tribe, whereas to win according to the rules covered the individual and his tribe in glory and honour, what every Bedouin longed for. The code was based on justice: you only fought against those who could defend themselves; women and children were not touched, nor any guest, nor the boy guarding the herds. Surprise attacks were possible, although war was usually declared beforehand, but it would have been shameful to attack at midnight or at dawn, when everybody was asleep. According to the Bedouin, when a man is asleep his soul escapes through his nostrils and wanders around.

One morning the Taamireh were attacked, at sunrise (this was within the rules, as it gave the victims all day to recover their scattered flocks) by the Revdat, an enemy tribe. When they reached the camp they divided into two groups: one to take away the sheep, the other to stop the horses from being used to pursue them when they left.

In an hour, everything had been ransacked – sheep and camels stolen, the camp devastated. There had even been a man killed, a Bedouin trying to protect his sheep with a sword, who had been trampled by the horses. The Bedouin did not, on the whole, like to spill human blood, even though their hard lives made them relatively indifferent to suffering and death. The purpose of a raid was theft, not murder, and the death of this Bedouin was a serious matter.

As the wives and children of the defeated could not be left destitute, the Revdat gave a camel to each of the Taamireh women, so that they could reach their nearest relatives in other camps. Apart from this, the Taamireh had nothing, and were desperate. They held a council to decide what could be done: sometimes the nobler type of raider could be persuaded to give back stolen camels and horses, if they could show that the theft had been dishonest, but these were fierce enemies, and jealous too, of the Taamirehs' recent good fortune.

The Taamireh, however, bore no grudge against the Revdat tribe, because what they had done was perfectly normal: after the hot and difficult days of summer, the Bedouin always started planning *ghazu*, raids on the camels and flocks of neighbouring tribes. For them it wasn't really theft, but almost an exchange – after all, were they not acting in the name of Allah? They themselves had often planned and carried out similar surprise attacks, in an atmosphere of secrecy and excitement. It wasn't the actual raid that worried them; they had suffered many raids before, often for months at a time and over long distances; mounted raids, to double the amount of camels taken, and others when every man had brought his own flour, dates and water, so as to be self-sufficient in case they were dispersed. Their leader, a strong and passionate man, eloquently reminded them of all this. No, what really worried them was that the raid had been caused by news of the scrolls and the money. The leader spoke to the tribe in the ruins of the camp:

'We have provoked the rage of Allah, and drawn the evil eye upon us. It is those scrolls that made us so rich. Allah has given and he has taken away: this means that he does not wish us to be rich. We will no longer sell the scrolls.'

The Bedouin greeted his words with relief; the rage of Allah had been explained. If they followed their leader's advice, they would be spared.

It was the end of summer, and both men and animals needed water. They had pitched their tents near a water hole, but the drought had been severe, and it was almost dry. It was a particularly hard August, still very hot, and for several days they had been worriedly scanning the sky for signs of rain.

One day, soon after the leader's pronouncement, they saw flashes of lightning, and immediately sent men to find out where the rain had fallen; the scouts came back a few days later, and the whole tribe raised camp and set off towards Jordan.

The night they reached the Jordanian desert and pitched their tents, a great storm broke over the sleeping camp: the air became oppressively hot, then a cold wind blew. There was an ear-splitting crack of thunder, and the desert was lit up like day by a flash of lightning. The men ran to their remaining camels, and the women to protect the children in the tents. Everybody waited, frozen, for ten minutes, while the distant rumbling grew deeper and louder. At last the rain came, gentle at first, then cold and heavy. There were cries of joy, echoing over the sand, as the hollows around the camp filled with water; when the rain slackened, men, women and children ran out to collect it in any receptacle they could find, bowls and pots and pans. Then they sat with their faces turned up, drinking the rain. The men woke the camels and made them drink litres of the cool brown lake around the camp; everybody was delirious with happiness. They had been blessed. All were convinced that this was because they had abandoned the sale of the scrolls. God, who had judged, punished, and now recompensed them, was great.

In the early light of dawn, they gathered to pray and give thanks. Each tent was like a small ark on a sea of fresh water. Summer was over. The rain had brought pastel colours to the desert, now an opalescent green. Life resumed its course, and the now impoverished Bedouin would manage; they had water, at least, the essential element for any new start.

When one day the man from the desert reappeared, with more jars and more scrolls, the leader told him firmly that they had sworn not to touch them any more, and begged him to leave with his merchandise.

The next day, there was a bad sandstorm, a veritable pea soup poured onto the desert. Inside the tents they had to light lamps and try to protect their faces, clothes, food and belongings from the all-invading sand. Nobody emerged for two hours: the sand blew so fast that anyone in its path could be badly hurt.

The sheikh in his tent wondered: 'Does this come from God? Perhaps Allah is angry because we saw the man yesterday. Perhaps he is taking revenge on the man.' For the man had left the previous day, and must still be in the desert, at the mercy of the storm. Men were often lost in sandstorms; it would be hard to survive in such a violent one as this. But he might be experienced enough to make his camel kneel down and crouch under its flank.

Several uneventful days passed, and then, one evening, there was renewed panic: the sky shook, and there were strange rumblings of thunder. Tents began to collapse. Some people started praying, others climbed to the top of a small dune beside the camp to scan the horizon. What they saw filled them with horror: in the distance, for as far as the eye could see, the horizon was on fire. The sky and stars were shrouded by black, smoky clouds. It was like a belt of fire beneath a leaden dome; a deep purple tornado racing towards them.

They ran into their tents, to pray to Allah and beg forgiveness. They lowered the drapes and held onto the cords, as they always did in bad sandstorms. An icy wind blew: when they looked out they saw the thing approaching, but it was not fire. The wind turned to hail.

Then they understood: it was a red sandstorm. What had looked like black smoke in the sky was just thick dust, now spreading everywhere. The great tongues of fire, regularly rising and falling, were whirling columns of dust that rose from the ground as if by magic. Crackling electrical discharges followed by rumbling thunder seemed to presage the end of the world. In a very few seconds, the camp was entirely covered with red sand.

After a few hours, the thunder passed over, giving way to a cool breeze. Then the Bedouin began to chant *al-hamadu li'ilah*: 'We have never experienced such a revelation. We thought the fire of God was about to devour us, and that the end of the world had come.' But their joy was muted: it had been a terrible experience. They spent the day resting, and in the evening ate a meagre repast coated in red dust. The sky soon cleared, but the whole landscape was the colour of brick.

The next day, they struck camp and set off towards the north, where they thought they might find a milder climate and some greenery. But their troubles had not ended: after a few days of travel, they were about to settle in a calm green spot near the Jordanian frontier when an undulating carpet appeared on the horizon. As it came closer they saw that it was a close-packed cloud of all-devouring locusts.

The yellow and black wave kept coming for three days, and left nothing in its path. The Bedouin caught some of them to eat, spreading out carpets and covers. Camels, dogs and men all feasted on them, but it was meagre consolation for what they had destroyed: every grass and bush, everything that makes the desert habitable, had been devoured. The land looked as though a bomb had dropped: the fields were empty, and only desert was left. With no grass the sheep were doomed, and the men not much better off. The Taamireh felt that they were being hounded by the Devil.

One morning soon after the locusts had left, as the first rays of the rising sun touched the camp, the men emerged from their tents into the still cold air and knelt down on the sand. Then the sheikh began to speak to the assembled tribe, including the women who were called from their tents, where they were praying or preparing the morning meal.

'This is why I have assembled you this morning,' he said. 'Allah has given us warnings of his anger, signs that show we have sinned. Thieves took our animals and killed one of our men; we suffered the tempest of red fire, announcing the end of the world; and now the locusts have taken the little we have left. All this has happened because Allah is angry; he is angry because of the scrolls. They are cursed!'

'But we don't have them any more. We sent the man away, and he is probably dead,' said one of the Bedouin.

'We sent him away, yes. But Allah is still angry with us. It must mean that one of us took the scrolls. He must confess, now, so that we can be saved from the wrath of God. He must give back the manuscripts, and then disappear for ever from our sight.'

They were silent. Each man looked suspiciously at his neighbour. Then one stood up: Falipa, Yohi's father.

'I took them,' he said. 'I didn't mean to do any harm, and I didn't think I was offending Allah. I just wanted to regain our fortune.'

'Where are they now?' asked the sheikh.

Falipa hung his head. 'I have already sold them,' he confessed.

The next day he was found dead in his tent.

When a murder is committed in the desert, the man responsible must usually take refuge with a cousin in a tribe as far away as possible to escape the revenge of the murdered man's family, and from there negotiate a sum for blood money. If there are no reprisals in the days that follow the murder, money is accepted to the value of fifty camels for a relation, or seven for a man from another tribe.

In this case nobody left the tribe, and nobody offered money. It was clear that the Bedouin had agreed to kill him, in order to escape further plagues. So Yohi went to the sheikh, to claim vengeance.

The sheikh called together a gathering of wise men, and after a long debate it was established that Yohi's father had acted disloyally, and had placed the whole tribe in danger by attracting the wrath of God. One of the wise men insulted the name of his father by saying that he was probably in Hell, and Yohi was narrowly prevented by the others from striking him.

For a Bedouin, Paradise was a place where it was always spring, with abundant grass and water, with perennial springs and rivers; it was a place where there was no hunger and no thirst, no parched fields and sick animals, where tribes lived together and nobody grew old. Hell contained all that was worst about the world: hot dry summers in which water for thirsty camels had to be carried on men's backs. To wish somebody in Hell was the worst thing a Bedouin could do. Yohi left the council sad and dejected. The whole tribe was against him, and he would not be able to avenge his father.

It was then that he met Yehudi, at the festival of Lag Baomer, who, in exchange for information about the scrolls, offered him the chance to leave the tribe, which he immediately accepted.

'What happened to the man who brought the scrolls?' I asked, when he had told his story.

'He didn't die in the sandstorm. At first he went on walking. Then, thinking he was lost, he stopped. Eventually the storm stopped and he went on.'

'How do you know?'

'Because I saw his son.'

'When?'

'Yesterday. He came to find me.'

'What did he want?'

'The same as Yehudi. He wanted to know if my father had kept any unsold scrolls.'

'And had he?'

'No, he sold all the ones he had.'

'But how did you hear about the scrolls?' I asked Yehudi.

'The rabbi sent me to find them. Since he read about them in the papers, he's been trying to find out about them. He met Hosea several times.'

I had an idea. I asked Yohi one last question. 'What was the name of the man whose father found the scrolls, the man you saw yesterday?'

'Kair. Kair Benyair.'

When I got back to the hotel, I found Kair with Jane.

'Listen,' I said at once, 'I've just met a man from the Taamireh tribe, called Yohi. Does that mean anything to you?'

He didn't answer.

'There's no point lying. He told me everything.'

'I escaped to go and find him, and then I came back to the hotel.'
'Why did you go and see him? How do you know him?'
No answer.
'Where do you come from?' I shouted. 'Who are you? Where did your father find the scrolls? What's your connection with Hosea? Answer!' I would have grabbed him, but Jane held me back.

He answered all my questions by saying he knew nothing. I didn't want to bring Shimon into it before trying to find my father myself; I was afraid of poisoning the situation, and bringing in elements I could not control.

'Very well,' I said, picking up the telephone. 'If you won't answer, I must call the police.'

He stopped me with a gesture. 'My father found them in a cave. I'll show you where.'

'First tell me where you come from, and how you met Hosea.'

'When my father found the scrolls, he wanted to sell them, but didn't know how to. That's why he went to the Bedouin and Falipa. But then they killed Falipa and didn't want any more to do with the affair. When my father died, I went to the place where Falipa used to sell them, the place my father told me about. That's how I met Hosea. He's the one Falipa used to sell the scrolls to.'

'How did you find them? Are you a Bedouin?'

'No. Tomorrow I'll show you where I found them. There are lots more there, and a treasure. Hosea found a good part of it, but the most precious pieces are still there. It's all written in the manuscript. Perhaps we'll find it, and your father too.'

I decided, for the moment, to accept these explanations. I didn't understand how or why, but if he could take me to the hidden caves of Qumran, that was a good start.

II

The next day we set off for Qumran in a hired car, which Jane drove. Kair seemed to be following us as well as leading us. There was no need to guard him: he was greedily impatient to find the legendary treasure.

I felt a strange mixture of apprehension and sadness at seeing the Dead Sea landscape again. In the distance, the powdery white mountains of Qumran, without shade or trees, grass or moss, their only horizon the salt sea with its dried mud and moving sands, seemed more threatening than ever. Puny scrub struggled feebly in this lifeless landscape. Leaves drooped, weighed down by salt. The sea did not gleam; it seemed tarnished by the cities that lay beneath it, gradually sinking, into dark caverns where no living creature could survive. There were no trees, birds or greenery on its banks; all the misery of the world seemed to be contained within that bitter, heavy water, unrippled by the wind. The Dead Sea, without port or sails, seemed a desert sea surrounded by desert. One instinctively approached it, thinking it a source of life, and one was constantly deceived by the lack of fresh water.

We reached the desert. The earth, between the arid beaches and the rocks which hid Qumran, became sandy and rock-strewn, and we were alone among empty, secret spaces. The wind blew ever stronger. It sounded like sails flapping on the roof of the car, as though a malevolent force were shaking a cloth above our heads. The sun was high, and beat down mercilessly. Mica shone darkly on the ground, where not a single plant grew.

And so we arrived at Ain Feshka, the site of the remains of the Essene dwellings. People here lived in tents, huts and caves, and between Ain Feshka and Qumran was a cultivated plain, several kilometres long. If you scratched the soil, you could find date stones: there had been palm trees here in Essene times. Nowadays there were just a few saplings, meagre and sparse, watered by springs from the mountains to prove that the place abandoned to reeds and tamarisks could be restored to cultivation.

Inside the ruins, one could see solid foundations amongst the constructions. There was one long wall, about a metre thick, around the edge of the irrigated area, which appeared to be the foundation of a high tower, and formed a proper enclosure of bricks on top of stone, marking the limits of a rebuilt town. Halfway along it was a small building, a simple square, open to the east, facing the plantation, with a courtyard and three rooms; it looked half-built.

The main site was close to the Feshka spring, at the southern end of the fertile area and two kilometres north of Ras Feshka. This was a huge square, slightly irregular, leaning against the enclosure wall, with a shed on the northern side opening inwards. Next to this was a large building comprising a courtyard bordered by small rooms; a staircase showed that there must once have been another floor.

Finally, at the northern end, three cisterns, linked by canals, were dug from the rock; huge and still usable, they were the best-preserved part of the ruins, as though they were still waiting to baptise souls in search of ultimate forgiveness.

Everything was still there, like a watch that someone had forgotten to wind up, but whose mechanism is still in good condition. All that was needed was a little water from the falls of Wadi Qumran to pour into the main basin, and flow out through the canal, crossing the courtyards and service buildings, fill up the smaller basin and the big circular cistern, as well as the two rectangular ones. To the west it would feed the mill, whose well-cemented walls and tightly packed chambers were built to hold as much flour as possible. Through another branch of the canal, it would pass the sluice by means of which the refectory and assembly hall could be flood-cleaned, flow around the reservoir towards the small basin, then end up in the great cisterns. The potter would use it to soften his clay in that dusty air, before letting it mature in the little pit, turning it on the archaic wheel, worked by foot, and finally baking the pieces, large and small, in the kilns.

We stopped in front of the scriptorium, where scribes copied Biblical manuscripts and transcribed the works of the sect. Here again, the men were gone but the tools of their trade were still there: the main table, high and wide, made of clay; the remains of two smaller ones; and amongst the debris, the two inkpots, one bronze, the other terracotta, unused but still the true masters of the place. I was suddenly moved to see again the dried ink I had noticed when I had come here with my father, looking as though it had been abandoned a few weeks before, rather than thousands of years ago. Further on was the great room which served as refectory, the grain silos, the kitchen, the forge, the workshops and the pottery, with its two ovens and plastered shelves.

Seeing all these concrete objects, a whole world seemed to come to life: an organised community, whose activities had as their only purpose the support of the most important work of all, that of the scribes. Imagined again, the ruins seemed alive, like the burning bush which is never consumed. They seemed hardly twenty or thirty years old; a speck of time. These were rough sketches, not ruins.

'Do you think they were massacred by the Romans,' Jane asked, 'or did they manage to escape?'

'I don't know. It doesn't look as though these buildings were destroyed. They never found any evidence of a massacre.'

'But if they escaped, where did they go?'

I looked towards the caves. 'Not far – a place they knew well, where they would shelter from time to time, and which could be the perfect hiding place, if necessary.'

Ever since we had reached the site Kair had seemed nervous. But he seemed to know the way, up steep slopes and along paths hidden from sight, and we finally reached the caves. Before us rose the almost vertical wall of rock in which they lay. We walked on in silence, following the ancient path of the Bedouin towards their encampments around Bethlehem. We held our breath, afraid both of the danger and of not finding anything. As we climbed, the air became softer and sweeter than it had been down by the Dead Sea, freshened by the nearby springs. All around us were steep ravines, protecting the galleries of caves from the outside world.

Then, in front of the entrance to the first cave, Kair stopped, and looked solemnly at us, as though asking us to prepare for danger. With a strange presentiment, I turned to Jane.

'Don't come.'

'But Ary, I want to be with you.'

'No,' I said firmly. 'You may be able to save our lives. Listen: go back to Jerusalem, and if we're not back tomorrow, raise the alarm.'

'If that's what you want,' she said, resigned.

We exchanged one last look, trying not to appear as frightened as we felt. Then, without turning round, I plunged after Kair into the depths of the earth.

At the back of the first cave, there was a small crack in the wall. We squeezed through it. The sides were crumbly, and trickles of earth fell around us, as if to bury us. The passage opened into a second cave, identical to the first; I inspected the sides with my torch, until I discovered another opening in the right-hand wall.

After several hours, we found ourselves in a much bigger cave, like a huge circular room cut from the rock by man. It was cold and dark, and the air was damp. I ran my torch over the walls and ceiling: thousands of disturbed bats began to fly around us in a terrifying dance, with piercing screams. We blocked our ears, and stood still in the midst of the chaos; eventually the bats returned, one by one, to their silent hiding place. We moved forward cautiously, and the light fell on a large bronze chest in a corner of the cave. The Qumran treasure, I thought excitedly – the treasure of the Copper Scroll.

Kair rushed to the chest. While he was trying to prise it open with his knife, I noticed an enormous brown leather sack near the entrance to the cave, close to the chest.

I opened it: it was full of human bones.

In a flash, I realised what was about to happen.

I turned to warn Kair not to open the chest. But it was too late: he had opened it.

Gas poured out, asphyxiating him on the spot, and spreading through the cave.

I fled back to the opening we had come in by: it was not there. I was suffocating; with a handkerchief over my face, I pushed further along the rock face – and there, right at the far end, was a small stone door.

Barely breathing, I pushed it open with difficulty and found myself in a smaller, dark room. Hastily slamming the door behind me, I caught my breath, and as my eyes became used to the darkness, gave a start.

There was a man at the back of the cave, coming towards me.

I prepared for the worst, but found the best. It was my father.

My fear dissolved, unable to restrain my joy, I began to sob. At this blessed moment I momentarily forgot that a man had just died and we were deep in a labyrinth of caves; caves I had come to in search of my father, without knowing why. I had only one thought in my mind, and it was something I had stopped daring to believe: he was alive. I was fortunate: my prayers had been answered. I tasted pure happiness, unalloyed by the anticipation of danger. I could have left then, without the scrolls or any further enlightenment. He was there. What more could I want?

I told him rather disjointedly what had happened since his disappearance, and how I had got here. 'But we'll talk about it later,' I said. 'Let's get out of here.'

I threw myself against the little stone door I had come in by, but it was firmly closed and impossible to move. I turned, and understood from the look on my father's face that it was hopeless; that he had already spent long hours trying. We were shut in, prisoners of the rock.

Our eyes gradually became used to the darkness. Not knowing what to do next, we sat down and my father told me what had happened to him: how he had been imprisoned, then taken to Israel, to the Samaritans, and nearly sacrificed, replaced at the last moment by a lamb. How he had been convinced that he was about to die horribly, and the passing hours had increased his agony; how he had thought of my mother and myself, and how this had made his suffering even worse, as he did not know if I were alive or dead. After this ordeal, his kidnappers had taken him away again, still ignorant of his fate, on a car journey to a very dark place, which he recognised at once. Blindfolded, he could smell the hot, acrid breath of the Judaean desert, and the damp stone of the Qumran caves.

'Then I knew who they were,' he continued. 'I knew them well: they were the brothers I had left when I was eighteen.'

'Your brothers?' I asked, disconcerted.

'My Essene brothers had come to take me back.'

I didn't understand. There had been no Essenes for thousands of years; I thought perhaps he had gone mad.

'Everyone thought they had all disappeared, either massacred or swallowed up by an earthquake after the Roman invasion. In fact they fled to the caves, where they lived for all those centuries – and *still live now*. I never told you, Ary; nobody knows, not even your mother, because when I left I swore to keep their secret. But the Essenes still exist, and I was one of them until the creation of the state of Israel. Then I and some others decided to leave, to experience the thing we had been longing and praying for down all those centuries.

And I wanted to meet other Jews, to live on Israeli soil in the open, away from the Dead Sea and the desert dunes, out of the subterranean caves. I wanted to see Jerusalem. Can you understand that?'

His voice trembled, and tears flowed from his screwed-up eyes. 'They wanted to question me to find out if I had betrayed them, and because they were searching for their stolen manuscript. They kept me prisoner, but they didn't dare kill me, because I'm a Cohen, one of the high priests, and they respect hierarchy. And besides, they believed what I said – they knew that I knew nothing.'

'So it was only when you got here that they unmasked themselves?'

'Yes, or they couldn't have held me; they knew that I would be worried about you and try to find you, and would have argued with them, used my authority.'

Lowering his voice, he added: 'They're the ones who stayed here after the creation of the state of Israel: they don't want to live there until the Messiah comes. They believe events have accelerated and now they're hoping for a divine intervention, which they believe is imminent and pray for all the time. But I think they've gone mad, living in these underground caves, while so much has happened outside.'

'They didn't hurt you?'

'No.'

It was the first time he had ever spoken to me about his youth, and it was almost a digression, a scientific fact that just had to be explained, that I had to understand. In other circumstances I would have wanted a thousand explanations, and it would have taken me days to get used to the idea; I would have gone over the whole thing over and over again. But there, it all seemed quite natural and obvious, and I understood quickly. Everything suddenly became clear: his reluctance to embark on the mission, his fear of discovering terrible things, and his wish, too, to help his Essene brothers. I understood now the vestigial superstitions that had always seemed to underlie his scientific certainties.

But much as I wanted to know more, I wasn't given the time. As he was telling his story, a man appeared in the cave and brusquely interrupted him.

He was of medium height, and although he looked and dressed like a Bedouin, his skin was not bronzed and leathery like theirs. In the light, indeed, it looked dead white. He approached me, looking surprised.

'It's my son, Ary,' said my father, who seemed to know him. 'Don't hurt him. He came to find me.'

'If he's your son, he's a scribe, the son of a scribe,' the man said. 'Therefore he must stay here.'

He handed us some parchments, an inkwell and a pen, and said in an antiquated language, ancient Aramaic that might have come straight from the steles my father used to study: 'Here's what you'll do. You must complete your mission. Write down what I tell you.'

Then this man, who was the leader of the Essenes, the high priest, began to tell his story. We listened in silence.

'There was a time when my valley was a long, continuous lake, and the rocks were at the bottom. When the waters dropped, caves appeared in the rock they had eaten into, and the underwater city became a viable dwelling place for men. They are mostly very hard to see. Some small cavities are completely hidden, and one has to clear the entrance to get inside. They are valuable hiding places, too, both for men and for treasure hidden by men. Ours was never discovered, it is far too deeply buried, and even I only know of it through the old stories. You have to walk a long way, and bend double to reach it, because it is deep in the mountain. When, three thousand years ago, David hid in one of the caves of Ein Gedi, King Saul took thousands of men to search for him, but instead of finding him, went to sleep in the very cave where he was hiding, without seeing him. In the same way the cave of the scrolls was not discovered by the Bedouin: it was far too deep for that, and had resisted man's efforts to find it for two thousand years. It is somewhere to the north of Ain Feshka, in a desert of stone; its entrance is a tiny hole in the rock, and on its floor were the clay jars, sealed and intact, with the scrolls inside them. But we know how they found the caves and why. How could anyone believe that the Bedouin, who had been around for centuries, only discovered them so late, and because of a lost goat?

'For a long time we were many in the caves, until the return of the Jews to their land. We had been expelled by the Romans, but we hid the scrolls in the caves to keep them safe, and then decided to hide there ourselves, unknown to anybody. For hundreds, then thousands of years, our community dwelt there, sheltered from the changes in the outside world, living according to the Law and our rituals – but we abandoned celibacy, because we needed children to perpetuate ourselves. We had before us the law of God, we bore it on our arms and on our foreheads, and we touched it as we entered our dwellings, thanks to our mezuzots. We told time by our records and our calendar, with which we could follow the movements of the stars and the seasons.

'As is the will of God, we follow the solar year, reduced to three hundred and sixty-four days, and divided into four parts of ninety-one days each. We begin each section on a Wednesday, and we have two thirty-day months and one of thirty-one days. We have holy places, where we hold liturgical gatherings, read texts and take our meals. We read the Word of God in Hebrew from the top of the ambo, and we recite psalms, canticles, hymns, benedictions and curses. Each day we take a purifying bath and, cleansed of sin, gather for the messianic repast. At the rising and the setting of the sun, we gather to pray together, except for the priests who have a special function, the office of light. On Sundays, we commemorate the creation and the fall of man; on Wednesdays, the gift of the Law to Moses; on Fridays we beg for the forgiveness of sins; and the Sabbath is a day of praise.

'Our whole life was perfectly regulated, and we survived for thousands of years, unknown to anybody, hidden in the rocks. But when, at the beginning of this century, the first Jews came back to rejoin those who had always stayed, and others followed, and then came the final return of the people to this land, and the creation of the state, everything changed. We heard of it when we went into the towns, disguised as Bedouin. So some of us decided that the time had come to live in the open, and rejoin our people scattered in the diaspora. For them the time of expiation was over, and we were entering a new Messianic era. But others disagreed; they felt they could not return until the Temple had been rebuilt, and there is a golden dome on the site, which prevents this from happening. For them, the Messiah had not yet come, and they felt that they must remain in the shelter of the caves until the moment of salvation actually arrived, and do nothing without his help.

'Surely this return to Israel after the great disasters was a sign from God? Had the war not taken place, the war of Gog and Magog, between the forces of light and the forces of darkness? Had not our brothers suffered more than usual? said some. Others replied that as long as the hand of God was not revealed by the Messiah, we should not emerge. Some thought that the leader of the fight for Israel's independence was the Messiah. Others said he was only a military leader, and, as long as blood was being spilt, we could not return.

'And so the community was split; one part wanted to live in Israel, the other to remain in the caves. Those who left swore a solemn oath never to reveal where they came from, or speak of their brothers who had remained in the community. The secret which had kept them alive, the secret of their isolation and their solitude, must be respected.

'Then one of our number spoke, for money; he who gave our manuscripts to the Bedouin to sell. This man was Moshe Benyair. He met Hosea by chance, in the course of a deal. Hosea was one of us too, an apostate who had become an Orthodox bishop. These two scoundrels between them revealed our secret to the whole world. They searched for our treasure, found it, sold it and vilified it.

'We held a council to decide how to punish this wicked, concupiscent traitor who had sold our treasure for gold, and might betray us, reveal our hiding place and prevent us from accomplishing our mission. That was when we decided to execute Hosea. Moshe escaped before we could reach him, but his son has returned and is dead because of his greed. We brought back all the sacred objects from the Temple that Hosea had in his chamber. With the money we took from him, and using you, too, David, to be a hostage for their ceremony, we bought the rest back from the Samaritans. It is all here now, in the chest, and will be kept until the coming of the Messiah.'

'But why crucify these men? Why crucifixion? And why kill the others? They weren't Essenes,' I cried.

'Three other people had had access to the scrolls: Matti, the son of Eliakim Ferenkz, Thomas Almond and Jacques Millet. We crucified them in the same way as Jesus was crucified thousands of years ago. Crucifixion has been our ritual form of execution ever since. It was our way of killing our enemies and those who wished to steal our history. *An eye for an eye, a tooth for a tooth.*'

'But why Jesus? Was he one of you?'

'That is our secret.'

'What about the Shapira affair? The man who killed himself, whose manuscripts were never found? Were you responsible for that?'

'Yes, our ancestors did that. He had found the scrolls, and was about to reveal our existence. So they killed him in Holland, and took back the scrolls.'

'And why did you crucify them on those strange crosses of Lorraine, not ordinary crosses? Was it to add torsion to the pain of crucifixion?' I asked.

The man did not appear to understand my question. I repeated it, but he still said nothing: my father intervened.

'That was the only sort of cross they knew, Ary. It was the sort of cross the Romans actually used. The one we know is the result of a later change in the shape. Jesus's cross is a decapitated cross of Lorraine.'

'You knew about all this from the start?' I asked.

'I suspected it.'

'Why didn't you say anything?'

'What could I have said? I couldn't betray them. That's why I accepted the mission – I thought, and feared, that they might be involved. And I didn't want anybody else to discover their existence. That was why I wanted to give it all up, after those atrocious crimes. I could no longer understand what was happening, nor wanted to keep their secret.'

'But what is this terrible secret in your past, that you're so desperate to hide?' I said.

'You cannot know that yet,' said the Essene priest. 'Now,' he said, turning on his heel, 'write.'

Two men appeared and pushed us to the depths of the cave, threatening us with antique knives. We went through a door which led to a subterranean passage, down which we were forced to walk further and further along labyrinthine paths, sometimes so low and narrow that we had to bend double. After about half an hour of damp and darkness, we reached a cave with a door carved into the stone. We went in and they shut the door behind us.

This was our home for forty days and forty nights. For the first three days we had no food or drink. I curled up in a corner of the cave, while my father tried in vain to remain standing, his legs weakened by hunger. Jane was my only hope. I knew that she would be worried, and would by now be doing all she could to find us. She must surely have understood that we had fallen into a trap, at the heart of the Qumran mystery. She knew where the entrance was – but how would she find this place? I did not know who she would go to, either; Shimon perhaps, whom I had told her about, or Yehudi, or the Israeli authorities. I longed with all my heart for her to find us, and yet a part of me felt that the Qumran secret must be kept – even though I didn't yet know what it was.

As starvation weakened my body, I felt my physical and mental powers waning. My mind wandered, and strange disconnected thoughts, beyond space and time, clashed violently in my head. And then, in the discipline imposed by abstinence, with an intense effort of concentration, forcing myself to forget my body and its suffering, I entered a state of *rapture*.

I saw unforgettable things, images from the time of Qumran. It was an evil world, in which divine creation was arrogantly mocked by the profane and the lewd. It was clear that such a world must be destroyed, and such destruction could only be imagined in a place like the edge of the Dead Sea, three hundred feet beneath sea-level, between the sour and stagnant lake and the bare and menacing cliffs. There, where the sun beat down mercilessly, where even the wind was hot and poisonous, where living beings could hardly survive, there was no place for a world. Hell seemed to have come to the surface in this dark hole, beneath the burning sun. I was primitive man observing the scene of God's judgement of human sin.

Fire rained down on Sodom and Gomorrah. A gigantic cataclysm was taking place; bitter salt tears flowed from the sea beneath stormy skies. Everywhere, huge oil and bitumen wells exploded in great sheets of mingled steel and fire. Above, the Gohr pursued its melancholy way through Jordan. It was an endless saga. The crust of the earth shook with rage and from its entrails rose a primitive roar, heralding a massive primeval earthquake, which, clashing with a previous one, threw up thousands of tons of oil, burning the inside of the earth's crust and causing huge sulphurous explosions. Fire and hail, mingled with blood, scorched the earth, and any vestigial trees and greenery on the shore of the lake. The sea was red with blood, all living things upon it dying, ships sinking. A huge star crashed through the burning sky.

Then the rivers and springs caught fire, the sun and the moon darkened, days lost their brightness and nights their luminosity. Stars fell, leaving columns of smoke, as from a furnace. Locusts spread over the earth, like scorpions, or warhorses. They had gold crowns on their heads, and human faces.

Then a great crowd of men, from all nations and tribes, speaking every language, stood before the celestial throne and the Lamb of God, wearing white robes and carrying palms. All proclaimed out loud: 'Praise to God on his throne, and praise to the Lamb of God.' And all the angels around Him fell before Him, faces to the ground, and worshipped God.

With this great movement the earth disappeared. A new sky and a new earth appeared – the previous ones had gone, and the seas with them. I saw the new Jerusalem descend from the sky, a bride prepared for her wedding night. A voice from the throne said that the time was near, and that we no longer had to be silent or keep the secrets of the books. *Behold, he cometh with clouds; and every eye shall see him, and they also which pierced him: and all kindreds of the earth shall wail because of him. Even so, amen, I am Alpha and Omega, the beginning and the ending, saith the Lord, which is, which was, and which is to come, the Almighty.*

It was the victory of the sons of light over the sons of darkness, the army of Belial, the band of Edom and Moab and the sons of Ammon, and the multitudes of the sons of the East and the Philistine. The sons of darkness were suffering the hardships of the desert, and war would break out against them: the exile of the sons of light was over; they had returned from their desert to dwell eternally in Jerusalem.

After this final war, the nations returned from the diaspora. *He* emerged in a violent rage to fight against the kings of the North, and, in His anger, to destroy and wipe out His enemy. This was the time of salvation for the people of God, and of disarray for the sons of Japhet: the domination of evil was over, impiety wiped out, leaving no trace, not a single survivor amongst the sons of darkness.

Then I saw the Essene encampments in the wilderness; they had been hounded from Judaea by the persecution of the high priest, and forced to live in exile in the land of Shem. I saw the deportation into Babylon at the time of Nebuchadnezzar, and I saw the whole subsequent history of the Jews, a story of destruction and injustice, massacre and catastrophe. I saw the executioners, the victims, and the witnesses.

Then I saw the sons of light gradually illuminating all the corners of the earth, until all the dark times had disappeared. Then I saw the moment when His greatness shone forth for all time, with happiness and blessings, glory and everlasting life for the sons of light.

And I saw a battle, unending carnage, on a very dark day, fixed by the Lord, a long time ago. On this day, the congregation of gods and the assembly of mankind met for the final confrontation. It was a time of suffering for the people who had been absolved of their sins; of all the miseries Earth had suffered, there had been nothing as bad as this, until finally the Redemption came. For once, the sons of light were stronger than the sons of darkness.

They came from the edges of the lake of asphalt. Nowhere else on earth had nature and history conspired to bring themselves to an end, and to bring a new order. After these times of ill-omen, with the coming of the Messiah, when rough places would be made smooth, all would see that God had saved them in this very place, on the desolate edges of the Dead Sea.

I fell into a trance, all my senses agitated by a fever. And then I understood the truth I had been concealing from myself since the moment I had known it: my father was a scribe, and all my ancestors were Essene. So, whether I wanted it or not, I too was an Essene scribe. At this thought my mind seemed to fall apart, and I threw myself against the rocky walls of my prison.

After three days, they decided that we had learnt the lesson, and brought us food and drink; they told us to do our work and write down what the leader had told us. We could not escape from the cave: the only door was blocked and the roof too high for us to climb out of – though we could see a ray of light from a hole at the top of it. We had no choice but to obey them. We ate and came slowly back to life; then we set to work.

We lived there, in the belly of the earth, at the heart of the mountain. We did not know why we were there, nor whether we would ever escape, but we did not despair. Indeed, I believe we felt safe there.

My father was convinced that, above us, the end of the world was approaching. Perhaps because of this return to his origins, never entirely forgotten, he was experiencing a return to mysticism. He believed that we had been sent here to shelter from the apocalypse, and that, eventually, we would emerge onto a devastated earth, to follow the Messiah and found a new world.

These prophetic speeches were unlike him. I had never heard him speak of the Messiah before, but now all the prayers and lessons of his childhood came back to him, along with a belief in salvation that had long been suppressed by his faith in science. Now he even looked like a Hebrew prophet, with a grey beard, grown in the last few days, his conversation interspersed with incessant quotations from the Bible.

I knew – he had often explained it to me – that apocalyptic prophecies and Messianic predictions only occur in times of crisis and desperation. I realised, too, that this place was suited to a belief in the end of the world. But I was equally convinced that if there were to be an apocalypse, it would not be in this cave, amongst these manuscripts.

So we wrote down what the leader had told us, as we had been ordered to do. And after writing, we deciphered the precious scroll which I had kept ever since Jane had given it to me. As the Hebraic letters were back to front and we had no mirror, we began by copying them out on the back of the scroll we had been given.

And so we found out the truth about Qumran.

As soon as we knew, we understood that it had to be suppressed until the Messianic advent. We didn't know what the consequences of such revelation would be, but we knew that what we had learned could never be spoken, only written and kept secret. I couldn't forget the vision I had had during my trance, when I had been ordered to write down what I knew. Was I not a scribe, the son of a scribe?

In that place and at that time, when there was nothing we could do but hope, study and talk, my father at last began to tell me about the Essenes. Memories came back to him piecemeal, sometimes painfully, sometimes flooding out in interminable recitations he couldn't stop, as though he had to unburden himself of all he had suppressed during those long years.

They had been the elite of the chosen people, the chosen among the chosen. For their contemporaries they were just a small unknown sect, without power or influence, and with no historical importance. But this was not how they saw themselves: they knew they were destined to play an all-important role in events that would change history. The world as it existed would come to an end, and a new cycle, very different from what had come before, would begin, in which the sect would play a dominant role. They believed the Jews were the people chosen by God, with whom he had made an exclusive covenant: however, not all Jews had been faithful to the contract; many did not understand what the promise meant, nor what its consequences would be. They and they alone, one particular sect of one particular race, were the ones who would be used by God to prepare the way to the new order, with the Anointed at their head. And all humanity would be redeemed by Israel alone.

They also believed they were the only ones who held the key to the scriptures. So they had their own library, always maintained and increased by the copying and re-copying of Biblical texts, to which they added their own scrolls. These were the sect's real treasure: they interpreted the past, and clarified the meaning of contemporary events. They also issued prophecies and dictated precisely how each one of them should live his life.

The sect had its own specific way of observing the country's history: it treated myth as literal truth, and legend as fact. Above all, they believed they were the people chosen by God for the first covenant with the Law of Moses. The Sinai was the site of a cosmic intervention, in which God had made an eternal pact with the children of Israel. But the priests and the governors had betrayed that pact, and all Israel had rejected it. Only they had remained true, and God had made a second covenant with them, the chosen of the chosen.

Certainly God had consolidated his alliance with David, who was also 'anointed', which is why David's victories were a foretaste of Israel's triumph. But there had been Zadok, as well as David, the greatest of the great priests of Israel. They were the true Zadokists, as opposed to the false ones, the Sadducees, who profaned the altars of God, and amassed undeserved riches, plundering the fruits of men's work. And, with the second covenant, God had announced the coming of a prophet, Elijah, who would continue the tradition of Amos, Isaiah, and Jeremiah. To consecrate the alliance, the arrival of the Master of Justice would inaugurate the new era.

'What happened to the Essenes?' I asked.

'The Roman occupation of Judaea was very peaceful at first. The Roman governors were rapacious, but less so than the native rulers. Antigonus, the last of the Maccabees, was succeeded by Herod the Great in 37 BC. He built many splendid buildings, founded the port of Caesarea, and embarked on the rebuilding of the Temple, which wasn't completed until 64 AD, and was destroyed six years later. When he died there were some genuine mourners. After Herod the kingdom was divided. Antipas, the governor of Galilee, married his brother's wife, and killed John the Baptist when he criticised this. When he lost his battle against Aretas, father of his abandoned first wife, it was widely seen as his punishment for having beheaded John. He ruled until 34 AD. In Judaea, Archelaus ruled for ten years, but his reign was so disastrous that Augustus revoked it and made Judaea into a Roman province, run by minor officials; one of them was Pontius Pilate, who was eventually recalled and banished to Gaul.

'Tension continued to grow between Romans and Jews. The Romans couldn't understand these people, whom they regarded as religious fanatics, and the Jews couldn't abide the Roman desecration of the Temple. Pilate was surprised and infuriated by the level of Jewish resistance to the Roman military empire. Until then nobody had challenged their religious idolatry, so why was Judaea fighting it? Emperor Caligula ordered that his statue be placed in the Temple, and he was assassinated. After that, the whole of Palestine fell under Roman domination. But the Jews continued to challenge the occupiers. Provoked by the Roman governor Antonius Felix's frequent recourse to crucifixion, one sect, the Sicares, began to assassinate Romans. Judaean affairs reached a low point: robbery was rife and the government incompetent. Rebellion, sedition and war were in the air. To deal with the crisis, the Jews formed an emergency government, and put Flavius Josephus in charge of defending Galilee. He fought unsuccessfully, and in the end went over to the enemy. The Pharisees, whom the Romans trusted, vainly tried to instil moderate policies, but eventually lost power. The furious Zealots took control, which meant the end of all moderation.

'Had Israel been more united and less corrupt, the war might have been won, but as things were, it was bound to end in tragedy. Jerusalem was torn apart by rival factions; Jew was killing Jew; the fratricidal quarrels only increased Roman massacres. At the end of the summer of 70 AD, the outer courtyard of the Temple was set on fire, and the fighting went right up to the burning altar. As Jesus had prophesied, the Temple was destroyed. The priests of Qumran, seeing one calamity follow another, believed the Day of Judgement had come at last, and that the Messiah was about to appear. It was true that the moon was not yet soaked with blood, nor had the stars fallen from the sky, but nevertheless the impious who had been governing Jerusalem were being destroyed, and it was time for God to turn his wrath on the Kittim. They waited. They knew the Romans would come. This was when they placed their precious manuscripts in jars and took them up to the caves. One day, when the battle was over, they would go back and fetch them, and when they returned, the scriptures would always be their treasure, and the Messiah of Aaron and Israel would preside over the holy meal on the day of the Lord, at the coming of the kingdom of God. This was the time when history lost all trace of them, and the early Christian sects began to appear. What had happened was that, after hiding the manuscripts, they went into hiding at Qumran, to prepare again for the coming of the Messiah. And there they stayed, unknown to the world, through all these centuries.'

And so my father talked on, telling long-buried stories about his past, and the times before that, for hours on end. I listened to all he said, so that I would be able to remember it, and later write it, as it was my duty to do. He told me about his life and that of his people, as it had been throughout his childhood, how it had followed a rigid calendar of dates and festivals; of the monastic existence of the community, in retreat for thousands of years, sheltered by the Dead Sea desert. They had, however, been aware of time passing, and they knew that, far away, their brother Jews were lost in the outside world, while they remained, guardians of the scrolls; they were forbidden to leave the Qumran caves, except when, disguised as Bedouin, they went to gather news at the festivals. But still nobody knew of their cave existence.

After forty days and nights, we heard the sound of pickaxes in the passage: someone was coming. We thought, at first, that it was the Essenes bringing our daily rations and checking the progress of our work. But the sounds came from a different direction; they got closer and soon echoed through our vaulted cave, only a few metres away.

Then three silhouettes appeared out of the shadows and the rocks. We held our breath – then recognised Shimon, with two other men.

He had been alerted by Jane and, following her directions, had for the last few weeks been searching the caves, unable to find anything in the labyrinthine passages. He explained that when we did not return, Jane had looked through my papers in the hotel room and, finding Shimon's number, had at once alerted him.

We set off again through the caves. Outside, we were dazzled by the light, blinded for several minutes. Then we found ourselves in Shimon's car heading for Jerusalem, suddenly shattered by the months of tension and suffering.

'So?' said Shimon.

'So, what?' said my father.

'Did you find the manuscript?'

My father shook his head.

*

Shimon dropped us off in front of my parents' apartment. 'Goodbye,' he said. 'Get some rest. I'll come back and see you in a few days, to talk about what happened.'

'Thank you,' said my father, shaking his hand. 'I believe we owe you our lives.'

'No,' he said. 'I was the one who sent you there. See you very soon.'

We stood for a moment on the pavement. We felt lost, watching the car drive away: it all seemed unreal, and we couldn't quite believe it. Here we were, as though nothing had happened, outside our home, where my poor mother had been waiting all this time in a torment of anxiety.

But our troubles were not over. We walked slowly towards the entrance, and then stopped in amazement. There, standing in the hall of our building, was Yehudi.

'Yehudi?' I cried. 'What are you doing here? How did you know we were coming?'

'Jane told me yesterday that they were about to find you. I've been waiting since this morning,' he said darkly.

'Jane? Where is she?'

His expression changed. 'Listen, Ary, if you want to find her . . . You must come with me at once.'

'Now?'

'At once. I'm not joking. She's in danger.'

So, without even going home, we went to a little synagogue I knew so well from my days in Mea Shearim, where the rabbi and his followers usually prayed. It was on the second floor of a shabby building at the end of a yard, off a long and narrow street. It was a bastion of orthodoxy, where the 'blackest' rabbis, scholars and students of Mea Shearim would gather. Venerable old men with grey side-locks and long white beards, in big hats and traditional clothing, they spoke only Yiddish amongst themselves, and had devoted their lives to study, the Law, and the education of their many children. Now they were old they had become the wise men of the community, a gathering to be consulted on all sorts of problems. They were regarded as the true masters of the tradition, the true guardians of the Torah scrolls. There were twelve of them.

When we arrived, it was three in the afternoon and the synagogue was deserted. Prayers were due to begin two hours later.

The rabbi was there waiting for us, but not Jane. He was standing on the stage, as he always did, with his elbow on the table where two scrolls of the Torah lay. He must have been reading through it, to check the writing and to see that there were no mistakes.

'So?' he said. 'Have you found it?'

'What are you talking about?' I replied.

'Ary, don't be a fool. I mean the parchment. The Scroll of the Messiah; the one that disappeared.'

'No,' I said. 'We don't know where it is.'

'But I do,' he said, pointing at the bulge in my father's jacket. My father had put the two scrolls there, rolled together, our copy and the original, when he left the cave. 'Give it to me,' said the rabbi.

'No,' said my father. 'It doesn't belong to you. It belongs to the Essenes.'

To my amazement, the rabbi began to laugh. A huge roar of laughter, strangely evil, echoed round the walls of the synagogue.

'Don't you realise? Come!' he said, as though speaking to a pupil who had made an elementary mistake in his Talmudic argument. 'Your people and my people are the same. Don't you know that the Essenes are called Hassidim in Talmudic literature? Don't you know that I am the Messiah of the Essenes, and that the time has come for me to take possession of the whole world? My ancestors go back to the rabbi Juda Ha-Hasid, who in the twelfth century forbade the marriage of his nieces to establish celibacy – he was an Essene who had emigrated to Germany. We have been Essenes for generations, passing our mission down from father to son – to prepare for the coming of the Messiah, to wait for the end of the world. And I had the revelation – I am the Messiah. Do you understand? Now give me the scroll.'

Then my father, defeated, handed him the parchment.

'No!' I cried. 'What are you doing?'

He turned to me and murmured hopelessly, 'I'm a scribe. He's a high priest. I have to obey.'

'What are you saying?' I shouted. 'You're not a scribe! You're nothing! You left them!'

The rabbi took the parchment and held it towards the flame of the synagogue's candelabra.

'What are you doing?' I screamed. 'Who are you trying to fool with your Torah – you don't even obey its commandments! You're a false Messiah, a usurper. You'll see the Last Judgement all right, and you'll suffer in it!'

'The Wicked Priest persecuted the Master of Justice, engulfing him in his fury,' the rabbi recited calmly, as if fulfilling the prophecy.

'You are that priest, and your ignominy is greater than any glory.' The words came out of my mouth before I could stop myself. I knew that I might be blaspheming, but anger had robbed me of reason.

The rabbi gave me a strange look. 'What about you, Ary? What were you doing in America when your father had been kidnapped? Were you thinking of him, or were you fornicating with a shikza? I'll tell you. You went into paths of drunkenness to quench your thirst. You call yourself a Jew, but in your heart you are not circumcised. You committed abominable deeds in the city. You soiled the sanctuary of God, you went into forbidden places, you went into churches. You sinned.'

'Who told you all this? Were you spying on me?'

'The Williamsburg rabbi told me everything . . . the dens of vice you visited. I warned you, Ary, of the risks you were taking, I told you always to breathe the air of Machiach. But you didn't believe me, and now you blaspheme against me; you didn't believe the words God placed in my mouth, telling what would happen to His people and to the world. I, Ary, am the mouthpiece of God, I and no other know all the secrets of the revelation.'

'You are a man of lies,' I said, full of hatred and shame, caught in his trap. 'You announce false oracles, you gain trust by graven images and false idols. But they won't save you on the day of judgement, when God exterminates those who serve false idols, as well as the impious of the earth.'

'That day is coming, Ary.'

'God decides His own time.'

At this the rabbi flew into a terrible rage, lips trembling and eyes flashing.

'How dare you contradict me? You are a blasphemer disguised as a *baal teshuvah*; you wear the cloak of truth, but your heart has not changed. Blasphemer you were, and blasphemer you remain! You have abandoned our God, betrayed our precepts, sinned with a woman; you have stolen our scroll and tried to possess its riches, you have revolted against God and wallowed in impurity!'

'You,' I cried, 'are like the priests in Jerusalem who amassed riches by robbing the people. "The prophet of lies has led the people astray to build his city on death and deceit".'

'"And the fury of God will drown him in misery and pain".'

With these last words, the rabbi held the double scroll to the long flame of the candelabra.

'No!' I cried. 'Don't do it!'

But it was too late. The scrolls had already caught, and disintegrated immediately in brilliant flames. They gave off a strong and bitter smell, like human flesh burning – a skin stretched, tanned, tattooed and finally ravaged. The scrolls burned without unrolling, opaque and closed for all eternity; licked, devoured and digested by the flames. I watched, mesmerised, as the little black letters folded and melted in the heat, and then dissolved into dust and ashes, while thick smoke rose to the ceiling and seemed to travel through it up to the sky. The scrolls had been obliterated forever on the altar of the synagogue. They had withstood time for so long, and now it was as though they had never existed, as though those two thousand years in the Qumran caves had never happened; as though they had never been stolen, found, stolen again; never searched for, longed for, written or read. It all had been in vain. One vengeful moment had destroyed something immortal.

I was overcome by invincible fury – the anger of Elias when he killed the forty false prophets on Mount Carmel, or that of the murderous, blasphemous Wicked Priest. I seized the velvet-covered Torah with its heavy silver hoops and edging.

'A day will come,' I said, 'when the proud and the wicked will be like chaff in a brazier; and when that day comes, says the God of Armies, they will be consumed root and branch.'

I brought the book down on the rabbi with all the strength of my anger, and he collapsed to the ground.

I don't know what happened next; I passed out. Later I heard that my father and Yehudi between them decided not to say anything. Yehudi was shattered, but he felt that my going to prison wouldn't change what had happened, and that the rabbi, if he was the Messiah, would soon rise again. Also he felt guilty for having set us up and did not want my life to be destroyed by what he had done – for it had been he who told the rabbi about Jane's presence, and who, on his orders, had imprisoned her. So he agreed to tell the world that the rabbi had had a heart attack.

It was also decided that I should disappear for a time to a safe, fortified place where no one would follow me. Thus it was that, without seeing Jerusalem again, without even having kissed my mother, I found myself, for better or worse, as though it was fated, back at Qumran.

III

The Essenes greeted me as though they had been expecting me. They believed I had come back as a novice, to take up the torch.

For a long time I saw nobody. I was appalled by what I had done. I tried, unsuccessfully, to understand; the reason for my deed, and its effects, were beyond any understanding. I was ashamed to be a murderer. Then I saw my father, who came to visit me several times, and, once or twice, my mother, to whom he had finally told the whole story.

I kept myself busy by writing, and learning to live like an Essene in the Judaean desert.

What struck me first was the silence. No sound or movement disturbed the solemnity of the place. The silence, somewhere between sobriety and serenity, was a powerful mystery, the very essence of the harsh, scorched desert with its secret inhabitants, these reclusive penitents. One day we went, disguised as Bedouin, far into the desert, to a remote cemetery similar to the one at Khirbet Qumran, filled with tombs that all lay on the north-south axis: this was where they buried their dead, in the soft warm breeze, amid the same deep silence as that of the caves. When I asked why the tombs were arranged like this, they replied that Heaven was to the north, it was written in the *Book of Enoch*, of which they were fervent readers: *Dead, awaiting the resurrection, they lie with their heads to the south, dreaming of their future land during this brief sleep. When they awake, they will rise, facing the north, and walk straight to Heaven, the holy mountain of the celestial Jerusalem.*

Then I felt I understood the meaning of their silence: it was like a deep sleep in this life, with seraphic dreams of the next. I realised just how much the Essenes were men of the desert; they belonged not to the world, but to themselves and to God. I understood how far we were exiles from the world, how estranged from this alien land without buildings, houses, towns or any familiar object. The desert was the world of the second day of the creation, when God had only made earth and sky, but no trees or grass, no rain, and no man to cultivate the soil.

Others, like God, transform dry earth into fertile soil; bring greenery, and grass followed by fruit. But we were a part of the desert, of that early chaos. We were no relief party; we wanted death to triumph, and the desert to reclaim its lost territory; we wanted the jackals and hyenas, the wildcats and the vipers to return, and the demons as well. We were outcasts: our desert was no Garden of Eden. It was a desert.

I grew to know it intimately. It was not like other deserts; this was no Negev, swept by the white-hot winds of eternity. It wasn't even quite the desert of the second day of creation, more like that of the third day; with the occasional bush to remind one what the earth could be like, and a bitter sea as a reminder of water, and rocks carved by wind, an echo of what man might do. The peaks of the dunes were as sharp as scimitars, and the wind had drawn rough waves with regular crests, and lunar curves. Sometimes the sky fell to the ground, leaving traces of stars. On some nights, when the sounds of the desert were carried on the breeze, we could hear the big palm trees talking to the young that sprouted from their trunks.

Stretched out on the ground, I would taste the salty sea flavour of the stones, and breathe in its particular odour of sulphur from the Dead Sea. I gorged on the thousand varieties of multi-coloured dates. My favourites were the 'fingers of light', yellow, crunchy and sour. Some liked them very ripe, and would wait for time and the sun to sweeten them on the tree before picking them. I liked them young, with a hint of the sweetness to come, but still juicy beneath the shrivelled skin; smooth and golden, sharp and vigorous.

There was a whole secret city in the caves, with streets, districts, houses, shops and a synagogue. Not many Essenes remained – many had left in 1948 – only about fifty, mostly men.

They lived in darkness; not the gloom one might experience in an ill-lit room in a town, but the profound darkness of night. Torches cast rays of light through the obscurity; I used to try to seize the light in my hand. When we went out we were blinded: it was like seeing God. It was like the beginning of the world, when light and dark were still one and the same thing, just as good existed at the very heart of evil, before it became an independent entity. Here light moved around in the heart of darkness, with no conflict between the two.

This isolated community was self-sufficient; everything necessary for survival was made on the spot. Huge caverns had been divided into grain silos, bakers' ovens and potteries; there were mills, and kitchens stacked with crockery for all. Other spaces had been made into bath houses, workshops, cisterns and bathing pools, which were fed by a complicated system of canals. One long, narrow room served as the refectory and main meeting place, where the community gathered twice a day. I could not attend these meetings until I had been there two years, but I used to see them filing in in silence, as if to a holy shrine; the baker would distribute bread in hierarchical order, and the cook would ladle out the food. The priest would say a prayer before the meal and, in place of Israel's Messiah until he should reveal himself in flesh and blood, broke the bread and blessed the wine, thus daily re-enacting the last supper. When they had eaten, they removed the white linen robes they had worn for the meal and worked until the evening, when another meal would take place.

Each person had a different task. All rose early, before sunrise, and did not stop until well after dark. The farmers worked outside the caves, in a small corner of fresh air and greenery among the rocks, fed by an undergound spring; shepherds took their flocks to the same place. There were bee-keepers and artisans, working in pottery and ceramic. Everyone received a wage for his work, which he handed over to an elected treasurer. Like the food, clothes were held in common: they all wore the same thick grey coats in winter, and brown-and-white striped tunics in summer. What belonged to one belonged to all, and vice versa.

Before 1948, they had lived as families until marriage, which for them had only one purpose – the continuation of the sect. They explained to me that they would examine the woman they wanted to marry for three months: she had to be purified three times, to ensure that she would be able to have children, and only then would they marry. Now, however, there were hardly any women left, and they lived a monastic life.

The true centre of their existence was the daily purifying bath, the baptismal rite that was even more important than the meal. The men, dressed in linen loincloths, would totally immerse themselves in the icy water of the pool – like Western man, although his daily shower is not generally perceived as a preparation for the coming of the Messiah. Then they would emerge, dry themselves and put on a holy garment. They said that those who did not purify themselves would have no part in the future world.

One day, they took me to the scriptorium, a vaulted room lit by a dozen torches; there were several long narrow tables, covered with piles of parchment and small earthenware or bronze inkwells. I spent most of the day there, leant over the table, dipping my pen in the ink, my only companions a few other scribes and the fresh, humid smell of the rock.

I had a room, too, where I slept; it was a little monastic cell, with a bed carved out of the rock, and a table and torch hooked to the wall: some caves had bigger dwellings and beds mattressed with hay, but even the old family rooms were extremely bare. The Essenes were not content with professing poverty; they lived a truly ascetic life, in accordance with their principles.

Like any novice, I was to undergo a two-year probationary period, a cleansing and a gradual separation from wordly corruption and material things, which would eventually allow me to join the sect and take part in communal activities. Secret doctrines were not revealed during the novitiate. I knew that the purpose of this retreat into the desert was to carve out a way for the Lord, to cut a path for his steps, to conceal his doctrine from the wicked, and instruct the good.

One of the priests, whose name was Yacov, was charged with initiating me into their doctrines. He taught me many things about the nature of man and the two spirits that reside in each of us; about the Divine Visitation, and the presence of God in this world since the creation; about the God of Knowledge, whence comes all that is and all that shall be. He had planned everything before human beings existed, and they could only carry out His glorious plan, without changing it.

Yacov taught me to distinguish between the spirit of truth and the spirit of perversity. He told me that when man's heart is inflamed by the light of truth, all true paths to the justice and judgement of God become clear: the spirit of perversity brings about cupidity and injustice and all the abominable sins committed in the lustful pursuit of impurity. He taught me that the two instincts have been in conflict throughout the generations. God distributed them in equal amounts, for the abomination of perversity is essential to the search for truth, as the abomination of truth is to the pursuit of perversity, and the battle between wisdom and folly will continue in each man's heart until the great renewal, when retribution comes. But when the final moment comes, God in His glorious wisdom will put an end to perversity for ever, and then truth will shine forth throughout the world. And God will cleanse each man of his sins and the spirit of truth will burst upon man like clear water.

These concepts were already familiar, both in theory and in observance. I could understand why the rabbi had said that the Hassidim and the Essenes were the same: both were possessed by the pursuit of virtue, to the point of fleeing the modern world and withdrawing from the rest of humanity; they both lived on the margin. But their interdictions were not restrictions: they praised God at all times and in all circumstances, with beautiful and strange melodies, accompanied by lyres, lutes, harps and flutes. Such was their way of life that their asceticism was a solemn and joyful period of waiting.

And how they longed for an end to their wait! Mashiah, they cried in their hearts. They awaited the Messiah of Aaron, the priestly Messiah, the Cohen descendant of the high priests. Every day, they fervently recited the words: *a star has come from Jacob, and a sceptre has risen in Israel, and it will shatter the time of Moab and decimate all the sons of Seth.* I certainly felt at home: the Hassidim also longed for the end of time, the coming of the reign of God and the extermination of the impious.

I would appear periodically before the high priest, who would examine my progress and evaluate my intelligence and my capacities. One day, after a year, he decided that I was ready to join the Covenant of God. Even though I was the son of an Essene and not a stranger, I had been brought up outside the community and so had to undergo the usual ceremony.

All the members of the community gathered in the refectory. The twelve priests sat at the high table, presided over by the high priest. Standing before them, dressed in white linen, I made a solemn vow to obey the Law of Moses – that is, the Law as interpreted by the congregation.

'I swear,' I said to the assembly, 'to act according to what God has prescribed, and never to turn away from Him through fear, or because of any ordeal.'

Then the priests narrated the acts of God and his great works, and proclaimed all the graces of divine mercy towards Israel, and the Levites denounced the iniquities of the sons of Israel, and their wicked rebellions and the sins committed during the empire of Belial. Then it was my turn to confess: 'I have been wicked, I have revolted, I have sinned, I have been impious, I and my fathers before me have gone against the precepts of truth.'

The priests said, 'Let the men of God be blessed, who have clearly seen His way.'

The Levites responded, 'Let the men of Belial be cursed.'

'Amen,' I said, bowing down before them. Then I lay down on the ground and, with my arms stretched out, swore to love truth and persecute liars, never to hide anything from members of the sect, and never to reveal it to the outside world, even if I were tortured to the point of death.

'I promise,' I said, following the traditional formula, 'never to communicate to anyone the doctrines I have learnt, nor any I learn in the future. I swear the strictest observance of the rule of obedience, by which I submit totally to the authority of the majority of my fellows, whatever decisions they take over my life or my death. For they will decide the fate of all things, be they about the law, goods or rights. I surrender to the community any evil leanings or insubordination that are within me, and will participate in all trials and judgements of those who transgress against the precepts.'

After this ceremony I still could not take part in the ritual baptism, or the sacred meals; I would have to wait another year for that. However, I was allowed to play a greater part in the life of the community, and also to leave the caves for a day.

Can I say it? Dare I admit it? In my mind, my oath had been as much a renunciation as a promise: during all this time I had not forgotten Jane. I had not seen her when the rabbi had imprisoned her to make me come to him; I had not seen her since the moment I had first entered the caves. I knew from my father that Yehudi had freed her as soon as I had left, and she had returned to the United States. He heard from her from time to time. Then one day he came to see me in the caves, and told me she was in Jerusalem and would like to meet with me.

I had often thought of her, remembering our discussions, and the battle we had fought alongside one another. Was I so certain of myself, so solidly anchored in my beliefs, that I could not experience love? Perhaps I had become lost in this eternal rest, which gave me a sense of security and identity, a mission and a community and principles to depend on. I decided to use my day of freedom to go to Jerusalem.

We met early one April morning in a café in the pedestrian precinct of Ben Yehouda. When I saw her, all in white, with her long blonde hair on her shoulders, I felt the same as when I had first laid eyes on her: this was an angel. Perhaps she was my guardian angel, who would watch over me wherever she was, as I did her.

For the first time since she had known me I was not in a long black coat and side-locks, although I still had a thin beard. My clothes were dark, but unadorned, in the Essene style: a loose-weave tunic and simple trousers. She looked at me carefully.

'It's odd, but I feel you're no longer yourself in those clothes. Other people dress like that nowadays. I hardly recognise you; you could have given it all up and become like anybody else. You're more antiquated than ever, and more modern as well.'

We looked at each other, slightly embarrassed.

'So,' she said, 'you've chosen to prolong your retreat?'

'I took the oath the other day; I've joined the community.'

'I'll keep your secret, Ary. I'll never say a word about it to anybody.'

'I know.'

'You're happy there, aren't you?'

'Yes.'

'You know,' she continued, 'the doctors never understood what had happened to the rabbi. They thought he had had some sort of seizure, and, given his age, they left it at that.'

'I know. I don't need to hide any more; nobody would question me about the death. But I must do my penance.'

'What do the Essenes say about the crime? And what about their horrible murders? What do you think about all that, Ary?'

'The Essenes no longer mention the lost scroll. But their terrible secret, all those horrible deaths, has united them. They're brothers in love and brothers in crime, joined for ever in secret complicity. They are both sons of light and sons of darkness, and they'll guard their secret as closely as they guard their treasure. One day they opened the chest in front of the whole assembly and showed us all the precious objects – the holy vessels, jewels and gold crowns, a two-thousand-year-old wonder waiting to shine forth again, when the Messiah comes.'

She smiled sadly. 'I always knew you were a Jewish monk. I told you, didn't I?'

There was another silence. I felt she was suddenly very moved, although she didn't show it. We hadn't spoken about ourselves since New York and the symposium, but I sensed that even after all this time she was still attached to me. It gave me a feeling of comfort and security that in a way appeased my longing for her. I had never thought that one day we would really be separated, for eternity, and was quite unprepared for the idea. When I had waited for her at the café table, I had assumed that she would always come, whenever we wanted. I had waited for her as if it were the most natural thing in the world, and when she had come and sat down opposite me, it had never occurred to me that it might be for the last time.

Now I realised what was about to happen, and it seemed catastrophic. Heart thumping, I tried to control the wave of feeling that overcame me. I remembered how much I had desired this women – how much, indeed, I had loved her, though I was not allowed to use the word 'love' for this forbidden, extra-marital emotion. It had grown from small beginnings to something huge, beyond words; now, when she rose and left the table after our conversation, I felt a powerful heartache as she walked off down the street; then I was as suddenly overcome by torpor. My love lay unfulfilled, stillborn within me, a non-event, still strong but now inert. The dam had burst under pressure, and everything was being swept away, the years of construction, of thought and calculation: she was going; *I would never see her again.* She was about to disappear from my life, leaving me to face it, face death, alone. She was going. I was alone.

I thought I was about to faint, but with an effort of will, I called her, though it came out as a wordless cry: her face was all that mattered, and the moment had to be seized, without thought of the future.

She turned, hesitated for a moment, and then walked on, faster. I stood by the table for several minutes, my arm frozen half-raised in a gesture of farewell, or welcome.

I never heard from her again. I don't know what would have happened if she had turned around that day and walked, with her sprightly step, back towards me. I know that at that moment I cared only about her, and the pain was uncontainable. But I knew too that later reason would have resumed its implacable course, and I would have regretted it. I think she understood my cry, and in that split-second took it upon herself to decide our future. I don't know what her exact thoughts were at that moment, but I do know that not a day passes when I do not relive it, and see that slender figure disappearing down the street, bravely resisting my call, like a figurine disappearing from a treasure chest.

Did she, on whose breast I might have lain, know where I really belonged? Had her role simply been to help me find my true home: the silent Judaean desert, with its hot winds and cold nights, its golden dunes, its damp rocky landscape and struggling vegetation? To see again the ochre plains, smell the hazy salt breezes that rose up to our caves from the Dead Sea, leaving a bitter taste on the tongue and stinging the eyes. To screw up my eyes at the sparkling surface of the water, and the pink and gold of the steep cliffs by its side, the olive spurs of the mountains like a backcloth, and the purple hills of Moab and Edom; to close them before the twilight canyons and wadis, ragged with shadows, and the high cliff which stretches north to south, pressing against the salt banks, as far as Ras Feshka; at the foot of the cliff, the Ain Feshka spring and the terrace with the ruins of Khirbet Qumran and the silent caves silhouetted in the dusk. To know that there, hidden at the lowest point in the world, the wait goes on, dreaming of the dawn of a new era.

My initiation continued for another year. Then one day Yacov came and gave me a small scroll, the size of a pencil, which had been right at the bottom of the chest, to read and copy.

'Here,' he said. 'To add to the one you're rewriting from memory, the one the rabbi destroyed, the Lost Scroll, which told you our secret. That one was the past; this is the Scroll of the Messiah, the future. And you should know that the rabbi, the King-Messiah, will not be resurrected. When you read the Scroll of the Messiah you'll understand what happened, and what you have done. You will soon be able to identify the man you killed. But before you find out you must be purified. The time has come, Ary, for you to be baptised.'

He gave me a loincloth for the baths, and a white garment, and a small pickaxe, useful for life in the caves, as the sign that I could now participate in all the activities of the community; take my place at the table with the Many, and share the bread and the wine.

That evening, they laid the table for supper. They prepared the wine, and the bread to be broken up and distributed. We began by taking off our coats and, in the ritual loincloth, immersing ourselves in the holy water. Then we dressed again and went to the table.

But that evening was not like other evenings. Normally, I knew, the priest put out his hand and blessed the bread and the wine. Tonight was different: the wine was poured; the bread was ready on the table; but the priest did not begin his benediction in the usual respectful silence. He did not lift the cup of crimson wine to bless it before all. He did not break the bread. Instead, he turned to me.

I had lived among them for two years now, and was no longer a captive, if I ever had been. I understood then that the time had come to make before the whole community the solemn vow that would join me to the Essenes; to speak in public the oath that would bind me to them for ever, converting me to the Law of Moses, to all that he revealed to the sons of Zadok, to the priests who kept the covenant, and to the members of the covenant, following His truth and His will. The time had come for me to join that Covenant, to separate myself from perverse men following the paths of impiety, outside our realm; I would no longer reply to their questions about laws and observance, never eat or drink with them, nor accept anything from their hands. The time had come to dedicate my life to the divine sacraments.

But this was not what the priest expected of me. He raised his hand in a slow gesture.

And there shall come forth a rod out of the stem of Jesse, and a Branch shall grow out of his roots. And the spirit of the Lord shall rest upon him, the spirit of counsel and might, the spirit of knowledge and the fear of the Lord.

He shall remain hidden for forty days in the palace and shall show himself to no one. After forty days a voice coming from the throne shall call the Messiah and bring him out of the 'bird's nest'.

At this time the King-Messiah shall leave that part of the Garden of Eden that is called the 'bird's nest' and shall reveal himself in the land of Galilee. The world shall be tormented and all the inhabitants of the earth shall hide in caves and caverns. At this time the prophecy of Isaiah shall be carried out: 'Men shall flee to caves and caverns and the deepest parts of the earth, to hide from the anger of the Lord and the glory of his majesty, when he rises to strike the earth.'

For this was not an evening like any other. It was the night of Passover, the celebration of the return from Egypt, and the carefully prepared table had been arranged for the Seder.

No, it was not an evening like any other. They all knew it. They all waited for the priest to advance his hand in a slow gesture, and to do what he had to do.

Then he did it.

He gave me the bread. Then he gave me the wine.

Seventh Scroll

THE LOST SCROLL

I

In the beginning was the Word:
the Word was with God
and the Word was God.
Through Him all things came to be,
not one thing had its being but through Him.
In Him was life,
and that life was the light of men, a light that shines in the dark,
a light that darkness could not overpower.
A man came, sent by God.
His name was John.
He came as a witness,
as a witness to speak for the light
so that everyone might believe through him.
But his utterances were distorted
and his words changed
and the word became a lie
to hide the truth,
the true story of the Messiah.
The story that will remain veiled in darkness
never revealed
through the centuries, by the scribes, and the doctors of the faith.
Here is the naked truth, more terrible than death.
Here is the truth about Jesus,
here is his life,
and the secret of his death.

Eli, Eli, lama sabachthani?

These were his last words,
at the end of his calvary,
When at last he realised that all was over.
Then, bowing his head, Jesus gave up his soul.

The night before, Jesus had gathered his disciples,
To share with them the meal
In memory of the return from Egypt,
But that night was not like other nights,
For on that night
His hour had come,
The hour of Revelation.
He knew it was so,
And that was why he gathered his disciples
Around him for the last time
Before the great day.
Around the table prepared for the Seder,
There were thirteen of them.
On the right of Jesus, head bowed on his chest,
Was John, his host,
The disciple Jesus loved.
There were Simon Peter and Andrew,
James and John,
Philip and Bartholomew,
Thomas, Matthew,
James, son of Alphaeus and Thaddeus, Simon
And Judas Iscariot.
For he too was loved by Jesus
And he too had been invited to the last supper.

The room was large; the table laid,
The thirteen sitting.
Then he rose, took off his coat
And wrapped himself in a loincloth.
He poured water into a bowl,
And washed the feet of his disciples
And wiped them with a cloth.
When Jesus reached him, Peter cried:
'You, Lord, wash my feet! Never!'
   'If I do not wash you, you cannot share my destiny.'
   'Then not just the feet, but hands and head too!'
   'He who has bathed does not need to be washed, for he is entirely
      pure: and you are pure –
But not all of you . . .'

For Judas was there
And he knew he would betray him.

When he had finished,
He put his coat back on and sat at the table.
'Do you understand what I have done?
You call me "Master and Lord",
And that is what I am.
I have washed your feet,
I, the Master and Lord,
You too must wash each other's feet
For I have set the example:
What I have done for you,
You must do as well.
Verily I say unto you,
A servant is not greater than his master,
Nor a messenger greater than he who sends him.
Knowing that, you will be happy, as long you practise what I say.
I do not speak for you;
I know those I have chosen.
But so that the Scriptures shall be carried out.
A man who broke bread with me
Has betrayed me.
I tell you that
Before the event happens.
So that when it does happen
You will believe in me.
And verily I say unto you,
To welcome the man I send
Is to welcome me.
And to welcome me, is to welcome He who sent me.'

Then he added:
'One of you will betray me.'

Then they looked at one another,
And wondered which one he meant.
Simon Peter said to John,
The disciple Jesus loved above all others:
'Ask who he speaks of.'

The disciple leaned towards Jesus
And said to him:
'Lord, who is it?'
And Jesus said:
'It is the one to whom I give the bread I have dipped in wine.'
Then he took the bread,
And gave it to Judas Iscariot, son of Simon,
Simon the Zealot.

'What you must do, do quickly.'
Judas took the bread,
And left quickly.
With a rapid step he went into the night.

When he had gone,
Jesus said to the other disciples:
'Now the son of man is glorified
And God has been glorified in Himself.
My dear friends,
I will not be with you
For very much longer.
But you know that where I am going
You cannot follow.
And I say it to you now –
Before I go,
I give you a new commandment:
Love one another.
As I have loved you,
You must love one another,
And all will know that you are my disciples.'

Having spoken thus, Jesus went with his disciples
Beyond the torrent of Kidron.
There was a garden
Which he entered with his disciples,
Judas, who would betray him, knew the place,
For Jesus had taken him there many times.
He led the soldiers
And the guards supplied by the high priests
And the Pharisees,

And he reached the garden
With torches, lanterns and arms.
And Jesus, who knew all that was about to happen,
Stepped forward and said:
'Whom do you seek?'
'We seek Jesus.'
'I am he.'
Judas, who had betrayed him, was amongst them.

Then they fell back,
And trembled.
Again Jesus said:
'Whom do you seek?'
And they replied:
'Jesus of Nazareth.'
'I have told you, I am he.'

Then Simon Peter,
Who carried a sword, unsheathed it
And struck the servant of the high priest,
Cutting off his right ear.
Jesus at once said to Peter:
'Sheathe your sword!'
'What?'
'Am I not to drink from the cup
That my father has given me?'

For he knew
That his sentence of death was a commandment
Which he must not resist.
The militia and the Jewish guard seized him
And tied him.
Until then all had been perfect.
All had gone according to the plan
Exactly as predicted.

In the year 3760,
A star came from Jacob,
A sceptre rose in Israel.
And the Lord Himself had given the sign,

For, a virgin was with child,
And she gave birth to a son.
Eight days later,
He was circumcised according to the Law,
And named Yeochoua
God saves.
Then Joseph and Mary
Went to the Temple
To make a sacrifice to God
And to buy him back,
For he was their first-born.

He had brothers and sisters.
His family was numerous
And poor.
And his town was poor,
Because of the taxes
And the famine
And the wars.
He learnt the written Law
And the spoken Law.
His mind was quick,
And his thoughts secret.
He spoke little
Even to those close to him.
Often he would remain alone, meditating,
Seeking answers in prayer.
And often he questioned his masters
When there was a difficult question.

He grew up
And became a young man,
He was called 'rabbi',
Like the Doctors of the Law
And like the scribes, who said
Love the artisan's work
And hate the rabbi's rank.
For the scribes wanted every child
To learn a manual craft
And most of them did so.

Is there not amongst us, they said,
A carpenter, the son of a carpenter,
Who can answer this question?
Now Jesus was the son of a carpenter,
And a carpenter himself.
But he did not like the work
His father had taught him.
And he decided to leave.
He left his family
And cursed his own mother.
'What have we in common, woman?'

For the end of time was approaching.
It was no longer a time for families,
For all were his family,
And he thought that whosoever came to him
Must repudiate his father, mother, wife, children, brothers.
That is what they had taught him
So that he could leave his home
And accomplish his mission.
From his first meeting with the Essenes,
He knew that he would have to leave his family,
If he wished one day to join them
And go to the community
Far from others in the burning desert.
If he wanted to have for himself,
And be surrounded by,
The constant presence of the Holy Spirit.

This happened
When he was twelve years old.
His parents had gone to Jerusalem
For the feast of Succoth.
Mary and the child were there,
Accompanying Joseph on his long journey:
They walked for four days
And by night, like Daniel, they called on the Messiah,
And gazed upon nocturnal visions.
And so it was that he came with the clouds from the sky
Like the Son of Man;

He reached the Elder
And approached him.
They offered him domination and glory;
People of all nations and languages
Served him.

Then they reached Jerusalem
And climbed to the Temple
And showed the House to the child
The ninety marble towers,
The huge walls of Herod's palace.
The stones that blocked the horizon,
Reminiscent of the domination of ancient powers,
Tyrannical powers.
The Kittim whom one met
At every halt,
Who controlled even
The entrance to the holy city.
Who watched
From the Antonia tower,
The pagan cult they had introduced
To the heart of the Temple.
And Herod was subject to the Kittim
Who had dethroned the high priest.

And they stopped at the Mount of Olives,
Before entering the Temple.
They put down their bags
And sat for a moment
Singing the psalms of Hallel,
And said a prayer.
Then they went into the valley of Kidron
At the foot of the Mount of Olives.
They climbed the hill of Moriah
Where the Temple was built,
And they entered Jerusalem the beautiful
And went to the pool of Bethesda
To take the ritual bath,
So that they would be pure when they entered the Temple.
Then they went to the ceremony

Over which presided the priest Zacharias,
The cousin of Mary.
Eleven priests had come from the north,
They wore long and narrow tunics,
And crowns on their heads:
All went barefoot.
Before them walked the master of sacrifice,
He turned towards the north face of the priests' courtyard,
To the place prepared for the sacrifice.
The lamb was held by a Levite,
And the master of sacrifice placed his hand on the animal's head,
And identified the priest with the animal.
Then he killed the animal with his knife
And turned to the altar.
And the Levites gathered the lamb's blood in a bowl
And others skinned it.
The blood and the flesh were brought to the sacrificer,
And he poured a little of the blood onto the altar,
And burned the fat,
Removed the entrails,
And let the meat roast on the fire at the altar.
He went to the Holy of Holies,
And opened it with a double key.
He entered alone,
While the faithful prostrated themselves
With their faces to the ground.
In the sanctuary, alone,
The priest accomplished the final act.
He poured the blood into a bronze bowl,
He scattered the incense,
He said a prayer
Over the blood spilled before the altar,
For the soul of the sacrificer
And the sins of the flesh,
And those of the soul,
Such were the sacrificer, the altar and the victim.

Then he returned to the courtyard
And asked the priests to bless the faithful gathered there.
The Levites replied 'Amen'.

One of the priests read some holy verses,
Another took some incense in his hands;
The priests spread a cloth of fine linen
Before him
And they hid him
While he took off his clothes,
And bathed,
And put on his golden clothes again.
He stood up,
Removed his golden clothes.
He bathed
And put white clothes on again,
He washed his hands and his feet.
Then with his hand on his head
He immersed himself
Confessing his sins
He prayed out loud.

And Jesus watched,
And Jesus did not know
If he was the priest or the lamb.

The next day, for their return journey,
They went down through the narrow streets of Jerusalem.
Jesus walked behind his parents;
He was following them
When he stopped before an old man
Who spoke to him.
And Mary and Joseph continued on their way
Without realising that the child had stopped.
When he looked up
They were no longer there.
He ran for a long time to catch them,
But he could not find them
And was lost in the town.

A week later, they saw him,
He was sitting in the court of the Temple.
He had changed,
And they did not realise it.

He did not tell them what had happened to him
For he had been forbidden to do so.

He had followed a man,
A man dressed in white,
Who had led him to a place close to the Temple.
There were several of his friends
Dressed like him.
They spoke
And Jesus listened to them.
They spoke of the coming of the Kingdom of God
And of the imminent coming of the Messiah.
Then he spoke
And the men listened.
They fervently awaited the Messiah.

They lived beside the Dead Sea,
In the depths of the desert.
They had left their families
And devoted themselves to studying
And waiting.
Then they took him with them to a house
And taught him about the wait for the Master of Justice.
It had come to them when they saw the child:
They had found in the child the Master they longed for.
They told him to leave his family –
They would help him
Rejoin his brothers.

And so he left his family
Who thought he was mad,
They did not believe in him as the Essenes did,
For they had shown him the path.
His mother and brothers tried to approach him;
They spoke to him,
They begged him not to go.
But he replied:
'Here are my mother and my brothers!
Whosoever carries out the will of my Father in Heaven,
He is my brother, my sister and my mother.

Whosoever leaves home, wife, brothers, parents or children,
For the sake of the Kingdom of Heaven,
Will receive his reward now,
And in all eternity.'

They were used to living as recluses,
But they thought the end of the world was approaching,
And said that they must preach repentance to others.
Thus the Kingdom of Heaven would come,
The Kingdom that must be proclaimed
So that all might be saved.
What was the use of living as recluses
When the Messiah was coming?
Who deserved salvation
If not them?
What is the use of the truth
Without repentance and forgiveness?
A voice spoke
In the desert,
Prepare ye the way of the Lord,
In the plains
Prepare a highway for our Lord.
We must leave the dwellings of men of Evil
And go to the desert to prepare the way of the Lord.

Now there was an Essene called John,
The son of Zacharias and Elizabeth,
And this man left the desert
And proclaimed baptism for all
For the forgiveness of the sins of Israel.
They called him John the Baptist,
And crowds flocked to him,
Who came from afar to hear him.
Hundreds of men listened to his words
Of repentance,
Then they confessed their sins
And were baptised by him in the river Jordan,
According to the Essene rite,
Since by immersion, their sins were forgiven,
And they would escape the wrath of God.

And John demanded from them a preliminary penance
He wanted all Jews to embrace virtue,
And exercise justice amongst themselves
And worship God.
He said that the immersions
Only cleansed bodily impurities.
He said that sin keeps a man
In impurity.
He said there could be no immersion
Without a renunciation of evil,
And only the man who abased his soul
Before the teachings of the Lord
Could be purified in the flesh
When the water touched him,
And he could be sanctified in the water of purity.
So spoke the Essenes:
Water cannot cleanse the body
Unless the soul has been cleansed by justice.
And the soul shall be cleansed with repentance
And the spirit of sanctity.

When they heard
The words of love and justice,
The crowd burned with painful emotions.
Men and women confessed their sins,
And plunged their bodies into the water.
They became pure.
They begged for the gift of the Holy Spirit
To raise their souls from the mire of evil.

Jesus left his home
And went to join the Essenes
In the desert,
And they said to him that his place was not
In the desert,
But with John,
In public places.
For John proclaimed the coming of
The Son of Man
Greater than himself.

And so he went into Jordan,
Where John was,
He listened to him,
And knew that the years of waiting
Were coming to an end.
The spirit of the Lord,
The Eternal One, was upon him,
For he had been anointed by the Lord
To bring the good news to the miserable,
He had sent him to heal
The broken-hearted,
To announce freedom to those in chains,
Deliverance to prisoners,
To proclaim the year of grace.
When he was baptised by John,
The heavens opened,
And he saw the Spirit of God descend upon him
Like a dove.
They heard a voice,
Which came down to them:
This is my servant
The chosen one,
In whom my soul rejoices.
I have placed my spirit within him
So that he can bring righteousness to nations.

Then Jesus understood the words of the Essenes.
He had been chosen
He was the son
The servant,
The chosen of the chosen.
But they told him
That the path was long
For he who brings the news.
The path towards the light is a long one
For the people who walk in darkness.
It is a long path to the one true light,
For those who live in the valley of the shadow of death.
To him the task had fallen,
Whose name was *God saves*.

He went to Capernaum,
The land of Zebulon and Nephtali,
The land beside the sea,
Beyond the Jordan,
Galilee where he was born,
Under pagan domination,
Ruled by Antipas,
Son of their enemy,
King Herod.
Amongst them the Zealots fought furiously
With many arms.
This was why he could not reveal
Who he was,
For they would have killed him,
And he would not have been able
To spread his message to all.
That was why he spoke in parables,
So that spies and informers
Could prove nothing against him.

On the banks of the Tiberias
Lay Bethseda
Birthplace of Andrew and Peter.
On the banks of the Tiberias
Were two other brothers,
Fishermen in the lake
John and James,
Sons of Thunder
Sons of Zebedee.
There was also Simon, the Rock.
Like Elias calling Elijah
He called them.
The gathering of wise men was composed of twelve men
Who governed the Essene brotherhood
And twelve they had to be
In this assembly of sages
Who were to spread the word.
That was why he found twelve men,
To be his brothers
And who would agree

And promise
To follow him
And to help him.

Then he began to prophesy
And hurl invective
In the towns
Which had not yet repented.
Woe unto you, Chorozain,
Woe unto you, Bethseda!
If the miracles that had happened there
Had happened at Tyre and Sidon,
It is certain they would long since
Have repented
In sackcloth and ashes.
But for Tyre and Sidon
The day of judgement would be more bearable than for them.
And you, Capernaum, will you be raised to Heaven?
You will descend into Hell.
For if the miracles that happened in your city
Had happened at Sodom,
That city would still be standing.
Yes, I say unto you
For the land of Sodom,
The day of judgement will be better than it will be for you.
And with such words
With inspired prophecies
He carried out his mission
Throughout the land.

Then they told him
Who John the Baptist was.
He was the precursor,
The prophet of the end of the world,
The prophet Elias who would come before the Messiah,
The one who announced the coming of the Son of Man,
Who one day would finally
Bring the judgement of divine anger.
John had a single prayer,
A single reason for living,

Which was the coming of the Messiah.
John was alone.
Those he baptised
Went away at once;
Those who had been cleansed
Returned to their homes.
He sent each man
Back to his work.
Passionately
He longed to know
If what he hoped for had happened.
So he sent two messengers
To ask
If he was really the Messiah,
Born of man.
For Jesus said
Repent,
The Kingdom of Heaven is nigh.
For Jesus taught
In the synagogues,
And Jesus cured
Sickness and languor amongst the people.
And the prophecy of Malachi
Would be accomplished
See, I send you Elias the prophet.

So John's messengers said to Jesus:
'Are you he,
Or should we wait for another?'
And Jesus replied:
'Go and tell John
What you hear
And what you see:
That the blind can see again,
The lame can walk,
And the deaf can hear,
And the poor will be saved.
Happy is he who believes in me!
The spirit of the Eternal Lord
Is within me,

For the Lord has anointed me
To bring the good news
To the miserable;
He has sent me to cure
The broken-hearted,
To free the captives
And bring deliverance to those in chains.

'All illness comes from the Devil,
And the Kingdom of Heaven is at hand
When Satan, the evil counsellor,
The tempter, the serpent,
Is at last conquered,
And is silent
And powerless.'
Jesus saw Satan falling from the sky
Like lightning.
When he healed,
When he expelled
Evil demons,
He was the victorious conqueror
That all awaited,
The enemy of Satan, without whom the Kingdom of Heaven cannot
    come.
Throughout the land
He dispensed blessings.
He preached to the poor.
The spirit of the Lord God was upon him
For the Lord Had anointed him With the Holy Oil,
The oil of balsam.
And he brought
Salvation to the meek,
He bandaged their bleeding hearts,
He gave freedom to the captive,
Redemption to those in chains,
He foretold a year of grace
From the Lord,
And a day of vengeance as well
To console the afflicted.
So it was

The spirit of the Lord was upon him,
And the Essenes had anointed him
To bring salvation to the meek
And to the poor.
He went into the desert to see them,
To tell them of his travels,
And to hear their words.
And when he returned
He told his disciples
All that they had said.

He did not want to abolish the Law:
They wanted it carried out.
He despised false priests:
They hated all priests and scribes.
He had not come to convert the Gentiles:
They wanted to draw back the poor in spirit,
The meek, the lost sheep of Israel,
The strayed and the sinners.
They taught him their science and their magic.
He worked miraculous cures
On the Sabbath –
Not to disobey the Sabbath,
But to fulfil it.

Then the messengers left Jesus
To report all this to John the Baptist.
And Jesus addressed the crowds.
'What did you look for in the desert?
A reed waving in the wind?
A man dressed in fine clothes?
But those who wear fine clothes dwell
In the palaces of kings.
So what did you go there for?
To see a prophet?
Yes, I say unto you,
And more than a prophet!
It is he of whom it is written:
See, I send my messenger
To prepare a path for me.

It is not a place for the courtiers of Herod Antipas dressed in fine
    clothes,
For those who dwell in the palaces of kings.
And for those who bend
Like reeds waving in the wind.
The reed can withstand the storm
Because it can bend in the wind,
Whilst a strong tree
Which cannot bend,
Is often uprooted in the strongest storms.'
He said that John was a prophet,
That Elias had at last returned,
Resurrected to accomplish his task.

So spoke the Essenes;
If John is the greatest
Of the children of man,
The smallest in the Kingdom of Heaven
Is greater than him.
John made the breach
Through which the light could shine.
They reminded him of the celestial message
The divine voice which he had heard
Telling him, at his baptism in the Jordan
What his mission was.
So spoke the Essenes.
'You cannot become the disciple of John,'
They said.
'It is for you to cross
The villages at the edge of the lake
To announce the coming of the Kingdom of God.'

Then John doubted no more.
With all his heart and all his soul
And all his strength
He preached
Announcing the impending coming.
'Hurry!' he cried,
'Hasten your step,
There is still time,

But soon it will be too late
And you will have no part of it.
Come quickly! Come and repent!'

Then his fame spread
Throughout the country.
King Herod feared him
Feared that he would attack the Kittim.
At the urging of his wife,
Who hated John,
He had him arrested
And locked up in the fortress of Machaerus.
He had him executed.
Salome, worthy daughter of a wicked mother,
Brought his head in on a silver plate
Dancing a wild dance
To celebrate the victory
Of the Sons of Darkness.

Then the Essenes said
That Elias had already come,
That they had not recognised him
But treated him as one of their own.
It was then that they made their plan:
The end had come,
The battle had started –
The son of man would have to suffer.

And so began the war
Between the sons of light
And the sons of darkness.
Sons of darkness were
The teachers of religion,
The makers of rules, precepts and commandments,
Doctors of written and oral interpretation,
Apart from the scrupulous,
The Pharisees.
They too believed in immortality,
In Heaven and Hell,
In the resurrection of the dead
And in the Kingdom to come.
The sons of darkness
Flew the proud flag of the House of the Maccabees,
Hating the Pharisees,
Favouring the Royal House,
Conquerors in the civil wars
Against the Pharisees,
On their proud throne in the Temple in Jerusalem
Where they could influence the important people,
The Sadducees
Who denied the oral tradition
And mocked the popular belief
In eternal life
Who said that nothing could be stated,
Nothing could be known,
Who like the Greeks believed in free will.

And the Master
To whom the crowds were not indifferent,
Undermined their efforts,

Freeing people from the yoke of the commandments they had taken
       such pains to define,
Eating with publicans
And fishermen.
So they wanted to be rid of him.
Let the sons of darkness
Bring to Jerusalem
Erudite scribes
Who would tell the world
That he was possessed by the devil.
This was the plan:
Let the doctors of the people
And the leaders
All hate him
Let the war begin!
For the end of time approaches.

They hated the Pharisees,
Whom they called
Misleading interpreters
And lying hypocrites
With false tongues
Who had led the people astray,
'Observe,' they said
'All that they say;
But do not model yourselves on their actions,
For they speak but do not act.
A curse upon you,
Scribes and hypocritical Pharisees
Who build the sepulchres of the prophets
And decorate the tombs of the righteous.
If we had lived in the time of our fathers,
We should not have joined them
In spilling the blood of the prophets.
And so you bear witness against yourselves
You are the sons of those who murdered the prophets.
You are the sons of darkness.'

And the Essenes
Hated the Sadducees

For they had left their Temple
And taken away their treasure,
The treasure of King Solomon.
In the desert they had built
A new Temple
In place of the old one,
A new covenant between God and his people
With another exodus
And another conquest
Of villages and towns
Where they established themselves
With women and children
In purity
Far from the Temple sullied
By impurity
And reigned over by the Sadducees
And their impious priest.

They told him that he must fight,
He who had never ruled
Never exercised power
Who knew only villagers
And the poor in spirit, the humble, his own people,
The country of Galilee,
Its flowers and trees,
Its fields and orchards.
They taught him
To turn the left cheek
When the right one was struck.
Not to resort to violence,
Which strays from the path of God,
To spread the word
Not to other nations,
But to the lost sheep of Israel.
'In all things,' they said
'One must love one's neighbour
And exercise mercy towards him,
In that way you imitate the actions of God.
For the justice of God
Is His mercy,

And God gives Himself above all
To the poor and the oppressed,
And fear of the Lord
Is more important than trust
In the strength and power of man.'
They taught him
About the righteous and the sinners,
The sons of light and the sons of darkness
The righteous on one side, the sinners on the other.
They taught him
That man's sins against his fellow man
Would be atoned for at the Day of Reconciliation,
To be at peace with his fellow man
He must show mercy
Just as God is merciful.
If one forgives men their failings,
The Holy Father will also forgive.
But if one does not forgive,
The Father will not forgive either.
In a better world, the just man
Will receive justice to the full,
And the sinner punishment to the full.
But in this world,
Only the love of your fellow man deserves the approval of God;
And hatred of your fellow man attracts His wrath.

'Judge not that ye be not judged,
Condemn not that ye be not condemned,
Forgive that ye shall be forgiven,
Give and it shall be given unto you.
Love your neighbour as yourself,
Fear God as Job did,
Love God as Abraham did.
Love is above fear.
It is better to serve God through unconditional love
Than through fear of divine retribution.
Flee evil and anything that resembles it
Follow the lesser commandments
For they are as important as the great ones.
As the wise man Hillel said,

Love God more than you fear Him.'
So said the Essenes.

'Preserve yourself from the stain of history,
Idolatry,
Adultery,
By respect for the law
Which is a barrier and a protection,
A difference and a separation.
Did not Noah climb into the ark
To escape depravity?'
So said the Essenes.

'Be holy
Because then God remains your ally,
Be the holy remnant withdrawn to the desert
Alone maintaining the covenant,
Be the chosen ones
Anointed by the holy Spirit,
Like Moses or Aaron,
The anointed of God.
Israel is the remnant of nations
We are the remnant of Israel
In the new covenant,
Cut off
By the perpetual grace of God.
Things hidden since the beginning of time
Have been revealed today to the Saints and the Perfecti.
We live here and now in fulfilment
Of the prophecies and just laws.
Our heart is renewed
Our spirit freed from the darkness of matter
We are joined with the angels and saints on high.
The heavens tell of the glory of God
And we sing with them daily.
The present is already the future,
The elsewhere is present here.
The will of God is done
On earth as it is in Heaven,
The Messiah comes now

To our common table
Around which we share the holy word,
The eternal and definitive covenant
God is with us.'
So said the Essenes.

They taught him poverty,
For the true sons of light
Are the poor chosen by God,
So said the Essenes.
And they believed that the Messiah
Would establish a new order.
They looked backwards,
They read the holy scriptures of Israel
The forces of darkness were the Kittim
And their agents in Judaea,
The elimination of evil
Would come with a bloody religious war.
Then would come a period of renewal
Of peace and harmony.
The final victory
The destruction of evil
Would be the result of divine predestination.
Then they told Jesus their secret,
The infallible arm of victory.
During a long night
They read
I will not avenge anybody,
I will pursue the man
Doing for him only what is good,
For God judges all living things,
And it is for Him to take retribution.
I will not wage war against men of destruction
Until the day of vengeance comes,
But I will not abate my anger
At wicked men
And I will not live in peace
Before the day of judgement fixed by him.

To conquer evil by doing good:
That was the secret
Powerful in its very weakness
That they passed on to Jesus.

'The good man does not have the evil eye,
He is merciful towards all,
Even if some are sinners,
And if they conspire to do him harm.
'Thus,' they said, 'he who does good
Will be stronger than he who sins,
Since he will be protected by good.
If your intention is good,
Even the wicked will live in peace with you,
The debauched will follow you
And be converted,
The miserly will not simply renounce their passion for money,
They will give back the riches
To those they have swindled.
A good intention is not double-tongued
Blessing on the one hand
And cursing on the other,
Reviling
And honouring,
Afflicting
And rejoicing
Pacifying
And provoking,
For hypocrisy
And for truth,
For poverty
And for wealth.
It can have only one feeling for all.
It cannot include two ways of seeing or hearing,
Whereas the work of Belial is ambiguous
And has no simplicity.'
So said the Essenes.

And Jesus replied:
'We have learned that it is said:

An eye for an eye
A tooth for a tooth,
A hand for a hand
A foot for a foot,
A burn for a burn,
A wound for a wound.
But I say
Do not resist the bad person,
And if anyone hits you on the right cheek,
Turn the other one,
If he wants your tunic
Give him another one too,
And walk for two miles
If one is necessary.
And give
To whoever asks,
And give
To whoever takes your goods
And never ask him to give them back.'

And Jesus spread their words.
He denounced the danger of earthly goods.
And the first shall be last
The last shall be first
The sorrowful shall be comforted.
To those whose spirit has been broken,
Eternal joy is promised.
Blessed are the meek,
The poor in spirit, the afflicted,
They would be comforted.
The Kingdom of Heaven was theirs.
Like Elijah feeding the crowd,
He fed the people.
Like Jonah mastering the storm,
When God brought a great wind onto the sea
He calmed the tempest.
Then he went to a synagogue in Galilee,
It was the holy day of Sabbath
They gave him the scroll of Isaiah
He unrolled it

And found:
'*The spirit of the Lord is upon me*
For he has given me the unction
To announce the good news
To the poor.
He has sent me to proclaim
Freedom to those in chains.'
When he had read,
He rolled up the parchment and sat down.
He said:
'*Today, this scripture is fulfilled*
For you who hear it.'
But they were sceptical:
No man is a prophet in his own country
He reminded them of the long line
Of prophets rejected and persecuted
Elias and Elijah
More welcome amongst the pagans
Than in their own country.
People were filled with anger
And threw him out of the town.
'*The word of God to our Lord*
Sit at my right hand
Until I shall make a footstool
Of your enemies.'

Then they chose as messengers
Two of his closest disciples
Who would travel throughout the country in his name,
For they had received precise instructions.
They were only to speak to Jews,
Not Gentiles
Nor Samaritans.
Like the Essenes
They did not encumber themselves with luggage or money.
If a town or a house did not wish to receive them
They did not stay.

But nobody was moved by the call to repentance,
Galilee, his own country, his birthplace,

Rejected its prophet.
When Jonas,
The prophet of Galilee,
Declared that after forty days
Nineveh would be destroyed,
The people had repented
And they had renounced their impiety.
If God had accepted his suffering,
If his people had listened to him,
Jesus would have given his life.
We were all wandering like sheep,
Each following his own path.
And the Lord made the sins of all
Fall upon him.
'Race of vipers,' he said,
'How could you say anything good,
Wicked as you are?'
Then he went away again.
Whosoever puts his hand to the plough
And then looks back
Is not worthy of the Kingdom of God.

And the wicked king Herod,
Tetrarch of Galilee and Peraea,
Watched the activities of Jesus,
When he learned that a preacher
In Galilee was announcing the coming of the Kingdom of Heaven
And drawing vast crowds
Like John before him
Like John resurrected.
This too was part of the plan.

But certain Pharisees
Of the House of Hillel
Who wanted to save Jesus's life
And knew what was being planned,
Came to warn him to leave,
For Herod wished to kill him.
'Go,' he said, 'and tell the fox this:
See, I cast out demons

And heal people today
And tomorrow
On the third day, I will have finished.
But today I must walk,
And tomorrow
And the next day.
For it is not right that a prophet should perish outside Jerusalem.'
And that too was part of the plan.

Then he went north to the sea of Galilee,
In the region of Caesarea.
He asked his disciples
What people were saying about him.
'Some think you are John the Baptist, Elias and Jeremiah.'
'And what do you think?'
'That you are the Messiah.'
'It is you that say it,'
He said,
'But you must not repeat it any more.
I say to all of you
You must keep the secret.
For it is too soon to reveal it.
My time is not yet come.
The time will come when I will go,
When I go to Jerusalem.'
Such was their purpose.
Then Jesus said to Peter:
'You are happy, Simon, son of Jonas,
For this revelation has come to you
Not from flesh and blood,
But from my Father in Heaven.'
For Peter was different
He had had a revelation
Different from that of the Essenes,
He was not influenced by them
That is why he could be happy
And different.

Then they began to teach him
That the Son of Man would suffer much,

Would be rejected by the elders,
By the sacrificers, by the scribes,
By the Kittim,
That he would be put to death
And be resurrected.
For it was said in the Psalm:
Protect what your right hand has planted,
And the son you have chosen!
Place your hand on the man at your right hand,
On the Son of Man that you have chosen!
And so God would not abandon him.

'I know,' he said,
'Those who will act against me,
The elders, the sacrificers, the scribes,
And the Kittim.
But I do not wish to fight against them.
I want to be on good terms with my enemy,
As long as I am
Still on the same path as him,
For fear that he will betray me to the judge,
And the judge to the guard
Who will throw me into prison.
I do not wish, like the Zealots,
To fight against the Kittim.
It is through the Holy Spirit
That I wish to free the world from its shackles
And I will wait
Until he reveals himself to us.
But I will not go alone
For my soul thirsts after God
The God of life.'

Then they said to him:
'Do not be afraid!
Is your name not Jesus?
God saves?
For you will be saved
By the Holy Spirit
Like Isaac

You will be tied
Like Isaac
You will be saved
At the last moment
You will not be abandoned.
And then all will know
That you are
The Master of Justice
And a Son of Man
No, believe it
God will not abandon you.'

Then he believed it
And then he went
To the Decapolis by the Sea of Galilee,
To the regions of Galaad and Basan,
And towards Lebanon and Damascus,
Where live the Rechabites and the Qenites,
With the Galileans,
Like the Essenes who had come out of the land of Judah
And were exiled in the land of Damascus
Thus they wanted to make the New Covenant
That the prophet Jeremiah had spoken of,
Promising to be free of all iniquity,
Not to steal from the poor, the widow or the orphan,
To keep apart the pure and the impure,
To observe the Sabbath
As well as other festivals and days of fasting,
To love their brothers as themselves,
To succour the unfortunate, the indigent and the stranger.
They taught him
That the community was a tree
Whose green leaves
Were food for all the beasts of the forest,
Whose branches sheltered all the birds.
But it had been overtaken by the trees of the water
Which represented the wicked world outside.
And the tree of life remained hidden by them,
Not thought of, not recognised.

It was God Himself who protected
And concealed His own secret,
So that the stranger saw without knowing
So that he thought without believing in the source of life.
For the Kingdom of Heaven was not just
The appearance of the reign of God,
But also a movement determined by God
Spread throughout the world
Amongst men.
It was not simply a realm,
But a Kingdom of God,
A region which spread wide,
Absorbing lands and people,
In which both great and small
Will inherit.
That is why Jesus assembled the Twelve,
So that they could be fishers of men
To heal
To bring salvation
To the poor, the indigent and the stranger.

Then Pilate, the governor of Judaea,
Thought that he would have to be put to death
For he was afraid
Of the New Covenant
Of the coming of the Kingdom of God
Which would end the Roman occupation.
He knew how many were listening to him,
And how many hated the Kittim.
Some of his disciples were Zealots
Who were causing trouble throughout the land
Who believed in one God
And who longed for freedom
From the invaders.

Then Jesus took the road to Jerusalem
He left Galilee,
And travelled through Samaria,
Stopped on Mount Gerizim,
Where the Samaritans awaited him

He left there a part of the precious treasure of the Essenes
The ancient treasure
Of the priests of the Temple
The magnificent treasure of Solomon
In this place
Where nobody would search for it
Where it would be safe
With the Samaritan scribes
Who were friends of the Essene scribes.
Then when the war took place
Between the sons of light and the sons of darkness
The treasure would not be stolen
And when the Messianic era came
They would reclaim it and take power.

He continued on his way
And along the road
He hid other parts
Of the treasure
Then he went to Jerusalem,
Holy city with the dwelling of the Lord,
The predestined centre of the kingdom
Whence redemption and blessings would spread
To all nations.
Jerusalem disgraced
Pagan Jerusalem
Betrayed by the Kittim
Profaned, soiled
By those who watched the courtyard of the Temple.
They must repent
Or else
All the city, from the greatest to the smallest
Would perish in agony.
He came to Jerusalem
At Passover.
He stopped at Bethany
Where he was welcomed by Martha and her sister Mary.

Then he came to Jerusalem,
Where he knew what awaited him.

He was no longer amongst his own Galileans,
But in Judaea where the dangers were greater
Where he must confront the sons of darkness,
The Jewish and Roman supreme authorities,
The Roman governor, Pontius Pilate,
And the Wicked Priest, Caiaphas,
Who held the sacred position
Of high priest,
Which he had attained with gold from his well-filled chests.

Passover was celebrated in the first month,
To commemorate the miracles that took place in Egypt,
When God delivered his people from slavery.
They ate the paschal lamb
Who that night was Jesus.

And the unleavened bread of his body
And the bitter herbs of humiliation,
For the paschal sacrifice would take place according to the
      Scriptures,
The blood of Jesus would be spilled like wine at a feast.
And then he would be glorified,
For the first fruits of the barley were consecrated to God.
The day after the paschal Sabbath
When they prayed for the dew
This is what was written:
Let the dead live again!
Let the bodies rise!
Awake and be joyful,
Dwellers in dust,
For your dew will revive us
And the earth will bring back light after darkness.
I will redeem their ingratitude.
I will be like the dew for Israel.
For God would not abandon him.

Then he went to Jerusalem
For he was to reveal himself to Israel
With the name of Messiah.
Then his time would have come.

The time for the arrival of the Kingdom of Heaven
The final and beautiful time
And the time for an end of
The master of the depths and the darkness.
No, God would not abandon him.

Then in Jerusalem
The Sanhedrin convoked an extraordinary meeting.
The high priest Caiaphas spoke thus:
'Can you not understand that in your own interests
It is better to see one man die than the whole nation?'
And the Council decided to condemn Jesus.

And he knew that,
For his friend John
The disciple he loved above all others,
His friend and host,
His secret ally, his spy.
John was a priest with the Sanhedrin
And knew all that had happened
And repeated it to Jesus his master.

Then Jesus left Bethany
And went to the town of Ephraim,
At the edge of the desert.
Then he returned to Galilee,
To perform the paschal pilgrimage
With the Galileans.

Then he came to the outskirts of Jerusalem
To Bethphage.
Lazarus had been given the task
Of acting according to the plan prepared
By the Essenes.
The donkey would be tied up
At the entrance to the village of Bethany.

But none of the disciples knew about this.
The order had been given
To let him go with messengers who would say:
The Master needs him.

The messengers came back with the donkey,
They were filled with wonder
For, according to the prophecy
The Messiah would arrive on a donkey.
They laid cloths along the way
And cut palms to lay beneath his feet.
At Bethany, Martha had prepared supper.
She rubbed onto his feet a precious oil of nard
And then his hair
So she was already embalming
Her Essene brother.
Jesus had asked her
To bring holy oil
Without explaining why
So that one of his disciples, exasperated, would betray him
And the prophecy would be fulfilled
The very man with whom I was at peace,
Whom I trusted
Who ate my bread,
Has raised his hand against me.
For this was the sign:
Riches and death
This was the plan of the Essenes.

Then he went to Jerusalem
Like a king
They sang the Hallel,
And they shouted *Hosanna*!
Blessed is he who comes in the name of the Lord!
Some of the Pharisees were scandalised and asked him to silence
    them,
So that he would not be killed,
So as to save him,
But he replied:
'*I say to you, if they are silent, the stones will cry out*!'
He allowed himself to be acclaimed by the Jewish crowd,
A sign of provocation
A sign of treason against Caesar.
He was accompanied by a crowd of pilgrims from Galilee.
And the Kittim had orders to allow the Jews who were singing
To get close to the leader of their cult.

In the court of the Gentiles,
The part of the Temple which was accessible to all,
Jesus attacked the merchants.
With a whip made out of broken ropes
Used to tie up animals destined to be sacrificed,
He lashed out
Upsetting the moneychangers' tables
And the seats of the sellers of doves,
Not in the holy place,
But just in front of it,
In the courtyard of the Gentiles
Where money was changed
To buy sacrificial victims.
He said to them that it was written:
My house shall be a house of prayer
And you have made it a thieves' den.
And he added:
'I will destroy this Temple made by the hand of man
And, after three days, I will build another
Not made by the hand of man.'
This prophesied the destruction of the Temple.

This was the plan
And the catastrophe was inevitable.
For the Temple was the only refuge for the Sadducees.
And now he announced the end for the Sadducee priests.
And the end of their Temple.
For the Temple had been soiled
By the illegitimate priesthood
With their unlawful calendar
Which fixed holy and profane dates
According to their own ideas.

This was war, the revenge
Of the sons of light against the sons of darkness,
The exiles from the desert
Against the armies of Belial,
The inhabitants of Philistia,
The Kittim bands of Assyria
And the traitors who helped them.
Then the sons of darkness asked him questions

In order to trap him.
'On what authority do you speak?' they asked.
'According to you, is John's baptism
Divinely inspired or not?' he replied.
'We do not know.'
'In that case,' he said,
'I do not need to tell you
On whose authority I act.'
People had been placed in the crowd
To ask questions
To trap him.
But he knew enough
Not to let himself be trapped.
'Should we pay tribute to Caesar?' they asked.
For the tax fixed for a census
Broke the law which forbade
The counting of the population.
'Why do you try to trap me?
Show me a denarius.'
They showed him one
But he refused to touch it
So as not to offend the Zealots
Who supported him.
'Whose is this head and inscription?'
'Caesar's.'
'Then render unto Caesar what is Caesar's
And to God what is God's.
For God is the only Lord,' he said.

Then Jesus celebrated the feast of Passover
On Tuesday, according to the solar calendar of Qumran,
And not according to the calendar of the impure Temple
As he had always done
With the members of the community.
At the end of the day,
He left the Temple for the last time,
He spent the fourth day at Bethany,
And the evening with Simon the leper.
On the fifth day began the feast of Matzoth
When the paschal lamb was sacrificed
Which that night was Jesus.

III

Then he went to Jerusalem
For the last supper
Which was the Passover supper.
He gathered his disciples,
To share with them the traditional meal
Taken in memory of the return from Egypt.
But that night was not like other nights
For that night was his last night on earth.
His hour had come,
He suspected it,
He knew it.
But was it his last hour or that of the world?
Was this night his last *in the world*
Or the last *of his life* in the world?
He decided to gather his disciples
For the last time
There were thirteen of them around the table
Prepared for the Seder.
Amongst them was Judas Iscariot.
For he too was a disciple,
Loved by Jesus,
And invited to the last supper.

The twelve disciples had sat down
Around Jesus, who stood up,
Put off his coat
And wrapped himself in a loincloth
He poured water into a basin,
And began to wash his disciples' feet
And to dry them with a cloth.
This was according to the Essene rite
So that no one should feel superior

And all were perfectly equal.
Then came the turn of Simon Peter.
'You, Lord, wash my feet!
Never!'
For Peter was not a member of the sect
And wanted no part in the plot.
'If I do not wash you
You cannot share my destiny,' said Jesus,
For he believed that the Essenes
Held the key to the Kingdom of Heaven,
'Not just the feet,
But also the hands and the head,'
Replied Simon Peter
And so he accepted the baptism
Of the Essenes
For he believed in Jesus.
'He who has bathed does not need to be washed,
For he is entirely pure
And you, you are pure,' said Jesus,
'But not all of you.'
For Judas was there.
And Jesus knew that he was going to be betrayed.
For Judas, son of Simon
The Zealot,
Was the strongest of the Essenes
And the one who believed the most in Jesus
To the point of sacrificing his purity.
More than Peter
And more than all the others
Judas believed that Jesus was the Messiah
And believed in God
Judas thought
Judas knew
That God would not abandon him
Judas had to betray him
To bring about the Kingdom of Heaven
The Kingdom of the King-Messiah
The Kingdom of Jesus.
And he had to be strong
To bear the impurity

And he had to be a Zealot
To bear such a sacrifice
The sacrifice of eternity
The ultimate sacrifice.

When he had finished,
Jesus put on his coat again,
And sat at the table
And said:
'Do you understand what I have done?
You call me "Master and Lord",
And you are right
For that is what I am.
If I, the Master and Lord,
Have washed your feet
You too must wash each other's feet
For I have set you an example,
And what I have done for you
You must do as well.
Verily I say unto you
A servant is not greater than a master
Nor a messenger greater than he who sent him.
Knowing this, you will be happy
As long as you put it into practice
I do not speak for you
I know those I have chosen
But let the Scriptures be fulfilled.
He who has broken bread with me
Has raised his hand against me.
I an telling you this
Before the event happens,
So that when it does happen
You will believe that I am what I say.
Verily I say unto you
Receive him whom I send
And you will be receiving me
And to receive me
Is to receive He who sends me.'
He wished them to perpetuate the brotherhood

Of Essenes, of the poor,
In case he did not return
For he knew the risk he was taking
By accepting the plan
He knew he was risking *his life*.

Then they ate the meal
Similar to that of the Essenes
And Jesus said:
'Verily, I say unto you
I will not drink this wine again until the coming of the Kingdom of
    God.'
And so he revealed himself to his disciples
As the Messiah
He revealed to his disciples
That he would no longer participate in the holy meal
As a communicant,
But as the true and visible Messiah,
Since confronting the priests.
For according to the scriptures of the Essenes
It was said that the Messiah of Israel
Should hold the bread in his hands,
And after praying,
Share it with the whole community.
And Jesus followed this ritual,
As he was in the habit of doing
When he celebrated Passover
With the Essenes.
While his disciples ate,
He took the bread,
And blessed it,
Broke it
And gave it to them.
He waited until the disciples had begun to eat
Before performing the sacrament
As he did
When he celebrated Passover
With the Essenes.
Then Jesus spoke thus to the twelve disciples:

'I have longed to share with you this paschal lamb
For I say unto you
I will not eat again until we are in the Kingdom of God.'

Then he took a cup of wine
Gave thanks
And said:
'Take
Share this amongst you.
For I say unto you,
I will never again drink the fruit of the vine
Until I drink it again in the Kingdom of God.'
For he believed the Kingdom of God
Would soon come.

Then he made the holy gesture
That of the Messiah.
He took bread
Gave thanks
And said:
'This is my body.'
So he pronounced the last words of the meal,
Identifying the bread with his body
And the wine with his blood.
But on this evening, he did not repeat the Essene prayer,
Which said that the food represented the absent Messiah.
For the bread was sacred
It was the symbol of food.
He identified himself with the bread,
Which represented
The Messiah in the sacred meal,
He did not say
As he had been in the habit of saying
'This bread represents the Messiah of Israel'
But he said:
'This is my body.'
So he revealed himself to them
For he believed
The Kingdom of God
Would come soon

And that soon
He would be saved
And all would be saved.
Then he declared to his disciples:
'Verily I say unto you,
One of you will betray me.'

Then they looked at one another,
And wondered who he meant.
One of them, John, the priest
The one Jesus loved,
Was next to him.
Simon Peter said to him:
'Ask whom he is speaking of.'
For it was only to John
That Jesus spoke
From his heart
To him
He said all
For he was the priest
Who was close to the Essenes
And who observed all that happened at the Sanhedrin
And told him all.
The disciple leaned towards Jesus's breast
And said to him:
'Lord, who is it?'
Then Jesus said:
'It is he to whom I give this mouthful
That I am about to dip.'
Then he took the mouthful that he had dipped,
And gave it to Judas Iscariot,
Son of Simon
Simon the Zealot.
And Jesus spoke words of complicity to him
For they had sealed a pact together
'What you must do, do quickly.'
And since Judas held the purse
Of the Essene community
Some thought Jesus was telling him to buy
What was necessary for the celebration

Or to give something to the poor.
But it had been agreed between them that at these words
Judas would betray him,
And he would give
The money he received
To the treasure of the Essene community.
He took the mouthful
And left at once.

As soon as he had gone,
Jesus was relieved
For they had not weakened
The two of them together
And he had gone,
As they had arranged,
As they had chosen
Following their plan.

He said to the others:
'Now the Son of Man is glorified
And God has been glorified in Himself,
And soon will glorify him.
Before I go,
I give you a new commandment:
Love one another.
As I have loved you,
So you must love one another.
And if you have love for one another,
All will know that you are my disciples.'

The plan was that of the Essenes
For they wanted him to be confronted
By the Truth,
So that through him,
Their truth would triumph,
They believed that God would save him
As he had saved Isaac
They wanted the final revelation
And for that,
They believed they could precipitate matters

Take God as a witness
And make him intervene.
Force him to reveal the Messiah.

This was their plan
This was their plot:
A plot for God,
A plot against God,
To betray Jesus, his messenger,
To the Kittim,
And to the Wicked Priest.
Not like the lamb on the altar,
But like Isaac on the altar,
He would be saved at the last moment.
And Jesus had accepted this pact
For he believed in them
As they believed in him.

After the meal
Jesus and his disciples
Left the town
And went to the Mount of Olives.
They climbed to a place called Gethsemane.
Then he asked his disciples to remain there
And told them
To pray.
Then he advanced,
And threw himself to the ground
And prayed:
'Father, if You wish it,
Take this cup away from me,
But let Your will be done,
Not mine.'
He would do nothing of his own will,
But would only wait for a sign from God.
He would not save himself.
He would wait for Him to save him.
He went to find his disciples
Who had gone to sleep.
Then he said to them:

'Why do you sleep?
Rise
And pray to keep me from temptation.
The spirit is willing
But the flesh is weak.'
For he was afraid that he might not complete his mission,
That he would weaken
And flee.
But he was able to conquer the temptation
That had taken hold of him,
Irresistible,
Called 'fear'
To use the darkness
To flee the gardens of Gethsemane.

Then Jesus went with his disciples,
Beyond the torrent of the Kidron.
There was a garden there
Which they entered together.
And Judas, who was betraying him,
Led the soldiers
And the guards sent by the high priests
He reached the garden with torches, lamps and arms.
Then the Temple guard appeared
With the Kittim
And the son of the Zealot
Who approached Jesus
They kissed one another
To give each other hope
And encouragement
And to say goodbye.
Jesus went to them
To give himself up,
And said to them:
'Whom do you seek?'
'We seek Jesus.'
They stepped backwards,
They trembled violently.
At that moment
He could have fled.

But still
He persevered.
Again he asked them:
'Whom do you seek?'
And they replied:
'Jesus of Nazareth.'
'I am he.'

Then Simon Peter
Who carried a sword,
Unsheathed it
And hit the servant of the Wicked Priest,
Cutting off his right ear.
He at last saw what had been planned,
And he wanted to save Jesus.
He would like to have cut off
His own ear
Which had been half-closed.
But Jesus at once said to Peter:
'Put your sword back in its scabbard!'
'What?'
'Should I not drink from the cup my father has given me?'

Then Peter understood:
For between Peter and the Essenes,
Between Peter and John,
The disciple that Jesus loved,
It was they,
It was he,
Who had won.
Sword, rise up
For my shepherd
And for the man who is my companion!

The soldiers and their commander
And the Jewish guards seized Jesus
And tied him.

In the evening
Judas was not a traitor

He was the purest and the most faithful
The son of the Zealot
He who hoped most for the final Deliverance
Who had the most faith in the Messianic victory
That of Jesus
Against the sons of darkness,
He was the most convinced that he was the Messiah.
Even Peter, the Beloved,
Denied him three times that night.
For Judas was the brother of Jesus,
Sent by the sect to denounce him
So that the Truth would emerge
That he was the Messiah,
That the Kingdom of Heaven was come,
That the sons of light would defeat
The sons of darkness.
They wanted to bring on the end of the world
Through the war
Between the sons of light and the sons of darkness.

And Jesus knew it
Before the high priests
He had said that the owner of the vine
Had sent a servant to the vine-workers
To ask for his share in the fruit of the vine,
But the vine-workers had beaten him
And sent him away.
He then sent another servant
And they beat him too
And cursed him.
He sent another
But they wounded him
And threw him out.
He sent his son,
Thinking they would behave well towards him.
But seeing him,
The vine-workers said to one another:
'He is the heir.
Let us kill him,
And we will inherit!'

And they threw him out of the vineyard
And killed him.
What will the master do to them?
He will come,
And the workers will perish
And he will give the vineyard to others.
The high priests had understood
The murdering vine-workers
Were themselves,
The wicked priests
Who had power over the people of God
And the vineyard was the people of Israel.

That evening,
There were thirteen of them,
Sitting around the paschal table.
There was Jesus
The Twelve,
And in the place of honour
The master of the house,
The beloved disciple, John,
The Essene who went into the house of the priests
The priest who had become an Essene.
And when Jesus was arrested,
He ran to the house of the priest Ann
Son of Sen, the old high priest.
For he knew where Jesus would be taken.
During that time
Jesus had been taken before the priest.
And he was asked
What he taught.
'Why do you interrogate me?' said Jesus.
'Ask those who have heard what I say.
They are the ones who know.'
Then Ann sent Jesus before the Council.
The Sanhedrin gathered
And he kept silent
Like a silent lamb
Before the shearer,
He did not make a sound.

'Have you nothing to say in your defence?'
Asked the high priest Caiaphas.
But Jesus was still silent.
'Are you the Messiah?'
'Yes, I am.
And you will see the Son of Man
At the right hand of the Lord,
Coming on clouds from the sky.'
Then the priest tore his tunic.
'What do we need other witnesses for?
You have heard his confession of treason.
What will you decide?'
For he was the Wicked Priest,
And the Council decided that Jesus deserved to die.
He had blasphemed
Not against God
But against Tiberius Caesar.
They were the denouncers
They formulated their accusation
Against Jesus before Caesar's representative.
And Jesus had not blasphemed against the Law
So he was not stoned
For he had not pronounced the sacred name of God.
The following morning
He appeared before Pontius Pilate.
They said that he was creating subversion
At the heart of the nation,
That he forbade the paying of tribute to Caesar
That he claimed to be the Messiah, the King.
Then Pilate came onto his balcony
And asked: 'What is happening?'
'This man is a criminal.'
'In that case, take him
And deal with him according to your law.'
'It is not a religious crime.'
'Are you the King of the Jews?'
'It is you that say it.
Or have others told you?'
'Am I a Jew?
It is your people, the chief sacrificers,

Who have delivered you to me.
What have you done?'
'My kingdom is not of this world.'
'You are a king?'
'I am king, you said it,
I was born
And came into this world to bear witness to this truth.
Whoever values truth will listen to me.'
'What is truth?
I have no charge against him.'
'He makes the people rise up by teaching
Throughout Judaea,
From Galilee,
Whence he came,
To this place.'
'He is Galilean?
In that case he comes under the jurisdiction of Herod Antipas,
The tetrarch of Galilee,
Take your accusations to Herod.'
Then the Wicked Priest took him to Herod
But he remained silent
And the Wicked Priest made accusations against him.
He sent the prisoner back to Pilate.
Then the Wicked Priest gathered his slaves
And their friends in the judgement hall.
But Pilate said Jesus should be whipped
And then released
For it was Passover.
Then, urged on by the Wicked Priest,
The crowd shouted that they wanted Barabbas
And not Jesus.
Jesus was whipped
And dressed
In a red cape
And a crown of thorns.
And the crowd shouted
That he must be crucified.
Then Barabbas was set free
And Jesus was condemned
They put a sign on the cross

Jesus the Nazarene, King of the Jews
For Jesus was a Nazarene
Like the Essenes who called themselves
Nozerei Haberith
The keepers of the Covenant
The Nazarenes.

And Jesus was taken by the Roman guards.
He went by the western gate of the city.
But nobody knew
What had happened on government hill.
It was the beginning of the festival
All the events had happened quickly
And in secret
And nobody knew
Of the plot that was being hatched.
By the cross
Was his mother
And John, the beloved disciple.
Mary Magdalen,
Mary, mother of James,
Salome, mother of James,
John, son of Zebediah.
The soldiers drew lots for Jesus's tunic
As it is written in the psalm.
They pierced his hands and his feet
As it is written in the psalm.
The chief sacrificers and the scribes mocked him
As it is written in the psalm.
They cried:
'He has trusted himself to God,
Let God save him if he loves him.'
As it is written in the psalm.
Then they gave him vinegar.
As it is written in the psalm.
His side was pierced by a lance.
As it is written in Zaccariah.
These things happened,
So that the plan should be carried out
And the Scripture fulfilled.

The crowd, urged on by the priests,
Called for the death of Jesus.
The Wicked Priest shouted
His hatred for the Saviour.
The Pharisees were not there.
For they were close to the Essenes.
Judas was not there,
The sacrificed one,
The pious one,
The strong and honest man
Who believed in Jesus and in God
And who understood
And who gave the money
Not to the Essenes
But to the priests
And who killed himself.

For it was too late
The time of confrontation had come
And nobody could do anything more
In this world.

That evening
The Essenes fasted
They prayed through the night
For divine intervention.

To dark Golgotha they dragged him
They nailed him to a cross
His clothes were shared out
By drawing lots.
With him were two robbers
One on his right
One on his left.

He surrendered his back
To those who beat him
And his face
To those who tore out his beard,
He did not hide his face from insults

Or spitting.
Oppressed and ill-treated,
He did not open his mouth,
Like a lamb being taken to the altar.
He suffered pain and anguish
And humiliation.
And of those of his generation,
Who had believed that he would be cut off from the land of the
    living
And beaten for the sins of his people?
And worse, he was a worm, not a man
Despised and rejected.
All those who saw him mocked him,
They opened their mouths,
Shook their heads:
'The Lord will save you,
Because He loves you.'
'I am like water flowing away,
And my bones fall apart;
My heart is like wax,
It melts into my entrails.
My strength is drying up like clay
And my tongue sticks to the roof of my mouth,
You have reduced me to dust.
For the dogs circle around,
They have pierced my hands and my feet.
I could count all my bones.
They look, they watch
They share out my clothes,
They draw lots for my tunic.
My heart breaks with shame
And I am ill.
I wait for pity
But in vain.
I find no consolers.
They put gall in my food,
And to quench my thirst,
They give me vinegar.
For they persecute the one you beat,
They tell of the suffering of those you wound.

And they look towards me,
The one they pierced.
They will mourn him
As one would mourn an only son,
They will cry bitterly
As one would cry for a first-born.'

Passers-by insulted him
And said:
'You who would destroy the Temple
And rebuild it in three days,
Save yourself
By coming down from the cross.'
And the Wicked Priest
With the scribes
Mocked him:
'He has saved others,
But he cannot save himself.
The Messiah,
The King of Israel,
Let him come down from the cross,
So that we can see!'
Those crucified alongside him cursed him too.

The kings of the earth rose up
And the princes joined with them
Against the Lord and His Anointed.
Despised and rejected by men,
A man of sorrows and familiar with suffering,
A man to make people screen their faces;
He was despised and we took no account of him.
The stone the architects rejected
Has become the keystone.
His enemies said of him:
'When will he die?
When will his name perish?'
All his enemies whispered against him amongst themselves,
They thought his misfortune would cause his ruin,
And if they asked him:
'Where do those wounds on your hands come from?'

He replied:
'I received them in house of those who loved me.
Sword, turn against my shepherd.
Beat the shepherd, and the sheep will go astray.
They speak against me with forked tongues
They surround me with their hateful words
And they make war against me for no reason.
Whilst I love them,
They are my enemies.

'When I walk in the midst of distress,
You give me life,
You set Your hand against the anger of my enemies,
And Your right hand saves me.
The Lord will act to help me.
I was surrounded by the silence of death,
And was caught in the net of death.
In my distress,
I called upon the Lord.
From His palace
He heard my voice,
And my cry reached His ears.
The earth shook
And it trembled,
And the mountains shook.
He stretched out His hand from on high
And saved me from my powerful enemy.
Come, let us return to the Lord,
For He has wounded
But He will heal us.
He has struck
But He will bandage our wounds.
He will give life back in two days
On the third day
He will raise us,
And we will live with Him.
I have the Lord always before me,
He is on my right,
I will not falter.
And my heart is full of joy

And my spirit of happiness
And my body rests in safety.
For You will not deliver my soul to the dead,
You will not allow your dearly beloved
To witness corruption.
You will show me the path of life,
With abundant joy before You,
And eternal bliss.
God will save your soul from the land of the dead,
For He will protect me.
Eternal Lord! The king rejoices in Your powerful protection!
Your help fills him with happiness!
You have placed a crown of pure gold on his head.
He asked for life,
You gave it to him,
Perpetual life.
His glory is great because of Your help,
You have crowned him with magnificence and glory.'

'Put up your sword,'
He had said to Peter,
'Do you think I could not call on my Father,
Who would place more than twelve legions of angels
At my disposal?
How then could the Scriptures be accomplished,
According to whom it must be like this?'
He thought,
He believed he would be saved.
He knew it right up to the moment
When he finally understood that it would not happen.
And that God had abandoned him.

On the day the Messiah gave up his soul,
The sky was no darker than on other days
There was no bright light,
No miraculous sign.
The sun hid behind thick clouds,
It was a day like any other.
And this normality was not the omen
For a lack of omens.

The death was slow and difficult.
His breathing dragged out into a long groan
Of infinite despair.
His colourless hair and beard
No longer reflected his vigorous wisdom,
Like a treatment or a cure.
His eyes no longer blazed
With the flame of passion
With his wise words
And prophecies
Announcing the advent of a new world.
His body, ravaged and twisted like a cloth,
Was no more than an open wound,
With bones jutting from the flesh
In macabre ridges.
His flayed skin
Was like a cloak
Shredded to pieces,
A shroud ripped in two;
It was a scroll unfolded and desecrated,
A decayed parchment with letters of blood
On scratched lines.
His stretched limbs,
Stabbed by needles
Purple-stained with bruises,
Blood flowed from his pierced hands,
Clenched with pain.
A warm gush rose from his heart
Into his parched mouth,
Void now of the gentle words he so loved to speak
His breast
Leapt up as if the heart would burst out
A naked, shining sacrifice.

Then he stiffened,
Drunk with his own blood
His half-open mouth and eyes
Wide in innocence.
Had he rejoined the Holy Ghost?
But the Holy Ghost had abandoned him

At the very moment when,
With a final glimmer of hope,
He had invoked him,
Calling him by name:
'God with us, God save me.'

But there was no response, no sign for him,
The rabbi, the miracle-worker,
Redeemer, consoler of the poor
Healer of the sick, the mad and the crippled.
Nobody could save him now,
Not even himself.
They gave him water
And sponged his wounds.

At three o'clock,
He knew that all was over.
In despair,
In solitude,
In desolation,
And disappointment
Jesus cried:
'Eli, Eli, lama sabachthani?'
Then he died.

Who has risen up to Heaven,
And who has come down?
Who has gathered the wind in his hands?
Who has made appear the ends of the earth?
What is his name,
And what is the name of his son?
Do you know it?

They had said
That God would not abandon him
And that to accomplish the mission they had planned
They wished him to carry on to the end
So sure were they that he was the Messiah
And that they would win their battle.
They wanted to provoke the final battle.

The confrontation with the priests
With the Kittim
To show to all those
Suffering the evil domination
That Jesus was the Messiah they awaited.
It would be the beginning of the last war,
Before the coming of the Kingdom of God,
At the end of which they would be saved.
They were tired of waiting for this war.
They wanted to act
And they felt strong enough to precipitate events.
Their emissary was called Jesus.
They did not wish to see him die
They believed they would win.

Why this tumult amongst the nations,
These empty ideas amongst the peoples?
Why did the earthly kings rise up?
And the princes join with them
Against the Lord
Against his Anointed One?
In the last days,
The impious will be in league together
Against the Master of Justice to destroy him,
But their plans will fail.
The Kittim rule many nations.
The princes
And the elders
And the priests in Jerusalem who govern Israel
With the help of their impious Council.
He knew the fate that awaited him,
His return in glory
To reign over nations
And to judge them.
Thus they had convinced him.
And they had had him killed.
They were so ashamed
That they solemnly swore to conceal amongst themselves
The true story of Jesus.

*

Some waited
For the miracle to happen,
For him to be resurrected in an apotheosis
Or for a cataclysm to carry everything away, as in their
prophecies.
Others saw a bright light cross the sky.
Some said
That they had seen him in a dream.
But down here
There was only the world, nothing else.

One day he will come
He will be of the line of David
Of the line of Essenes
He will be a great man on earth
All will venerate and serve him
He will be called great and his name will be
The Son of God
They will call him the Son of the Highest.
His kingdom will be like a shooting star
A vision.
They will reign for several years
On earth
And they will destroy everything.
One nation will destroy another
One province another
Until the people of God rise up
And throw down their arms.

He will be anointed
By the man of nations
The righteous man who was sacrificed
He will fight against the sons of darkness
Against the Wicked Priest
In his time
He will conquer them.

In the year 3793
By John the Essene, the secret priest, the disciple whom Jesus
    loved.

For *he who has seen must bear witness,*
A truthful testimony
For *that man knows that he tells the truth.*

Eighth Scroll

THE SCROLL OF THE MESSIAH

He will return, the one they called Jesus,
God saves,
For God did not save him
The first time.
He was the son
He became the Holy Ghost
He will become the father
And so he will return
And he will be tied
Like a lamb
And saved
For God must save
For his words to be fulfilled.

And a sucker will grow from his roots.
And the spirit of the Eternal will be within him,
The spirit of wisdom and intelligence,
The spirit of advice and strength
The spirit of science and the fear of the Eternal
Will be in his son.

And nothing will happen
Before the war, the revenge
Of the sons of light against the sons of darkness,
The sons of Levi,
The sons of Judah,
The sons of Benjamin.
Of the exiles in the desert
Against the armies of Belial,
The inhabitants of Philistia,
The bands of the Kittim of Assyria
And the traitors that help them.

And the Sons of Light
Will reconquer Jerusalem
And the Temple
And this war against seven countries
Will last for more than forty years.

And this will happen
After the century of destruction
Of catastrophe
Of hatred
Of illness
Of fratricidal war
Of genocide.

And this will happen
When the Son of Man comes
From the line of David
From the line of the sons of the desert.
He will be anointed
They will pour over his head
The oil of balsam.
By the man of nations,
The just man pierced,
Elias and John resurrected
Will he be announced.

And he will be tempted
By the devil in the forest.
Three times
He will conquer
He, the King of Glory coming in clouds from the heavens,
The weakling plant
Growing feebly from the dry earth
The humble king riding a donkey
The suffering servant
So said Hosea
I will go, I will return to my home,
Until they admit they are guilty
And seek me.
The hand of the Lord was upon me.

*

And all those who eat his bread
Will raise their hand against him.
They will speak evil of him,
In a perverted tongue,
And all those who have been associated with him.
They will slander him to the sons of darkness,
But so that His voice shall be raised up,
Because of their sin,
He has hidden the spring of intelligence
The secret truth.

And others will add to his distress
They will imprison him in darkness,
He will eat the bread of sorrow,
And drink tears without end.
For his eyes will be dimmed by sorrow
His soul will be suffocated by daily sorrows.
Fear and sadness will envelop him.

Then war will come
Throughout the world
He will fight against the sons of darkness
He will pursue them
Mercilessly,
And he will fight
Against the Wicked Priest,
And he will defeat him
He will kill the Wicked Priest
With the Law.

And during these times, all will be ready for the coming of the
Messiah
All will be prepared in the desert
There will be a treasure
Precious stones and holy objects
From the ancient Temple,
So that he can go to Jerusalem
Covered in glory
So that he can rebuild the Temple
And he will rebuild the Temple

As he saw it in his vision.

And the Son of Man will have an army
Sprung from a landscape of bones.
Lo, there will be a great many of them
Dry in this landscape.
And then the Lord of Armies will say:
'Son of Man, could these bones live again?'
And he will reply:
'Eternal Lord
You know that it is so.'
Then he will say:
'Prophesy upon these bones,
And say to them
You, bones that are dry,
Hear the words of the Lord.
This is what the Lord has said:
Bones: I will place the spirit within you,
And you will live again.
And I will put nerves in you
And flesh will grow upon you
And skin around you
And the soul within you
And you will live again
And know that I am the Eternal Lord.'
So he will prophesy
As he has been asked to do
And as soon as he has prophesied,
There will be a great noise
And quaking,
The bones will join together.
He will look
And see,
Nerves will form,
Flesh will grow
And skin,
Souls will enter them
They will live again
And stand,
And form a great army.

And he will lead his army
And go to Jerusalem
He will enter by the Golden Gate
He will rebuild the Temple
According to the vision he saw,
And the Kingdom of Heaven
So long awaited
Will come through him
The saviour
Who will be called
The Lion.

And all these things will take place
In the year 5760.

ALPHABETS

1	2	3
א	א	A
ב	ב	B
ג	ג	Γ
ד	ד	Δ
ה	ה	E
ו	ו	Y
ז	ז	Z
ח	ח	H
ט	ט	Θ
י	י	I
כ	כ	K
ל	ל	Λ
מ	ק	M
נ	נ	N
ס	ס	Ξ
ע	ע	O
פ	פ	Π
צ	צ	
ק	ק	
ר	ר	P
ש	שׁ	Σ
	שׂ	
ת	ת	T

1. Hebrew alphabet contemporary with the Qumran scrolls.
2. Modern Hebrew alphabet (definitively established from the fifth century), called 'square' alphabet.
3. Corresponding Greek alphabet

GLOSSARY

Ashkenazi: Jew from Germany or Europe.

Baal teshuvah: Non-religious Jew who becomes practising.

Bahurim: Pupils of the yeshivah.

Bar Mitzvah: Jewish ceremony at the age of thirteen, marking the beginning of adult life, with a reading from a passage from the Torah.

Belz: Hassidic group in favour of peace.

Devekut: Highest spiritual state of mysticism for Hassidim.

Chollah: Bread eaten on the Sabbath.

Gabbaï: Treasurer, collector of funds for the community

Galut: Exile, diaspora.

Gour: Polish Hassidim, who devote their lives to study.

Goy: Originally 'people', then non-Jewish.

Guemara: Rabbinical commentary on the Mishnah.

Guertl: Long ribbon of plaited silk separating the top and bottom halves of the body.

Habad: Messianic missionary movement throughout the world, believing that the Messiah will not come until all non-practising Jews have converted.

Hagganah: Clandestine Jewish movement for the defence of the Jewish people and the liberation of Israel.

Hannukah: Jewish festival commemorating the Maccabean victory over the Romans in 167BC

Hassid (pl. Hassidim): Literally 'pious'. A member of an ultra-orthodox Jewish community, under the authority of a rabbi.

Holoth: Black gown with short round lapels and wide edges.

Kaddish: Prayer for the dead.

Kiddush: Prayer made before drinking wine.

Kapel: Hat.

Kipah: Hat.

Kosher: Fit to be eaten. Wider sense: conformist.

Kvitl: Written request to a rabbi.

Mashiah: Messiah.

Matzo: Bread eaten at Passover.

Midrash: Jewish method of interpretation of texts using images and parables.

Mezuzot: Small boxes attached to the lintels of doors, containing verses from the Torah.

Mikveh: Ritual Jewish bath.

Minian: Quorum of ten needed to conduct prayer.

Mishnah: Rabbinical law written by rabbi Judah Ha-Nassi towards the end of the second century, the core of the Talmud.

Mitzvah: Commandment, law.

Parnas: Senior lay leader of community.

Passover, Pesach: Easter festival, commemorating the return from Egypt.

Pilpul: Casuistic method of rabbinical interpretation.

Sanhedrin: Rabbinical tribunal.

Seder: Ritual meal on the night of Pesach.

Sephardi/Sephardim: Jew/Jews from Spain and the Mediterranean.

Shiksa: Pejorative term to describe non-Jewish woman.

Shofar: Ancient instrument blown on Rosh Ha-shanah, made from a hollowed-out ram's horn.

Shohet: Ritual butcher.

Sofer: Scribe.

Sukkot: Feast of tabernacles.

Talmud: Torah in writing, composed of the Mishnah and the Guemara.

Tallit: Prayer shawl.

Taref: Non-kosher.

Teshuvah: Return to religious practise.

Tefillin: Phylacteries; black leather boxes containing verses from the Talmud, attached to left arm or upper forehead.

Tikkun: Reparation or redemption.

Tishri: Banquet at the end of Sabbath.

Torah: Pentateuch, the written law, foundation of Judaism. Bible.

Tsahal: Israeli army.

Tzimtzum: Key word of the Caballa, meaning the retraction of God to make way for his creation.

Vishnitz: Moderate Hassidic group.

Yeshivah (pl. yeshivoth): School where the Talmud is studied.

Yiddish: Vernacular language of Ashkenazi Jews, originating in about 1000 AD in the Rhine and Moselle valleys, a mixture of Hebrew, German and Aramaic.

Zohar: Pivotal book of cabalistic literature, written down by Moses of Leon (1240–1305) in Castile at the end of the thirteenth century.